W9-DEU-227

By Anthony Marra

Mercury Pictures Presents

The Tsar of Love and Techno

A Constellation of Vital Phenomena

MERCURY PICTURES

· PRESENTS ·

MERCURY PICTURES · PRESENTS ·

| a novel |

ANTHONY MARRA

LONDON / NEW YORK

Mercury Pictures Presents is a work of fiction. Names, characters, places, and incidents are the products of the author's imagination or are used fictitiously. Any resemblance to actual events, locales, or persons, living or dead, is entirely coincidental.

Published in the United States by Hogarth, an imprint of the Random House Publishing Group, a division of Penguin Random House LLC, New York.

HOGARTH is a trademark of the Random House Group Limited, and the H colophon is a trademark of Penguin Random House LLC.

Library of Congress Cataloging-in-Publication Data
Names: Marra, Anthony, author.
Title: Mercury pictures presents: a novel / Anthony Marra.
Description: London; New York: Hogarth, [2022]
Identifiers: LCCN 2021049651 (print) | LCCN 2021049652 (ebook) |
ISBN 9780451495204 (hardcover) | ISBN 9780593449165 |
ISBN 9780451495228 (ebook)
Classification: LCC PS3613.A768726 M47 2022 (print) |
LCC PS3613.A768726 (ebook) | DDC 813/.6—dc23
LC record available at https://lccn.loc.gov/2021049651
LC ebook record available at https://lccn.loc.gov/2021049652

Printed in the United States of America on acid-free paper

randomhousebooks.com

First Edition

Book design by Susan Turner

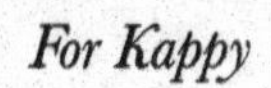

For Kappy

Was this artificial "return" mere playacting? I cannot believe it.

—Thomas Mann, *Doctor Faustus*,
written in Los Angeles, 1943–1947

PART I

SUNNY SIBERIA

1

WHEN YOU ENTERED THE EXECUTIVE OFFICES OF MERCURY PICTURES INternational, you would first see a scale model of the studio itself. Artie Feldman, co-founder and head of production, installed it in the lobby to distract skittish investors from second thoughts. Complete with back lot, sound stages, and facilities buildings, the miniature was a faithful replica of the ten-acre studio in which it sat. Maria Lagana, as rendered by the miniaturist, was a tiny, featureless figure looking out Artie's office window. And this was where the real Maria stood late one morning in 1941, hands holstered on her hips, watching a pigeon autograph the windshield of her boss's new convertible. She'd like to buy that bird a drink.

"It's a beautiful day out, Art," Maria said. "You should really come have a look."

"I have," Artie said. "It made me want to jump."

Artie wasn't known for his joie de vivre, but he usually didn't fantasize about ending it all this close to lunch. Maria wondered if the Senate Investigation into Motion Picture War Propaganda was giving him agita, but no—the crisis at hand was on his head. His bald spot had finally grown too large for his toupee to conceal.

Six other black toupees were shellacked atop wooden mannequin heads on the shelf behind his desk, where a more successful producer might display his Oscars. They were conversation starters. As in, Artie began conversations with new employees by telling them the toupees were the scalps of their predecessors.

As far as Maria could tell, the six hairpieces were the same indistinguishable model and style, but Artie had become convinced that each one crackled with the karmic energy of the hair's original head, unrealized and awaiting release, like a static charge smuggled in a fingertip. Thus, he'd named his toupees after their personalities: The Heavyweight, The Casanova, The Optimist, The Edison, The Odysseus, and The Mephistopheles. Artie had never felt more at home in his adoptive country than when he learned the Founding Fathers had all worn toupees, even that showboat John Hancock. The only one who hadn't was Benjamin Franklin. And look how he turned out: a syphilitic Francophile who got his jollies flying kites in the rain.

"Maybe the toupee shrunk," he said, still hoping for a miracle.

"I think you'll need one with more coverage, Art."

"That's the second time this year. Christ, when will it end?"

"Life's nasty and brutish but at least it's short."

"Yeah? I'm not so optimistic."

Artie didn't believe in aging gracefully. He didn't believe in aging at all. At fifty-three, he maintained the same exercise regime that had made him a promising semi-professional boxer before a shattered wrist forced him into the only other business to reward his brand of controlled aggression. (He still kept a speedbag mounted to his office wall and liked to pummel it while in meetings with unaccommodating agents.) Sure, maybe he lost a step; maybe his knees sounded like a pair of maracas when he climbed stairs; maybe the boys in the mailroom let him win when he challenged them to arm-wrestling matches—but he wasn't getting *old.*

Or so Maria imagined Artie telling himself. In truth, she'd begun to worry about him. In four days, he would sit at a witness table on Capitol Hill, where he would testify alongside the heads of Warner Bros, MGM, Twentieth Century–Fox, and Paramount. It was shaping into a pivotal confrontation between campaigners for free speech and crusaders for government censorship. But as far as Maria could tell, Artie was more preoccupied with his toupee than his opening statement.

On the topic of censorship, he said, "Have you heard back from Joe Breen?"

"Earlier this morning."

"And? Will he approve the script for *Devil's Bargain*?"

Maria said nothing.

"I'm going to pull the rest of my hair out, aren't I?"

"I'm afraid so," she admitted.

Maria had started working at Mercury a decade earlier, rising from the typing pool to the front office. At the age of twenty-eight, she was an associate producer and Artie's deputy, a job that demanded the talents of a general, diplomat, hostage negotiator, and hairdresser. Among her duties was getting every Mercury picture blessed by the puritans and spoilsports who upheld the moral standards of movies at the Production Code Administration. The grand inquisitor over there was Joseph Breen, a bluenose so distraughtfully Catholic he'd once bowdlerized a Jesus biopic for sticking too close to the source material; apparently, a foreign-born Jew advocating redistribution smacked of Bolshevism to Breen. Committed to making pictures gratuitously inoffensive, Breen withheld Production Code approval from any movie dealing with contentious subjects. Throughout the 1930s, if you only got your news from the local picture house, you'd find the American South untroubled by Jim Crow and Europe untouched by fascism. But by late summer 1941, not even a force of blandness as entrenched as the Production Code could keep the European crisis from the screen.

In response to pro-interventionist messages in recent movies, a group of isolationist senators accused Hollywood of plotting with Roosevelt "to make America punch drunk with propaganda to push her into war" against Germany and Italy. Congressional hearings were hastily arranged to investigate these charges and propose legislative remedies. And Artie Feldman, ever reliant on the free publicity of controversy to find an audience, wanted to both undermine the legitimacy of the investigation and capitalize on his newfound notoriety with Mercury's next movie.

Maria passed Artie the script she'd received back from the Production Code Administration that morning. Joe Breen had rerouted scenes with the frantic arrows of a besieged field commander. *Devil's Bargain* was a clever idea—no matter her misgivings, Maria would admit that much. Written by a German émigré, it retold the Faustian legend through the story of a Berlin filmmaker who agrees to direct indoctrination movies in exchange for the funding to finish his long-gestating magnum opus. In a pivotal sequence, a visiting delegation of American congressmen watches one of these propaganda films and leaves the theater persuaded that the real enemy to peace is not in Berlin but in Hollywood. Of course, insinuating that US senators were easily duped conspiracists ensured the script would never receive Production Code approval. Maria supposed she should feel disappointed, yet for reasons she would not admit to Artie, she was relieved Joseph Breen had sentenced *Devil's Bargain* to death by a thousand cuts.

"I'm surprised he didn't censor the spaces between the words," Artie said, flipping through the blue-penciled script. Maria's marginalia were heavily seasoned with profanity and exclamation points. "Breen's always had it in for me. I've never understood it."

"You did call him a 'great sanctimonious windbag' in the *New York Daily News*."

"I was misquoted. I never called him 'great.'" Artie tossed the script on his desk and peeled off his hairpiece. His liver-spotted scalp resembled a slab of pimento loaf. Maria always found the sight of it oddly moving, a sign of the trust established over the ten years they had worked together. Artie allowed no one else at Mercury to see him in between toupees. He turned to her and said, "What do you think—any chance we can salvage this?"

Artie assumed Maria's background made her a natural fit for supervising the production of *Devil's Bargain.* Long before she became his second-in-command, Maria and her mother had fled Italy as political exiles after Mussolini had her father, one of Rome's most prominent lawyers, sentenced to internal exile in the Calabrian hinterlands. Over the years their correspondence had imbued Maria with a contempt for censors and a talent for circumventing them.

Sometimes she felt life had professionalized her to hide in plain sight. Fascism and Catholicism had educated her in navigating repressive ideologies, and growing up a girl in an Italian family meant you were, existentially, suggested rather than shown. Gesture and insinuation comprised the Italian American vernacular, from mamma to Mafia, and coming from a diaspora where desires and death threats went articulately unspoken, Maria had a knack for smuggling subtext past the border guards of decorum at the Production Code Administration. Nevertheless, in the case of *Devil's Bargain,* she agreed with the censors' decision. Meddling in politics was for the rich, the powerful, or the self-destructive; she learned this from her father's example and had no wish to become him.

"I think this one is well and truly Breened," she said.

Artie nodded and tossed the toupee into the trash. He replaced it with the richer sable of The Mephistopheles. Its deployment was cause for hope, not least for its wider coverage. To conserve its occult charge, he spared The Mephistopheles for the most important negotiations. Artie was trying to establish a new credit line to ensure financing in case things went south in Washington. He and his twin brother, Ned, had a meeting that afternoon with Eastern National, a consortium of hard-charging Wall Street slicks who likely knew the etiquette for expunging drunk-driving fatalities from the legal record.

Securely helmeted, he swiveled around in his desk chair. "How'm I looking?"

The truth was that Artie exceeded his protégé's talent for euphemism.

"You don't look a day over twenty-five," she said.

This elicited a rare grin from Artie. As a master bullshitter, he encouraged his apprentice's efforts. Despite her sex and ethnicity, he knew Maria was, at heart, a Feldman Brother through and through.

"I pay them to lie," Artie said, nodding in the direction of the accounting department. "I pay you to be honest."

"Honestly, you look like Elmer Fudd's dad."

Artie winced. "I don't pay you to be *that* honest."

"Then you should pay me more."

"Let's not get carried away. But I suppose that's the impression we want to make on these East Coast bankers. It takes a genius to know when to be taken for a fool."

Maria smiled. "In that case, you're a regular Einstein, Art."

"Hey, you laugh, but you of all people should know being underestimated is a competitive advantage. When these Mayflower Society Wall Street suits see me, they'll think they can use my fedora as a bedpan. It goes against everything they've been taught to take a loudmouth immigrant in a bad rug seriously."

"You look like Elmer Fudd's dad," Maria said, "and the Yankee Doodle Douchebag across the table won't see who you really are."

"And who am I?" Artie asked.

"At the bargaining table? You're Mephistopheles."

Enlivened by the wig's demonic power, Artie felt ready to slay his enemies. He stood up and stuffed his arms into his jacket sleeves. A canary chirped at him from the brass cage at the end of his desk. The bird had been an anniversary gift from Mrs. Feldman. The accompanying note said Artie could use the companionship. Artie had named the canary Charles Lindbergh, on account of it being an excellent aviator but otherwise a real piece of work. There was comfort, Maria imagined, in reducing one's enemies to caged and easily throttled creatures.

"Where's the statement you plan to read before Congress?" Maria asked. "I'll edit it this afternoon."

Artie shrugged and said nothing.

"Art. You're flying to Washington tomorrow morning."

"I haven't prepared an opening statement," he admitted. All at once, he felt very much like the man he spent a great deal of psychological effort convincing himself he was not: a middle-aged narcissist whose bald spot had outpaced his toupees, a guy about to have his loyalties questioned and character maligned on the largest stage in America, an ex-boxer who could defend himself in a dark alley but not in a well-lit hearing room on Capitol Hill.

"It's going to be a show trial, Maria. It doesn't matter what I say. I just . . . I just don't see this ending well."

Rubbing his temples, he seemed taken aback by his own uncertainty. No matter how often he was proved wrong, Artie never stopped insisting he was right. Whether he was speculating on the physics of Joe DiMaggio's swing, the name of the capital of New Zealand, or Rita Hayworth's natural hair color, his confidence made you nod in agreement, even if you knew he was talking complete crapola. And now he dropped into his chair as if crumpling beneath the weight of what he did not know and could not predict.

The bleak foreboding in his face concerned Maria. Artie could be maddening, capricious, and self-absorbed, but he had done more to support her career than anyone else. He had promoted her over the protest of male colleagues. He respected her opinion and had faith in her abilities. When he learned another executive had tried to get handsy with her, Artie slugged the guy and gave Maria his job. Editorials denouncing Artie for rending the nation's moral fabric papered his office wall in lieu of good reviews, but there was no one whose morality Maria admired more than his.

"Listen, how about I come with you to Washington," she suggested. "We'll prepare your opening statement on the flight in."

"You really want to watch me get fed to the lions?"

"I'm from Rome. My people invented the sport."

"That's very reassuring," Artie said.

"Besides, my father was a defense attorney in the early days of Mussolini's regime. I'm not unfamiliar with show trials."

Artie gave her a grateful nod. "Book yourself a seat on the flight out of Mines Field tomorrow."

They walked out to the lobby, past the miniature of the studio lot. Out on the street, the heat radiating from the asphalt painted sedans and roadsters in impressionist smudges. Due north, the mansion-heaped hillsides looked like a plutocratic favela. When they reached Artie's Lincoln, he gave her a letter. "Do me a favor. Get this in today's mail, will you?"

The envelope was addressed to German-occupied Silesia, to the last known address of Artie's older sister. He wrote her every day but hadn't received a reply in months. It was thin enough to contain nothing at all, yet Maria accepted the envelope in both hands as the true weight drained into it from Artie's downcast eyes.

Maria put her hand on his shoulder, squeezed once, and slipped the envelope in her purse.

Wanting to change the subject before she could offer words of sympathy, Artie said, "It's a real pity *Devil's Bargain* didn't receive Production Code approval. Can't you just picture me touting it in my congressional testimony?"

Maria could. Inevitably, the most creative aspect of any Mercury production was the publicity campaign promoting it.

"I bet no one's ever plugged a movie before Congress." Artie turned to an imaginary camera. "If the senators here really want to learn about the dangers of propaganda, I'm happy to offer them complimentary tickets to *Devil's Bargain,* opening this December in a theater near you. Remember I'm under oath when I say *Devil's Bargain* is the best motion picture of the year—that's the truth, the whole truth, and nothing but the truth."

"You can thank the Pope of the Production Code for saving you from perjury."

"The Pope of the Production Code, huh," Artie said. The phrase sent a flicker through his glassy eyes. "You're from Rome. You must know what's his name. The pope's house painter. Michael Angelo."

"Michelangelo," Maria corrected.

"Whomever. The point is, that Sistine Chapel is something, isn't it? You want to know what I think?" She didn't, but Artie's opinions moved with the tottery insistence of a drunk barging past the maître d'. "I think this Michael Angelo character must've been the Preston Sturges of his time."

"Sure," Maria said, smiling. "He was okay."

"Okay? *Okay?* Somehow Michael Angelo got away with painting peckers on the pope's ceiling. And mind you, we're not talking one or two. There must be dozens up there. I bet the pope can't raise his eyes to God without getting flashed by some smart-ass saint."

"Michelangelo had a sense of humor, I'll give you that," Maria said.

"I can't show a husband and wife faithfully married for fifty years sleeping in the same bed without that two-bit Torquemada Joe Breen farting brimstone on me. And yet the pope's private chapel has more southern exposure than a ballpark bathroom at the bottom of the seventh."

Artie looked at Maria and across that long stare the musculature conjoining their intuitions flexed.

"You know what? I think Michael Angelo would have done very well in Hollywood. To get away with that, and on the *pope's* ceiling. How do you think he did it?"

Maria folded her arms and leaned against the hood of Artie's Lincoln. "Clearly, he and the pope reached an accommodation," she said, trying to visualize the Sistine Chapel. "Michelangelo could paint peckers to his heart's content, so long as he painted them small."

"Bingoski."

Maria understood what Artie was getting at. For years, Maria had devised strategies for smuggling the profane beneath the most sensitive censorial snouts. At her best, she passed more colorful bullshit than Babe the Blue Ox. Through charm, flattery, faux naiveté, and veiled threats, she convinced censors of Artie's honorable intentions the way her father had once persuaded courtrooms to believe in the innocence of the incorrigibly recidivistic. When meeting with Joe Breen to discuss a Mercury production, she dressed demurely, low hemlines and high necklines, no jewelry but a golden cross. She so credibly explained away the innuendos Breen unearthed that the head censor would begin to fear that *he* was the pervert. Ten minutes later, Breen would be hotfooting his way to midday Mass and Maria would have a Production Code seal for a picture called *Aren't They Cousins?* Beneath her cross she was all killer.

"I'll make you a deal," Artie said. "You find a way to get *Devil's Bargain* past the censors and I'll give you the producer's credit."

Maria eyed him warily. She'd been an associate producer for several years now and had yet to receive a screen credit, but she distrusted any transaction that gave her what she wanted. "Why now?"

"Because you've earned it," he said, offering her his hand. After they sealed the deal with a handshake, he added, "Now go knock Michael Angelo down a peg or two."

IT WAS HALF PAST NOON, and Maria thought she might catch Eddie in the commissary before he went back on set. She found him wedged between a couple extras, with a makeup man's tissues still tucked into his collar, opining on the dearth of serious theater in Los Angeles.

He was well acquainted with the topic. Eddie Lu was a self-taught Shakespearean actor and the night clerk of the Montclair, the residential hotel just off Hollywood Boulevard where Maria lived. Though he radiated the leading-man exoticism that catapulted Valentino to stardom, Eddie didn't benefit from even an Italian's off-brand whiteness, and thus Fu Manchu villainy was the most he could reasonably hope for. Unreasonably, he hoped for more. He knew by heart the leading lines of the major tragedies, but the stage was no less miserly with opportunity than the screen. He'd lost the lead in *Hamlet* to a corn-fed idiot from Iowa who wanted to give his notes to the playwright. "If Hamlet were the Prince of China, you'd be my first choice," the director had told Eddie apologetically.

In addition to being an immensely talented and unemployable actor, Eddie was Maria's boyfriend. They had consummated their ongoing flirtation two years earlier at the New Year's Eve party, where they tested the sound insulation of Mercury's recording booth. Maria moved into the Montclair the very next day.

"All's well on set?" Maria asked, taking the chair beside Eddie.

"I'm beginning to think *The Landlady Dreams of Arson!* isn't the masterpiece of emotional restraint I was led to believe," he said. Maria steered bit parts to Eddie now and then, if only to keep him in good standing with the Screen Actors Guild, and he could only accept her nepotism by hating every single second of it.

"Tell me what you really think," she said.

"I really think the mascot of this place should be a gutter. Why do you stay here, huh? Forget Paramount, you could work anywhere."

Several months earlier, she'd been offered a job at Paramount. It was twice the salary but a tenth of the power of her current position, and despite Eddie's urgings, she had declined.

"Artie promoted me out of the typing pool. He brought me up in this business. That means something."

"It means he can take advantage of your gratitude," Eddie pointed out.

"If I wasn't so concerned about maintaining domestic bliss," Maria said, "I might wonder aloud why someone so unhappy with his career is so eager to advise me on mine."

Eddie smiled sheepishly and raised his hands in surrender. "Those who can't do, teach." He nodded to the woman who sat alone at the table nearest to the exit, extinguishing a cigarette in the dregs of her cantaloupe and cottage cheese. "Speaking of new hires, who's she?"

"Anna Weber," Maria said. "One of the Germans. We took her on a couple months back. She did some of the miniatures for *Metropolis.*"

More and more exiled Europeans had appeared at Mercury in recent years. You could map the march of fascism across Europe based on Mercury's employment rolls. In a moment of uncommon candor, Artie had confided that his only professional expectation of these émigrés was that they ease his conscience by cashing their paychecks. A number had never worked in movies before. So, Maria had been pleasantly surprised to find that by hiring Anna, Artie had brought on a miniature architect in complete command of her craft.

"From *Metropolis* to Mercury." Eddie shook his head at the injustice of it all. "What a shame. Speaking of which, it's about time I return to the great debacle."

He reached under the table and squeezed Maria's hand. As he passed Anna's table, he said, by way of introduction, "Welcome to sunny Siberia, Mrs. Weber. It only gets worse."

Maria helped herself to the last bites of Eddie's apple pie and unfolded her notes on the table, but instead of *Devil's Bargain* she found herself thinking of the scale model of Mercury. She didn't know what drew her to it. Perhaps it was seeing Mercury through a medium anathema to that of the movie factory it depicted. So much of a movie's meaning came down to who it deemed worthy of a close-up, a perspective, a face. But within the zoomed-out omniscience of the miniaturist's gaze, all were worthy, as if the camera had pulled back until it held every bit player in its frame.

If you were to pull back right then, you would see Anna, the miniature's architect, alone at her table, sketching a Berlin tenement on her napkin. Pull back farther and you would see Artie coasting west on Santa Monica Boulevard in a cream-colored Continental, each block bringing him nearer to the brother he loathed. Pull back farther still and you would see Union Station, where a Calabrian fugitive traveling on a dead man's papers was stepping off the train with Maria's address in his pocket, a cigar box in his carpetbag, a knot in his throat.

And you would see Maria pass an equatorial jungle, a Gothic castle, a brownstone street as she crossed the back lot to her office. You would see her linger at the Italian Piazza set. Change the signage and it became any European village, but Maria had modeled the set on the little piazza in Rome where every Sunday her father had taken her to the cinema. It was a small square encircled by clay-roofed buildings, cafés, and shops, all false fronts. The marble and travertine were painted plaster and plywood. Standing there, Maria repopulated the empty piazza with the evening passeggiata: pigeons bolt from footfall, sleek signorinas glower from the imperious heights of their heels, an old man's part wilts over his forehead as he scoops steaming balls of horse manure into a fertilizer bag. In the alleyways, loaded laundry lines lift imperceptibly with each droplet of evaporated weight. Everyone watches one another, yet no one sees Maria. She's twelve years old, walking beside her father. Their footsteps rise and fall, rise and fall, like sewing needles stitching them to the city, and it seems impossible that this is about to end, that it's all about to disappear, that outside the confines of a Hollywood set, she will never see Rome again.

The landscape of exile was loaded with trapdoors like these. A misstep and the ground fell away. She was back in the place she fled, even now, in her office, at the Olivetti she had inherited. Long before it sat in a second-tier studio, her typewriter was stationed on her father's desk, where the legal appeals it recorded had overturned dozens of guilty verdicts. No matter the termination notices or ultimatums she had composed on its chromium keys, Maria still regarded her father's typewriter as an instrument of mercy.

Even now, all these years later, she could feel her father's eyes on her. He watched and waited to see what she did next.

2

IT WAS INEVITABLE: WHENEVER MARIA THOUGHT OF ROME, SHE RE-turned to that final summer when every Sunday her father took her to the air-conditioned cinema instead of church.

Those outings had been a wonderful, worrisome development, her father's attentiveness one more sign of their reduced circumstances. Historically, he relied on a draconian Scottish governess to facilitate his infrequent excursions with Maria. But the governess, maid, and cook had been dismissed that spring, leaving the apartment vacant and forlorn with only her parents in it. Her father saw things differently: parenthood had been more agreeable to Giuseppe Lagana when someone else looked after his daughter, and without hired help to contain the twelve-year-old, the six-room apartment on the Aventine had never felt more unmanageable and overrun. If nothing else, it was educational. For instance, Giuseppe learned that the more time he put into cooking dinner, the less of it Maria would eat. He learned that she refused to use an alarm clock like a civilized person and just getting her out of bed in the morning was a half-hour ordeal of escalating threats that left him winded and exasperated. He learned that her favorite color was mint green. He learned how swiftly she could send his thoughts swerving from the homicidal to the enchanted. Now, on the first Sunday in August, he felt outnumbered when he met Maria at the front door and followed her into the late afternoon light.

"Don't tell your mother, okay?" He locked the door behind him. "She might not appreciate our . . . program of cultural enrichment."

"Because she thinks we're going to church."

"Hey, if you'd rather we go to—"

"No," Maria said quickly. Her Calabria-born mother had an arriviste's disdain for common entertainment, instead preferring to be bored in uncomfortable shoes at marathon operas and gallery openings. These outings with her father were Maria's only chance to visit the cinema.

"Then don't tell your mother." Maria mouthed the words as her father spoke them.

Giuseppe studied his daughter, this befuddling creature in a gray dress and red bow. She kept her buoyant black curls spring-loaded within bobby pins that sparkled in the sun. Somehow, they had become a couple of fellow hobbyists with a shared interest in deceiving his wife. It was a nice change of pace, given that his relationship with his wife was based on him deceiving himself. Ever since Giuseppe confessed the extent of their financial predicament, he and Annunziata largely spoke through Maria. She served as messenger, translator, and negotiator, a purportedly neutral broker they both tried to co-opt with bribes and blandishments. The faculty Maria had developed for playing her parents off each other—extracting concessions that in peacetime neither would consent to—might have frightened Giuseppe had he not actively encouraged it.

They ambled down the Aventine Hill, passing beneath stained-glass saints while trolley wheels skated over rails with the sound of swords honed for combat. Across the Tiber, steeples and spires wrinkled in the heat. This was the first summer the Laganas hadn't fled the city for the seaside resorts on the Adriatic. As if to defy the weather—or to punish himself for marooning his family in it—Giuseppe wore his herringbone three-piece. A serious suit, crisply ironed, lapels as wide as shark fins. It was much too hot for winter-weight wool, but when he recognized in the mirror the fussily dressed lawyer he'd once been, a vanished sense of adequacy returned to him.

By the time they entered the public gardens, he'd begun to melt. An old man skull-capped in a wet handkerchief watched with amusement from a park bench. "Bet he has some regrets," the old man told the dog panting at his feet.

If anything, the old man understated the case to his dog: regrets were all Giuseppe Lagana had these days. It seemed unbelievable now, but as recently as last autumn he'd still been among Rome's most sought-after defense attorneys, a lawyer who could wield a technicality like a battle-ax. Once you could have entered any prison in Lazio and found jailbirds reciting his courtroom poetry like schoolboys quoting Dante. By spring that time in his life had ended. Newly enacted legislation outlawed opposition to the fascist regime and instituted the Special Tribunal for the Defense of the State, a system of extrajudicial show trials to try and sentence political subversives. Giuseppe had made his reputation defending socialist, anarchist, and communist agitators following the Great War; now those potential clients had either fled abroad, renounced their prior allegiances, or been sentenced without trial to terms of internal exile in the south. It rendered a defense attorney with Giuseppe's particular talents and clientele increasingly unemployable.

Each morning he lifted his hat from the stand, popped his head into the kitchen, and cheerfully announced he was off to "work." He overestimated his ability to mislead his family while underestimating his ability to mislead himself, a shortcoming of the professionally equivocal. At night he waited to come home until after Annunziata had retired to the guest room in which she had taken up permanent residence. Whatever confidence he projected in the morning had burned out by evening. He'd need another seven hours of sleep to convincingly lie to his wife for another thirty seconds. He hung his hat in the darkened foyer and crept into the kitchen, where Maria sat at the table in her pajamas. Her body drained its drowsy warmth into his chest as she leaned against him. Sometimes his fear of failing her astonished him.

"I thought we agreed you wouldn't wait up for me?"

"I woke up," she said. "A bad dream."

"The crocodiles again?"

"Not me. Mamma had a bad dream."

"How do you know?"

"I heard her."

Giuseppe resisted the urge to ask more. For years, the sedative Annunziata needed to fall asleep submerged her in a dreamworld she struggled to wake from. In her nightmares she drowned: kicking, flailing, gasping for air as the tsunami pulled her under. Back when they shared the same bed, he would wake to her furious movement, alarmed by how little he could help the thrashing woman beside him. Taking Annunziata's hands in his own, he would whisper reassurances until his voice reached through the ocean roar and guided her to the surface.

"Your mother's fine," Giuseppe said. "We're all completely fine."

After putting Maria to bed, he went to his study, locked the door, and ratcheted a fresh sheet of paper into the Olivetti. Ever since his employment had dwindled to long hours staring at a silent telephone, he kept himself busy with . . . well, what exactly could you call this document that by now had sprawled to fill six accordion folders? Not a series of appeals, though that was what they were. In the evenings while waiting for his wife to fall asleep, he ventured across the city to interview the families of those convicted through the Special Tribunal. He cataloged the meager and fabricated evidence, chronicled the departures from settled law, measured the mauling of his mother tongue in the rulings issued at drumhead trials. That this was a futile exercise did not dampen the fervor with which he pursued it; that the clients could not pay him and the Special Tribunal had no appellate court he could petition was irrelevant: if he was not a defense attorney he was nothing. And who better than a defense attorney to document the state's ruthlessly inconsistent application of the law? Who was more sensitive to the drift and swerve of justice? Into the early hours you could hear paper trembling like umbrella silk under the hailstorm of keystrokes. The appeals he wrote would bring no relief to their subjects. Instead, he was submitting them to posterity via his desk drawer, where long after this era had eased into history's flow, perhaps a reckoning would be possible. Perhaps one day, far from now, the evidence gathered in these pages would serve as a Rosetta Stone to the lingua fascista. A dictionary to decode the reality enciphered within the fantasy of Mussolini's Italy. More likely it was just the final motion of a defeated lawyer before the defense rested.

In the morning, after her father left for the office, Maria went into his study, curious to see what had kept him at the Olivetti so late. Uncorrected pages billowed from the crash site where the typewriter had collided with his fingers. She carried a few to the window, drew open the curtain, and read. The lavishly adverbial contempt with which her father described the regime surprised her. Over the last year, he had tried to suppress his once ardent socialist activism. He no longer argued politics with friends. If he was in public when Mussolini came on the radio, he dutifully stood without complaint. Though he refused to join the Fascist Party, he showed no ill will to former comrades who had, saying one shouldn't judge a man harshly for doing what the times demanded. A year after he had resigned his Socialist Party membership, her father had so carefully restrained his political opinions that nowhere in his private or public life—nowhere, really, but in the pages passing through her hands—would Maria find evidence that he believed in anything. And though his legal arguments were incomprehensible to her, she could feel his anger by running her finger over the page: he had struck the keys so violently the typebars had dented the paper. She returned the pages to their messy heap, but for the rest of the morning she couldn't dispel the idea that inside her father there was a stranger.

THE TICKET OFFICE LINE SNAKED from under the marquee, across piazza cobbles, and into the evening passeggiata. Maria followed her father past the cat tails twitching over butcher scraps, the swishing of a grande dame's silken stride, the tiny mosquito wings vibrating in the heavy air.

"The line has never been this long," Maria said when they reached the end.

Giuseppe fanned his face. "Air-conditioning is popular in Hell."

A copy of *Il Popolo d'Italia,* Mussolini's favorite propaganda rag, eddied in the breeze. Families in their smartest suits and dresses promenaded around the piazza's perimeter.

"The Monster of Frankenstein," Giuseppe said, squinting at the hand-painted poster hanging outside the ticket office. "That came out years ago. It doesn't really seem appropriate for a twelve-year-old, does it?"

"Next week they're showing *Beasts of the Bordello.*"

"You're not reassuring me."

"We could go to church instead," Maria said. "Do churches have air-conditioning?"

She had him there. "What about dolls? Wouldn't playing with dolls be a bit more wholesome?" No, never mind, Giuseppe could just picture her playing Dr. Frankenstein with her very expensive British dolls, sewing them into a multiheaded monstrosity. He supposed he was to blame for her interest in the macabre. A few years ago, during one of his then still blessedly infrequent misadventures in fatherhood, he let Maria spend the day with him at his law office. While he was in a client meeting, she found her way into a file cabinet containing photographs of several thoroughly bespattered crime scenes. For weeks, she restaged the crime scenes with her very expensive British dolls. Giuseppe was imagining the indignities that awaited her poor dolls after a summer of movies like *Beasts of the Bordello* when the line began to move, funneling them through the theater doors and into soothing gusts of mechanically cooled air. At last Giuseppe felt dressed for the weather.

Years later Maria would still remember the cold air cycling through the theater while the rest of Rome smoldered. She would remember the impresario in black tails and white tie introducing the evening's entertainment, the pianist noodling on the black keys by candlelight, the scene when the Monster gazes through the window of a cabin in the woods, becoming one more shadow in the audience, peering into the lighted world ahead. Most of all, she'd remember the Fiat trucks roaring up to the cinema doors, the pianist falling silent, the squad of Blackshirts storming in.

The squad leader was a gelatinous man over-served into a uniform weighted with make-believe medals. He led his men down the aisle. The pummel of jackboot on carpet dented the hushed air. Maria felt her father's hand tighten around hers, but no warning was needed. She knew to sit still and silent, lest she draw the attentions of a liquored-up Blackshirt. Even as a twelve-year-old, she understood these punitive expeditions were safaris as much as campaigns of political terror. Before getting to whatever flimsy pretext brought them to the cinema that evening, the Blackshirts spread through the audience to hunt for trophies. They pitted coins from pocketbooks, stripped billfolds bare. The fascist dream of empire came to foreshortened fruition right here, in Rome, colonizing one's own countrymen in the capital city.

On the screen a torch-wielding rabble pursued the Monster into a cave. The actor portraying him stormed through the scene with an operatic expressiveness that rendered the dialogue title cards superfluous. No matter how powerfully the actor emoted, Maria could not hear him, just as he, of course, could not see the squad leader dragging the impresario forward by his beard, nor hear him declare the impresario a Bolshevik guilty of exhibiting degenerate entertainments, and it seemed outrageous to Maria that the actors on-screen would remain impervious to the drama playing out in their audience. She envied them their blindness.

The two Blackshirts waiting at the edge of the proscenium arch didn't hear the squad leader's command. Evidently, they were too caught up in the picture: the Monster discovered in the cave, the mob coming, the torches blazing. "The offending contraband," the squad leader repeated. The two Blackshirts hustled forward and unspooled film reels at center stage.

Inspired by the scene playing out on the screen, the squad leader pulled a matchbook from his pocket. The impresario's appeals for leniency were just whispers, really, panted pleas muffled by his beard, but Maria would remember them as echoes of the Monster's cries, whispers that broke the silent era's sound barrier.

The Monster of Frankenstein, like some ninety percent of all silent films, is lost to time, in no small part because it was printed on film processed from nitrocellulose, a chemical so combustible it was used as gunpowder.

The squad leader dropped the match and the flames on screen came to life.

Before Maria could think, let alone move, her father was pulling her to her feet and hurdling over the legs of the dazed spectators in their row. By the time the others began to stand, her father had hauled her into the aisle. As the others were stampeding toward the aisle, he was shoving her through the lobby and into the piazza. The summer air no longer felt oppressive. It took the carabinieri half an hour to cordon off the piazza while firemen doused the blaze and ambulances ferried away the injured. Rubberneckers in their Sunday best whooped when the projectionist, fireproofed within his asbestos-lined booth, emerged unscathed. "Slow breaths," her father said. "Just like that. Nice and slow. You're a natural." Maria breathed while her father dampened his handkerchief in fountain water and wiped soot from her face. She concentrated on the wet stripes his handkerchief dragged down her cheeks. She closed her mouth and breathed through her nose until the tingle of her father's aftershave replaced the taste of smoke.

"Don't tell your mother," her father said.

Maria watched reveling Blackshirts who would return to their shops and factory floors and classrooms in the morning. "Will the police arrest them?"

"I don't think so, Maria."

A few paces away the impresario lay on the ground with tears puddling in the potholes of his deep-set eyes.

"Don't worry. The police won't arrest him either. These geniuses burned all the evidence."

Maria's hair still smelled of smoke early the next morning when she pushed open the heavy wooden door to her father's study. She could barely remember the order the maid once imposed on the room—the dusted shelves and replenished flowers, the alphabetized books and neatly stacked files. Now the study had reverted to a state of nature: overdue bills spilled from the wastebasket, coffee cups doubled as ashtrays, and heaps of paper and reference books sprawled across the floor. One look was enough to see that her father was unable to care for himself, let alone her mother, to say nothing of her.

Newspapers crackled underfoot as she made her way to the desk. She didn't know what she was hunting for beyond reassurance that her father knew what he was doing, that the Blackshirts who came for the theater impresario wouldn't come for him too. Instead, on the page cranked through the Olivetti, she found his account of the previous evening: physical descriptions of the squadristi, names where he had them, a summary of the crimes he witnessed, a list of corroborating witnesses he would later interview. He was forever admonishing her to think before acting, but what action was more thoughtless than assuming you were exempt from the very retribution you cataloged and recorded?

She tore the paper from the Olivetti, and in a cold rage gathered the accordion folders brimming with appeals that incriminated the lawyer who prepared them. Who was her father to privilege the freedom of these strangers over the safety of his family? She dragged the accordion folders to an alley down the street. She emptied the first folder into a metal pail haloed in rust and struck a match. It hissed against the alley stone. She daubed the flame along the edges of the paper. The pages puckered and curled as the flames consumed the arguments for mercy her father memorialized in typewriter ink.

When she later tried to account for her actions, she construed them as an act of misguided love, because in those violent years whom would you risk saving from themselves if not your family? In the inferno of a Roman summer, whom would you build a fire for if not your father?

She had incinerated half the documents when a neighbor, smelling smoke, called the police and then ran outside to restrain her before she burned down the block. The officer wore a creased uniform and a listless shirt in a boxy, bureaucratic cut. He scanned the unburned appeals and, realizing he was out of his depth, summoned agents from the OVRA, the regime's secret police. Maria refused to answer the OVRA agents' questions, but it was too late for her silence to matter. The neighbor told the officers where the Lagana family lived.

Giuseppe was brushing his teeth when he heard the pounding at the door. He dropped the toothbrush as the first OVRA agent pushed him to the floor and cuffed his wrists. The second agent questioned Annunziata while the first one ransacked his study. He didn't know what to do with the toothpaste in his mouth. Spitting on his own floor was one indignity too many and so he held in the foamy lather as men in cheap shoes stepped over him. He didn't notice Maria return to the apartment. When she appeared at his side, he assumed the tumult had woken her. She brought him a bowl to spit in and a glass of water to rinse his mouth. Because his hands were cuffed behind his back, she brought the glass to his mouth. She didn't have time to clean his face before the OVRA agents led him away. Her father, the most civilized man she had ever known, was pushed onto the street with his shirt untucked, his shoelaces untied, and minty spittle leaking from the corners of his lips.

The OVRA agents took him to the Regina Coeli, where the three-man Special Tribunal sentenced him to confino—internal exile—at the Calabrian internment colony in San Lorenzo.

• • •

SEPTEMBER PASSED AS A SLOW-MOTION burglary. First the jewelry and furs her mother no longer had occasion to wear, then the good silver laid out for guests who no longer visited. As their debts mounted, the furniture disappeared. Maria developed passionate attachments to pieces she'd scarcely noticed until they reappeared in the windows of neighborhood pawnshops. How she wept over the chaise! How she grieved for the ottoman! Her mother marshaled her full powers of repression to meet the moment.

"What ottoman?" her mother said—threatened, really—when Maria asked where it had gone.

The money her mother raised bought the false assurances of charlatans. Annunziata knew the bribes were wasted, but when you're desperate, every open pocket is a wishing well. Finally, Annunziata delivered herself to the office, then the lunch table, then the hotel suite of a deputy minister who inflicted his sexual inadequacies on the wives of men whose incarceration he oversaw. The deputy minister wasn't wearing socks when he answered the door of the elegantly appointed suite. For the next half hour, she willed herself to become an extension of the impersonal decor, no longer human, exactly, so much as a hard surface easily wiped of fingerprints. When it was over, she went home, hair disheveled by fat fingers, dress wrinkled from being hastily thrown on and run in, the deputy minister's breath still damp in her ear: "I have made inquiries and only the Duce can commute your husband's sentence."

Annunziata didn't remember coming home, didn't remember Maria greeting her, didn't remember the forty-five-minute bath, the sedative knocked back with a glass of brandy, the stumble to her bedroom. Instead, she remembered the whiplash of animal reflex snapping open her eyelids at two in the morning when the sheets peeled back and her daughter eased into bed beside her.

"What's wrong? What happened?"

"It's okay, Mamma," Maria whispered. "You were only dreaming."

Over the following weeks, Annunziata combed through Mussolini's speeches, making the case for clemency with the Duce's own words in letters dispatched to the Palazzo Venezia. The exercise was as futile as shouting Bible verses at the sky, but whose words would an omnipotence heed if not its own? But no matter whom she wrote, begged, or inveigled, no matter the favors cashed, strings pulled, or threats issued, she elicited only repellent pity, empty promises, deafening silence. Part of her didn't understand why she was exerting such time and energy on behalf of a man she might very well leave the moment he was freed. Hadn't she warned Giuseppe time and again that no good would come of his dalliance with the antifascists? Hadn't she told him to stick to defending murderers and frauds and embezzlers, those normal, decent criminals whose crimes did not offend the government?

In the end, she had no choice but to write her aunts in Los Angeles, and by December had secured two passports, visas, and steamship tickets. Only one item of outstanding business remained. Ten days before their ship sailed from Genoa, Annunziata and Maria boarded the night train to Calabria.

It was the first time Annunziata had returned to Calabria since leaving it nearly twenty years earlier. To friends and neighbors, she claimed descent from minor Mezzogiorno gentry, and for sixteen years of marriage obscured her trail from the bloodhounds patrolling the lower limit of high society. But follow her swept-over tracks and you'd reach the ruins of Gallico Marina, on the Strait of Messina, a few miles from the epicenter of the most lethal earthquake in European history.

What Annunziata remembered of that unspeakable day in 1908 was not the earthquake itself, but the subsequent tsunami—a moonlit range snowcapped in sea foam rising higher and higher until it obscured all of Sicily but the ruby corona of lava reflected in the clouds over Etna. The tidal wave swallowed and regurgitated towns along the Calabrian coast. Tottering through the wreckage, Annunziata couldn't imagine how these million strewn pieces had ever fit together. All around, strange sea creatures drowned in the air. Limp marine plants dredged up and dragged inland slumped from broken rafters. The sky writhed with the air traffic of a hundred thousand departing souls. Several of her relatives, including her mother, had vanished into the water that day, disappearing with such finality it seemed they hadn't drowned but dissolved into the froth.

After Annunziata moved north and married Giuseppe, she purchased herself a plot in Rome's Verano cemetery. The mason she spoke with guaranteed his tombstones would remain legible for at least two thousand years. When her time came, she wanted her name inscribed in big, capitalized letters, so no one would have any trouble finding her.

Once she thought nothing would compel her to return to Calabria, but here she was, in San Lorenzo. The land still felt semisolid underfoot.

"Come, my dear." Annunziata took Maria's hand. The sun was pallid, underripe, illuminating without warming backstreets grooved by millennia of mule carts. Women screwed amphoras into yard dirt colonized by listless goats. Pigs feasted on rubbish chucked into alleys where sallow children pelted one another with rocks. Aside from the political detainees, the town was mainly women: emigration had conscripted most working-age men, mustering them to distant lands from which they were unlikely to return. Maria saw no looming citadel, no fences looped in barbed wire, just sun-bleached dwellings huddled on the Busento River beneath turbulent gray skies.

"Where's the prison?" Maria asked.

"I think it's all a prison."

There was nowhere Maria looked that didn't glare back accusingly. Not once during the torturous months her mother spent trying to hold her family together did Maria confess what she had done; not once did she admit, explain, apologize. And her mother showed little interest in learning what had led the political police to arrest her father on that scorching August day. Despite her efforts to conceal her Calabrian roots, her mother still brought a Mezzogiorno mindset to suffering: it was never explicable; it was only endurable.

"I didn't know you came from a place like this," Maria said.

"What, you thought I emerged fully formed from my boudoir?"

In fact this was more or less exactly what Maria had thought. "I can see why you left."

"My dear," her mother said, "you haven't the faintest idea."

Political prisoners could work and choose their own lodgings, provided they presented themselves for twice daily roll calls. Curfew began at 18:00, but during the day they could move within a two-square-kilometer zone. Outside of internment, passport photography was among the town's few growth businesses, and Giuseppe had taken a room above a studio run by the Picone family. He was waiting by the door for them. Maria was too ashamed to meet his eyes.

Had she passed him in the street, Maria might not have recognized her father. Over the previous half year, he'd lost twelve kilograms, half the black in his hair, and all the smile on his face. Months subsisting on slop unfit for canine consumption left his suit jacket sagging, his shoulder blades visible, his belt riddled with new holes. He tried to find work, but there was no hope for a lawyer who couldn't even castrate a pig. The locals viewed his academic credentials as diagnoses of dimwittedness. When one peasant asked if he knew how to farm, Giuseppe said he knew the threshing chapters in *Anna Karenina*. Even if he could farm, it wouldn't have mattered: the peasants might walk ten miles to work a couple patches of barren soil, but for Giuseppe the town, the country, the universe itself was no more than a few acres beyond which he was forbidden. To trespass those invisible and arbitrary borders was to descend to deeper misery: all roads from San Lorenzo led to solitary confinement. Giuseppe didn't know what he might have done had Signora Picone not given him room and board in exchange for tutoring her son.

Maria followed her father to his small, drab bedroom and her mother busied herself with unpacking a portable delicatessen of cured meats and hard cheeses. Transporting this motley assortment of secreting grease across three hundred jostling miles without staining her handbag required a genius for conveyance that approached teleportation. Maria watched her mother nimbly undress the salumi and cheese and, for the first time in months, felt safe: these hands would carry her across the ocean without spill or breakage.

For several minutes they made uncomfortable small talk, and Maria was relieved when a boy appeared in the doorway. He was a few years younger than her, nine or ten, crowned in a messy doodle of dark hair, the scent of darkroom chemicals on his hands—Maria would remember this when she met him again many years later.

"This is Nino Picone, the young gentleman of the house," her father said. "Nino, why don't you show my daughter around."

She followed the boy past portraits photographed in the moody style of Emilio Sommariva, downstairs to the terrace where scarred pigeons hopped around in wire coops. The Sila Massif rose to the east, a sweeping ridge of browns and greens that cupped San Lorenzo like a hand around a match. Trying to look bored, Maria answered Nino's questions about life in Rome while water whispered through the river rocks below. Where she lived and what she did for fun and if she'd ever seen the pope. He was an earnest, friendless, overly mothered child whom Maria felt embarrassed for. At the same time, she couldn't remember when a stranger had last spoken to her with curiosity uncontaminated by pity or judgment. She wanted to hold on to that feeling.

"California," Nino repeated. "I envy you."

"Then you're an idiot," Maria said.

"Hey, you get to live where Valentino lives."

"Valentino's dead."

"His last couple pictures weren't so good, but I'd hardly call him—"

"He died in August," Maria said.

"What?"

"It was in all the papers."

"We don't get all the papers." Nino sank his fists into his pockets and kicked a pebble off the terrace. "How did he die? Was it of a broken heart?"

"I think it was peritonitis."

The pebble plinked into the river below.

"Then never mind, I don't envy you. What good is California without Valentino?"

The existential implications of this question lay beyond Maria's grasp.

"Do you want to see the portrait studio?" Nino asked.

In the darkroom, trays of processing chemicals shimmered beneath an amber safelight and drying prints bobbed on clotheslines. There was a closet with silk dresses and serious suits for sitters to pose in. Behind the cash register, halves of torn passport photographs hung on a corkboard. Each tear bisected the sitter's face. Some had hung so long their features had dissolved into a milky void.

"Who are they?" Maria asked.

Nino said that because emigrants who came for passport photographs were largely illiterate, his mother developed an extra print, tore it in half, and asked the emigrant to send his half back when he reached his destination. When the two halves were puzzled together, it was known the emigrant had safely arrived.

Nino pulled a black photo album from beneath the cash register. It detonated dustily on the countertop. Its pages held hundreds of passport photographs pieced together, fixed with paste, provisioned with names, dates, destinations. The left half of each was punctured by a pushpin but otherwise unblemished. The right half, however, was folded, stained, and faded by each weatherbeaten mile of its journey. Maria couldn't fathom the distances compressed into the seams of these reassembled passport photographs.

When she looked up, Nino had a camera in his hands. "May I take yours?" he asked.

UPSTAIRS, ANNUNZIATA HAD CLOSED THE door when the children left. The imprecations she intended to bring down on her husband had kept her furnace lit, her fury stoked these many months. Now? Now she couldn't summon the energy. Growing up in Calabria had made her an autodidact of failed institutions, matrimony included. Sixteen years into theirs, outrage had gone the way of the other passions, better in theory than practice.

"You're the stupidest man I've ever met, you know that? The very stupidest." Her reproach had a touch of admiration, the variety deployed to acknowledge achievement in fields of endeavor best left unexplored (modernist music, competitive eating).

Giuseppe conceded the point. His eyes were duller than she remembered, the dim brown of dry cough drops. "I take it you're leaving for Los Angeles?" he said.

Annunziata was no stranger to broken hearts. In her betrothal years her demurrals had turned one suitor into a priest, another into an atheist, and a third into a melancholic who scribbled love poems by moonlight. Whatever heartache she dispensed was repaid the moment Giuseppe said he knew she would only visit him to say goodbye.

"You should have had an affair like a normal man. An affair I could understand."

"I've never been unfaithful." He spoke with the haggard triumph of a castaway who'd survived months at sea without turning cannibal. How narrowly you define betrayal, she thought. How you reduce it to a legalistic technicality.

Suddenly exhausted, she lay back on the lumpy mattress. It was rutted with the impression of her husband's body, a newly laid narrowness that tilted her toward him. She rested her head on his thigh. "Don't get any bright ideas," she warned.

"You'll have to smile like an idiot in America. They expect that sort of thing over there."

"As if the Protestants weren't bad enough."

"I'm sure some are okay."

This she would accept. "A denomination founded on divorce can't be all bad."

"You'll stop at divorce? I figured you'd want my head."

"And do what with it? I don't even like your hat." She drew a finger along his unsteady trouser crease. "Who's pressing your pants?"

"I do my ironing with a kettle."

He ran his hand through her hair. She closed her eyes and everything vanished but the springy circumference of her curls unspooling on his fingers.

"Will you find yourself a cowboy?" he asked.

"I've had quite enough of cowboys, thank you. I'll find an American who has affairs and doesn't vote."

Giuseppe smiled and slid another inch closer to her. She was worried he would kiss her, but he just went on running his fingers through her hair.

"You'll never meet another one like me," he said. "America isn't big enough."

"I hope to God you're right." She tucked her hand into his and brought it to her lips. His fingers were engineered for elegant penmanship the way certain lithe legs were made to pirouette. The craquelure of notched skin on his knuckles made her think of old museum paintings, and when she had first kissed his hands, in the Ostia hotel, the thrill of trespass was no less than if she had brought her lips to the surface of a Caravaggio. They had been, what, twenty back then? Unmarried and registered at the hotel under false names, Signor and Signora Rossi. One morning he woke early and, thinking she was still asleep, began to dress in the dark. She lay still in the sheets and watched. His popped collar stood like a tomcat's perked ears and his beautiful fingers passed a half meter of navy silk through the tie knot. The post-pubescent perfection of his skin and the faint whisper of tightening silk aroused transgressive thoughts. He looked so far from death, and how was that possible if they were the same age? If she could save ten seconds from all their years together, it would have been those she spent in the cheapest room of an Ostia hotel, watching him tie his necktie in the dark.

Now he hooked his fingertips beneath hers and lifted her to her feet. There was no phonograph or wireless, no instrumentation but the clop of goat hoof on cobble, the ruffle of pigeon feather, the scrape of phlegm on the back of her throat. She felt his ribs through his baggy suit jacket and wanted to remember where each one went, precisely how their bodies had fit together in this bleak little room where they swayed as the river breeze played over the coo of captive birds.

"How has Maria dealt with everything?"

"She thinks we don't know what she did," Annunziata said.

"That's good. Let her think that."

"Sometimes I could just strangle her for what she—"

"She's just a kid. It's not her fault."

"Oh, believe me," Annunziata said, stepping out of Giuseppe's arms, "she's not the person I blame."

He reached under the bed and passed her a small pouch puckered by a drawstring. Inside, six coins caught the last of the daylight.

"I owe you both more, I know that. But even Protestants take gold."

The coins were imprinted in imperial profiles, Roman numerals, Latin inscriptions. They clinked solidly in her palm. "Where did you get these?"

He nodded to the window. On the terrace Maria and the boy stood at the pigeon loft.

"Nino found the first in the riverbed. I found the rest."

He told her that at night, after the final roll call, he went down to the Busento to swim. A series of bridges spanned the river, manned by militia soldiers with spotlights and rifles, but if he swam on moonless nights he was invisible. He would dunk beneath the surface, paddle to the riverbed, and down there, in the underworld, he was an oysterman harvesting gold.

He had one more thing to give her: the brown leather suitcase he'd brought from Rome.

"But you'll need it," she said. He kissed her forehead and in the ensuing silence she glimpsed the miles and years she would journey without him.

The day before she and Maria left Rome, Annunziata carried the brown leather suitcase to the Verano cemetery. In her last act as a resident of Italy, she packed the earth of her plot. The soil hissed as each shovelful slid into the silk lining. She stared into the hole, dwarfed by the fury lumbering within her, and felt the distances she had traveled, from driftwood debris to salon parquetry, and how even years after the ground had stopped shaking the memory of the earthquake could still grip her in a rattling panic that took all her self-control to suppress. She had done everything asked of her and her reward was the grave she packed in her husband's suitcase. She fastened the clasps and heaved it off the ground. The weight tightened the bowstring of tendon in her forearm. It was cumbersome, ungainly, a heaviness too impractical to bear, and yet she carried that portable grave across the Atlantic, then across America, because she would not surrender the piece of Roman ground she had gone so far to stand upon, and, if she died in exile, she would at last return home.

3

IN THE CITY OF ANGELS THERE WAS A BUNGALOW OF SAINTS.

Saint Francis of Paola looked out the front window of the Lincoln Heights home Maria's great-aunts—Mimi, Lala, and Pep Morabito—had shared since fleeing Calabria following the 1908 earthquake. It was a cozy kit-bungalow with lapped sidings and overhanging eaves. The look, Maria was told, was Sears Roebuck Revival. Her mother was horrified to live in a house that arrived in the mail from a department store selling underwear.

Coming through the front door, you entered the parlor where Mimi, Lala, and Pep spent their free time hiding from their enemies' envy. There were chintz drapes, a coffee table steadied by matchbooks, a davenport no one was ever allowed to sit on. The only book on the bookshelf was the Bible. To the bungalow's residents, Job was the most relatable character.

Monday through Saturday, when Maria's great-aunts ran their North Broadway trattoria, the parlor was unoccupied. On Sunday, however, it filled with widowed friends and neighbors whom Mimi, Lala, and Pep had always lived beside, first in Gallico Marina, then in Lincoln Heights. In their black dresses and sunglasses, they looked like Grim Reapers going as Greta Garbo for Halloween. They played briscola and scopa, kept an oral record of one another's sins in case Saint Peter lost count, and cursed their enemies in ornately genealogical profanity. ("She is more vulgar than the sweat on the testicles of the horses that carted the coffins of her ancestors to Moorish brothels to be used as latrines on a Sunday," Mimi said after learning Signora Spadafora had slandered her grilled swordfish.)

The saints watched over it all. A dozen plaster figurines stood sentry throughout the house in little shrines encircled by votive candles and withered fronds from Palm Sundays past. "The boys," as Lala called them. Pep could rattle off their names and patronages like a broadcaster reeling through the batting order and career stats. The figurines, part of a series sold by the Los Angeles diocese, were each depicted in their martyrdom, affixed with arrows or striped in claw marks, hemmed by flame or cradling decapitated heads. Maria couldn't brush her teeth or sneak a late-night snack without confronting the torment of some hapless martyr. Her great-aunts' understanding of Catholicism was so fickle you couldn't really call it monotheism. It was a protection racket. Mimi, Lala, and Pep provided prayers and offerings, and expected each saint to deliver on his patronage. If a saint failed to keep his end of the bargain, Mimi would nice and casually leave a hammer beside the figurine. If the saint continued to malinger, he would find himself hostage to escalating ultimatums that ended with his re-martyrdom.

Martyrdom was a subject Maria's great-aunts were well acquainted with. Their husbands had passed in swift succession and, in the decades since, they had waited for God to reunite them. On this point, they were disappointed. God condemned any Morabito woman who survived childhood to ninety years of life. Each night the great-aunts intended to pass in their sleep. Each morning they arrived at breakfast in black dresses billowing like an armada bearing bad news.

"Do you see this?" Pep said, reading the death notices in *L'Italo Americano,* one of Los Angeles's two Italian-language papers, which the Morabito sisters preferred for its more robust obituary coverage. "Signora Agostino. Heart failure."

"Some people have all the luck." Mimi stirred her coffee. "My heart failed me long ago and I'm still here."

"In a manner of speaking," Annunziata said, sifting through the paper for news of the living.

"You poor girl," Lala told Maria with genuine pity. "You have your whole life ahead of you."

Despite their love of cigarettes, physical inertia, and bootlegged grappa of questionable potability, the great-aunts exuded immortality. Perhaps credit went to their Mediterranean diet. The olive oil served as embalmment, the fats and salts as preserving agents, endowing the Morabito sisters with the suspect agelessness of filling-station pastry, a three-pack sealed in cynicism, nonperishable people dreaming of decay.

Planning her funeral was one of the few pleasures Mimi allowed herself. She fantasized about it as she once had her wedding, selecting the flowers, music, and verses, preparing a list of slights suffered at the hands of her family to be nailed to the coffin lid (there was a bit of the opera in Mimi). Yet she kept outliving her undertakers. The most recent in her employ was Ciccio Scopelliti, a snake-oil salesman and director of the Lincoln Heights Funerary Society. For fifty cents a month, he guaranteed a plot, casket, service attended by one professional mourner, an exuberantly embellished obituary, and a selection of seasonal flowers laid on your grave each month.

"It's the only lottery you're guaranteed to win," he promised Mimi, after failing to sell her on his various panaceas. Only a few pins stood in the spare frame of his lower gum, but he had a full head of hair and his own hearse. Halfway handsome, if he wasn't smiling and the sun was in your eyes.

"I'll go quick to get my money's worth," Mimi said.

"Maybe I'll convince you to stick around."

"Maybe someone'll wash out that mouth of yours."

"Maybe you have soap," Ciccio said. He wasn't smiling and the sun was in her eyes.

A few days later, he returned claiming he'd forgotten what flowers Mimi wanted on her grave. "Cactus," she said, and slammed the door. She listened to Ciccio sing a few bars of Caruso as he clomped down the stoop. His brilliantine stained the air with teak and mint, a scent medicinal and fiery in the sinuses. She stood there while the tingle diffused into her capillaries and then went to the backyard to slaughter a chicken. The next morning she found a potted cactus ribboned in red on the porch.

On a Lincoln Heights lot dominated by a brick façade and green awning, Trattoria Contadina remained impervious to progress since the Morabito sisters opened its doors in 1909. Same daily specials, same customers, same time on the same stopped wall clock. A paisan living in the wrong year and country—such as Ciccio Scopelliti, now approaching—could feel at home here.

According to the tax authorities, Trattoria Contadina was a red sauce joint with a history of underreporting. To its regulars the restaurant was an employment bureau, matchmaker's parlor, accountant's office, confessional, time machine. The checkered tablecloths were cured in Lala's matronly perfume. Across those tablecloths unfurled fields of plenty: ricotta balls, ciambotta, 'nduja, fileja, and an endless variety of seafood for Italian diners. For the Americans, they served elephantine meatballs, agita-inducing lasagnas, and a dish ominously referred to on the menu as "meat recipe." Dishes contadini in the old country might only eat at weddings, wakes, or feast days, but it bespoke the conditions of American overstatement that the staples of celebration and calamity were daily fare.

One week after delivering the potted cactus, Ciccio Scopelliti took a seat. The generations of the Morabito family appeared in reverse order: Maria bussing tables; Annunziata serving mugs of sacramental wine, courtesy of a local priest's entrepreneurial interpretation of Prohibition's religious service exemption; Mimi, Lala, and Pep hovering over pots and pans, decanting well-aged grievances into one another's ears.

"What do you want?" Annunziata asked Ciccio. She showed customers the same brusque dismissal she would door-to-door salesmen. Ciccio, himself a door-to-door salesman, was desensitized to rejection.

Ciccio scanned the menu. "I'll take the Mimissima."

Every family is a palimpsest and most days, in the kitchen, Mimi felt herself the half-effaced, hardly legible text overwritten by the energetic bluster of her successors. She took no pleasure in the satisfaction of her customers, whom she dreamed of poisoning. To coax her from the kitchen, one must order her signature dish, the Mimissima.

At a distance, the Mimissima resembled a liquified traffic cone, the vivid hue of hazard. Once in a while you'd find a soggy pea the color of sun-bleached billiard felt, such as the one presently mired in the sauce. Disconcerting given that no other item on the menu contained peas, but Ciccio chose to take it as an omen of good fortune, a pearl produced by the pressure of two cups of cream, a stick of butter, a pound of pasta, and half a pig.

Mimi exited the kitchen. Ciccio set down his fork as the dish's eponymous author approached. The Mimissima was her autobiography and treatise. A disquisition in starch on the consolations required to endure this sorrowful world.

"Well? How is it?" Mimi asked, a weary interrogator who needs a witness to confirm the abundantly obvious. Less a question of culinary enjoyment than one of mental competence, like knowing the correct year and sitting president. A question to which there was but one answer: "It's perfect, signora."

CICCIO SOON BECAME A FIXTURE in the Morabito bungalow. You could map his movements by the snail's trail of brilliantine he secreted on headrests and seat backs; Lala dispensed doilies behind his head like a hostess throwing coasters beneath sweaty tumblers. He left an indelible mark on their furniture. Maria's mother initially disapproved of Ciccio, but his nitrogen-rich hair-growth formula did wonders for her vegetable garden. Fertilizer—or its principal component—was Ciccio's bread and butter. Though he'd emigrated from Catania and had never been naturalized, he claimed he was "born an American" as if it wasn't a nationality but an astrological sign. There was nothing he wasn't willing to fail at. Besides denying his racism, it was his most American quality.

Long before it became the hub of the film and aviation industries, Los Angeles was the capital of the quackery business. The terminally invalided, the arthritic and consumptive, those who just wanted to look twenty-five forever, they all flocked to Southern California for the supposedly therapeutic climate. Naturally, the snake-oil men followed, Ciccio among them. His medicines were entirely side effects. His skin cream gave you vertigo, his weight-loss formula induced hair loss, his cure-all cured nothing, and his anti-aging tonic was an alarmingly fast-acting laxative. After enduring a course of Ciccio's nostrums, a person was so enfeebled, dizzy, nauseous, bald, and dehydrated they were easily persuaded of the advantages of joining his Funerary Society without delay. "I get 'em coming and going," he told Mimi. She rolled her eyes and said, "Yeah, coming and going to the bathroom." That a man driving a hearse convinced anyone he knew the secret to eternal life was testament to the charisma with which he promised miracles.

One summer, when Maria was fourteen, Ciccio hired her as his secretary. Having a secretary answering his calls, he assumed, would give him a veneer of professionalism. Each morning they went to Ciccio's "office." It was hard to imagine Ciccio having anything as respectable as a place of business, but Maria climbed into Ciccio's hearse and they drove beneath the singing trolley wires, over the slimy stripe of the Los Angeles River, toward downtown where the blade signs of movie palaces layered the lower horizon in verticals of fuming neon.

"Here we are," Ciccio said, pulling to a stop. The Eastern Columbia Building drew its paradisal color scheme from a booster's vision of Pacific splendor. Thirteen stories of turquoise terra-cotta detonating with golden sunbursts and spandrils. It looked like the royal treasury of Atlantis had been dredged from the deep, given a fresh varnish, and relocated to downtown's gray-beige busyness.

"You don't work here," Maria said.

Ciccio reached into his wallet and fished out a business card. The addresses matched. The names did not.

"Who's Dr. Charles Scarborough?" Maria asked.

"You're looking at him in the flesh," Ciccio Scopelliti said. Maria was impressed that a man with a second-grade education had the brass to pass himself off as a doctor. She was less impressed to discover the business card's telephone number belonged to one of the public booths inside the lobby. Ciccio opened the booth's accordion door. "Welcome to my office."

"It's a telephone booth."

"It's an executive suite."

"How'd you manage this?" Maria asked.

"A guy I know," Ciccio said. The guy in question was the doorman who made a nice profit renting telephone booths to hucksters, bookies, and professional perjurers selling their services as defense witnesses. When the phone rang, Maria took messages for Dr. Scarborough while Ciccio read the sports pages. At twelve sharp, they returned to the hearse and made whatever house calls had been scheduled that morning.

From everywhere came the crooning vernacular of the city street: the razzle-dazzle of baseball broadcasters on a barbershop wireless, the accounts of amorous adventuring provided by switchboard girls on their lunch hour, the promises of theosophical cultists and sidewalk faith-healers—Maria inhaled it all. Once she wandered into a speakeasy gents room and beheld in the wall-scrawled vulgarities the sense of expressive possibility Monet must have felt when he saw his first waterlily. If it was a slow day, Ciccio would buy his secretary an Orange Julius and they would take the elevator to the City Hall observation deck. At thirty-two stories, City Hall was three times taller than the neighboring buildings, as pronounced as an exclamation mark on the skyline. From the observation deck, you could see Chinatown a few blocks to the north and Little Tokyo a few blocks to the east. You could see the Beaux Arts façades framing

Pershing Square. You could see Wilshire Boulevard, the high street built on a game trail and traversed by mastodon, missionary, and movie star. The Burbank test pilots shearing the underbelly of clouds. The reticulated grids of Craftsman bungalows and courtyards, the tartan weave of lawn and pool unfurling toward the Santa Monica Mountains, beyond which rumors of development prowled like chimeras at the borders of medieval maps. If you went high enough, you might even see Lincoln Heights sandwiched in the sprawl.

Down there, Maria's mother was lost in the city too. Annunziata felt no more at home in Los Angeles than the day she arrived: without English or an automobile, she was marooned in Lincoln Heights in the company of widows waiting to die. Her daughter made things no easier by flaunting the relative ease with which she assimilated, never missing an opportunity to roll her eyes when Annunziata needed help translating a document, or speaking to the bank teller, or navigating the numberless tasks made impossible by barriers of language and culture. To avoid her daughter's condescension, Annunziata consciously narrowed her life until it was small enough to live without Maria's assistance.

When Maria turned fourteen, Annunziata tried to teach her the facts of life. This had nothing to do with reproductive biology (in a Catholic family all births are virgin, all conceptions immaculate). It had to do with the postures of aggression and dissimulation an Italian woman needed to survive. And there was no better place to hone this faculty than the market. Annunziata went to the market as Greeks went to war: armed with guile and under the protection of powerful gods. She didn't shop for food but for shopkeepers. An ideal negotiation ended as outright robbery, with the shopkeeper staring at his shoes, the spine of his spirit snapped, begging her to take what she wanted and leave.

But Maria had no interest in learning the lessons her mother wanted to impart. Maria was trying to acclimate to California and her mother was only interested in perusing butcher-shop gore for parts whose consumption probably violated bestiality statutes.

"What would you rather eat?" Annunziata asked.

"Jell-O."

Oh, the girl knew how to make her mother hurt. Annunziata had suffered worse culinary affronts—the casserole, the abomination!—but never from the mouth of her own daughter. How could the blood of her blood define as food an invertebrate blob of unholy brightness made of horse hooves and . . . and science! American cuisine was not fit for a civilized person. When applied to gun violence or tax audits, *American* connoted ruthless proficiency, yet when applied to life's pleasures (food, seduction) it suggested blandness and impotence. And what did it mean when applied to her daughter? She feared to imagine.

On her free afternoons, Annunziata went to La Grande Station. Inside, the terminal's vaulted curves cupped echoing footfall. Condensation beaded the walls, body heat patterning weather into the empty overhead. On the loudspeaker a clerk announced delays with the dour precision of a dry drunk enumerating the days since his last bender. She stood beneath the Santa Fe Railway departures board and tried to imagine the cities spelled in those spinning tiles, the mileage spooled within the wheels of cantankerous engine cars. It would be so easy to buy a ticket and disappear. She'd done it once before, after the earthquake. Simply left the ruins behind her. What was keeping her here? Her daughter? Please. Maria never overlooked an opportunity to show her mother how little she was needed. The only place in Los Angeles where Annunziata felt welcome was the train station departures hall. A few times she even brought the brown leather suitcase, certain today was the day she would leave.

One July afternoon, Maria went with Ciccio to La Grande to peddle his ghastly green cure-all to arriving tourists. Maria was waiting in the hall, listening to the idle patter of salesmen enthroned on shoeshine stands, when she noticed her father's suitcase; she recognized the case before she recognized the woman sitting beside it. Her mother was wearing the green silk dress with a navy collar and belted waist she reserved for those outings when she had to make a good impression. She was leafing through a folded train schedule with an expression of serene expectation.

For the rest of the afternoon, Maria conjured excuse and justification, telling herself that she hadn't really seen her mother at the train station, or that if she had, there was an innocent explanation. Long before she went to work in the pictures, she understood that the true temptation of fantasy wasn't its outlandishness but its aching plausibility.

When she arrived at the restaurant that evening, her mother was polishing wineglasses with a drab apron as if today were no different from any other. Maria said nothing as she walked past. After the dinner rush ended, when they sat together to eat at the table closest to the kitchen, she broke her silence. Admitting she had seen her mother in the departures hall was out of the question; instead, while describing her day, she offhandedly mentioned that she and Ciccio had gone to La Grande Station.

A drop fell from her mother's spoon and pinged in the bowl. "Did you?"

"Yes."

Her mother set down her spoon, folded her hands, and studied her. Hours manning the steaming stove had wilted her waved curls to a listless bundle trawled up by her hairnet. She was exhausted and overworked, a shadow of the poised woman Maria had seen in the departures hall. The whole of her mother's vitality was expressed through the roving omniscience of her eyes. Not even a long dinner shift sapped them of the power to see through Maria.

"There's something I've wanted to tell you," Maria found herself saying. Tomorrow her mother might board an eastbound train; if Maria didn't tell her now, she might never have the chance. "About when Papà was arrested."

"You want to tell me about your father?"

"No, about me."

"My dear, please don't."

"Why not?"

"Because it won't change anything. It certainly won't make you feel better."

"But Mamma, I—"

"There's nothing you could say that I would want to hear," her mother said, startling Maria with her forceful dismissal. "Why don't you listen to me for a change? Let me tell you a story I heard from some of your great-aunts' friends who come from the mountains around San Lorenzo. Apparently the most interesting thing to ever happen there happened a couple thousand years ago. Have you heard of Alaric? He was the Germanic king who sacked Rome back in ancient times. Real piece of work, if you ask me. From Rome, he pillaged his way down the peninsula until he died in whatever San Lorenzo was called back then. His army diverted the Busento and press-ganged the locals to dig a tomb in the riverbed big enough to bury him and all the looted treasure of Rome. Now, Alaric's men went to a lot of trouble moving the river this way and that, and naturally, they wanted to conceal the location of the body and the treasure. And this is the point of this particular anecdote: Alaric's men knew how to keep a secret. They slaughtered every last gravedigger to ensure no witness was left living. And guess what? To this day no one has discovered Alaric's tomb."

"What? Don't change the subject. I'm trying to tell you something important and you're—"

"And what I'm saying is more important: You didn't kill the witnesses, Maria. You left survivors."

That evening at the corner table was the closest she and her mother ever came to acknowledging the ways they'd hurt each other. Her mother knew; of course she knew. How could Maria have imagined otherwise? How could she have hoped to hide a secret that large from a woman so sensitized to scandal she could smell an impure thought blooming in her daughter's brain?

What Maria didn't understand—what she might never understand—was this: her mother relished making her feel guilty, usually for what Maria couldn't control or hadn't done. So why had she kept quiet about this? Why had she declined to hold her daughter culpable for the one great wrong Maria had committed? If you can't forgive your daughter, perhaps the kindest thing you can do is pretend she isn't asking you to. For Maria, this was no kindness at all.

Over the following years, her relationship with Annunziata dwindled to banal commentary on the weather outside or the meal on the table, the kind of disposable small talk that eases passage in the company of a stranger you're unlikely to meet again.

Left alone with her cumbersome feelings, Maria began to write her father more and more. In the letters she typed on the Olivetti, she described Los Angeles in sweeping volleys of verbiage. When she was fifteen she wrote her first impressions of her high school, a halfway house between child- and adulthood populated by the hormonally unbalanced and emotionally disturbed. When she was sixteen she told her father about the fishmonger's son, Angelo, a regularly pantsed pushover for whom Maria nursed a socially self-destructive crush. In all seasons she told him about the restaurant regulars, the competitive nostalgists and stooped day laborers, the friends of her aunts whose archive of local sin swelled with their acquisition of tabloid English.

When Universal released James Whale's adaptation of *Frankenstein,* Maria saw it opening night. To the Italians who patronized the Lincoln Heights theater, the movie house was a classroom. Here you could study the conventions of your adoptive country from the anonymity of the audience. Here you learned whom to desire and dread. The *Frankenstein* source material and later adaptations depicted the experience in the scene when the fleeing Monster comes upon a cabin in the woods. Forlorn and exiled, the Monster watches the family through the cabin window, thinking that if he learns their customs and culture, they will welcome him in from the cold. That's how Maria saw herself in the darkened theater: a monster at the window of a house where she did not belong, trying to find her way to the lighted room within. She told her father this too. She told him everything but the one thing that mattered.

Giuseppe's replies, when they arrived at all, arrived censored. Dissected by razor blade, whole sentences and paragraphs surgically excised. Maria and her father resorted to a coded language of innuendo and allusion. Sometimes she larded her letters with political references to satisfy the San Lorenzo authorities' appetite for expurgation. Make excess blatant and the censor will overlook understatement. Other times, the censor worked so haphazardly the only purpose was to frustrate communication. What survived of Giuseppe Lagana in these missives that were little more than collections of lacunae? Not even his name: without fail, the censor cut out her father's signature.

"SHE'S NEARLY EIGHTEEN. SHE'LL FINISH school this spring," Lala announced. A heavy, windless movie rain thrashed the windowpanes. "Time, isn't it?"

To Mimi, Lala, and Pep, love was a venereal disease of the heart, curable by marriage. Like any invasive procedure, it was best to get matrimony over with while you were young enough to bounce back. They studied young men in church, on alleyway handball courts, in the feast day processions for San Vittoriano and the Madonna delle Stelle. Finding a suitable husband took the research required to buy a single-use item secondhand—that a man was on the market and in your price range suggested fraud or defect. They judged the sons of butchers, tailors, and fruit vendors: all geriatric souls smuggled into youthful bodies and rendered romantically inert to Maria by her great-aunts' approval. The idea of Maria marrying one of the "foreigners"—as her aunts called Americans—wasn't entertained, even in desperation. Americans had invented the Packard backseat, the motel do-not-disturb, and the Nevada divorce, which explained why their marriages had the average life expectancy of a Calabrian newborn.

Maria protested that she was too young to marry.

"You've used that one before," Mimi said.

"When I was fifteen."

"And when you were fifteen I said let Maria wait until she's sixteen to get married. Blood of my blood, you can only fool me once."

"Seventeen and not pregnant," Lala said. "It's a disgrace."

"You know what they'd call an unwed seventeen-year-old where we're from . . ."

"A child?" Maria said.

"A child, don't make me laugh."

"Nine months is all that should ever separate childhood from motherhood."

". . . they called her a miserable old maid," Mimi said. "Like my sisters."

"Better to be unwanted than wanted by the likes of Ciccio Scopelliti." Lala patted Mimi's hand. "How I pray God will end your suffering soon."

"At least in Heaven I'll be an only child." Turning to Maria, Mimi said, "A miserable old maid doomed to spend her days talking to cats. Is that how you want to spend your life, talking to heartless animals?"

"I am talking to heartless animals," Maria said.

"The language she uses. And on a Sunday."

"An infamy, that language, on a Sunday."

Notwithstanding their conviction in their own irrelevance, Maria knew her great-aunts were giants. To have come where they came from, and do what they did, so late in life. As an expression of desire through motion, emigrating had been their great dance. They were ballerinas in black dresses.

". . . what I would do if I was her age."

"You'd throw yourself from the nearest bell tower, I know, I know," Maria said.

"One word," Pep said. "Just a word."

"You? Keeping yourself to one word? Now I've heard it all," Mimi said.

"One word I'd tell myself. One word."

"What would you tell yourself?"

Pep, the least fatalistic of the three Morabito sisters, looked at Maria as if staring back through time and gave her grand-niece the one word of advice she wished someone had given her: "Run."

MARIA DID. CICCIO COVERED HER. After five years living in sin, he proposed to Mimi in the dining room of Trattoria Contadina on an unseasonably warm Tuesday in March.

". . . and you can't be made to testify against your spouse. It's in the Constitution," Ciccio said, concluding his proposal after five minutes analyzing the tax and legal benefits of matrimony. Mimi understood his proposal as an effort to postpone Maria's own marital reckoning, but what could she do, in full view of the restaurant patrons, but accept? Maybe she'd use a cactus as her flower. That way she might enjoy tossing the bridal bouquet.

Amid the commotion of wedding preparations, Maria made preparations of her own. She circled classified ads for secretarial, typist, and switchboard positions in *The Hollywood Reporter.* She presented her woefully accurate résumé and cover letter to Ciccio.

"You mind if I give this a little make up?" he asked.

By *make up* he meant *made up*. He rendered her CV as faithless as a based-on-a-true-story biopic.

"I didn't go to secretarial school," Maria said, reading his revisions.

"Don't trivialize your accomplishments," Ciccio chided. "To present yourself honestly is to undersell yourself. You were the best secretary Charles Scarborough ever had."

The week before the wedding, she found a notice seeking competent typists fluent in French, German, Spanish, or Italian. The ad held considerable promise: it had eighteen typos.

When Maria arrived at Mercury Pictures International for her interview, she passed through a main office divided into cubicles. Like a casino, there were no clocks on the walls, a policy instituted to juice a few extra hours from the workforce each week. It was among the more tenable of the measures the studio had taken to keep afloat. Screenwriters were fired on Friday evening, rehired Monday morning, and asked to work through the weekend. Sets were occasionally hired secondhand from pornographers commanding predictably lower rental fees than legitimate studio prop suppliers. Mercury had been among the most successful studios of the silent era, but the onset of the Depression and the advent of the talkies had reduced it to a shadow of its former glory. Maria felt as if she were walking through a once grand palazzo that had fallen into ruins.

"Excuse me, I have a job interview with Mr. Feldman," Maria told a man hurrying toward the exit.

The man chortled heartily and pointed down the hall.

Art Feldman, Vice President and Head of Production was stenciled in neat black letters upon his door. *Head of Publicity*, *Head of Accounts*, and *Head of Sales* had been hastily scrawled on paper and taped below.

Maria knew little about Art Feldman beyond what she read in the framed waiting-room news clipping that detailed the libel suit the Ku Klux Klan had brought against him for his "overly accurate"—Mr. Feldman's words—portrayal of their activities in one of his social message dramas. "The greatest testament to my character is the character of my litigants," Mr. Feldman boasted in the kicker.

Maria knocked on the door. Inside, an adamant voice bellowed, "No!" Unsure what to do, Maria knocked once more and let herself in.

Four typewriters sat on the desk, each loaded with pages of script, production memorandum, advertising copy, and inadequate public apology. The life cycle of an exploitation film in four movements. Artie was a one-man quartet, juggling the counterpointed melodies as he swiveled from typewriter to typewriter until he saw Maria in his doorway and asked just who the hell she thought she was.

Maria introduced herself. "I'm here about the typist position."

"Oh, I see. I thought you were here about the misfortune." Seeing her confusion, he added, "An actor in a Western we just made shot himself."

"My God," Maria said. "I'm sorry for your loss."

"Losses," Artie said, accepting her condolences with a solemn nod. "It'll be another ten grand to redo the ending. Frankly, this happens more often than I'd like to admit."

"I'm sorry—how often do your employees kill themselves?"

"It's been happening more and more. And not always with a gun, mind you. It's happened several times with a bow and arrow. Once even with a tomahawk. So, you're here about a job?"

While Maria struggled to reconcile the physics of a self-inflicted tomahawk, Artie explained that to keep costs down amid the Depression he employed the same actors to play multiple roles in the same picture. "Somehow this nitwit gets himself cast as both a cowboy *and* an Indian. He gets shot by himself in the fifth reel and no one noticed until today."

"But . . . he's still among us?"

"No." Artie smashed his cigarette into the tray. "I fired him this morning."

Before he wasted time remembering her name, Artie dictated a letter to his distributor regarding his policy of rereleasing failed movies under new titles until they turned a profit. Maria noted the typewriter's exclamation mark had worn smooth from overuse. Artie clocked her words-per-minute, accuracy, and tolerance for profanity. Satisfied she met these prerequisites, he offered her a cigarette.

Artie had always liked Italians. When Hollywood was in its infancy, none of Wall Street's Ivy League anti-Semites would lend to movie men. The Hollywood lender of choice was A. P. Giannini, founder of the Bank of America, née Bank of Italy, up in San Francisco. Giannini was technically gentile, but in California an Italian was just a Jew with the wrong sabbath. Artie had respected Giannini—a rarity in their businesses—for democratizing banking the way the pictures had the theater. "Your character is your collateral," Giannini had told Artie and Ned Feldman the day he lent them the capital to start Mercury. Artie was never late on his repayment. He signed each check himself.

He explained the position: "At night we shoot foreign language versions of our pictures for export. French, German, Spanish, and Italian immigrant actors use the same sets, wear the same costumes, and replicate scene for scene in their native language what was shot in the English version that day. We can make five movies for not much more than the price of one. So, in addition to your services as a typist, you would need to translate English scripts into Italian."

As the only fluent English speaker in her household, Maria had extensive experience translating into and out of Italian.

"You're a Catholic, I take it?" Artie asked. "You have any clout with the local bishop?"

"No, sir."

"That's too bad." Artie lit a cigarette and leaned back. There were already two lit in the ashtray, but as with typewriters and hairpieces, Artie craved excess. "I could use a good word with the top banana. The Production Code just installed a Grand Inquisitor named Joseph Breen. One hell of a Catholic, apparently." His gray eyes sparkled with grim irony. "In my experience, when a Christian comes to town to clean things up, it rarely ends well for the locals."

Artie swapped his cigarette for one of the others smoldering in the tray.

"Now, Breen assures me the goal of his asinine moralizing is to secure the movie business's long-term prosperity. Who knows? Perhaps a devil can quote scripture for his own purposes. Shakespeare said that. Me? I say this Joe Breen is as intellectually disingenuous as the thoughts before prayers. He doesn't want patrons; he wants parishioners." Artie switched cigarettes. "Religion isn't the opiate of the masses because the masses pay good money for opiates. Now, if you can't give away religion on a Sunday morning, how the hell am

I supposed to sell it on a Saturday night? You can't. No one wants it. It stinks. So, tell me, Miss Lagana, as someone fluent in Catholicism, what do I do?"

"I'm just here for the typist position," she reminded him.

The smile soured on Artie's lips. "Great. Another dummy."

Maria gathered her purse and walked to the door. She dreaded the empty expanse of sidewalk, the long Red Car ride back to Lincoln Heights, and then the evening ahead, wiping down tables and washing dishes at Trattoria Contadina. She turned back.

"You want to know what I'd do?" she said. "I'd give Mr. Breen plenty to satisfy his censor's pen. If he expects you to go a mile over the line, he's less likely to notice when you put your toes over."

Artie stared at Maria curiously. "How the hell would you know your way around a censor?"

She told him about her father. A small serving of admiration poured into Artie's voice as he asked her to have a seat. He scanned her cover letter. His finger stopped halfway down the page. "You worked for Dr. Charles Scarborough?"

Maria frowned. "You know him?"

"Yeah, I know him." Artie lifted his toupee off his head. "I drank a bottle of his weight-loss formula. I gained fifteen pounds and my hair fell out. To be perfectly honest, we could do with that kind of moxie. You can start next week." He nodded to his four Underwoods. "Have a typewriter."

"I have my own."

Out on the sidewalk she paused beneath the studio gates. A stucco arch rose over the guard shack with the words *Mercury Pictures International* affixed in black swoops of cursive. The Temple of Mercury once stood on the Aventine Hill where Maria had grown up. Thousands of years ago, travelers, translators, and letter writers climbed the Aventine to leave offerings to their patron deity before beginning a journey. Still standing beneath the studio gates, Maria rummaged around in her purse until she found a single penny. She laid the coin on the sidewalk and hoped it was enough to buy the protection of the ancient god of passage.

THE SUNDAY BEFORE MARIA STARTED at Mercury, Mimi made her way to the altar of St. Peter's Italian Church. She refused to wear white ("Who'm I kidding?") and settled on a grayish dress her sisters insisted was lavender. The pews filled with neighbors, Trattoria Contadina regulars, and gossipmongers scandalized by the December-December romance. Ciccio's side of the aisle was populated by his fellow Eastern Columbia loiterers and members of the Funerary Society. His creditors made a good showing.

After the ceremony, the priest looked green. Over the last few years, Mimi had stopped airing her own sins at Saturday confession. The thrill was gone, and so, for sport, she confessed fictitious affairs with prominent parishioners rendered in gruesomely vivid detail. The priest was a known hypochondriac, and Mimi liked watching him squirm the next day, following Holy Communion, when he had to slurp down the sacramental backwash in full knowledge of the sullied places his parishioners' lips had probed. From the anonymity of the confessional screen, the priest had tried to picture this mysterious adulteress. He imagined she was in her thirties with red hair. He only recognized the disembodied voice behind the bridal veil as Mimi pledged her everlasting fidelity.

The pipe organ blasted as guests and well-wishers flooded the street. There was applause and shouts of "Auguri!" Lala and Pep dabbed their eyes. Every cheek was kissed. The front grille of Ciccio's hearse was loaded with flowers and he drove his bride down Alameda Street to Italian Hall, where waiters maneuvering with the synchronized cheer of a musical chorus laid out the antipasti. The wedding reception was a public works program. Profits pocketed from the only two businesses to thrive in Hoover's Depression—the snake-oil and funeral trades—plowed back into the local economy via fourteen courses of animal, vegetable, and mineral, an eight-piece Sicilian band, enough white wine to rub out the red wine stains, and enough red wine to satisfy a wedding in Cana. A dozen local businesses and a criminal defense firm balanced their books on the back of Ciccio and Mimi's wedding. By the time the bonbonnière of sugared almonds was opened, and the Sicilian band started playing tarantellas, Maria had slipped into the sweet lethargy induced by rising blood alcohol, falling inhibitions, and the spectacle of her great-aunts dancing barefoot to a bawdy folk song about the sexual prowess of a butcher, a farmer, and a fisherman.

When no one was looking, she left.

Annunziata noticed her daughter's absence an hour later. She asked wedding guests if they had seen Maria. None had. She asked the groom. "She'll be fine, Nunzia," Ciccio said. "She'll be just fine."

The bungalow was empty when Annunziata returned. She called out but no one answered. Was she too late? She crossed the hallway and peered into Maria's bedroom. A brown paper bag had split open, disgorging Maria's carefully folded clothes onto the floor. Maria was sitting outside on the back stairs.

"There you are."

Annunziata reached for her daughter, as if only then, in the shadows, she saw Maria well enough to recognize her. Maria endured the embrace as a physical aggression she couldn't overpower or outrun: she played dead.

Night insects jeered from the garden.

Annunziata stepped back and smoothed the front of her green silk dress. The transgressing suddenness of her affection, this breach of the restraining order set by family culture and expectation, had taken her by surprise too. Feeling Maria recoil in her arms validated her longstanding belief that loving your children is a compulsion best tended to alone and without their knowledge.

"Ciccio told me you got a job."

Maria nodded.

"Where will you live?"

"I got a room in a women's boardinghouse."

Annunziata considered how to move through the next moments without causing irreparable harm. "Will you be okay?" The anger ebbed in Maria's eyes, and it saddened Annunziata to see how little her daughter trusted her. The night air was cool, perfumed in jasmine and wood smoke. Moths caroused dizzily around the lamp. The weatherworn stoop groaned as she squatted on the steps.

"We should celebrate your good news. Get us a couple glasses."

When Maria returned from the kitchen, her mother was walking back from the shed with a watering can encrusted in flaky layers of rust and dirt. She reached into the watering can and pulled out a bottle of Old Crow.

"Whose is that?" Maria asked.

"Whose do you think, Einstein?"

Along with short hair and long pants, the imbibing of hard liquor regularly featured in her mother's remonstrances against "American ladies," a phrase she invested with the raised-eyebrow incredulity of outlandish contradiction. Maria didn't know why she was surprised to discover that her mother drank booze. Her mother had an incumbent's effortless flair for accommodating hypocrisy and abdicating blame.

"So you're a boozer," Maria said.

"What, you thought I was a gardener?"

Annunziata poured two fingers into both glasses. The mellow amber caught the glint of a distant streetlight and the heat of the alcohol diffused into the cool night air. Maria gave the liquor an uncertain sniff, and something about that tentative little snuffle—the suspicion and naiveté it implied—made Annunziata wish she had been kinder to Maria back when kindness was all her daughter wanted from her. "A hundred years," she said, clinking her glass against Maria's. In garden shadows, where no one could see them, she taught her daughter to drink Kentucky bourbon neat.

Maria took a belt and as the comet's tail plunged down her esophagus, she folded over in a fit of dry heaves. "There's something wrong with mine," she gasped.

"I poisoned it."

Maria's laughter led into another outburst of coughs. She felt her mother's palm between her shoulder blades, patting her back until she could breathe. "Exhale when you drink," Annunziata said. "It goes down easier that way. Like this." Maria watched her mother sip the flammable liquid without flinching. The sip left a glistening waterline on her upper lip. Her lower lip printed a ruby crescent on the rim. Her mother drank bourbon in the moonlight with an effortless air of unattainable elegance.

"You make it look easy."

"My dear," Annunziata said with regal self-possession, "I make it all look easy."

"I never knew you drank liquor."

"What you don't know about me would fill a library."

It was true. Her mother was a library whose volumes she was prohibited from opening. "I don't know about the earthquake. You've never told me about it."

The earthquake was the great unutterable, a topic so taboo Maria knew it only by the suddenness with which its mention would stop a conversation.

Annunziata exhaled. "It left little to tell."

Maria could hear Verdi drifting from a neighbor's Victrola, the cars passing down Griffin Avenue, the running commentary of a radio weatherman. There was much they would never tell each other. "I've always wanted to understand."

"You think you can understand a thing like that?"

"Not the earthquake. You."

Annunziata marveled at her daughter's folly. The better you know someone the less understandable they become. That's what intimacy is—not a threshold of knowledge but a capitulation to ignorance, an acceptance that another person is made as bewildered and ungovernable by her life as you are by yours.

"Please, Mamma. Help me."

Annunziata set her glass on the weatherworn step. With as much tenderness as she could muster, she turned to her daughter and said, "I don't know how."

She waited for Maria to return inside before straightening her green silk dress, setting the bottle of Old Crow in the watering can, and returning it to the shed. The scent of basil and thyme rose from twine-plotted rows in the garden. Annunziata returned to the house, went to her closet, and hauled out the brown leather suitcase. She lugged it outside, careful not to let the screen door crash. On her knees, she scooped the Roman earth from the suitcase and spread it across the garden. Moonlight glazed the tomato cages. By late summer those little tornados of wire would loom with the towering leafiness of Corinthian columns, and Annunziata would crouch there many August evenings, sneaking nips of Old Crow as she tended to what grew in graveyard soil.

When she finished, she brought the suitcase back inside, brushed out the lining, and set it beside Maria's bed. "It's still a little dirty, but better than a torn bag." Maria unfastened the scratched bronze clasps and peered inside. This was the only piece of luggage Annunziata had brought to the La Grande departures hall. It was all she wanted to keep. And now it was her daughter's.

Annunziata washed her hands in the kitchen sink, luxuriating in the heat as soapy spindrift whirled around the drain. She dried them on a dishtowel and telephoned for a Red Top cab. It would be simpler for everyone if Maria was gone when the wedding party returned home. First Gallico Marina, then Rome, now this: the third great parting of Annunziata's life. She had never imagined she would be the one left behind.

Headlights pushed shadows across the wall. The taxi idled outside.

Plaster saints watched from the windows as Annunziata carried the brown suitcase while the cabbie set the Olivetti in the trunk. The cabbie returned to the driver's seat and slammed the door. Mother and daughter stood beneath overhanging leaves gilded in the streetlamp's glow.

"There's something I should say before I go," Maria said.

"No, there isn't."

"There is."

Annunziata hung her head, resigned to whatever Maria needed to confess.

"You've done a good job, Mamma."

Annunziata laughed. "You're so full of shit."

TWO SUNDAYS PASSED BEFORE MARIA returned to Lincoln Heights, and her visits became increasingly infrequent as she worked her way up the ranks at Mercury, first translating scripts for the Italian casts that shot at three in the morning, following the French-, German-, and Spanish-language versions, and then overseeing the Italian-language productions themselves, beginning with a picture called *Unanticipated Descents.* It was about a plane crash, an illegitimate child, and madness. After much familial inveiglement, she invited them to see the Italian-export version of *Unanticipated Descents* one Sunday in the projection room. Lala brought a pair of opera glasses. Ciccio asked what this place was paying for its bathroom soap. Maria dimmed the lights and signaled the projectionist. Her family seemed genuinely—perhaps alarmingly—moved by a picture plotted to extract the most pun from its title. Only when her mother said, "These make more sense when you understand what they're saying," would it occur to Maria that her family had never seen a picture in their own language. To them, Maria had invented sound.

Over the next few years, Maria's family piled into Ciccio's hearse on Sundays and drove to the studio lot to watch Mercury's Italian exports. On their way to the projection room, Maria led her mother through the back-lot sets, where the distant corners of the earth were suddenly accessible to Annunziata: London, Paris, New York. The destinations Annunziata fantasized about in the La Grande departures hall were now within walking distance. All week she waited for Sunday to see where her daughter would take her next.

They would picnic in the projection room and watch screwball comedy and schmaltzy melodrama shot by a skeleton crew in the predawn hours. No matter the genre, Annunziata watched with a sense of exhilarating clairvoyance. All the Italian-language versions, even the ahistorical fabulism of Mercury's period pieces, seemed transmitted from a future she wouldn't live to witness. On the screen people who looked and spoke like her navigated this bewildering nation as respectable citizens, unencumbered by legal status or language barrier or nativism. The actors and actresses were immigrants from Sicily, Calabria, Campania, Puglia, Basilicata, who in English-language productions were no more than extras, bit players, dago heavies. But in Mercury's Italian-language versions, they starred as scientists and newspapermen and detectives and captains of industry invested with the full rights and privileges of citizenship. Only in a fantasy country produced for export would Annunziata find the place she belonged.

In 1938, Maria received a letter from her father. Amid the strokes of the censor's razor, an important line survived: "I'll see you soon." It was the last letter she would ever receive from him. The Sunday picnics in the projection room ended not long after, when Mussolini banned imported American pictures and Mercury ceased producing Italian-language versions of its films. After the last reel, Maria walked with her family to Gower Street and said her goodbyes. She thought back to the evening she had stood beside the idling taxi and reassured her mother that she would be only seven miles away.

"My dear," her mother had said. "It may as well be Rome."

For a time, on a Sunday, it was.

THE BIGWIG

1

AT THE SAME TIME MARIA WAS SITTING IN THE STUDIO COMMISSARY, thinking about the German miniaturist's scale model of Mercury, Artie Feldman was armored within several thousand pounds of Detroit steel, coasting west on Santa Monica Boulevard, top down, wind raking his "hair."

His week-old Lincoln was a vanilla sundae of a coupe: all cream and chrome, rounded curves and stretched lines. The automobile was the Angeleno exoskeleton, and each year, on his birthday, Artie treated himself to a new one, believing the Lincoln lineup's annual upgrades would offset and restrain his own corporeal deterioration. He knew he couldn't die behind the wheel of a new car.

Beverly Hills tasted of orange blossom, Chanel No. 5, and tailpipe. The Pacific Electric Red Car jangled to a stop on his right. Disembarking tourists strolled beneath the trellised pergolas and leafy canopies of Beverly Gardens. Beyond that lay the flatlands where, in the 1920s real estate bubble, you could buy a lot with only your hat as down payment. After the flatlands you hit Sunset Boulevard and the famous foothills where movie colony royalty resided among patchworks of Spanish tile, putting green, pool water, and bared navel. Artie and his wife, Mildred, considered buying a place up there, but even more than the covenants against selling Jews certain tracts, it was the ordinance prohibiting for-sale signs larger than one square foot that offended Artie, who saw the billboard as the most elemental unit of personal expression. An awful lot of la-di-da for a place that was one big bean field twenty years ago.

Still, Artie showed his face in Beverly Hills at least once a week. It was paradoxical that a business reliant on the exploitation of youth would operate by the rules of an old folks home: if you weren't seen, you were presumed dead.

Continental lunch at the Victor Hugo, drinks beneath the Zodiac Bar's domed clock, dancing at Ciro's amid the cancan-costumed cigarette girls. Artie ate at places that listed celebrity patrons atop the menu as if they were served by the slice as a starter. On weekends he attended Beverly Hills backyard bashes modeled on the garden parties of East Coast gentility, all charming banter and "Blue Danube," the staid tastefulness corralled within red-and-white-striped tents. If an out-of-towner wanted to experience the seedy whoopee of tabloid lore, Artie had to take them downtown to the Main Street honky-tonks that pandered to the expectations of midwestern vulgarians.

But if you wanted to be seen conducting business over lunch, few places offered better visibility than Romanoff's on Rodeo Drive. It was a panopticon of banquettes thoughtfully arrayed to ensure you were visible to everyone but your dining companion. You could chart rising and falling careers purely based on whom the maître d' seated where. Artie felt eyes on him when he walked in. He heard the wingbeats of unfurling tablecloths. The bright chime of silverware on porcelain. The pianist lunging through Schoenberg with the violent elegance of a cat stalking a butterfly across the keyboard.

The eponymous owner stood at the maître d' stand stroking his pencil mustache.

"Hiya, Prince Mike," Artie said, tossing his keys to a red-vested valet.

Prince Michael looked up with those dark, melancholic eyes that had witnessed empires end. To hear him tell it, Prince Michael Romanoff was of *the* Romanoffs. It never ended well for the children of families whose fame was confirmed by the definite article. The Romanoffs. The Frankensteins. The Donners. Once Michael Romanoff was nephew to Nicholas II and now he managed a restaurant that served pineapple and cottage cheese salad.

But as Artie well knew, Prince Michael Romanoff was neither Romanoff nor royal. He was Harry Gerguson, of the Brooklyn Gergusons, and before becoming a prince he pressed pants for a living. It was hard not to love a town where a pants presser could rise to the rank of deposed royalty. Everyone knew that Michael Romanoff was as fake as his Oxbridge accent, and anywhere else this revelation would lead to social excommunication, but here? Here, Michael Romanoff *was* royalty. Who among his regular clientele hadn't changed their name? Who wasn't an airbrush artist of autobiography? You couldn't help admiring a guy for doing what you were doing, only less restrained by shame or plausibility.

What got Artie, however, was that even though everyone knew Michael Romanoff was a fraud, he was still paid to consult on pictures about the Russian Imperial family. It was an ouroboros of bullshit: a man who built his artifice from movie fantasies became the authority legitimizing and propagating those fantasies. They weren't remotely realistic, but then again, what kind of masochist enjoys realism? Realism is everywhere. It stinks. Artie had emigrated from Europe to escape all that dour realism. If Manhattan critics privileged with Anglo surnames and Ivy League pedigrees fetishized realism, it was because they resided in realms more artificial than any Artie conjured.

As a young man, after long days training at the boxing gym, Artie had worked as a doorman at a Broadway theater where the Park Avenue set paid top dollar to watch Ibsen jerkoffs get screwed six ways to Sunday. The lesson was that rich people would recognize the humanity of poor people, provided the poor people weren't real. Artie had vowed never to cater to people who read reviews, or went to the theater, or had Park Avenue property beyond what they erected on a Monopoly board. He understood what his audience understood: No one truly touched by reality believes it worth honoring. What monster or dullard provisioned with Hollywood's godly powers would reproduce life as it was, without revision or redemption? And if the world narrowed to what you could revise or redeem, then for Artie Feldman it scarcely existed beyond the borders of the film frame.

He followed Romanoff to his table and stashed Ned's birthday present beneath his chair. "If you see a Republican with a shit-eating personality, send him here."

A few minutes later the other Mr. Feldman arrived. A quarter-inch taller and eight minutes older, Ned Feldman looked the way Artie aspired to feel: youthful, or at least well-preserved. They were identical twins who had never been mistaken for each other. Ned was crowned in chestnut hair as luxuriant as mink pelt and forever looked like he'd just finished a fortifying breakfast. The remnants of weekend sun glowed in his cheeks. Released from the death trap of his first marriage, Ned had jettisoned thirty pounds and a quarter century of recriminations. He'd started eating avocados and exuded the hale glow of second chances. (The stenographer in Artie's head captured Ned more succinctly: *jackass.*)

Ned took a seat and crossed his legs. The vigorous scent of citrus cologne issued from his unbuttoned collar.

"Art," Ned said. The tumult of Artie's polka-dot on plaid elicited a wince from his older brother.

"Ned," Artie said. Each name, in the other's mouth, fell between loveless greeting and expletive. There wasn't a time when they hadn't been at each other's throats. Raised in Silesia, at the eastern reaches of the German Empire, where anti-Semitism was all the Prussians and Poles had agreed upon, Artie and Ned had outlasted their state, their kaiser, their real names. In 1901, their older sister, Ada, raised the money to send Artie and Ned to live with relatives in New York, where ten years after immigrating, the brothers opened the Titanic, an unfortunately named nickelodeon furnished with seats rented from a funeral parlor.

They expanded quickly, and in 1918, Artie wrote Wilhelm II to inform the deposed kaiser that though his family had endured generations of persecution at the hands of the Prussian state, he was pleased to offer the unemployed king an entry-level position at any of his six picture palaces. "I can always use a fellow with managerial experience," he wrote the former head of state. But the theater chain grew too big too fast, and soon the Titanic met the same end as its namesake. Artie and Ned Feldman decamped to Los Angeles to remake themselves in a land far from their lenders' lawyers. At the corner of Gower and Sunset, they founded Mercury Pictures International, an institution in the silent era that reaped windfall profits through much of the twenties, until the arrival of sound films and the Great Depression reduced it to a second-tier studio producing movies that passed over the eye without lingering in the brain.

Through it all, Artie and Ned were hostile combatants in a war whose ceasefire was poorly articulated and haphazardly enforced. Mortal enemies to be sure, but mortal enemies whose shared time in the trenches made them closer than kin. In a business where friendship had a high turnover rate, the Feldman brothers' animosity was a stabilizing force. Artie would give Ned an organ, but wouldn't lend him a five-spot, handkerchief, or kind word. Some days their admiration for Cain was their only common ground. That and ownership stakes in this tinpot crapola factory. Hardly anything. Nearly everything.

The only way to successfully run a family business was to put three thousand miles between the family members. For nine years Ned Feldman had been based in Manhattan, where he kept Mercury's finances afloat. He lived on Park Avenue, attended the theater, read reviews. He took elocution lessons from the same acting coach who taught Mercury's beautiful buffoons to talk like Cary Grant, and now spoke with the transatlantic accent native only to cinema screens and certain New England yacht clubs. Ned's aspirations to gentility seemed pathetic to Artie. He owned a sailboat he didn't sail, a library he didn't read, and oil portraits of dead aristocrats he'd never met. He wasted thousands of dollars on Republican fundraisers but popped into every studio bathroom he passed to flip off the lights. It was rumored that Hoover had wanted to appoint Ned as ambassador to Paraguay until he met him. Most heartbreaking of all, and known to no one outside Ned's family, was his collection of celebrity autographs. Ned didn't collect autographs from movie stars, but from the politicians and business leaders he wrote to under various pretenses to receive their signatures on letters addressed to him. Ned judged himself by the stature of his correspondents. He was the president of a studio and an autograph hound. He embodied the prim hypocrisies Artie had spent his life subverting, and yet the sentiment he most often elicited from Artie—after anger, disdain, envy, loathing, indifference, hatred, embarrassment, and spite—was pity.

"How's little Billy?" Ned asked, unfolding the menu.

Artie detected a repressed smirk smuggled into his youngest's name. If Ned knew about the boy's latest infamy, it meant that Mildred was talking with Ned's ex-wife. If lines of communication had opened between those two, there was no telling what crosscurrents of hearsay Mildred was privy to.

"Billy?" he said. "What can I say about him? He's my son. I'm his father."

"That, my friend, is a tautology," Ned said. That was Ned in a nutshell: adventurous enough to use a word like *tautology* only because Artie probably thought it was Ancient Greek for knot-tying. "I hear he's quite the marksman."

Ned did know. Wonderful. *Family secret* was as oxymoronic to the Feldmans as *happily married* or *brotherly love.*

The pertinent facts: On a nightly basis for the last few months,

Artie's eleven-year-old had sleepwalked into the master bedroom to take a leak in Artie's laundry hamper. So said Mildred, the boy's defense attorney. Artie wasn't buying the sleepwalking alibi. The preternatural consistency of Billy's aim—always Artie's hamper, despite its proximity to his wife's—required a suspension of disbelief even a showman like Artie found implausible. The laundryman had started giving Artie funny looks. Probably thought Artie was one of those movie people who hosted weird "parties" full of "Europeans" who "socialized" with "each other." Already he could hear the laundryman's ironic lilt italicize every other word with insinuation.

Having kids in this country . . . you might as well open a looney bin for uninsured anarchists. The noise, mess, and mutiny, they were goddamned rabble-rousers, his three kids, protesting everything from bedtime to vegetables. Every parent is a failed dictator; it was nearly enough to inspire admiration for the real ones. A few years back, before Mussolini joined himself to Hitler's hip like a colostomy bag, Artie had read Il Duce's autobiography for parenting tips. It was written in semiliterate bombast, its pages damp with autocratic spittle, the reading experience akin to literary lobotomy, and yet, Mussolini's leadership style made for inspired parenting ideas. Artie had imposed curfews and pledges of fealty. But here you had Billy, performing nocturnal reconnoitering of Artie's laundry hamper like a resistance fighter ready to blow the railway depot. If Artie wasn't so embarrassed, he might've been halfway proud of the little renegade.

"Mildred's taking him to the psychoanalyst next week."

"I bet it's the Oedipus complex," Ned diagnosed while surveying the menu. "Say, how are the sweetbreads à la king?"

"You only want the best for your children, but what do they want, huh?" Artie asked. "Only to kill you and bang your wife."

"I hear Romanoff's makes some mean sweetbreads."

"You know, you never used to hear about boys trying to kill their fathers. But now? Now it's patricide all the live-long day."

"Kids today," Ned said. "Who knows what makes them tick?"

"When we were boys, the fathers were the ones trying to kill the sons, weren't they?"

"It's a grand tradition. Judeo-Christian belief is premised on it."

"I bet Abraham brought Isaac to the mountaintop after catching him pissing in his hamper one time too many. Hell, I'm one soiled undershirt from bringing Billy to the top of Bunker Hill."

"Then there's Jesus," Ned pointed out. "Whose hamper did he foul up?"

"Talk about a fella who needs psychoanalysis. Poor guy thinks his dad's God and his mom's a virgin. No wonder he has a messiah complex. Still, I must admit, I like Jesus's politics. Feeding the hungry, blessing the meek, wearing a robe to work."

Ned frowned; a junior nobody from Columbia had a better table than them. "The problem with Christianity, of course, is the Christians."

"It's like communism. A belief system based on human dignity that somehow incites its adherents to mass murder."

"You know," Ned said, "I met a five-hundred-dollar-a-week writer who used to send his scripts to the psychoanalyst to find out what was wrong with them."

"How'd that work out?"

"He's an English professor now." Ned folded his menu and studied his brother. "C'mon, Art. How's Billy really doing?"

So Ned had heard about that too. Fantastic. "He's still getting bullied at school," Artie said. "Tough little guy, in his own way, it's just this punk in his class, this Dennis Bleecker. The kid's mother is a mover and shaker in isolationist circles: the Mothers' Movement, the America First Committee. Given everything happening in Washington, I'm sure she's pouring poison into her son's ear about me."

"Then I don't really blame Billy. I'd probably piss in your hamper too."

"I've tried to teach him to box but he'd rather wander around the garden looking at bugs and flowers with a magnifying glass."

A waiter came by with fresh drinks, thank God. Artie killed a third of his in one gulp. "Enough about me. How are your kids?"

Ned's children were a pair of precious little shits. There was Rachel, hand-reared by a Parisian governess in such demure privilege she probably sneezed rosewater. Then there was Adam, a Little Lord Fauntleroy who insisted sailing was a real sport. But Artie shouldn't be too harsh. The poor bastards were overburdened by Ned's longing for respectability, more worthy of lenience than scorn.

At the mention of his children, Ned's face flattened.

"You know Rachel married Jack last month," he said. "Thanks for sending the china, by the way. Rachel thinks it's swell. Jack's from a good family. A perfect match for Rachel. So, even though I'm already coughing up for a Waldorf-Astoria reception fit for Kubla Khan, I ask Jack what he wants for a wedding present. You know what he asks for? A job. He wants a fast-track position at Mercury."

Artie winced. "What a disappointment. I'm sorry, Ned."

"And that's not even the worst of it. Adam's in his second year at Dartmouth. Do you know how difficult it is to get into Dartmouth? I had to *buy* them a building. The worst extortionists I've ever dealt with, and I've been in arrears to Murder Incorporated. Adam's been there two years and he could be anybody. A judge, a diplomat, a politician. Some days I'm so proud of him I'm sure the milkman's his father. Now? Now he wants to leave school and work for me. Over my dead body, I tell him, and you won't believe how he tries to convince me: his good grades."

"If he assaulted a professor I'd say, okay, maybe he's got what it takes. But good grades?"

"Thank you—finally, a voice of reason." Ned pestled his knuckles into the mortars of his sockets. Crestfallen that the son he so adored admired him enough to follow in his footsteps. "I sit him down and tell him that, frankly, he doesn't have the aggression necessary to make it in Hollywood, and you know what he does?"

"What's he do?"

"Starts weeping."

"Unbelievable."

"I want to tell him that this, here, the waterworks, is why he'll never succeed in the picture business. Art, our children could never survive the world we've come from, and we could never survive the world they're going into. By bettering their lot in life, we doom them to misunderstand us. I want to tell Adam that I became a bulldozer so he could become a racing bicycle."

"You told him that?"

"Pfft. Of course not. He's at Dartmouth. Thinks he knows something. I sent him there so he wouldn't have to learn about the world. But what do I do. He thinks he knows something."

"You've done what you could."

"I do what I can."

"Hey, you bought a college a building. How many people do that for their children, huh?"

Ned flagged the waiter. "People like you and me, Art? The sons of furriers and cobblers and glovers who've been in the business since the battles with the Edison Trust? We came out here to build ourselves a broken kingdom where only the broken prosper, and then, our children, they hold it against us when we make them whole."

"Our children aren't whole. They're just broken in more delicate ways by finer instruments."

"Being broken delicately is what I call whole," Ned said. He reached over and patted Artie's shoulder. "You're a good father, Art. You know how I know? Because your son is pissing in your hamper instead of trying on your clothes."

THE APPROACHING WAITER WAS A jiggly man in a snug vest. His pen hovered impatiently over his notepad.

"How's the sweetbreads?" Ned asked.

"No one's died yet," the waiter guaranteed.

Ned folded his menu. "Who could say no to that?"

Artie ordered the squab.

"Very good, sir." As he collected the menus, the waiter asked Artie if he had any more upcoming vacations.

"Vacation," Ned said, as if naming the war god of an ancestral enemy. "This business forgets me if I spend too long in the john, and you go on vacation."

"I had no choice," Artie said, ordering another martini and a preemptive aspirin. "I had to save my marriage."

The previous year, the prospect of divorce had gathered in gloomy thunderheads on the horizon. Artie loved his wife, of that there was no doubt. Few had the fortitude to share an elevator with him; Mildred had shared a life. She had an endurance runner's resolve, a prison warden's temperament, and if twenty years handling Artie's prickly personality had left her callused and nettled, what but love had kept her from leaving? She was his person, the only one on God's green earth who could stand the sore sight of him. She enjoyed wine spritzers, Virginia Woolf, probing the depths of his bellybutton, having affairs with men half her age, and buying overpriced paintings of people with their eyes and ears all mixed up. She liked her weekends in Santa Barbara, exploring sanatorium country. She was the only person he knew who wasn't lying when claiming to enjoy opera and caviar. The heights of spectacular outrage her five-foot frame rose to still rendered Artie speechless with desire. The compact opulence of her build was downright subversive in this city of willowy starlets. She was Rubenesque, and, like both painter and deli sandwich, irrefutable proof of Creation's genius.

The problem was that two decades of marriage had so entwined their lives that she had become subject to his self-loathing. The gloom had fallen over him like a bell jar ever since the State Department rejected in form-letter finality his sister Ada's visa application two years earlier. He stayed in bed until noon, afflicted with lockjaw of the eyelid. Darkness unrolled over his brain and he couldn't find the light switch. There was a seductive, corporeal thrill in surrendering to it. Artie took an unhealthy interest in Billy's Scouting knots and quietly passed evenings contemplating the load-bearing capacity of the ceiling fan. His family was provided for. Like other luxuries, suicide was an indulgence only the rich could afford. He ran through the beats: the dry-cleaned suit, the glass of special occasion scotch, the dog leash tied nice and tautological, the mute weight of the dining chair toppling onto the Persian rug. The trick was to let your imagination skate over the gruesome reality to the dreamlessness where pain ceased. His children would still hate him—Billy would probably take a leak in his coffin—and he wanted to believe himself worthy of Mildred's grief, but really, who could begrudge him taking the trapdoor from a world as inhospitable to life as ours?

Being inside his brain was like being a deer in the forest in hunting season. To survive, he had to get lucky every single second of every single day. The hunter? Depression? That cruel bastard only had to get lucky once. In the end, Artie never ginned up the moxie to go through with it. Instead, he brought his self-destruction to bear on his marriage. Divorce: the survival suicide, the true coward's way out. He started gambling away mountains of cash, ordering made-to-measure shirts by the dozen, buying twenty-dollar haircuts even though he wore toupees. His checking account statements read like the *Hindenburg*'s altimeter. He started an affair with a young bookmaker named Betty Ludlow, and after a few months of carrying on, had succeeded in driving Mildred to the brink of the Nevada border. His depression subsided. In an attempt to mend their marriage, he took her on a cruise.

"Just you two on the high seas," Ned said.

"Just Mildred and me. And Betty."

"You brought your mistress on a cruise to repair your marriage?" Ned smiled despite himself. "And my kids wonder why I pour Milk of Magnesia on my cornflakes each morning."

"Every man has his Everest. Mildred's mine."

"So, what? Betty's your porter?"

Artie shrugged and lanced the loose olive in his martini glass with a toothpick. "Mallory had furs and climbing equipment. I have anger issues and feelings of inadequacy."

"You know, Art, Mallory did die on Everest."

"Yeah, well, his Everest *was* Everest. He was too literal for his own good. Me? I keep my Himalayas where they belong," Artie said, patting his breast pocket, where his Everest stood behind a packet of cigarettes and a roll of mints.

"So how *was* the cruise?" Ned asked.

ARTIE HAD GONE IN WITH the best intentions, but how could he summon the strength to repair his marriage without the emotional support for which Betty was lavishly compensated? He arrived at what he thought of as a "European" solution, the continent being less a landmass in his mind than a state of moral limberness. He purchased two berths on either end of the ship. By day, he and Mildred sunbathed in the first-class commiseration of Previously Important People. Mildred was an early riser, in bed by 9:00 P.M., and when she slipped off, he slipped out in a tuxedo and dancing shoes. He'd even brought his most prized possession, the top hat Marlene Dietrich had worn in *Morocco,* purchased for three grand at a charity auction.

Mildred had begun to laugh at his jokes again, Artie had begun to feel himself again, it had all gone splendidly, really, until the third night when Artie stole into Betty's cabin to discover two bodies tangled on the bed. One was Betty. The other wasn't Artie. Wasn't even the same genus. In the bedsheets a disembodied arm flexed with muscles Artie had last sighted on his own body during the Coolidge Administration. The Other Woman had Another Man. At this revelation, the world went dark. Artie assumed he had passed out. He'd only closed his eyes. The scene rematerialized on his retinas in pinpricks of unbearable clarity: the man's broad, smooth shoulders; the plates of sinew shifting under his back; his abdominals as neatly segmented as a beetle's exoskeleton; Betty's fingers gripping his rich mane without fear of yanking it off.

When he saw Artie, the other man leapt naked from bed. His reproductive faculties appeared to be dispiritingly operational. He didn't need a fig leaf. He needed the whole tree. This being the high seas, he availed himself of the nearest lid, which he lifted from Artie's head and clamped over his pecker.

Betty turned to the naked man and, with self-assurance that left Artie aghast with desire, said, "Now, Ralph. Don't you know you shouldn't wear a hat when a lady is present?"

The interloper had the concussed Gary Cooper look that had done so well for Paramount. Christ, he was young enough to be Betty's age. It was obscene.

"Who is Ralph?" Artie stammered. "Who are you?"

"Ralph Ludlow, Mr. Feldman." He offered Artie his hand and Marlene Dietrich's top hat hung freely on its peg. "It's a pleasure to finally meet. Betty's told me so much. I must thank you for taking me on this cruise."

"I'm paying for *his* ticket?"

"I'm sorry, Art," Betty said, robing herself in bedsheets, "but we never had a proper honeymoon."

"Who hasn't had a proper honeymoon?"

"Why, Ralph and me," Betty said, and reached for her husband's hand. The news that Betty was married rubberized Artie's knees and unmoored his feet. Was nothing sacred? The cabin floor tilted and the goose-feather mattress swung up to catch him.

"He thinks I'm a monogamist," Betty said, the word exotic and faintly deviant in her enunciation. She loosened Artie's bow tie and fanned his face with a folded *Life*. "It's been a rough year for Art. The studio he runs with his brother is going bust. A family business. Incest usually is."

Artie imagined the force of his hyperventilation would pop his lungs inside out, like a pair of dirty socks. When he finally caught his breath he asked how long this had been going on.

"Our marriage? Three years come October."

"This was supposed to be a romantic vacation, and you went and made it a honeymoon."

"You did bring your wife," Ralph pointed out. It was a reasonable objection, but Artie was in no mood to reason with a man wearing his three-thousand-dollar top hat as a jockstrap.

"Betty, I invited you because Mildred and I haven't been having relations."

"Unless you get off on crying yourself to sleep because your children don't like you, then we haven't been having relations either, Art." Betty's smile popped open like a switchblade. "How about that, Ralph? I *am* a monogamist after all."

Artie left the cabin and shuffled past exhaust manifolds whose burbling gas provided a wellspring of convenient metaphor. Low in the sky, the sickle moon was the bilious white of a pack-a-day smile. Its beams slithered over indigo swells tufted in foam. Artie patted his pockets for a cigarette and added his own hot air to the steam.

He heard the slap of bare feet on deck wood. Betty? He'd accept her without condition. He'd have the captain marry them in international waters. He was a terrible person, a lousy husband, a derelict father, and he'd abandon everyone to become anyone else.

"Mr. Feldman?"

It was Ralph.

"You forgot your hat, sir." Ralph doffed Marlene's top hat from his pelvis and returned it to Artie's hands. Artie peeled a couple bills from his money clip and told the handsome simpleton to treat himself to some underwear.

Not that he could admit any of this to his brother, and so when Ned asked how the cruise had gone, he just said, "Acapulco is lovely this time of year."

THE WAITER RETURNED WITH A couple plates of sweetbreads and squab. Ned oared his spoon through the sludge, but at first glance rumors of its edibility had been exaggerated.

Across the dining room, Artie spied Ernst Rosner, head of Accounting, the most creative department at Mercury. He was a harried man with eyes clouded in resignation and a misplaced faith in the magnetism of bow ties. He looked like someone's ex-husband. Working in close quarters with the Feldman brothers had made Ernst Rosner a sommelier of antacids and sleeping aids. His curriculum vitae had long wandered the wilderness in search of a new home. Helming Mercury's accounts was like being chief meteorologist on a Mesopotamian plain oft hit with brimstone and deluge. Properly performing the job meant inciting panic, lamentation, and notions of divine betrayal.

Ernst spotted the Feldmans, walked over, and apologized for his tardiness. "I don't trust the valet with my new Cadillac."

Ned made room. "It's a beautiful automobile."

Ernst scooted in. "You've seen it, haven't you, Art?"

"I've seen it," Artie said. "I've seen less phallic penises."

"That wouldn't surprise me at all," Ernst said. Like everything else in their business, one's car was another means of asserting power. Artie made a point of only driving Ford's Lincoln line, feeling it subtly but tangibly evinced his allegiance to American ingenuity and industry. Only after Henry Ford's promulgation of anti-Semitism and assembly-line efficiency found its apotheosis in Polish towns synonymous with Hell would Artie consign his collection of Lincolns to the junkyard, where they would rust and corrode among other cars with bodies in the trunks.

"I come bearing good news for a change," Ernst said, pulling a file from his briefcase. "Eastern National is offering a million-dollar credit line to get us through the next few quarters."

Artie frowned. The thermodynamics of fate demanded that news this good be offset by countervailing grief. "But?"

"But for collateral they want an option on thirty-three percent of the company's stock, roughly half what you two own."

Artie rubbed his eyes. "Let me get this straight: we have to put up a couple million in stock to collateralize a million in credit."

"Now, before you start using four-letter words on me, Art, may I remind you that you were the one who asked for this loan . . ."

"True," Ned chimed in.

". . . because you're the one getting hauled before Congress for being such a pain in the ass."

"Also true."

"Now, that's the worst of it," Ernst continued. "Eastern National wants Ned back in LA permanently to keep an eye on things, and they want a few board seats. If you're a nickel light on the payments, you can bet these boys will have you on the curb before you can pat your pocket for change. They don't want to loan to you. They want to own you."

Artie ignored the news of Ned's relocation to Los Angeles; it was one bad tiding too many. Instead, he sank into the leather banquette and thought of all the moguls who had lost their studios to the gentile banking conspiracy: Adolph Zukor, William Fox, Jesse Lasky. When the business was in its infancy, none of the patrician investment firms would lend to Jewish showmen selling shadows on a wall. Only once those showmen proved the profitability of their shadows did the Wall Street vultures swoop in to pick the meat from their bones. Take Carl Laemmle, the founder of Universal. He was forced to put up nearly six million in stock to collateralize a seven-hundred-thousand-dollar loan and his lenders still walked off with his studio. If that's what the gentile banking conspiracy did to Carl Laemmle, a pint-sized giant who'd gone up against Thomas Edison and *won,* just imagine what they would do to Artie Feldman.

"You've walked us into a bank to get sticked-up, stick-upped . . . stuck-up . . . *robbed* by the teller."

Smirking at Artie's maverick grammar, Ernst said, "Sure, these bankers are stickup men. But who knows, Art? Maybe you can outrun a bullet. You two survived worse. You're the Feldmans."

The Feldmans. Artie grimaced. Billy was well and truly screwed.

Ernst reshuffled the papers he had extracted from his briefcase. "Now, there is a silver lining in all of this. Eastern National are major shareholders in Warner Bros, and they're pushing Warners to reallocate its capital toward prestige pictures, hoping to build Warners into a rival of Metro. Which means Warners will need more

B-product to fill out their blocks. Eastern National assures me they can get yours released through Warners' theatrical holdings."

Artie blinked, waiting for a reversal that didn't come. "Are you serious?"

"I'm wearing a bow tie. Yes, I am serious."

"Did you know about all this?" Artie asked Ned.

Ned nodded. "We've wanted this a long time. A chance to get back on top. Entrée to the majors."

As soon as they vanquished the Edison Trust, the movie moguls had co-opted their nemesis's monopolistic inclinations, consolidating production, distribution, and exhibition into vertically integrated cartels. The big five—Metro-Goldwyn-Mayer, Paramount, Twentieth Century–Fox, Warner Bros, and RKO—kept smaller outfits like Mercury sidelined through block-booking and blind-bidding, practices that required unaffiliated theaters to book a studio's entire production slate to acquire the handful of star-powered A-pictures that drove ticket sales. Sinking back in the banquette, Artie tried to imagine his pictures opening in first-run deco picture palaces again, his name bannering cathedrals of light.

"I don't know," Artie said. "We risk forfeiting our position as majority shareholder to Wall Street sharps so slick they have to clothespin their hats to their hair, and all for the amount of money L. B. Mayer spends on the movies he doesn't make."

A waiter passed; Ned pointed to his empty glass. "It's only thirty-three percent."

"Thirty-three percent and three board seats," Ernst said, helping himself to Artie's squab. "One million means they're overpaying by about one million. If I wasn't so good at playing hide-the-insolvency, you'd be lucky to get five brown bananas and a how-do-you-do. Renting the back lot to other studios' productions is all that's kept you in the black this year."

Sensing Artie at the bottom of the scrum, Ned piled on. "And I'm sorry, Art, but we're in this mess due to you and this propaganda investigation."

"These investigations always end up being a lot of hot air," Artie said. "Remember when the Dies Committee was trying to smoke out Hollywood reds? They called Shirley Temple a communist. The richest goddamn ten-year-old on the planet, and they think she has something against capitalism."

Ernst surreptitiously investigated his left nostril and wiped his findings on his trousers.

Ned jabbed his finger at Artie. "For years these politicians have been rooting around Hollywood for Jewish necks to lay on the chopping block. Rather than keeping your head down, you've sent them your collar measurements."

"You know what else has a lot of Jews in it?" Artie asked.

"The Bible they're bludgeoning you with?" Ernst suggested.

"The front office of every major in this town," Artie said. "We're the only Poverty Row studio invited to testify on Capitol Hill."

"Don't you dare call us a Poverty Row studio," Ned interrupted. "We've just had a few bad years."

"That's exactly what I'm saying. At the witness table, we'll be right there alongside Warners, Paramount, the rest of them again. Now, I know I sound like I'm panning for gold in a river of shit, but this could be a good turn, Ned—we could never buy this kind of publicity. Maybe this is where our comeback begins."

Ned blinked slowly and took a few deep breaths until the murder in his eyes cooled to manslaughter. "That is the stupidest fucking thing I've ever heard. Ernst, is there a small man with a big mallet behind my brother . . ."

"Hard to say."

". . . because I swear every time he opens his mouth, he sounds like he's had his brains bashed in." Ned leaned forward and dropped his spoon into the pond of creamed calf gland. "The US Senate is fixing to give you a pedicure with a pair of pliers, but yeah, having your martyrdom broadcast on national radio is a great way to get our name out there."

Artie stared into the dregs of his martini and made a metal note to start taking his liquid lunch for breakfast. "Okay, Ned. You've made your point."

"Have I? Because you sound like a comedian instead of a killer. I've been pounding the pavement on Wall Street for the last month to keep the repossessors from selling your toupees to the taxidermy museum. Every banker I spoke to thinks Senator Nye will beat the stuffing out of you next week. 'Oh, no,' I told them. 'I met Senator Nye once. I've even donated to his last campaign. He's no match for my brother Art. I trained Art myself at the Borough Park Pugilist Gym. Senator Nye isn't going to know what hit him.' But you know what? I should've told them you traded your boxing gloves for clown shoes."

Ernst muttered an excuse and slipped away.

Ned reached over the table and kneaded Artie's shoulder. The pressure of palm on plaid generated enough warmth to animate the illusion of a relationship uncomplicated by fratricidal ideation. "I'm worried about you, you big galoot," Ned said. "You look like crap, even for you."

Artie hated to admit it, but Ned was right. He didn't know where it came from, the anger and depression and dread that into his early fifties still buffeted him. He had built a studio with a thousand employees and his name on the gates. When measured by his origins, his was a wild success story. The dirt square he'd grown up on had been renamed for the Feldman brothers eight years earlier in a ceremony that inspired Artie to underwrite its paving as well as the construction of a stone schoolhouse on its north side. And yet nothing soothed the outrage herniating his heart. Now that he'd been reduced to shoestring budgets, outrage was all he could bring forth with greater quality than his better leveraged competitors. It was his main business strategy. He couldn't outspend, outproduce, or outadvertise Metro or Fox or even Columbia, but he could out-outrage them all. He'd fought the Republicans, the Democrats, the Communists, the Chamber of Commerce, the forty-hour work week, the defenders of daylight savings time, the idea of men's sandals, the Los

Angeles Country Club, and his own accounting department. He was *still* a fighter. And maybe that's why he was so unhappy.

"This is none of my business," Ned said, "but a little bird told me your blues have come roaring back. Another little bird told me you've been burning through a lot of cash."

"What, you live in a fucking aviary now?"

"Are you back at the card tables?"

Artie dropped his gaze to the tablecloth while shame seeped through his cheeks. Legends of Artie's card playing were legion. He'd gamble all night with rival studio executives at the Clover Club or the Trocadero or the casino barges anchored three miles off the Long Beach shore, just beyond the jurisdiction of federal and state authorities. The poker table was a cage match for men in cuff links. It's where Artie paid tribute to the muses of fortune, where his showman's belligerence, subterfuge, and instinct were tempered and honed.

The recent marital rupture, which necessitated the cruise, had begun when Mildred discovered his weekly decimation of their checking account and let her imagination dash to the most logical finish line: gambling run amok. Artie wasn't sure which pained him more: the extensive history, footnoted with witnesses and evidence, that Mildred cited to substantiate her suspicions, or his inability to admit the truth.

"I'm not playing cards any more than usual." Artie waved away the suggestion. "Besides, my cholesterol? I play Russian roulette every time I order a fried egg."

"Then what's going on?" Ned's scrutiny swept over him, a Geiger counter alert to the hot frizzle of hazard. "Wall Street is parachuting in big bags of money and you look as somber as a mortician's closet."

Artie cupped his face in his hands. The tabletop blurred. His retinas felt daubed in Vaseline. "I've been sending cash to Ada."

Ned looked across five hundred miles of tablecloth with a tenderness Artie hardly recognized. "Oh, Art. You big fucking galoot."

When Ada sent Artie and Ned to live with distant relatives in a Lower East Side tenement, she was already married to a local inn-keeper and remained behind. Artie saw Ada for the first time in three decades when he returned for the square naming ceremony. He'd been raised by her, really. Over the years he'd lobbied her to join them in California, promising to buy her a lovely little hotel on the Pacific, but her inn was thriving and Artie respected her reluctance to abandon the business she had built with her own hands. Then it was too late. Artie hadn't received word from her in over a year, not since she added Peru to the atlas of countries that denied her visa application. Yet every weekday, he mailed a hundred dollars to her. Each C-note purchased false hope on the installment plan. He was too ashamed of himself to stop, too proud to tell his brother about it any earlier.

"You never know," Artie said. "Maybe one gets through."

"You never know," Ned conceded, though certainty steeled his voice.

"The Polish postal system is so consistently unreliable it must mis-deliver mail to the right address now and then."

"Art, it's the German postal system now. They've renamed Feldman Square."

"To what?"

"Himmlerplatz."

They sat there in the polluted silence. There were no chips or cards, no green felt or waistcoated dealer. No referee or gloves. There was nothing but empty martini glasses, pigeon bones, and his brother's fingers lotioned in creamed calf gland, but Artie felt flush with the vitality he experienced only at the poker table or in the boxing ring, those venues where he judged himself not by what he won but by what he risked and how much he hurt.

"Okay," Artie said. "You deal with the bankers and I'll deal with the senators. But I want your word that if I find a way around the Production Code, you won't give me grief about *Devil's Bargain*."

Despite self-interest, common sense, and political expedience, Ned found himself asking if Artie could be subtle.

"I am subtle," Artie said, regretting his decision to wear polka dot on plaid. Much later, it would become obvious that even then, at Romanoff's, when they made the pact that would destroy their studio and family, Ned had been playing the longer game. By the time Artie had occasion to ask these questions it was too late. He couldn't know that the bargain struck at Romanoff's would lead him to lose Mercury, become a multimillionaire, and spend his evenings in midnight rumination beneath the ceiling fan. He would stand there one night, a year hence, thinking of this very moment, right now, when he shook his brother's hand. Watching the ceiling fan spin like a film reel unwinding time, he'd wonder if it was inappropriate to ask Maria—who for years had ghostwritten his anniversary, birthday, and Valentine's Day cards—to pen his letter, for he wouldn't want Mildred to think his suicide note was written by a stranger.

After they paid the bill, Artie reached under his chair and retrieved the gift-wrapped box. "A belated birthday present," he said.

"Let me guess. It's a dead skunk." Ned unwrapped the bow. Inside was a top hat.

"You'll need it when the Mayfair Club or Hillcrest takes you," Artie said.

Ned touched the brim of the top hat. It was a beautiful gift. Even though they'd been born eight minutes apart, Artie usually forgot his birthday. "This is nice, Art. Thank you."

Setting the top hat snugly on his brother's head, Artie said, "You'll never guess who's worn it."

2

"IS IT TRUE?" VEDETTE CLEMENT, MARIA'S SECRETARY, WAS PRECEDED by the chloroforming intensity of her perfume, which had an enfeebling effect on the occupant of any room she entered. Maria assumed it was a defense mechanism to tranquilize wandering executive hands.

In the doorway Vedette was up to her blond curls in a blue dress. Her wrists were braceleted in bands of coral-snake reds and yellows.

"Is what true?" Maria asked.

"Are Artie and Ned selling the studio?" Vedette was the vector of the most virulent strains of studio rumor, specializing in adultery, alcoholism, and the shifting fortunes of personnel, which she packaged in the prim superciliousness of cautionary tales, lest anyone accuse her of gossiping. At other studios, you knew your days were numbered when your subordinates stopped reading your memos. At Mercury, you knew your pink slip was printed when Vedette stopped pumping you for dirt.

"Of course not," Maria said. "It's just a loan. Listen, Vedette, call TWA and get me a seat on Artie's flight tomorrow."

"You're going to Capitol Hill? I'm envious."

"Why? You can go to the conference room if you want to watch men in bad suits interrupt one another."

"Sure, but I can't take an airplane to get there."

Maria smiled. "Fair point."

"Anyway, I stopped by because there's a fellow at the gate for you, but he's not on your schedule. Shall I tell him to take a hike?"

"What's his name?"

"Vincent Cortese."

"I'll see what he wants."

It had been three and a half years since Maria last received a letter from her father, years more since she received one untouched by the razor of the San Lorenzo censor. Not even an innocuous description of a swim in the Busento during a spring shower had survived the censor unscathed. None of the former confinati whom Maria contacted knew what had become of him. That she accepted he was missing or dead did not preclude her from indulging the hope that he would one day show up out of the clear blue. Sometimes she even entertained the idea that she could get her father a job in the studio's legal department; if there was one thing Artie Feldman always needed, it was a good defense attorney. In the meanwhile, she still waited for another envelope with her name on it.

A man with a blue carpetbag leaned against the gatehouse. He looked a bit like the boy who had taken her passport photograph on that distant afternoon in San Lorenzo. But that had been a long time ago and his name hadn't been Vincent.

His eyes brightened when he saw her. He had come a long way and he had news.

THE POSTHUMOUS LIFE OF VINCENT CORTESE

1

THE DAY HE ARRIVED IN SAN LORENZO, GIUSEPPE LAGANA STEPPED OVER the line in the road where the zone of confino ended. Here, liberty looked the same as captivity, but when he closed his eyes, no one could tell him what he saw.

A week later, he ran away with his eyes open. No plan, no provisions, nothing but an animal craving propelling him toward his family. With his shoe leather doused in ammonia he made it nineteen miles west before the bloodhounds sniffed him out. Near enough to the sea to smell salt through the police truck's bars. Domenico Gallo, San Lorenzo's newly appointed podestà—an executive office created to ensure control of local government rested in the hands of a single loyal functionary—watched the police truck pull up with an expression of stern satisfaction.

The punishment for runaways was the Vault, a small cellar beneath Domenico Gallo's office. A few feet by a few feet by a few more. Only a chamber pot for furniture. It was the darkness that did you in. Once the earth closed its eyelid over you, you wouldn't see until you had served your time. And they didn't say how long you'd be down there. That was the punishment too. The last man imprisoned in the Vault was named Michele from Genoa. Giuseppe felt the name carved into the stone wall with a screw.

There was no timekeeping in the unbroken night. Not even meals adhered to a schedule consistent enough to define a day. To maintain his sanity, Giuseppe paced his cell. Three steps to the wall, three steps back. He mapped his steps on what he remembered of the Appian Way. Walked home, three steps at a time.

It was only a month on the surface, but time passed differently in the underworld. A decade filled those thirty days. The man who emerged blinking and bearded wasn't recognizably the one sent down. According to rumor, the first thing Michele from Genoa did once released from the Vault was walk to the Ponte Zupi and drown himself in the Busento. Giuseppe wasn't one to break with tradition, but when he reached the Ponte Zupi, the spirit didn't move him. Still, he came back to the bridge most afternoons, watched the sunlight crinkle on the water, and wondered what in the river had seized Michele from Genoa by the soul.

There was a rowboat docked below the bridge. A shirtless boy paddled it out October afternoons and jumped into the river.

One afternoon, the boy didn't come back up. Giuseppe saw the empty rowboat draw taut on its mooring, the white-capped current erasing the ripples where the boy had sunk. He had to do something, that was clear, but what? He could double back down the bridge to the embankment and climb down, but the boy would drown well before then. The only way to collapse that space in such little time was to jump from the bridge. Which hadn't worked so well for Michele from Genoa.

Every tendril of sanity stretched its roots through Giuseppe's heels, grasping dry land, but he felt himself pulled aloft by . . . what?

Not courage or nobility or any of the empty virtues that had led him astray. It was a coin flip, double or nothing. A wager on the life left in both bodies, above and below the water. He had no spare change; he made himself the coin. He stepped onto the bridge parapet. His legs pistoned into his leap. For one weightless spell, he felt perfectly free. Then the earth inhaled him.

The surface water caved beneath his back. A tuning-fork hum raced up his spine. Somehow he missed the rocky outcrop and plunged to a depth so narrowly unobstructed it felt tailored to his floundering figure. Silty river water singed his pupils. There, a dozen feet off, the boy lay across a strip of sand and rock. Balls of air rolled from his head like funny-page thought bubbles; down here, the world of land and sky was no more than the dream of the drowned.

Giuseppe closed his eyes and paddled through the pounding blindness. He pried the boy's clasped fist from where it had wedged between two rocks, hoisted the lifeless thing over his shoulder, and kicked off as the pressure built and built in his chest.

Then he was lying on a rippling rooftop while air swooped into his lungs. He dragged the limp body to shore and hammered his palms into the boy's chest. Leggy river birds tottered in the shallows, unimpressed with the soaked man malleting a steady beat against the boy's rib cage until the drum inside carried the rhythm on its own.

The boy spurted river water in shuddering coughs. His fist relaxed, and right there, in his palm, a coin gleamed, heads side up: an imperial portrait carved in gold.

GIUSEPPE STOOD IN THE DOORWAY of Picone Photography, weighed down by ten pounds of waterlogged suit, an ache in the shoulders, a shiver in his spine.

Nino's mother, the town portrait photographer, clutched her ashen boy long enough to make sure he was breathing before she slapped him. The crack multiplied in echoes from the stone walls lining the narrow lane. Color drained into the imprint her hand stamped on the boy's face.

"You are?" she asked Giuseppe.

He introduced himself. When he said he'd been a lawyer, Signora Picone's head tilted, as if assessing the forecast of the weather between them.

"So you're smart," she said, clearly skeptical of this proposition.

"Intelligence doesn't naturally follow education. As my present circumstances attest."

"Where have they put you?"

Since sentenced to confino, he'd lived in hopelessness, in limbo, in the carabinieri barracks. Free to roam through the town by day, he was locked at night in the barracks, downwind of a colicky Neapolitan whose volition was so sapped by confino he spoke only in the passive voice. Giuseppe couldn't bear to ask Annunziata for money and thus could not afford to rent a room with the locals.

"You will stay here," the signora said. It wasn't a question or an offer but a command. "There's a spare room at the end of the hallway on the second floor."

"That's my room," Nino said in dialect.

"It *was* your room," his mother corrected.

"That's a kind invitation, but I can't afford it."

"I don't want what's in your pocket but what's in your head," she said. "You're an educated man. My son is a stupid boy. You will teach him."

The Vault's worst torture wasn't the darkness but the brutal introspection the darkness imposed. The hours of unbroken rumination transformed every mistake into regret, none less forgivable than those surrounding Maria. He'd been so certain he'd have more time with her. Time to take her to more movies, to answer more questions, to say the things he wished his father had said to him. Time to make up for all the instances when he could have done more but instead did less. Now that he had all the time in the world, it was too late.

"I don't think so," he said. "I'm no good with children."

Signora Picone folded her arms across her chest and, with an exasperated sigh of one far too busy to be contradicted by a fellow in a waterlogged suit, said, "Take off your clothes."

"I'm sorry?"

"Your clothes. They're sopping. I already washed the floor this week."

A puddle of river water had widened beneath Giuseppe's feet. The adrenaline rushing through his veins had ebbed. He didn't have the strength to argue with this resolutely misguided woman, didn't have the heart to tell her that there was not enough of him left to give anyone.

In the lane, a couple of women carrying baskets of grain stopped to watch the most respected defense lawyer in Rome strip to his underpants right there for the Madonna herself to see.

"Make sure my boy doesn't die, okay?" Nino's mother said.

IT WAS A TALL ORDER. Nino was the sort of earnest, excitable child whom other children stuffed in barrels and rolled down hills. He was to neighborhood bullies what the Holy Family was to Raphael—a subject of inexhaustible poetry and regenerative possibility.

When even the most resourceful bullies grew bored, Nino made them fall in love with hating him all over again. For instance, after seeing an American picture down at the local cinema, he began dividing his hair down the center and shellacking it into a patent leather helmet. He'd asked the barber for the Valentino. He got the Vaselino.

Among the local children, the verdict was unanimous:

"It's a butt cut!"

"It's an ass hat!"

A passing confinato, a French teacher in his other life, joined the fun. "No, *mes enfants*. It is *derrière* hair."

Despite ironing it, then oiling it in brilliantine, the two wings lifted by mid-morning, as if his hair, upon realizing to whom it was attached, tried to take flight. Following Giuseppe's questionable advice, he began wearing his mother's silk stocking over his head to keep the part, strutting around the photo studio like a nine-year-old bank robber.

Weekends offered no respite from the antagonism of his peers. Every Saturday, Nino begrudgingly dressed in his little black shirt and green shorts to join in the military exercises mandated by Balilla, the fascist youth organization. They practiced getting mowed down by automatic fire and gouging out the eyes of communists. The troop was led by a local baker, a pocket-sized autocrat who promoted social Darwinism via physical education, assigning the boys feats of strength that divided them into predator and prey, mouths and meals. He had a habit of waxing lyrical on the wisdom of the ancient Roman practice of infant exposure whenever Nino tried to do a push-up.

It was only natural that a boy who hid from the eyes of predators would feel safest in the darkroom, printing his mother's photographs. From Picone Photography, the photographs might travel thousands of miles. A father in Australia only knew his children through the portraits Nino's mother took. A daughter in Argentina watched her parents age in monthly portraits until the February morning she received a photograph of her father dressed in mourning and standing alone. Nino's mother taught him how to light a photograph according to its purpose, its audience, its subject. "We will make him fall in love," she assured an anxious young seamstress who came to have her portrait taken for a prospective suitor. The suitor, a stonemason in Ohio whom the seamstress would be buried next to seventy-three years later, saw the love of his life for the first time through the eyes of Nino's mother. She taught her boy everything she knew and relied on Giuseppe to teach him what she could not.

Despite his poor record where parenting was concerned, Giuseppe found himself growing reluctantly fond of this boy he pulled from the water. It was hard not to pity his nearly athletic faculty for getting the crap kicked out of him. If Giuseppe were a boxer, he'd have taught Nino to fight. But he was a lawyer. He taught Nino to think. When Nino was ten, Giuseppe gave him Plato's *Crito*. When Nino was eleven, Giuseppe gave him Dante's *Divine Comedy*. And when Nino was twelve, and his mother succumbed to malaria, Giuseppe gave the boy his Bible.

A GRAY NOVEMBER MORNING, THE crackle of stones underfoot, the river a glistening mirror of clouds.

"Signora Concetta is family," Giuseppe lied. "A distant cousin."

"I've never heard of her," Nino said.

"A very distant cousin."

His mother had been in the ground for two months, but when he closed his eyes, Nino still saw her in the narrow cardboard coffin. Asleep, his mother was more liquid than solid, expanding to fill each corner of her bed. How would she rest in that narrow cardboard coffin? She had never slept so compactly in all her life.

He managed to stay dry-eyed during the church service and burial, but after he came home and failed to find a single image of his mother's face among her thousands of negatives, he dropped his head into his hands and wept for the sublime portraitist who, mindful of wasting film, had never turned the camera on herself.

He had relations in Reggio, but due to an ancient family feud, whose precise origins had been forgotten several generations earlier, they refused to take him in. Giuseppe had come to an arrangement with the widowed Concetta Cortese: for two hundred lira a month, she would look after Nino.

Now Nino flung a stone into the river. "You promised my mother."

"The podestà could transfer me to a different confino colony. He could throw me into the Vault again. I'll still see you every day after school, but I'm in no position to be your guardian."

With all the puny savagery his twelve-year-old voice could summon, Nino said, "You're a coward."

They walked in silence along the riverbank and Giuseppe watched several gravediggers in waders struggle to flatten a topographical map against the breeze. Over the centuries, the hopes of innumerable treasure hunters had died on the banks of the Busento, where the lost tomb of the Germanic king Alaric was said to reside. Now the podestà, in an effort to drum up positive headlines for San Lorenzo, had proposed the largest excavation yet.

"Here we are," Giuseppe said, nodding to the low stone house ahead, where Concetta Cortese was stepping out of her chicken coop. She was four eleven and eighty-five pounds in her church shoes. Her hair, hoisted in a white kerchief, was the color of overcast clouds. Her left eyebrow was burned off, her right was arched, and she clutched a spasming chicken by its feet.

Giuseppe made introductions.

With one clean wrench, Concetta snapped the chicken's neck. "Come here," she said, pulling Nino to her bony chest and kissing his cheeks. The last volts of life pulsed through the chicken's body. Nino felt the feathery carcass convulse against his shoulder as Concetta welcomed him.

Concetta's sole surviving son watched from the doorway, one thumb casually hooked through a belt loop. Nino recognized Vincenzo from his infrequent appearances at school. He was a stout, hotheaded kid blessed with early onset puberty, a hormonal freak of nature who probably began shaving at nine and fathering illegitimate children at ten. Quick to scrap, he entered conversations looking for the pretext to punch someone in the face. Whether Vincenzo was violent by temperament, or whether violence was the inevitable effect of too much testosterone throbbing through a twelve-year-old's brain, Nino didn't know. All he knew was that this brooding, volatile loner was uniquely qualified to make his life even more miserable.

Giuseppe passed Concetta several folded bills.

The sight of the money disappearing into his mother's dress shifted the light in Vincenzo's eyes. It promoted Nino from meal to meal ticket.

The following day, a couple schoolkids tried to make Nino eat a live lizard. Calmly, almost indifferently, Vincenzo broke their noses, pulled Nino to his feet, and tossed the lizard into the undergrowth. "I'm not your friend," Vincenzo said, lest Nino get the wrong idea, but from then on, Vincenzo's pugnacious physical presence rarely left his side. Winter nights they huddled together for warmth beside the stove. Summer evenings, when they swam in the river, Concetta would leave a lamp burning in the window so her boys could find their way home in the dark.

When Nino turned seventeen and received a scholarship to study law at La Sapienza, courtesy of one of Giuseppe's old professors, Vincenzo went to Rome too. By then it had been a long time since Nino last wondered if Vincenzo was his friend.

THREE YEARS LATER, WHILE THE afternoon light blinked in the wings of five million starlings over Rome, Nino absorbed Vincenzo's news. "America?" he said. The word nearly stung him.

"America," Vincenzo repeated. "My boss needs someone to look over his interests in New York."

When they left San Lorenzo, Vincenzo was the hanger-on, the junior partner to their friendship, but look at him now: his whole body one flexed muscle of self-assurance, a hustler in a homburg with a golden toothpick seesawing between his incisors. The only avenues of advancement for a Calabrian of Vincenzo's talents ran through the underworld. Advance he did, first working as a heavy, then bodyguard, then associate to a black marketeer who smuggled contraband past the customs officers at the Port of Civitavecchia. Now he was advancing right across the Atlantic.

Nino tried to muster enthusiasm for his friend but couldn't hide his disappointment.

Ignoring Nino's dourness, Vincenzo slipped his golden toothpick behind his ear and fired up a cigar. "We'll see if it takes. I hear adults drink milk with dinner over there. What kind of country is that? Where men still drink milk?"

"What about your mother?"

"If New York becomes a long-term proposition, I'll come back for her. As for you?" Vincenzo reached over and mussed Nino's hair. "You keep hitting the law books so you can get me out of jail someday."

But Nino had stopped going to class months earlier. Instead of legal texts, Nino studied antifascist pamphlets published by Giustizia e Libertà, clandestine editions of *l'Unità,* Trotsky speeches translated into Italian via Spanish, French, and German. Be they socialist, communist, or anarchist, the most competent doctors and teachers in San Lorenzo were its confinati. Who offered as commendable an example of how to be a citizen as those revolutionaries? Why had he imagined he could become a lawyer when everyone he admired was an outlaw?

The circle of leftists remaining in Rome was small enough to spiral down a drain, and that autumn, in the meetings Nino attended, the civil war in Spain was all they had discussed. Mussolini was sending soldiers and materiel to aid Franco's nationalists, while antifascist exiles in Paris organized a brigade of Italian volunteers to fight alongside the Spanish Republicans. Several of Nino's comrades had already headed to Barcelona.

"These communists, Nino, they're idiots," Vincenzo said. "Getting their heads blown off and for what? To get screwed over by politicians who wear a red star instead of a black shirt?"

"They want to make the world a more decent place."

"Like I said, they're idiots."

"That doesn't mean they're wrong."

"Please tell me you're not considering joining these wackos."

"Maybe," Nino admitted. He'd been seriously considering it even before Vincenzo announced he was moving to New York, but now the notion took on new urgency. He was jealous of Vincenzo's exciting news. He didn't want to be the one left behind.

"Does Giuseppe know about this?" Vincenzo asked. "No, of course he doesn't. Because he'd tell you exactly what I'm telling you. And I hate to bring up ancient history, but kicking your ass was a rite of passage for an entire generation of San Lorenzo schoolkids. You're no fighter. Have you ever even held a gun?"

"I only want to shoot a camera."

A few weeks earlier, he'd seen a Robert Capa photograph that captured a Republican militiaman falling as a bullet passed through him. It was among the most disturbing, somber, eloquent photographs Nino had ever seen, the first to make him think of the camera as a machine for converting light into evidence.

Vincenzo told him he was naïve, but was it naïve to believe documentary photography could serve as an antidote to the propaganda poisoning the body politic?

"No," Vincenzo said. "It's fucking crazy."

But a week later, when Vincenzo was on a steamer somewhere south of Greenland, Nino received a package at his boardinghouse. Nested in tissue paper sat a Leica 35mm camera, the same model Robert Capa used. There was no note, no card, no question who sent it.

Nino never reached Spain. An informer in his cadre had alerted the secret police, who took Nino and six others into custody at the French border. The Tribunal hearing Nino's case could have sent him to the Sicilian penal islands, but one of the judges pitied the deluded young man who had thrown his future away and sentenced him to confino in San Lorenzo.

EVERY MONTH GIUSEPPE WENT TO the piazza to watch new confinati arrive manacled to an iron chain. He was crestfallen but unsurprised to see Nino on that open necklace of pain. Nino's teachers were enemies of the state and he was a diligent pupil.

When Nino returned to San Lorenzo, Giuseppe had already begun working at the Busento excavation site, where, under the command of the podestà, the search for Alaric's tomb and its treasure commenced. It was hard labor, but the best paying work for miles. They erected a city beneath the earth, a series of tunnels and caverns buttressed on wooden struts and illuminated by hanging sodium lamps, so labyrinthine in design and immoderate in execution it seemed less like the excavation of an ancient tomb than the construction for a king to come. One day the diggers came upon a mass grave. The thousands of skeletons belonged to the locals enslaved to dig Alaric's tomb and slaughtered upon its completion. The podestà telegrammed Rome with news of the discovery. Feral dogs broke into the excavation site, and for months afterward Giuseppe could hear the ecstatic crunch of stray dogs gnawing on human bone.

Mussolini, ever alert to the political power of historical spectacle, notified the German regime. Berlin propagandists accustomed to reaching into mythic murk for precedent saw much to mine in the Busento riverbed: who was Hitler if not Alaric resurrected, the king who ended empires and dragged the curtain of the Dark Ages across the continent? And as the Italian and German regimes had begun discussing a military alliance, it was mutually decided that an excavation of their shared past could prove an invaluable propaganda exercise to sell their shared future. A few historical literalists in Rome bristled at the idea. Alaric had sacked Rome, plundered and massacred his way down the peninsula; it had taken Italy a millennium to recover the civilization it lost. These concerns were pushed aside. Every totalitarian knows you cannot change the future, only the past. San Lorenzo's telegraph wires trilled with messages incoming from Rome and Berlin. In spring 1938, Mussolini's minions descended on San Lorenzo to prepare for Heinrich Himmler's visit.

That spring, when Vincenzo returned to San Lorenzo to bring his mother over to New York, he found his oldest friend once more in need of his protection. "You fucking idiot," he said, kissing Nino's cheeks and then taking him in his arms while Giuseppe watched from the threshold where he once stripped to his underwear in the midday sun. "I'll get you out of here," Vincenzo said. "Okay? I'll get you out of here and we'll both leave this piece of shit town for good."

Nino shook his head. "No one gets out of San Lorenzo."

"Last year I moved twelve tons of contraband past the customs agents. You don't think I can move sixty kilos of idiot past a couple prison guards?" Vincenzo looked over to Giuseppe. "What about you?"

"It's a backwards country where the criminal gets the defense lawyer out of jail," Giuseppe said, shaking his head, thinking *Yes, yes, okay, I am ready now.* Twelve years since he emerged from the Vault, Giuseppe was prepared to try again.

2

ON THE DAY HEINRICH HIMMLER ARRIVES IN SAN LORENZO, VINCENZO elbows open the front door of Picone Photography and drops two jugs of gasoline on the floor.

Giuseppe puts a finger to his lips, walks to the radio, and dials up the volume at the behest of his inner paranoiac. Though he holds faith in the unwavering incompetence of the carabinieri, Giuseppe knows no one in Italy has more job security than wiretap stenographers. The transmission dunks in and out of static fizz. Nino can hear the echo and fade of radio waves bouncing off the surrounding mountains.

While Giuseppe safe-cracks the radio dial, Nino lugs the gasoline to the darkroom, figuring that if the militia makes one of its periodic house searches, it will go unnoticed among the canisters of developing chemicals. For the past three weeks, as San Lorenzo prepared to welcome Himmler, the three of them prepared to leave. The road out of town, studded with checkpoints and canines, heavily patrolled by militiamen who let no vehicle pass unsearched, has seen enough traffic that more and more cars are waved through with only a cursory inspection. And now the militia has begun letting all German vehicles proceed unimpeded. Vincenzo insisted they wait until Himmler arrived, assuming the most opportune moment was when all eyes were on the Reichsführer.

Vincenzo unrolls a map on the counter; topographical features coil within reverberating rings of elevation; the road to the shoreline is a dusty wrinkle. He has marked the checkpoints and roadblocks with asterisks, measured the distance between each, noted the shift changes, offered his assessment.

"You're in the wrong line of work," Giuseppe says, stroking the wings of his mustache. "You should be a general."

Vincenzo gives a modest shrug, but Nino can guess what Giuseppe's admiration must mean to a guy discounted as the sort of troubled soul prone to brawls and death by misadventure.

The plan Vincenzo had hammered out over the preceding weeks has minimized risk to a level only a man in a trade that budgeted murder into the business model would consider acceptable: Tonight, he will steal one of the black Mercedes the Germans parked behind the San Lorenzo carabinieri station. Tomorrow, he will deliver it to Nino and Giuseppe. Then they will say goodbye. With a little luck, and the two jugs of gasoline, Nino and Giuseppe might make it to Naples before their absence is noticed. From there, they'll head north, hopping along an archipelago of attics and spare rooms provided by former confinati, and finally slipping across the French border on foot. Meanwhile, Vincenzo would return to New York with his mother.

"Himmler delivered our getaway car." The idea still baffles Giuseppe, but it has a certain elegance. After all, the black Mercedes favored by the Gestapo is an automobile designed to spirit political dissidents away in the middle of the night. The car windows are tinted, a security measure for Himmler. Giuseppe and Nino could wear Soviet flags as togas and the checkpoint guards would still wave them through.

"I counted forty-two of them parked behind the carabinieri station, identical aside from their plates. It'll be days before anyone notices one is missing."

"And you still think you can get a key?"

"Now, that's the real beauty," Vincenzo says, his voice swelling with self-confidence. "Are you familiar with Elisabetta Bellino's closed house?"

"I may have heard it mentioned in passing."

Vincenzo smiles, but lets Giuseppe's demurral pass unopined upon. "Over the last few weeks, the brothel has made considerable improvements to show our German friends a good time. Tonight, they're having a little party for them."

"And?"

"And it's easier to pick the pocket of a driver when his trousers are on the floor."

While Giuseppe and Vincenzo discuss possible contingencies, Nino stands watch by the window, quietly asphyxiating. He loosens his necktie, still feels its phantom clutch, and realizes his collar remains buttoned. At twenty-two, he is too young to appreciate the ease with which he inhabits his body, the corporeal bounty he will one day covet from across time's pauperdom. Youth, like any natural abundance, is appreciated only after it is misused and squandered, or so says Concetta, Vincenzo's mother, who despite illiteracy possesses an aphorist's concise flair for exposing Nino's ignorance. That ignorance never feels more apparent than in the presence of her son. Look at him hunched over the map, in his gangster suit, whistling big band numbers that won't reach Italian shores for years, his golden toothpick spearing a ray of afternoon sun. In nine days, he will take the *Columbia* to New York with Concetta while Nino and Giuseppe hoof it across the Alps in cardboard shoes and jackets insulated with newspapers. His shoulders fill his trench coat's broad wingspan. The coat pockets, deep as shoe bags, seem tailored for American abundance. Once he rode Nino's coattails. Now? Now he wears them.

Among the contradictions of confino is the prohibition on locks. In dwellings where political prisoners reside, the bolts are unscrewed, the keyholes filled with glue. You might be bathing, sleeping, or plotting a jailbreak when the door swings open and a guard drags his dusty boots inside to collect the submission that is his tribute.

"Roll call," the guard announces.

Across the room Giuseppe calmly opens a newspaper over the map. Nino leans against the wall in a delinquent slouch, the slant running so deep he feels his spine italicize. He's learned to keep his face illegible to official scrutiny.

"Picone, Lagana." The guard, a sallow-faced bruiser whose myopia has overpowered his lens strength, squints at his ledger and checks them off. "And the proprietress?"

"Deceased," Giuseppe says.

It's testament to the resilience of administrative inefficiency that ten years since Nino's mother passed she's still called, twice daily, on the militia's rolls. Some days her name voiced by a guard is all that keeps her alive in Nino's mind. He remembers the strangest things: the coffee grounds she saved to fertilize her tomatoes, how she kissed old bread before throwing it out, the torn photographs she pinned to the corkboard behind the register. Once, she went to his pigeon lofts, selected one, and served it for dinner. "You know why you find pigeons everywhere?" she asked. "Because they're willing to eat anything." Her lack of formal education didn't diminish her genius for imparting memorable lessons. Not the least of which was how to leave San Lorenzo forever. Nino misses being a son. Ever since returning to San Lorenzo, he visited Concetta every few days with the misplaced hope that she would love him like her child. He'd chop firewood, carry well water, transcribe her letters to Vincenzo. He wrote for Concetta the letters he craved to receive himself, and as she dictated the correspondence, he'd catch himself imagining that he was hers.

As if picking up the frequency of Nino's inner oration, the guard tilts his head to the stranger in the trench coat. "You are?" he asks.

"Only a customer," Vincenzo says genially. It's clear why Vincenzo can't reveal his name. The guard's ledger will be scrutinized after they run, and any free citizen recorded in their company will fall under suspicion.

"Documents," the guard demands.

"It's not a good idea, sir."

"Give me your documents."

"Suit yourself." Vincenzo coughs heavily into his hand, then pulls out his passport. "It's only a touch of tuberculosis," he assures the guard. "I'm feeling much better."

As if suddenly seeing microbes squirm on the passport, the guard steps back and surreptitiously touches his testicles to ward off bad luck. He may have his doubts, but the local clinic is known colloquially as the Morgue for good reason, and one is rarely wrong in believing the very worst.

Once the guard is gone, Vincenzo takes the cigarette Nino left in the ashtray and kills the last inch in a single showboating inhalation.

"You decide what you'll do with yourself once you're in France?" he asks Nino.

"I'll carry on to Spain. The International Brigades are still there. I still want to photograph them."

"When did you become such a little hardhead? For such a good student, you can't learn a simple lesson, can you?"

"Maybe you were the one I was learning from."

Smiling, Vincenzo shakes his head and makes the sign of the cross.

"You shouldn't come back here, Vincenzo," Giuseppe warns. He scribbles an address and time on scrap paper and tucks it in the trench coat pocket. "I'll meet you there tomorrow. Bring the car."

"You bring this." Vincenzo slides his passport across the counter. Folded inside is his ticket on the *Columbia,* which will take him and his mother to New York next week. "I don't want it on me tonight in case the carabinieri shake me down."

As he leaves, Giuseppe gives Vincenzo one of the golden coins he'd unearthed from the Busento. Vincenzo insists he's helping them out of friendship, but Giuseppe knows nothing in San Lorenzo is free.

IT'S EARLY EVENING WHEN GIUSEPPE and Nino set out for the Busento. The sun flattens on the western horizon, casting a pink glow across the stone walls of the lane behind Picone Photography.

"Let's stop by the police station," Giuseppe says. "I want to pick up my mail."

Over the years he has described San Lorenzo a thousand times in letters to Maria and Annunziata. It's where confinati use the future tense to speak of the past. Where old men point to the slots in their mouths they will fill with gold when their children send money from America. Where the churchyard keeps a couple plots ahead of death and in the oppressive lethargy of a summer afternoon confinati climb into open graves with their newspapers to escape the heat. Where figs dry outdoors on bed springs and peasants sleep on stone floors. Where outside the grocer's a guard fearing tuberculosis unwraps the wax paper from a soap bar and licks it like vanilla ice cream.

At the police station, a clerk gives him his bundled correspondence from the podestà's office. It's composed entirely of lines cut from his most recent letter to Maria. Any given week, his incoming mail is mostly the extracts the podestà censors from his outgoing letters and returns to him. It's another form of punishment: knowing precisely how little of what he writes reaches his wife and daughter, how little of him escapes.

Nino peers over his shoulder. "Anything good?"

Giuseppe scans the clippings to see what the podestà's straight edge has expurgated. The majority of the letter is there, in neatly sliced-out rectangles, but to his surprise the words *I'll see you soon* have made it through. "It's good news," he says, and slips the bundle in his pocket to save for later.

A BULLHORN COMMANDS SAN LORENZO's citizens and confinati to gather at the Busento to greet the German delegation. Nino follows Giuseppe to the crowded riverbank, where several hundred locals wait, press-ganged into patriotism as mud seeps over their ankles.

On the Ponte Zupi flashbulbs pop and hiss. The grinding rotary of a newsreel camera devours a foot of film per second. Party grandees stand streaked in tricolor sash, boisterous with local pride yet pining for transfer to less malarial postings.

"The barbarians have returned," Giuseppe says.

A black Mercedes bannered in German flags stops when a cameraman waves it down. The cameraman whispers through the slit in the driver's window. The Mercedes backs up and approaches the bridge from a better lit direction.

Growing up in a photography studio, Nino long ago learned there is no more powerful an instrument of deception than one claiming objectivity. The camera conducts history on the bridge. Party members jostle into its frame. More than a witness or participant, it is a choreographer. The lens absorbs light but also emits its own kind of radiance. Even the podestà strains to bask in its gaze.

The Mercedes stops at the center of the bridge. A big shot from the Ministry of Foreign Affairs climbs out. One of Mussolini's inner circle, to judge by the medals on his chest. His boots crunch over discarded flashbulbs. His jacket sags beneath the clanging enormity of his distinctions. He opens the door for the guest of honor. The cameraman needs to change his film. The Ministry official returns to the passenger side and the second take begins. The carabinieri signal the crowd to applaud. The newsreel camera spins the stage-managed pageantry into the historical record.

Reichsführer Heinrich Himmler disembarks to clicking heels. He resembles none of the flamboyant monsters Nino imagined. Only an uninspiring pudge poured into a pear-shaped uniform and eye-patched in exhaustion. This was once the land of hydras and gorgons, cyclopes and sea creatures. Those mythic monsters didn't die, Nino thinks. They evolved into ulcer-prone bureaucrats the way dinosaurs evolved into pigeons.

A whistling flare unzips the night. With a thunderclap, drizzling fronds peel from the firework. More flares shuttle forth. Seams of light stitch the sky.

Himmler strides past the saluting phalanx and stares into the

Busento. The camera follows. Sixty feet over his rippling reflection, he raises one arm to hail the barbarian king in the water below.

A MILE AWAY, VINCENZO VISITS the brothel on Via Agostino. Elisabetta Bellino, the madam, greets him at the door in a silk dress knotted in fancy bows with pullable loose ends. Vincenzo exchanges his trench coat for a cloakroom ticket.

"Have you visited us before?" Elisabetta asks.

In fact, he had, when he was twelve years old. It had taken eight months hauling stone in a quarry on Saturdays to afford one hour of Elisabetta's time, and it remained the best investment of his life.

"My first time," Vincenzo says, pocketing the cloakroom ticket. The closed house isn't at all as he remembered. In preparation for the German delegation's arrival, it received municipal investment previously earmarked for an antimalaria campaign. The parlor expands into a commodious lounge wallpapered in golden satin. Moderne divans stretch with the sleekness of greyhounds mid-stride. Tiffany-style lamps open umbrellas of colored light across hightop tables where sternly dressed Germans banter with women brought down from the north.

Vincenzo maneuvers past two pressmen regaling a Tyrolian trio with stories of what Emil Jannings is really like. He orders a schnapps and takes a seat. Several women approach; he politely declines their company. He sits back and listens to the melodies uncoiling from the record player while jackboots and stilettos gently tap the dented parquetry. Will his mother like Brooklyn? Vincenzo hopes she will, hopes that after all the trouble he gave her as a boy, he can finally give her a bit of comfort and peace. When he told her about his new apartment, a beautiful four-bedroom a block away from a church where she could attend morning Mass, she said, "Four bedrooms? What do we need four bedrooms for? How will I ever keep them clean?" "Mamma, you don't have to clean. There's a Polish girl." "What am I supposed to do with a Polish girl?" "You're supposed to sit on the sofa and take a nap while she does the dusting." His mother liked the sound of that. She liked the sound of that quite a bit. Still, Vincenzo worries about how she'll do on the voyage over the next week, even though everything he knows of hardness and fortitude he learned from her.

As the evening dwindles, men and women pair off and make their ways to the bedrooms. Vincenzo searches out the lady of the house, gripped by the unaccountable wistfulness he mistakes for desire.

At the bar Elisabetta sits behind a pair of tortoiseshell reading glasses, tallying the night's take.

"You wouldn't be available for the evening," he asks. Whatever braggadocio he boasted has fled him, and once more he is a nervous adolescent in need of a professional's guidance.

She sets a hand on her hip, leans back into the pose, assessing. Then she flutters her fingers and Vincenzo catches the sparkle of a steel wedding band.

"Just my luck," he says. "I'll see myself out."

Instead, he ventures upstairs alone. Like all dwellings in San Lorenzo, the prohibition on locks extends to the brothel. The heavy carpeting muffles his footsteps as he moves down the hallway. He cracks open several doors until he finds a pair of pressed trousers folded over an armchair within easy reach. On the bed across the room, their owner's backside pistons with the precision his country is famed for. There are two things Vincenzo overlooks as he rifles through the trouser pockets. The first is the mirror mounted over the headboard, allowing the clientele to watch their performance. The second is the pistol the German brought to bed with him. Crouching on the floor, Vincenzo feels the cool jangle of car keys. When he looks up, the German is staring down at him, clothed only in a Luger. In bed, the woman watches with keen indifference.

While Vincenzo doesn't understand the particulars of the barked German, the gist is clear enough. He should drop the keys and backpedal from the room, but as his teachers can attest, Vincenzo never heeded instruction or authority. He plows his shoulder into the door and the fifty pounds of hardwood backhand the German and pitch him to the floor. Vincenzo runs. The hall carpet treadmills underfoot. The stairs fall away. He barrels into the night. He is pure speed, free fall on a flat surface, his shoe leather just glancing the cobblestones. Overhead fireworks explode and he's three blocks away when he slows to catch his breath. He stuffs his hands in his pockets and shivers in the evening air. His trench coat is still in the cloakroom. Five minutes later he reaches the lot behind the carabinieri station, where a few dozen black Mercedes line up in two neat rows. He goes to the end of the first row and tests the key in the driver's door. Amid the cascading fireworks, he doesn't hear the patter of bare feet on gravel. He doesn't hear the gunshots. The naked German snags his keys from the body's unclenched palm and returns to the brothel to fetch his clothes. A firework fills Vincenzo's empty eyes, a molten asterisk in the heavens to which the body on the ground is a footnote.

As boys, when he and Nino spent summer evenings swimming in the river, Vincenzo's mother would leave the lamp burning in the window for them, so they could find their way home in the dark. They'd wait outside his house, air-drying in the breeze while San Lorenzo adjusted to night. They'd listen to the gossiping river insects, the wolves howling in the mountains, the intermittent footfall of passing travelers. The door is there. It has no lock. Vincenzo looks back at his friend and knows he must go through this door alone. He need only push and he will be there. He'd like to linger in the melodies of this improbable world, but he should go inside, for his mother likes to know her son is home before the light burns out.

3

WHEN INSPECTOR ROCCO FERRANDO DREAMS AT ALL, HE DREAMS OF paper: stacks of it blowing through his slumberland, beautiful squalls of pristine pages to which he gives order and meaning. Ever since the higher-ups realized Ferrando was the only officer in San Lorenzo with a good grasp of spelling and grammar, he has been the desk-bound originator of all police paperwork. Clerical work is his calling. If he gets creative in the pursuit of justice—omitting evidence here, manufacturing it there—it's because justice thrives most plausibly within the margins of a fabricated police report.

In the dream he chases a windblown page along the bank of the Busento and as he reaches out to grab it the telephone rings. He shoots upright, slamming his head into the overhead bunk in the detention cell. He puts the telephone to his ear but only hears the anguished hiss of consciousness leaking into him through the hole in his forehead. The telephone continues ringing far away and Ferrando realizes that he's not holding the receiver to his ear but his shoe. And it seems he stepped in something.

There have been worse mornings, such as the morning one week earlier when his cat burned down his house—an unattended cigarette, a feline's curiosity. Due to Himmler's visit, there isn't a spare room for miles. Hence why Inspector Rocco Ferrando is waking up in the cell of his own jail, wiping whatever he stepped in from his ear.

In the other room, the telephone keeps ringing. Ferrando rises from the bunk and crosses the concrete floor. He takes the jail cell keys—worryingly, he's begun to think of them as house keys—reaches through the bars, and unlocks the cell door.

The telephone in his office is ringing for the forty or fiftieth time when he finally answers it.

"I thought you got locked in again," Giovanni Bellino, his sergeant, says cheerfully from the other end of the line. His sergeant's schadenfreude verges on insubordination, but Ferrando doesn't hold it against him. Bellino is an ambitious young officer condemned by fate, God, and bureaucracy to work under a bespectacled Genovese paper pusher who has never been tasked with investigating a crime more serious than public urination. But Bellino will only have to work under Ferrando for another twelve to eighteen months, this being the timeline offered by the doctor who found the spots on the X-ray of Ferrando's lungs.

"Stop by the podestà's office on the way in—see what he needs from us today," Ferrando says. He throws open the curtains and winces at the lemon spritz of sunlight. "Be careful, okay? About half the Ministry of the Foreign Affairs came down with Himmler from Rome. We're up to our eyeballs in assholes."

Bellino promises to call back from the podestà's office. Ferrando returns the receiver to the cradle and prepares for the day under the supercilious gaze of his roommate, confidant, and only friend, the cat.

"Don't give me that look," Ferrando tells the cat. "You're the reason we're in this mess. I turn my back for one minute and what do you do? You set the whole place on fire." The cat slinks over and wraps its fuzzy tail around Ferrando's shin. "You can drop the innocent act. I'm Inspector Rocco Ferrando. Brigands cower at the sound of my—" The cat nuzzles its head against his ankle. "Okay, okay. I love you too."

After shaving and dressing, he grabs one of the dozen books stacked beside the filing cabinet. Aside from the cat, they were all he saved from the fire. Of all the investigators to appear between a pair of yellow covers, his favorite, no question, is Sherlock Holmes. Sherlock Holmes is the Galileo of the left-handed human heart, trading the telescope for a magnifying glass to discern the order within the nearer darkness. In his company, Ferrando can imagine a world where an inspector is the restorer of justice rather than another instrument of its impoverishment. Now that he's twelve to eighteen months away from the end, this has become a fantasy he'd like to believe in again.

Though his creatively drafted police reports are celebrated by his superiors, Rocco Ferrando, the man, is considered a buffoon by his subordinates, incapable of resolving the most open-and-shut case without resorting to manufactured evidence and invented witnesses. Every now and then the podestà will ask him to document the carnal adventuring of the local gentry—though it would require a Bayeux Tapestry to fully chronicle some of their conquests—or look into the political denunciations with which locals settle old scores, dispatch rival lovers, ruin business competitors, and generally deploy for every purpose but reporting genuine political subversion, but honestly, Ferrando doesn't *want* to leave his desk. Though his sergeant views him as a pitiful functionary whose heart sings at the prospect of paperwork, Ferrando feels lucky to have a job where a man of his limitations can thrive.

In the station kitchen, he fetches a salami for himself and a boiled fish head for the cat. Bellino calls back.

"I'm over at the podestà's office and I've got good news and bad news," Bellino tells him. "The good news is that a body turned up and you'll never guess where."

"Where?"

"The carabinieri station."

Ferrando can't help laughing. "Jesus, the carabinieri cover themselves in glory once again. Was the victim one of them?" He feels a tingle of optimism for the first time since receiving the prognosis. The local police and the carabinieri are bitter rivals, devoting more time to sabotaging each other's investigation than they give to pursuing their own.

"That's the bad news: the guy who called it in says no. It looks like the victim got popped while trying to steal one of the Germans' cars."

"Okay. Swing by there to see if Chief Inspector Consoli needs help while I begin the paperwork. Let's see if we can't pin the murder on one of the carabinieri."

"You spend too much time behind the typewriter, boss," Bellino says. "I keep telling you you'll go blind reading all those little words."

"And I keep telling you you're a moron." Ferrando notices the cat has eaten his salami and left him the boiled fish head. You give a cat the best years of your life and what do you get for your troubles? A jail cell bunk for a bed, a welt on your forehead, and a fish head for breakfast.

"You never see an illiterate with reading glasses, that's all I'm saying." Bellino sighs. "Listen, I know this doesn't make any sense, but the podestà wants you down at the crime scene."

Chief Inspector Consoli, to whom Ferrando is inferior in rank and all other respects, is responsible for investigating all serious crimes. Whenever he requests Ferrando's assistance it is invariably of the most demeaning kind, such as holding his umbrella, fetching him a snack, or cleaning up after his dog. "How does Consoli intend to humiliate me today?"

"What, you didn't hear? The Greco inquiry took him to Naples. The podestà says the case is . . . well, God help us, it's yours."

Bellino must be mistaken. Surely Ferrando's record speaks for itself. "What do you mean the case is mine?"

"I mean the podestà is personally ordering you to lead this investigation."

And with those words the gilded age for San Lorenzo murderers begins.

FERRANDO COUGHS A TEASPOON OF pink phlegm into his handkerchief as he shoulders open the door to the carabinieri station.

"You see? Too much reading, it's bad for your health," Sergeant Bellino observes. Ferrando keeps hacking up bits of viscera-colored detritus. "Hey, Rocco, are you okay?"

"I'm fine," Ferrando lies. "It's just a spring cold."

Bellino nods and surreptitiously tucks his pocket square deeper into his breast pocket. Decked out in windowpane plaid, silver cuff links, and patent-leather wingtips, Bellino lives up to the loveliness of his name. He wears lavender oil on his neck and a flower on his lapel. His left cheek sports the ruby skid marks of a glancing kiss received while running out the door. Bellino couldn't tell you the ten commandments or seven deadly sins, but he can recite the eighteen measurements his tailor needs to stitch him a new suit from scratch. He's the best-dressed man for a hundred miles and he works for a guy covered in cat hair.

Once he catches his breath, Ferrando looks around the empty stationhouse. Photostats of wanted brigands share wall space with a portrait of Mussolini and a couple pinups of Doris Duranti and Clara Calamai. Though the local carabinieri aren't renowned for their industriousness, he'd expect at least some sign of activity at ten-thirty on a workday. "Where is everyone?"

"Anyone who might have witnessed anything was conveniently deployed a few minutes before I arrived," Bellino says.

No surprise there. Even otherwise honorable carabinieri refuse to cooperate with the local police; Ferrando chalks it up to the assimilative force of regional culture. To assist an inspector is to legitimize the law he upholds, and since time immemorial, locals have considered the law and its officers an apolitical and inscrutable evil. As despised and inescapable a feature of the landscape as earthquake and epidemic, a force countermanded with resignation and silence. This accounted for the improbable camaraderie Ferrando witnessed between peasants and political prisoners, unalike in every imaginable way, who nonetheless greet one another like survivors of shared disaster.

"What's that?" Bellino asks, nodding to the paper in Ferrando's hand on which eighty-odd German names are listed in order of unpronounceability.

"All the Germans in San Lorenzo," Ferrando says. "Nine are named Helmut."

"No wonder they're such a warlike people," Bellino says. "If I was named Helmut, I'd turn out a belligerent bastard too. Instead? Hey. I'm a little bit of beautiful, boss."

The body lies in the grassless lot behind the station alongside a few dozen black Mercedes. His well-cut suit and hair suggest he isn't local, but his complexion is pure Mezzogiorno, and instinctively Ferrando checks the pulse, though the brain and sinew unraveled across the gravel make clear the victim's timepiece stopped hours earlier. Mosquitos wet their wicks in the bloody halo. A few more buzz around the bullet holes in the chest, stomach, and pelvis. If not for those four bullets, he would have outlived Ferrando by fifty years easy, and Ferrando supposes that admiring the longevity of a corpse is a worrisome development.

"A shame for a thing like this to happen to a suit like that," Bellino says. "Look at that beautiful chalk stripe. You know, a nice chalk stripe pattern would look good on you, boss. It's very slimming."

"You think he's a confinato?" Ferrando wonders.

"If anyone missed roll call, we'd have heard."

Ferrando goes to Bellino's car and brings back a lacquered accordion box of a camera to photograph the murder scene. He unbuttons the man's jacket and rifles through his pockets. Bellino has already awarded himself the contents of the dead man's wallet as a finder's fee but left the golden coin and cloakroom stub in the left trouser pocket. There are no identity papers. Nothing to give the body a name.

He returns the man's jacket button to its hole, straightens his tie, folds his hands.

Bellino frowns. "What are you doing?"

"A man should look presentable when he's getting his picture taken. Isn't that what you're always telling me?"

"Well, yeah, but Rocco, it's a crime scene photograph."

"That's no excuse." It bothers Ferrando, not knowing the name of the man whose tie he straightens. This is his first homicide investigation—his first investigation, period—but he's seen how death renders you an object of unflattering study, a body stripped by strangers and dissected by a medical examiner who doesn't wash his hands after using the can. But a name is the deed on your personhood. A declaration of specificity against the oncoming anonymity. The least Ferrando can do.

Of course, Michele escaped these final indignities. Ferrando bought a rowboat and spent weeks trawling the Busento, but the river had swallowed him whole. Michele became a name without a corpse, and now, standing over a corpse without a name, Ferrando feels the perspiration prickle his forehead and an unnamable tumult in his brain.

"Let me see the cloakroom stub," Bellino says. Ferrando passes the evidence envelope and waits while Bellino mentally sifts through the brothels, taverns, gambling tables, and dens of iniquity he frequents.

"Elisabetta," Bellino says with a strange look. "She's the madam of the closed house over on Via Agostino."

"A brothel with a cloakroom." Ferrando wonders what the world is coming to. He stands, brushes the patches of dust from his knees, and volunteers Bellino's hat to cover the dead man's face. His sergeant's implacable smile wanes the moment the wool touches cadaver. "So, uh, where are the clues?" Ferrando asks Bellino. Bellino shakes his head in disgust. Ferrando has assisted Chief Inspector Consoli before—usually by fetching his laundry—but if he's honest, a practice he avoids, he would acknowledge that the little he knows about detective work comes from reading Sherlock Holmes. The problem, of course, is that Holmes lives in a universe explicable through the cool application of reason. Ferrando, for his sins, lives in San Lorenzo.

Foraging through brittle yellow grass, they find four brass 9mm cartridge cases. Etched into them are the two letters Ferrando dreads: *DR*.

"Deutsches Reich," he says. "What's the standard issue sidearm among our Himmler's entourage?"

"Luger 9mms."

Ferrando curses. It goes unsaid that they can't question their German guests without the podestà's approval. Which leaves them where? With a town full of murderers and a body without a name.

Bellino casts a final glance on the crime scene. "My money's on Helmut."

THE PODESTÀ DOMENICO GALLO IS a lean man sheathed in a black uniform and shaving soap. He paints heady foam across the folds and flutes of his neck with a badger-hair brush.

"You want strudel?" he asks. "I made it myself."

The sugared log lay on yesterday's *Il Popolo d'Italia*. Bellino helps himself to a slice. Ferrando abstains. According to legend, the podestà's interest in the culinary arts began in a POW camp where he'd subsisted on snow, boot leather, frozen mammoth flank, and a private from Puglia who drew the short straw. Hearsay, surely, but it tempers the appetite nonetheless.

"It's good," Bellino says. The oscillating desk fan sprays confectioner's sugar across his chest.

"It's Donna Himmler's recipe. I'm told she rolls the dough thin enough to read a ransom note through."

"A lot of ransom notes in her kitchen?" Bellino asks.

"When she bakes strudel."

The podestà's Calabrian accent thrums with the menace that is his true mother tongue. Public servants from here to Reggio parse his edicts with Jesuitical rigor, trawling the subtext for damnation and divinity, but you'd need a doctorate in sociopathy and the complete works of Machiavelli to decode the man. Domenico Gallo was born in San Lorenzo, and it's said he's turned down ministerial positions to remain the chief executive of this malarial backwater whose bureaucracy offers ideal conduction for a misanthrope's energies. He's cruel and capricious, a man who relaxes by censoring the letters of political prisoners, the architect of the confino colony and the Busento excavation. Or at least that's the impression Gallo tries very hard to make. Ferrando, however, knows that Gallo, unlike so many of the blackshirted tyrants who lord over cities in the south, is not motivated by greed but by deep loyalty to his hometown and a dedication to improving the lives of its citizens. Which makes him far more despicable than Ferrando and a much better man.

"Tell me, is your colleague a simpleton?" the podestà asks after listening to Bellino praise the cut of the Germans' uniforms.

"He's just quiet," Bellino says.

"I was talking to *him*."

Bellino's smile sags like a hat brim in a downpour. Ferrando confiscates the conversation before his sergeant hurts himself with it. Bellino busies himself with another strudel slab, then excuses himself from the room.

The podestà sets down his straight edge and fishes the golden coin from his pocket. "The archeologists tell me the coin you pulled off the victim dates from the late fourth century, just before the fall of Rome." He wipes the spumy blade on the washcloth, brushes more lather on his cheeks. "Growing up here, I heard all the stories of Alaric. They said the menorah from the Second Temple, Persian gold, Grecian sculptures, all the looted riches of the Roman Empire were right out there, buried in the riverbed. These are tales for children and simpletons"—his eyes find the Bellino-shaped hole in the office chair—"not something I would believe."

This gets Ferrando's attention. The ongoing excavation is pharaonic in scale, a network of tunnels and caverns to rival the town overhead. Why the massive expenditure of labor and resource if there is nothing down there?

"It's the future we're mining in those tunnels," Gallo says. "The only German barbarian I'm interested in is Himmler, who, to be perfectly blunt, is the kind of uncivilized brute who admires Alaric's program of massacring and looting. If—*if*—I can convince him to commit Germans to the dig, I can use their presence in San Lorenzo to pressure Rome into making overdue public investments. Infrastructure, sanitation, a hospital that's more than a mortuary—to make San Lorenzo habitable for Himmler's friends, Rome will have to make it habitable for us too. All of which is to say, I want you to limit your investigation to discovering who gave the victim this coin. Maybe there are more. We can bury them in the tunnels and dig them up during Himmler's tour tomorrow. It doesn't take much to impress these Bavarian savages."

"What about the murder?"

"I don't want the murder solved. That's why I gave the investigation to you. God knows that choirboy Chief Inspector Consoli would insist on bringing the perpetrator to justice."

"I'm sorry?"

"Accusing our guests of homicide would dampen the spirit of camaraderie and mutual interest. I read your police reports. They're very believable. Your gift for massaging the official record will prove useful in giving this a quiet, clean ending."

THE CLOSED HOUSE ON VIA Agostino is one of the three San Lorenzo brothels licensed and regulated by the state. Its bedchambers are refreshed with new prostitutes every other week, an occasion the town's stray men honor with the solemn anticipation of a religious feast. The bureaucratically rigid quotas—eight bottle blondes, eight brunettes, zero gingers, as many French ladies as can be mustered—appeal to that feature of male licentiousness Ferrando doesn't understand, the desire for infinite variety within a narrow band of uniformity.

Ferrando has never frequented the town's closed houses in an off-duty capacity. They are zoned for desperation, furnished with impoverished visions of opulence, staffed by the second daughters of families with only one dowry. They offend his sense of reason and his morality. Aside from the confinati, those San Lorenzo men sufficiently spry to frequent the closed houses are few enough to fit into a couple elevators going down. Yet they receive a biweekly bonanza of prostitutes, while the women whose taxes pay for the brothel upkeep receive neither medical care, nor adequate shelter, nor schooling, nor reliable work, nothing from the state but radio addresses extolling their unshakable fortitude and the reverence with which the nation honors them.

Elisabetta's has two doors: a front entrance for single men, and a backdoor for husbands. This being official business, Ferrando and Bellino approach the former. Bellino sneezes; on top of everything else, he's allergic to Ferrando's cat.

"You and the madam have a history together?" Ferrando asks.

"Like Greece and Troy," his sergeant admits, wiping his nose. Bellino, less a family man than a families man, considers his wedding band as he knocks on the door. "We are, well, technically, married."

"You don't say."

"We haven't been on the best terms since she discovered I've been having an affair with the madam of a rival establishment."

Ferrando isn't the least bit surprised.

Elisabetta leans defiantly against the doorframe in an ensemble of three-inch heels, silk stockings, and plunging neckline whispered to life by a wolf whistle. In her right hand she grips a large iron crucifix hatchet-like. She glares from the crucifix to Bellino's temple, calculating the densities and durabilities of the holy and profane.

"We come in a professional capacity," Bellino says, keeping one swinging crucifix's length away from her.

Elisabetta's skepticism registers on the rising altimeter of her right eyebrow.

"My darling, please, just a couple questions. You aren't . . . indisposed?"

Elisabetta holds up the crucifix. "I was praying."

"By yourself?"

"Me and the Holy Ghost," Elisabetta says. When Bellino steps within range, she swings the crucifix, clocking his temple with a satisfyingly hollow thwack. She holsters the crucifix in her silk robe's side pocket. The satisfaction of a job well done settles into her smile.

"You can come in," she tells Ferrando. Casting a final glance at Bellino, she adds, "So long as you take the trash with you when you leave."

Elisabetta pulls a cut of meat from the icebox behind the bar and slaps it against the welt where Bellino was touched by Christ.

"Hold that there. It'll keep your hands occupied." She punches out the indentation in Bellino's hat and tosses it onto the table. They sit. With the slab of loin still pressed to his head, Bellino passes over the cloakroom ticket. "We're looking for a coat," he says.

"They give you all the big cases, hmm?"

Something shifts in Bellino's ogle to accommodate and then encourage the flirtation in her voice. He offers her his outstretched hand. "That's right. Watch out or I'll catch you next."

Elisabetta taps cigarette ash into his upturned palm. "You wouldn't know where to start."

Bellino leans in. "I'd start with the handcuffs."

She leans in. "And then?"

"Search around for fingerprints."

Beneath the table, Elisabetta works Bellino's feet like a couple organ pedals. Ferrando looks away. "About that coat."

The trench coat Elisabetta returns with is oversized and broad-backed, tailored to emphasize the shoulder and conceal the gut. Ferrando slips his shirtsleeves through the silk-lined armholes. Obeying some boyish instinct, he spins on his heels, and the rising hems dervish around his knees. "How do I look?"

"In my professional opinion," Elisabetta says, "you look like a dick."

Ferrando pats the pockets and comes up with a couple unsmoked cigars, balled receipts, and a bit of scrap paper where a location (Piazza Vittorio Veneto bus stop), a date (today), and a time (19:00) were hastily scribbled.

Elisabetta sees the book crammed into the side pocket of Ferrando's suit jacket. She helps herself and flips to the table of contents.

"The Memoirs of Sherlock Holmes," she reads. She looks at Ferrando, then back to the book, then back up at him. She flips through the collection of stories, sees Ferrando's annotations and underlining, the investigative methods he's drawn from Holmes's example, and shaking her head in genuine pity, says, "No wonder they give you two the big cases. Unbelievable. Two Watsons in search of a Sherlock."

Bellino touches his temple, winces. "It's sad, this one. Ends with Sherlock Holmes taking a swan dive off a waterfall and . . . splat."

"Sherlock doesn't die, not really," Ferrando says, unable to restrain his pedantry. "He's trying to elude Professor Moriarty, his nemesis, but Moriarty is always there, a few steps behind him, pursuing him to the end. Sherlock confronts him atop Reichenbach Falls, the two of them grapple, each the other's equal. The only way Sherlock can defeat him is to sacrifice himself and they both plummet off the cataract, drowning in the water below. For years, everyone thinks Sherlock is dead: Dr. Watson, Scotland Yard, all of Sherlock's readers. But he isn't, and the only person who knew he was alive was his author, Arthur Conan Doyle."

Why this particular story draws its bow across his heartstrings is obvious, even to a middle-aged paper pusher all but impervious to self-awareness. To his relief, Ferrando sees that no one has been listening to him. Bellino is hand-printing the madam's thigh. She peels the frozen loin from his face. Her voice dials down to an agitated murmur, the tone of urgent news whispered in the ear of a guy on a podium, widening his eyes.

"You will make the most beautiful widow," Bellino says.

Elisabetta cocks her finger and blows a hole through Bellino's heart.

When they return to the car, the clouds above are marbled in charcoal gray.

"I forgot my hat," Bellino says.

"Your hat's on your head," Ferrando observes.

"My wallet, then. I forgot my wallet. Listen, why don't you get the crime scene photographs printed at Picone's and I'll meet you back at the station?" Bellino's face is flushed, his tie is crooked, and his hair is mussed from the madam's fingers. The look in his eyes is one of windblown wonderment and he hotfoots it back to the brothel with his hand still pressed to the hole in his chest where his wife slew him.

THE MUNICIPAL POLICE WOULD RATHER lose a fortune incrementally than spend the modest lump sum required to set up a darkroom of its own, and for years Picone Photography has developed crime scene photographs and mugshots. Ferrando has always liked the Picone kid. It went back to Michele, his childhood friend from Genoa who was sentenced to confino in San Lorenzo. After weeks of fruitlessly trawling the Busento, Ferrando stowed his rowboat under the bridge Michele had jumped from. Nino asked if he could use it. Ferrando didn't see the harm. He learned about the accident months after it occurred, and still feels tenderness for the boy who was resuscitated from the water where Michele had drowned.

When Ferrando enters the photography studio, Nino sets down a copy of *The Count of Monte Cristo* and says, "I didn't expect any business today."

"Me neither. And this poor bastard certainly didn't expect to become the business." Ferrando hands over the film. "Murder."

"What, is Chief Inspector Consoli out sick?"

Ferrando chooses not to hear the sarcasm blaring in Nino's voice. Most days he maintains his self-respect solely through the selectivity of his hearing. He wonders what it's like to work in a real police state. He can't imagine.

"Never you mind. Murder is serious business, not for the delicate ears of a college boy."

The light shifts in Nino's eyes at the mention of his time at university. Ferrando knows the general outline: the political prisoner Giuseppe Lagana wrangled Nino a scholarship to study law in Rome and his matriculation had been a point of civic pride. So many denizens of the educated and monied North had descended to San Lorenzo, and Nino Picone was that rare native son to stake his claim as a citizen of their country. Which made mystifying his decision to flush his future down the crapper by trying to photograph the yahoos killing one another in Spain. He could have gone anywhere. Now look at him: back where he started.

"When do you need these by?" Nino asks, writing out a receipt.

"Soon as possible."

"They'll be ready tomorrow."

Ferrando pockets the receipt and, at the door, looks back. "Were you at the festivities last night?"

"You missed it?"

"A privilege of rank," Ferrando says. "How'd Himmler look?"

Nino chooses his adjective carefully. "Unpleasant."

"Most murderers are."

When Ferrando returns to his office, his cat meets him at the door, its tail shivering with excitement. "I know, buddy." He strokes the cat's belly and it purrs with delight. "I missed you too." The cat follows Ferrando to his desk and leaps into his lap. Ferrando unfolds the slip of paper he pulled from the dead man's trench coat: *Piazza Vittorio Veneto bus stop, 1900 hrs.*

Ferrando decides to go see who the dead man was going to meet. Perhaps it's the very person who gave him the golden coin.

4

FIREWORKS ASH COATS THE EXCAVATION SITE, A GRAY DANDER GIUSEPPE kicks through to reach the work shed where he signs out a shovel and pickax from a guard who is Sicilian by birth, temperament, and mustache. The guard hands over the tools and Giuseppe recrosses the field to the excavation entrance. He nods greetings to the bedraggled night-shift diggers exiting the tunnel. Most are local peasants, women and men inured to the frustrations of tilling rocky and barren soil.

He wobbles across a wooden gangplank and into the darkness. As he descends, the air congeals into a cold sluggishness. Earth arches over the wooden struts lofting the tunnel walls. Giuseppe stoops until his third vertebra feels hinged. Sodium bulbs stapled to the crossbeams light his way.

To the diggers, the tunnels are without end, feature, or purpose. When one confinato, a professor of archeology transferred to Lampedusa, pointed out that tunneling and blasting bedrock would destroy the burial site the podestà sought, it became clear to Giuseppe that not even the author of this ill-fated epic believed the legends. The scope of the endeavor, the marshaled resources, the relentless spectacle, this is what the diggers mine in these alleyways of the underworld. Such scales make the production the product itself.

He tosses the pickax and shovel into a mining cart. The wheels grate on rail rust. The tunnel forks and forks again. When he arrives at its end, he reaches up and unscrews the sodium bulb. Standing in utter blackness, he swings his pickax. Only in the darkness can he see what he's truly digging toward.

In the late afternoon, Giuseppe returns to Picone Photography and climbs the stairs to the room where he's slept every night for the last twelve years. He will never sleep here again. Giuseppe will receive the Mercedes from Vincenzo at Piazza Vittorio Veneto at 1900 hours. By midnight, he and Nino will have driven through the last roadblock out of San Lorenzo. By morning, they'll be north of Naples. By next week, they'll reach the French border. In a month, Giuseppe will be in Paris, Nino will be in Spain, and Vincenzo and his mother will be in Brooklyn. And no matter the actual distances, Giuseppe knows Paris is far closer to Los Angeles than San Lorenzo. Perhaps by the end of the year he will see Maria and Annunziata again? He imagines his wife and daughter living in California splendor. What will they think of him, a stranger in threadbare trousers who years ago ceased being the man they remembered? Is it kinder to let that Giuseppe live in their minds than to replace him with the ghost he's become? A disturbing thought: what if confino has remade him into a person that his wife and daughter will not recognize, a person only at home in San Lorenzo?

After reviving himself with a cold bath, hot shave, and snort of red wine, Giuseppe dries and dresses. He checks under the bed and in the closet to make sure he's forgotten everything. There is nothing he wants to bring from this place, nothing but the red and white cigar box sitting beside his bed. He goes to the darkroom to check that the two jugs of gasoline are safely hidden. Then he pockets the passport and steamship ticket Vincenzo left here for safekeeping while stealing the car the previous night.

"I've been waiting for this day for a very long time," Giuseppe tells Nino, a bit too declaratively, when he returns downstairs to the storefront. "A very long time."

"I know you have."

"Are you ready?"

"I will be."

As he paces back and forth, trying to restrain his nervous energy, Giuseppe notices the film plates beneath Nino's dog-eared copy of *The Count of Monte Cristo*. "We had a customer today?"

"Inspector Ferrando," Nino says. "I told him I wouldn't have the prints ready till tomorrow afternoon."

By then, they'll be long gone.

Giuseppe studies the looming clouds, unsheathes an umbrella from the stand, and, glancing back into the recesses of the portrait studio, feels an urge to confide his fears in Nino. Instead he shakes his head and closes the door behind him.

Nino climbs to the terrace where many years ago Giuseppe's daughter told him that Rudolph Valentino had died. He watches Giuseppe hail the town bus. The bus is a rattling, rusting jalopy fueled by a wood-burning generator; every few hours the driver pulls over and has the passengers chop down a tree to feed the furnace. On the far side of the terrace, the pigeons coo in their loft. They are a piratical bunch: scarred, half-blind, hobbling on nubby bird ankles. Nino trained them as carrier pigeons until the guards began using them for target practice.

He sets his hands into the loft and the pigeons board his arms in a gray-lavender fluster. The downed birds are helmeted in emerald, their legs rhubarby and scaled in cloudy fiber. They hop and shuffle up his arms, fanning their feathers, and rimmed in broken pigeon Nino pads noiselessly on the flagstone terrace, his outstretched arms cutting through the air, carrying the grounded flock through the memory of flight. He will miss San Lorenzo.

It only takes ten minutes to pack. Easy enough when you can't take most of what you want to bring. Photographs compose the greater bulk in his blue carpetbag, a few reproductions of Robert Capa's and Gerda Taro's work, but mostly his own: diggers at the Busento, women filling clay jars with fountain water, a local fascist official getting a manicure at the beautician's. The Madonna dei Fiori feast day procession—Father Mancuso carries a candle the size of an elephant femur, followed by boys who plow snow shovels through bergs of wax and scrape the drippings into paint cans to later sculpt into cylinders, weave with wicks, and sell back to the priest. There are photographs of the carnival street theater, the impromptu and ad-libbed dramas performed by peasants powdered in quicklime and redrawn in ghoulish slants of burnt cork, supposedly religious reenactments that invariably veered into protest against the latest indignity the state imposed. A photograph of advertisements hanging upside-down from a grocer's storefront after a tax was announced on signage posted the right way up. The next picture, taken from the other side of the storefront, shows a dozen passersby craning their necks to read the day's specials. Photographs of a community so invisible he sees the exposures as proofs of life. This is what Nino will bring with him: only everything he runs from.

He carries his carpetbag downstairs and sets it by the door. He goes to the counter and opens the black album of passport photographs his mother reassembled over the years. As a boy, Nino had loved watching her piece the two torn halves together and seeing the complete face emerge. Now he hefts the black leather photo album in both hands, and even though it's bulky, even though it's all dead weight, he will bring it with him. This is what his mother left him: photographs of a thousand strangers' faces and not one of her own.

He and Giuseppe will enter France on foot, through the Maritime Alps, where the border threads through uninhabited wilderness and no visas or papers are required. Nonetheless, as the rain drumrolls on the clay roofing tiles, he goes to the studio and sets up the camera. His final picture of San Lorenzo is his own passport photograph. When the print has developed and dried, he tears it in half. One half he pastes into the black leather photo album. The other half he slips into his billfold. Once he reaches Paris, he will piece the two halves together. Only then will he believe he has made it out of San Lorenzo.

Inspector Ferrando's film plates sit beside the register. It's nearly seven. The bus will deposit Giuseppe in the Piazza Vittorio Veneto shortly. Figuring it's better to keep busy than worry at the wall clock, Nino takes Ferrando's film to the darkroom. He'll leave the inspector's prints out for him. They'll be his letter goodbye.

5

FOUL WEATHER CURTAILS THE EVENING PASSEGGIATA AND FERRANDO alone pushes through the drizzle into the piazza. Moonlight scallops damp cobbles. Crows shelter beneath patriotic statuary. Ahead looms the fog-frosted Bourbon palazzo where Himmler and company are quartered. Kneeling at one of the balcony balustrades, Bellino sweeps the piazza with a pair of binoculars impounded from a Peeping Tom in Palmi who claimed he was a bird-watcher.

Ferrando is wearing the trench coat, hoping their man will mistake him for the murder victim. He knots his belt to seal what little warmth he smuggled from the station and heads to the rendezvous. The Piazza Vittorio Veneto bus stop is a fashionable destination for local vandals and public urinators. Several lives ended and several more were conceived on its bench. Put a record needle to the fingernail scratches and you'll hear the traffic of souls shuttling into and out of the void.

He takes a seat and sinks his fingers into his face. Mussolini peers over his shoulder. The washed-out propaganda poster offers slogans declaiming Italian greatness, a sentiment belied only by the surrounding three hundred miles. Some iconoclast slit the Duce's neck with a slice of red paint. Just below it, a budding poet wrote *pony fart.* No doubt getting to the bottom of this crime will be his next big case.

At five to seven he unfolds a newspaper and dips his brim below the broadsheet's horizon.

There's a rusty wheeze and rumble. Bus headlights careen across the piazza.

Ferrando resists the urge to peek over the newspaper as disembarking passengers ruffle the mist with flapping raincoats and hoisted umbrellas. He feels eyes on him. About ten meters ahead a man stands still, watching him. Backlit by bus light, the figure's silhouette clouds the broadsheet like the shadow on the chest X-ray in the Reggio doctor's office.

A few steps more and the man will come near enough to cuff. Ferrando has never used his handcuffs before. What if he accidentally handcuffs himself? He'd give anything to be at his desk, submerged in paperwork, the one place on earth where he knows what he's doing. Then Bellino is yelping from the balcony and Ferrando drops the newspaper and occupying the space where the man stood is two hundred feet of fog and a brown mutt lifting its leg on a wall. All at once, Ferrando realizes what went wrong: from his balustrade bird's eye, Bellino can't make out anyone beneath the mounded umbrellas, and Ferrando, using the broadsheet to conceal his face, didn't see the suspect either. He heaves himself upright and into the piazza. Raindrops ricochet from roof tiles.

Neglected laundry hangs over the nearest alley. Ferrando moves with what plodding stealth his last legs allow. Farther down the alley, he hears breathing. He pats at his underarm, feels cool gunmetal, and unholsters the revolver he's never shot.

He commands the man to come out. He tastes the recoil of mammalian fear wafting from the alley shadows as he peels back the hammer and lowers his aim from the lethal elevations toward the knees. He gives the guy to three. Then to five. On twenty-eight, the gun slips and he accidentally shoots.

The muzzle emits a pupil-perforating flash and a clapper swing inside Ferrando's skull, and for a moment he's just a passenger on a thunderbolt, plunging through the storm.

When the dazzle dims he sees the bullet has blasted a Bolognese of brain tissue across the alley wall. Speechless, he does the only thing he can think to do: he removes his hat.

When he reaches into the shadows for the man's body, he touches fur.

Ten seconds later, he's loped back to the piazza, cologned in cordite, the taste of headless hound in his throat. He tries running, but his lungs roar with the backdraft of his sixty-a-day habit. How easily he forgets his only real exercise these days is coughing and constipation.

He can hear footsteps bolting from the piazza, but he's bent over, hacking up blood, trying to catch his breath. By the time he gets his wind back and lumbers out to the corso, the man, whoever he is, is gone.

Ferrando turns around but sees only the slow plod of women coming home from evening vespers, the shopkeepers closing up, the queue forming beneath the cinema marquee, the White Widows talking of their emigrant husbands, the streetlamps dousing the fog in hazy haloes, the silent camaraderie of sad men waiting for their families to fall asleep before they return home.

Bellino catches up with Ferrando and offers him an umbrella. Ferrando accepts it wordlessly. He's soaked to the skin, but beneath that denting dome of silk, the air is dry enough to light a cigarette.

AN HOUR LATER, FERRANDO CLOSES the passenger door, stomps through riverbank mush, and pops the Fiat trunk. "We're really doing this, huh?"

"Gallo's orders," Bellino says, as if naming an inexplicable act of God.

At the outer range of the mist-smudged headlights, Ferrando can see the pit where the discovery of fifth-century skeletons launched the flurry of communications to Rome and Berlin that culminated in Himmler's visit.

"You take the left arm," Bellino says.

Too much rides on the symbolic spectacle of resurrecting fallen empires and dead kings to risk investigating the murder of a Calabrian so forgettable no one remembered to report him missing. And where is a body less likely to call attention to itself than in a mass grave? It will take all his powers of prevarication to give this police report the clean ending Gallo requested.

They drag the body by its wrists to the exposed pit, a thirty-by-twenty-meter trench darker than the neighboring night. They slop back through muck ornamented in trampled grass and gnarled vines and retrieve a couple shovels from the Fiat trunk.

Ferrando mounts his shovel in the dirt. He hunches down, unties the dead man's shoes, peels each putrid sock. When he's naked, they heave the body into the pit. The slumped weight sends back a muddy splatter and skeletal crack. Ferrando waits for his sergeant to offer a few inadequately considered words, but Bellino just picks up his shovel and gets to work.

For a few minutes, there is no sound but water babbling and sediment whistling from shovels into the dismal night. The Milky Way speckles rifted rain clouds. The starlight must have traveled a few billion miles to flicker uselessly across an impoverished vista better left unseen.

"Look, you can make out O'Brian's Belt," Bellino says, hitching a thumb through his suspender.

"Orion."

"O'Ryan."

"O-r-i-o-n," Ferrando says. "Greek fella."

Bellino smears sweat around his forehead with a handkerchief. "I always wondered what an Irishman was doing up there."

Ferrando stomps his shovel into the murk and scoops five pounds of grit stitched together by earthworm. In the mist-clouded distance, he sees the bridge. When Michele threw himself from it, there was no goodbye, no explanation, only the locked-room mystery of his own mind. Some days it still breaks Ferrando's heart to think that if he weren't such an incompetent he might have discovered *why*. There was no answer. Even though Ferrando searched for weeks in his rowboat, there wasn't even a body to bury. Just a name on water and the empty coffin Michele's soul rode into eternity. Just Michele on the bridge, grappling with the Moriarty in his brain, and the only grace note was knowing Michele had taken his nemesis down with him.

"You want to say anything?" Bellino asks when they finish.

"Yeah, I'd like to say this is all completely fucked."

"I mean do you want to say a few words for the departed. A Hail Mary or something."

Ferrando removes his hat and tries to recall a Latin prayer. He wants to defang the bite of contrition in the devitalizing words of a dead language. Years earlier he stepped off the path of righteousness to take a leak and he never found his way back from the woods.

"You deserved a better friend than me," he tells Michele, and then, to the body he buried, he offers the kindest words he can summon in this deep hour of evening. "You can sleep in tomorrow."

He ladles a fedora full of fog onto his head and walks to the car.

6

THE PRINT MATERIALIZES WITH DREAMLIKE SLOWNESS IN THE DEVELOPing tray. Shadows and shapes creep across the photographic paper: a man lying beneath a glinting Mercedes hood ornament. The image emerges so leisurely Nino tells himself that he isn't seeing the full picture, that he's missing some vital and extenuating context. The tongs in his hands move the print from the developer to the fixer to the stop bath, operating purely on muscle memory now that he's floating several feet above his body. He feels drugged by shock but on some deeper level he isn't entirely surprised. Gangsters with Vincenzo's temperament tend not to die of old age and ever since Vincenzo began working as a heavy, Nino feared he would meet a gruesome end. But not now. Not here. Not yet. Vincenzo lies back with his tie straight, his suit jacket buttoned, his hands folded over his stomach, imperturbable, self-assured, and for a man with four bullet holes in him, strangely at peace. Nino slides back into his body on the downdraft of his next breath and that's when the pain begins.

When Giuseppe returns home, Nino is hunched on the darkroom floor, arms wrapped around his shins, eyes ringed in washed-out lavender, the red lightbulb transfusing color into his cheeks. Giuseppe pulls out a stool, sits down, and only then does he notice the photograph drip-drying on a bobbing length of twine. The gory circumference haloing the young man's cranium. The apertures through which Vincenzo Cortese's bluster blew.

"Oh God." Giuseppe averts his gaze. He feels inadequately engineered to bear the weight of a photograph held by clothespin to a shoelace. What a waste.

He asks Nino to describe Ferrando's visit that afternoon and realizes the inspector hasn't identified Vincenzo. How could he? Vincenzo left his passport and papers with Giuseppe to avoid being identified in case he was apprehended.

"One of the Germans must have shot him," Nino says. "When he was trying to steal the car."

"I suspect that's true."

"Then what do we do?"

Giuseppe wants to offer comfort or consolation but resists the urge. He straightens his tie, brushes the woolly prickle of his damp suit coat. It is paramount he remains cool and calm, keeps his composure glazed over, glacial, even if a few fathoms below he feels bergs crack in the swell. The most generous gesture he offers is a gruff hand on Nino's shoulder. "For tonight," he says, "we have done enough."

Once Nino has gone to bed, Giuseppe returns to the darkroom. He fires up a cigar and considers the coming hours with an actuary's eye for peril and profit. He can call off the attempt, relinquish the first real opportunity in years, and risk probable discovery. Or he can improvise. It is the costliest decision of his life. He makes it in under ten seconds.

He flips through the pages of Vincenzo's passport, past the American visa, to the ticket for the steamship on which Vincenzo and his mother would have embarked for New York the following week. Vincenzo Cortese, buonanima, is dead, but there is still life in his name.

AFTER FIVE HOURS TOO FITFUL to constitute slumber, Nino drags himself from bed and goes downstairs, where Giuseppe wordlessly slides a passport across the kitchen table. Nino flexes the cardboard wingspan. His own eyes stare up from the passport's identity page.

"I reprinted the photograph you took yesterday and did the rest by hand." Giuseppe's eyes flicker with the mixed satisfaction of succeeding at a deplorable task.

Nino's face is yoked by bureaucratic cursive to his dead friend's name. His photograph is stamped in the lower right corner with red ink, a thirty-degree slice completing the underlying seal of a Roman eagle. The cork stopper on the table is meticulously cut, engraved, and inked. Nino tries to imagine Giuseppe hunched over the wine cork, etching feathers on a coin-sized eagle with a sewing needle.

"I'm nearly thirty years too old to pass as Vincenzo Cortese. So, there it is. His name is yours. Bon voyage, Vincent."

"I can't, Beppe."

"You can't?"

"It's wrong."

"Wrong?" Giuseppe's eyes grow grave and overcast. "This isn't a passport. It is a lifeboat. If you don't take it, you deserve to drown."

The words hit their mark. Nino can feel the dismay sinking into the corners of his frown. "I can't afford it."

"It's a gift. It's an inheritance. Understand I would kill to keep what I am giving you."

Nino is silent.

Giuseppe squints over the copper rims of his spectacles and nods to the darkroom. "The inspector will come for those crime scene photographs in a few hours, no? And then? Then it's only a matter of time before Vincenzo is identified. You think he'll ever arrest a German? He'll pin this on our lapels."

"Ferrando is one of our best customers."

"And that will save you?" Giuseppe asks, moved to pity by Nino's faith in customer loyalty. To judge by his record, Ferrando believes in prosecution uninhibited by evidence, alibi, or innocence.

"What about you?" Nino asks.

"I'm coming with you," Giuseppe promises. "But we don't have much time. We need to leave this morning and you need to visit Vincenzo's mother."

Upon hearing those words, Nino's stomach caves in. He hasn't considered Concetta. Hasn't thought of her once.

"I'll tell her," Nino says. "She's been like a mother to me. I have to—"

"You can't do that. I'm sorry, Nino, truly, but the passport is only valid while Vincenzo is presumed alive and well."

"I can explain everything to her. We can bring her with us, can't we?"

"She won't leave San Lorenzo without burying her son. You know that as well as me. If you tell her that her son was murdered, she will go to the police to ask for his body. And then? Then Vincenzo's passport will be canceled." Giuseppe shakes his head. "Tell her not to worry. Tell her Vincenzo has gone away for a few days, but he's on his way home to her."

Though Nino is an atheist, he still relies on Catholicism's division of transgression: the venial sins, repented with a few laps around the rosary, and the mortal trespasses that devein the very grace from the soul. Taking a life is murder, the most mortal sin, this much is clear. But taking a death? For that is what Nino would do: steal Vincenzo's death from his mother. What is the name of this trespass, both murder's opposite and its equal? Not even Giuseppe, once among the great lawyers of Rome, can name the crime.

"This isn't a gift," Nino says, slipping the passport into his pocket. He cannot bring himself to name the price or who will pay it.

"This is San Lorenzo. Nothing here is free."

ONCE NINO HAS GONE, GIUSEPPE drags the two jugs of gasoline outside and their sloshing weight grunts through him. That said, he's surprisingly alert given the hour and the dismemberment going on in his shoulder joints. The sunlight flexing between the eastern mountains kicks a beat back in his circadian rhythms. By the time he reaches the excavation site, he is awake.

A sign hitched by yellowed rope over the tunnel entrance redirects traffic to the adjacent guardhouse, where two watchmen slumber. Giuseppe pads past, scissors his legs over the frayed yellow cord, and steps into the mouth of the tunnel. Whatever hope he held of leaving San Lorenzo by car died with Vincenzo. Now he can think of only one way out.

Twenty steps in and the ground pitches downward. Absolute darkness but his eyes are open. In the Vault, he'd learned to walk without light. A footpath of bouncy wooden planks paves the way. The air is heavy with the loamy scent of churned earth. He no longer hears the gurgle of the river overhead.

At the end of the tunnel, he sets down the gasoline jugs. He feels overhead for the electrical wire stapled into the crossbeam and strung with lightbulbs. He works the wire from its fasteners. It swings down and he gropes around for it. Applying the blade of a kitchen knife, he skins a few inches of rubber insulation. The frayed copper wire bristles as he slips it into the gasoline jug.

A few hours hence, a well-rested watchman would flip on the lights to prepare for the day's belated first shift. Electricity would spill down five hundred feet of copper wire and drain into two jugs of petroleum chemically refined to put the purr of satisfaction in the most finicky Mercedes engine. Where electron meets hydrocarbon, a case study in thermodynamics—the only laws inviolable to political coercion—would commence. The fire would leapfrog up the tunnel, igniting wooden struts like mountaintop signal towers until the darkness caves in on them. Perhaps the entire excavation site would collapse. At the very least, it would summon every guard, carabinieri, and militiaman from their habitual post, watchtower, and checkpoint, leaving the route out of San Lorenzo unmanned and unwatched. Fifty feet below the earth, the gasoline would fuel their getaway. Glossed in sweat, caked in mud, some ornate braid work gnarling his lower back, he nonetheless feels himself seized by the rapture of a simple and unexpected perfection: he has made a detonator of a light switch.

Riding the daredevilry a little further, he dips his finger in the mud and applies to the tunnel wall a sentiment whose lineage stretches from the Cave Paintings of Altamira to the lightless walls of the Vault. When finished, he steps back, seized by the desire to stay. It's no death wish, just the opposite. He wants to see his testimony when the light turns on. He wants to read, there on the tunnel wall, that Giuseppe from Rome was here.

7

WHEN FERRANDO RETURNS FROM BURYING THE BODY, HE'S TOO BE-numbed to feel more than the pins and needles of remorse, but by four in the morning, the paralysis ebbs and the memory of the Busento is a rawness in his brain gurgling to life. He soaps his face and hands, but the scent of unmarked grave persists. The rot no longer on but within him. Somewhere bloodhounds howl.

He's *just* nodded off when someone calls his name, he springs upright, and smashes his forehead into the bunk overhead.

On the other side of the bars, Bellino stares at the welt between Ferrando's eyebrows. "You should be more careful, boss."

There are times, while lost in dreams or the pages of a book, when Ferrando can imagine himself capable of courage or sacrifice or honor. But then the book ends, the covers close, he wakes up, he remembers who he is: a paper pusher in a provincial station, a loyal functionary whose only talent is fabricating police reports, a buffoon in a jail cell with a bump on his head, spots in his lungs, and cat hair in his nose, listening as his sergeant says a militia guard saw a stranger fitting the murder victim's description visiting Giuseppe Lagana and Nino Picone two days earlier.

8

CONCETTA CORTESE STILL LIVES IN THE SAME HOUSE VINCENZO WAS born in, a low-slung stone hut roofed in clay tile, sandbag, flowerpot, and napping tabby. Out front, a laundry line billows bed linen over tufted grass. Amphoras of aqueduct water stand in pocked soil. Suspicious of ostentation, wary of eliciting the malocchio, Concetta advertises the prosperity of her son, the gangster, only by the polished brass hinges on the door that Nino knocks.

She's a full head shorter than Nino, but there's never been a time when she hasn't loomed over him. She stands in the doorway with one hand holstered on her hip. Evidence of proficient butchery, spattered across her apron, spirits to sea whatever hope Nino still harbors. He apologizes for interrupting and promises to return another time.

"Inside," Concetta says. A virtuoso of the imperative mood, she easily converts any preposition to command. She lays the bouquet of dead chicken across her forearm, its white feathers disheveled from the final futile wingbeat.

The house is a large room of unadorned white stone, modestly provisioned and immaculately kept. A wicker basket hangs over the bed, suspended from a rafter by withered twine. Each of Concetta's six children slept in that basket. Three died in it. Of the three who survived childhood, two passed preventably and predictably, disease and vendetta. By the time Nino came to live with her, Vincenzo, her youngest, was the only child she hadn't buried in Father Mancuso's churchyard. And yet once she had rocked all her children in the wicker basket hanging from a rafter.

"What troubles of my hardheaded son have you come to lie to me about?" she asks, never more affectionate than when bemoaning the grief her boy gives her.

When Nino speaks, she raises a hand. Some of the all-time greats have lied to her, chief among them her husband, and she has no patience for amateurism.

"Don't even try to lie," she says. "I saw Vincenzo dressed to go whoring on Friday evening. You think I don't know the look of a man on his way to a brothel? I was married to his father, buonanima."

Concetta searches Nino's face for a flinch to measure her distance from the mark. Her pupils are ringed in irises of kaleidoscopic caramel, two black holes where something furious scorched through and burned out around the time she buried her third child.

"So long as he gets himself back in time to take me to New York," she says, "I'll forgive him whatever the Madonna won't."

"He'll be back soon." Nino barely gets the words out. "He wouldn't want me to tell you more."

"I should hope not." Concetta dunks her hands into a basin frothing with soap suds, then dries them on the clean side of her apron. Nino is looking at the Italian passport on the table, identical to the one in his pocket.

"Has Vincenzo told you where he and I will live in Brooklino?" Concetta asks. "A four-bedroom apartment. It comes with a Polish girl."

Tucked inside her passport is her ticket on the *Columbia*, departing Naples for New York next week. There's still time. Nino could tell her what happened. Perhaps he could even convince her to come with him? But Giuseppe is right. Concetta would never leave San Lorenzo without giving her son a proper church burial, would never allow Nino to assume his identity, would never consent to participating in this grotesque fraud. As she speculates doubtfully on whether the Polish girl can meet her exacting standards of tidiness, Nino looks to the bed in the corner where he slept every night for five years after his mother died.

He weeps openly, there at the table beside the slaughtered chicken. Concetta's first instinct is contempt. Like other bodily emissions, weeping is a solitary pursuit, taboo and unmentionable, a biological imperative you overlook in yourself and disdain in others. He is mourning her departure, she realizes. She draws her arms around Nino's shoulders. His unloaded bulk flattens her chest. The tightly tuned tendons at his nape ripple under her touch. She smells faded laundry soap and lemony pomade and the secondhand stink of Signor Giuseppe's cigars. Since sentenced to confino, Nino has come by her house several times a week to chop firewood or carry drinking water or transcribe her letters to Vincenzo. A good son, but he is not hers.

"Quiet now. We will see each other again. I'll come back someday," she says, but she will never return, not even if a mourner awaits her. If not for the merciless God of Calabria, she would be mourned by all her children.

"Pull yourself together," she says, "and do what you came here to do."

"What did I come here to do?"

The way he looks at her, she'd have thought the whole of his life trembles on her answer.

"To untie my basket from the rafter," she says. "It's time for me to pack. Vincenzo and I have a long journey ahead of us."

9

WHEN FERRANDO DRAGS HIS HEAVY HEART THROUGH THE FRONT DOOR of Picone Photography, he smells the unmistakable punch of gasoline.

"Hello?" he calls. No answer. Mud imprinted by busy footprints smudges the threshold, but the place is quiet. Ferrando searches the rooms. In back, there are a couple wooden braces deployed before the advent of flashbulbs to immobilize a sitter during a long exposure. Ferrando tries to imagine the emigrants lining up to get their passport photographs, or years later, their families coming to send a portrait, and it seems to him the allure of photography is the medium's faith, despite all contrary evidence, that people can see one another at all.

He climbs upstairs. His footsteps shimmy though the house's creaky woodwork. He opens the terrace door and there are pigeons perched on every graspable horizontal. A couple on the eaves prepare to skullcap Ferrando in guano.

Behind him the door swoops closed with a crash. All around the pigeons hop from their perches, unfold their underwings, and slowly scull the sky. The pumping white fluster draws down an image from memory's outer orbit: snow in August.

It had been so long ago, in the prelapsarian epoch when he wore his body like a freshly laundered suit, eighteen and eligible for immortality, undimmed, tumor-free, aglow in the crisp vigor of inexperience. It was the summer of the workers' strikes, when communists unfurled red flags from campaniles and unrest rocked the Genovese streets. That summer the August afternoons were sun-baked torpors stretching from mid-morning to midnight, and Rocco Ferrando spent them lugging twenty-five-kilo sugar sacks at a local import warehouse. Inside the warehouse it was always one degree below heatstroke, a languishing warmth that sublimated the distances to wrinkles and smudges. Then one day, miracle of miracles, Michele showed up with an electric fan. The four-bladed vortex was encased within a chromium grille, shiny and sleek, engineered to meet the onrushing future. The churning clip of its blades dredged up Arctic winds. Carved slabs sparkled on Rocco's face. The sensation of coolness like a beloved memory surfacing from amnesia.

They stripped off their clammy shirts and stood there as the gyring current glittered on their chests. Michele's skin was bright and flawless and stippled in beads of sweat that wobbled in the airflow. Rocco was standing so close to him. Anything could have happened. Then Michele kicked over a sack and the fan inflated the avalanching sugar to a whirling granular whiteness. It erased Rocco's eyes. A million sugar grains adhered to his wet skin. Five kilos of incandescence armored him. He couldn't see Michele through the snow-blind brilliance, but he felt the damp suddenness of a hand on his chest. The sugar crashing into his teeth provided rapturous synesthesia: in the whiteout he tasted the sweetness of Michele's touch. When Rocco opened his eyes, he saw Michele had peeled a perfect handprint from his chest.

The intensity of Michele's gaze seemed to coax a few extra photons from each sugar grain. Rocco Ferrando was a diamond, and he would grieve to remember how beautiful he'd been for a few seconds on an August afternoon a lifetime ago.

"Look at them," one of the other laborers said.

"A couple finocchi," said another with the lazy contentment of a stereotypist proven right. "Knew it the moment I saw them."

Ferrando turned to Michele and did what he had to do to protect himself from the person he loved: he punched Michele in the face.

Years later Michele was sentenced to confino for sexual deviancy, and when Ferrando learned that San Lorenzo was recruiting officers from the North, he volunteered. He wanted to make amends, to ease the internment of the boy who had put his hand on Ferrando's heartbeat a minute before Ferrando put him in the hospital. Michele claimed not to remember Ferrando when he introduced himself in San Lorenzo, but the recoil in his eyes was unmistakable. That evening Michele ran for it. The podestà's hounds picked up his trail at first light, and by the following afternoon, Michele was down in the Vault, then atop the Ponte Zupi. Was Ferrando Michele's Moriarty? A pursuing evil he could only shake by throwing himself from a great height? His body was never recovered, but Ferrando bought a rowboat and for months searched up and down the Busento, a tomb robber, a treasure hunter, searching for the resting place of Michele, the only body in the Busento worth recovering, the boy from Genoa who conjured snow in August.

The branches bob with alighting pigeons.

Ferrando knows where Giuseppe Lagana and Nino Picone have gone.

10

IN THEORY, IT'S A ROWBOAT. IN PRACTICE, THE HULL HALF-BURIED IN the riverbank is a visual index of local fungi and a nursery for deciduous saplings. The gunwale is moss and missing paint. The oarlock is a rusted oculus veiled in cobwebs. The thwart—carved with paired initials and proclamations of love—is a Rosetta Stone to adolescent bewilderment. The rowboat is so rickety it can't keep afloat on dry land.

"You know what?" Giuseppe says. "It's in better shape than I thought."

Nino counters that the rowboat has no shape. It is dimensionless. A heap of boat molecules insufficiently fused by mud and miasma.

Giuseppe knocks dirt from the oar blades. "It's important to keep things in perspective. It's part of our heritage."

"Our heritage, huh."

"That's right." Giuseppe hauls the bow's breast hook. "We're Italian. We're descended from the people who invented perspective."

Nino considers this patrimony in all its utility and merit. "I'd rather be descended from the fuckers who invented boats."

A half hour earlier, they rendezvoused at the studio and hoofed it through the side streets that entangle the old town in dovetails and dead ends. Each footstep Nino planted on the cobblestones sprouted into flourishing echoes behind him. They barreled down marble stairs eroded by a millennium of human passage; through lanes rutted by medieval wagon wheels; under wrought-iron balconies woven in canvas to prevent wayward eyes glimpsing matronly calves; past elderly men fixing cigars into holders carved from rabbit legs. By the time Father Mancuso tolled the church bells, Giuseppe and Nino had reached the Busento.

They've nearly dislodged the hull from the riverbank when, with the flip of a light switch, the ground slouches. Not an earthquake, just a stern reminder that you are but a small mammal riding the world's shoulders.

The trembling heaviness settles over the riverbank.

Black smoke rises in the south.

Siren light spins off San Lorenzo's stone façades.

Giuseppe's face tightens with grim ebullience. "Look. The guards are running."

Downriver the bridge sentries abandon their posts, racing by car, horse, and bicycle toward the imploding excavation site. The gateway from San Lorenzo is open and unmanned. Between the bridge abutments the river throbs its glassy brilliance.

Giuseppe unlaces his shoes, rolls up his trousers, noses the bow in the water. Miraculously, it floats. Nino climbs in. Giuseppe swings a leg in after him and immediately water seeps through the rotted plank at the center of the hull. He steps out and the rowboat regains its buoyancy.

"You have Vincenzo's passport. You have his ticket on the *Columbia.* Now you have this."

Giuseppe hands him a red-and-white wooden box of Tuscan cigars.

"You packed cigars?" Nino asks.

"It's a gift for my daughter."

Nino sets the cigar box on his carpetbag and turns to help Giuseppe in, but Giuseppe is putting his shoulder to the transom and pushing. Nino feels the lurching hiss of sand on stern. The rowboat scrapes down the last two feet of bank and springs into the river.

Nino's weight wobbles through the frame and he steadies himself on the gunwales. The current draws its fingers down the hull. Nothing but an inch of moldered planking between him and the water's dark pull.

Giuseppe watches the boat drift. He doesn't climb in. The hull is riddled with wood rot. It won't support the weight of them both.

"Come on! What are you waiting for?" Nino calls.

Giuseppe feels pinned to this vanishing point where his failures, regrets, and hopes converge. "I'm waiting for you to go," he says.

Nino's look leaves exit wounds as it passes through him.

Several years earlier, in one of her weekly letters, Maria confessed to the role she played in Giuseppe's arrest. She wrote that though she didn't deserve his pardon, she was immeasurably sorry. That sprawled self-reproach, tidied within typewritten script, radiated its bleak energies into Giuseppe's brain. In his replies, Giuseppe assured her it wasn't her fault. Of course it wasn't. He desperately wanted to release her from contrition, but every week, the podestà's straight edge expurgated Giuseppe's words of reconciliation, and the censored strips were returned to him, comprising nearly all his incoming mail. Those common and essential words—that he loves her, that he laments missing so much of her life, that she makes him ceaselessly proud—have never made it past Domenico Gallo's razor. The podestà exacted this painstakingly cruel punishment on Giuseppe for having the temerity to think he could ever make it out of San Lorenzo.

Maria's letter is now watermarked in finger grease and underarm sweat. It is seated in his breast pocket. The hood on his heartbeat. The envelope flap hangs over the lip of his pocket like a target pinned by a firing squad captain.

A few feet from the bank, the current hastens into glossy chutes. Boulders in the riverbed vein the water's surface with foamy comet tails. Giuseppe watches Nino scramble to the stern and torque his lean frame over the transom to extend his hand. Giuseppe need only reach out. Instead, he is transfixed by clarity. He will never leave San

Lorenzo. He can see that now. By nightfall the podestà will throw him into the Vault. There is, then, only one thing left before the defense rests. With a final push, he propels the rowboat into the current and watches the Busento carry away the boy he once pulled from the water.

11

FERRANDO GLIMPSES THE ROWBOAT BOBBING BETWEEN TREE TRUNKS AS he guns the Fiat downriver. All other vehicles funnel into the oncoming lane as every uniformed body from carabinieri to postman races to the collapsing excavation site, and the entirety of northbound traffic is divided between the rowboat and the Fiat.

He reaches the Ponte Zupi five hundred feet ahead of the rowboat. There is a wooden crate layered with the losing hand of an unfinished scopa game, a couple stools tipped where their occupants sprung upright, but otherwise the bridge is empty. He takes out his Beretta and uses the parapet stone to steady his aim.

The rowboat seesaws on the current. In the rower's seat Nino Picone plows the oars forward. White gouges break the dark river and clouds waver on the water. Watching the young man row toward mountains, Ferrando suddenly feels that twelve to eighteen months is a very long time.

He peels back the hammer, aims, and puts a hole into the heart of the universe.

There's no doubt the shot hits its mark. There is cordite residue on Ferrando's hands, should the podestà inspect them. There is an empty shell in the Beretta cylinder. His body bears the physical evidence to substantiate the final paragraph of the police report he's already drafting by the dim light of his good intentions: *One shot fired. Suspect hit. Search failed to recover body. Presumed drowned.*

It's a clean shot, leaving a blowhole in the water a couple hundred feet upriver from the rowboat. Nino Picone keeps rowing, unaware that he was killed by a bullet that missed him by two hundred feet, that on paper he is already another body unrecovered from the Busento.

Ferrando puts his faith in the power of his mighty paperwork. Only in paperwork is he an honest, honorable, and incorruptible servant of the law. Only in paperwork is justice possible. He can save the rower in the boat by killing him in the fiction that is the official record. He can call off the manhunt before it begins and no one will know the truth but the police report's author.

The rowboat disappears beneath the bridge where San Lorenzo ends.

On the other side, it emerges between the abutments.

The wingbeats of oar strokes carry its rower across the rippling sky.

When Nino looks up, Inspector Rocco Ferrando tips his hat.

OFF SUNSET

1

EVERY DAY THE WAR IN EUROPE PRODUCED MELODRAMA TO RIVAL HOLlywood's most indolent imaginations. Thomas Mann, Fritz Lang, Billy Wilder, Hedy Lamarr, Lion Feuchtwanger, Douglas Sirk, Alma Mahler, Robert Siodmak, Bertolt Brecht, Jean Renoir . . . all of them rode to Los Angeles on a series of coincidences and near misses as improbable as those that carried Nino Picone—or Vincent, as he now called himself—from San Lorenzo. For the past ten minutes, Maria had leaned forward in her desk chair, a blade of sinew sawing away at her lower spine, listening to him without interruption. Now, as he wound down his story, she asked the only question that mattered: "What happened to my father?"

He stared at his hands. "I don't know."

"It's been over three years since I last had a letter from him," Maria said. She spoke slowly, breathed deeply, because keeping her anger in check was a feat of cardiovascular endurance. "Three years. And in all that time, you didn't think to call, or write, or send a telegram?"

"I didn't know what to say. I still don't. I'm sorry."

She eyed him with disdain. "It's a rather long way to come to apologize."

"I thought I owed it to you to come."

"You owed it to my father to stay. He saved your life and you left him to die."

"It all happened so fast, and I—"

Maria raised her hand. Whenever she thought of her father, she felt divided by contradictory impulses. The desire to know and the craving to forget, yearning for absolution while rejecting the possibility of forgiveness. Sometimes she felt her life had folded in half the morning she went to the alleyway to burn her father's papers: it was and would always be the central event, the worst thing she would ever do, the most consequential, least condonable. Nino might have left her father in San Lorenzo, but Maria had put him there. They had both failed Giuseppe Lagana, and she regarded Nino with an intensity of contempt she usually reserved for herself.

"I didn't intend to cause you any more grief," he said, and collected his hat as he walked to the door. He reminded her of the young men her great-aunts failed to fix her up with—schnozzola as steep as a sundial, eyebrows as dense as Groucho Marx's mustache—but without their clean-cut geniality, prospects of steady employment, and character references supplied by neighborhood gossips. Hating him for leaving her father behind was natural; forgiving him for what she could not forgive herself was inconceivable; buying him a sandwich, that much she could do.

She would have liked to subject him to the gastrointestinal malevolence for which Mercury's commissary was renowned, but it had already closed for the day. Instead, they crossed Gower to Vick's Drugstore. Maria helped herself to one of the ruby leather stools that mushroomed in the shade of the countertop. Over the grill, a grease-spattered mirror reflected the various medicines, antacids, and syrups sold to mitigate the inevitable effects of what the menu called, with hyperbole verging on outright fraud, "quality dining."

Manning the grill, cobwebbed in hairnet, was the establishment's owner, Vick Reynolds. Despite having suffered the monstrosities he plated on checkered wax paper, Maria had begrudging regard for a man who so persuasively expressed his misanthropy through cuisine. He and Aunt Mimi would have gotten on famously.

She ordered the safest items on the menu—a couple chicken salad sandwiches and chocolate sodas—and turned to . . . well, what was she supposed to call him?

"You go by Vincent now?"

"It's easier that way."

"Knock yourself out. If Constance Ockleman can become Veronica Lake, I don't see why a Nino can't become a Vincent."

Vick slid their sandwiches across the counter. Vincent peeled the corner of his and eyed the innards skeptically. The indignities of the American palate regularly tested his resolve: hot dogs wolfed down beside pushcarts, pickles splashed on paper plates, tuna packaged in shoe polish tins. Then there were sandwiches. By design sandwiches were deceitful. Smuggling in their holds unknown cargos of so-called salads. To Vincent's mind, a salad should involve vegetables. However, at the American lunch counter, a salad was a glop of indeterminate meat predigested by mayonnaise, served by ice cream scoop, and blindfolded between flaccid slabs of white bread. Studying the sandwich, his heart broke for his stomach.

"You took the *Columbia* from Naples to New York three and a half years ago," Maria said. "Where have you been living since then?"

"Everywhere."

At first, Vincent really had intended on coming directly to California to tell Maria what had happened to her father. But what *had* happened to Giuseppe? He didn't know. Best-case scenarios were unspeakable while the worst were unimaginable. Until he knew what to say, he would say nothing. From New York he'd made his way across the archipelago of Little Italys that thinned as it reached westward: a winter shoveling snow in South Philly and delivering firewood in Pittsburgh's Bloomfield, then a spring working a steel mill, a coal mine, a strawberry field. A few months flopping on Mayfield Road in Cleveland, a week sweeping the floors of the Berry Brothers Bolt Works in Columbus, a summer as a lector reading Bible passages to illiterate slaughterhouse workers in Indianapolis. Those early months passed as a span of astonishment interrupted by dread, homesickness, and panic. The true sights were what locals passed without noticing: the neon signage and spinning barber poles; the living room drapes left open through the evening; the metered parking and overprescribed condiments. The emigrants whose passport photographs he had taken in San Lorenzo offered him a few feet of floor to sleep on, a warm meal, a job lead. After nine months, he'd saved up enough to purchase a dark box, gelatin emulsion, metal plates—everything necessary to produce cheap tintype portraits in under five minutes on any street corner in the country.

Working as an itinerant photographer, he traveled throughout the Midwest and Deep South, to impoverished towns with unpronounceable names where a five-cent tintype was a luxury. He set up his camera at fairgrounds on Saturdays and outside churches on Sundays, wore out his soles on boardwalks and town squares, advertised two tintype portraits for a nickel, five for a dime. Many thousands of American faces passed through his lens. A farmer's children pulling the ears of the family cow on a farm in Oklahoma; the hot-dog-eating champ of Sioux Falls and the beauty pageant queen of Amarillo; the happy newlyweds and happier divorcées on courthouse steps in Reno on a perfect spring day. For so long the traversable world had been no larger than the two-square kilometers of the confino colony, but in the expanse of inner America, the earth became endless. Only when he reached the Pacific, when he finally ran out of land, was he prepared to deliver the news he had been running from all along.

Now that he had, he wanted to put as much distance between himself and Maria as possible.

Maria sipped the beige froth hissing atop her chocolate soda. "So where to next?" she asked.

"San Francisco. I've saved up enough money to open my own shop in North Beach. Wedding photos, that sort of thing. Here—you remember this?"

He opened his black album of passport photographs to the one he'd taken of her in San Lorenzo a decade and a half earlier.

"I'd forgotten about this," she said, but she could remember following him into the darkroom where the air simmered with the taste of exotic chemicals. He had explained the process of developing and printing film with the painful self-consciousness of early adolescence. After the print dried, he tore it in two: one half he gave to her, the other he pinned on the corkboard alongside those still journeying emigrants. The first thing she did upon arriving to Los Angeles was mail her half back, so her father would know she had safely arrived.

She peeled her photograph from the album, crushed it in her fist, and tossed it on the counter.

"I wouldn't show these to prospective clients," Maria advised, paging through the other passport photos. "Brides generally don't want to look like impoverished emigrants on their wedding day. Even in San Francisco."

"A photograph I took of Italian volunteers traveling to Spain was published in *Pravda*."

"Never heard of it," Maria said.

"It's the official organ of the Communist Party of the USSR." He'd been disappointed to discover that *Pravda* had zero readership in the United States. Presumably, if it had an American edition, he wouldn't have been reduced to selling tintype portraits at state fairs for the past three years. "It's very well known in Soviet Russia."

"You poor schmuck. I wouldn't mention that to any brides-to-be either. Are you going to San Francisco today?"

"I'll leave from here."

"Good, that's for the best," Maria said, but neither moved from the counter. She wished he hadn't come at all, wished he hadn't dredged up what she kept tamped down through emotional detachment and the suppression her colleagues mistook for composure.

She still felt torn down the center, like the passport photograph in his album, wanting to make peace with her ghosts but unable to even look at them without hating herself.

More than anything, she wanted to ensure Vincent would prosper in San Francisco and never have a reason to search her out again. It was her wish to be rid of him forever that prompted her to suggest he stick around for one more day. "I'll put out a casting call this afternoon," she said. "By tomorrow morning, I'll have a few dozen extras in wedding dresses for you to photograph. They'll play better with the brides of San Francisco than glum peasants and communist organs."

"I don't think so," he said, taking the crumpled passport photograph from the counter and tucking it in his pocket. "All due respect, and thanks for the sandwich and everything, but I said what I came here to say. I'd rather not see you again."

Maria brightened to have her feelings of mistrust and hostility reciprocated. "I'm flying to Washington first thing. You won't see me at all."

2

"I'M NOT BUYING RADIO SPOTS IN MOBILE, BUT C'MON, LET'S SPITBALL this," Artie said, shouldering the telephone. "How about you get a . . . what do you call those things, the woolly ski masks? Balalaika? No, that's a Russky ukulele. Bala*cla*va, there we go. Hire a guy, put him in a balaclava and trench coat, have him wander the streets of Mobile with, say, a machete. He chases pedestrians down alleys, follows them into their homes, generally runs amok. When they start screaming, he says, 'If you think *I'm* scary, just wait till you see *The Night Stalker,* opening this Friday!' I don't know, Bob, I'm not a lawyer. It's Alabama. Nothing's illegal down there."

Artie waved Maria in and got off the line. The intervening hours had added a few more floors to the skyscraper of paperwork towering in his inbox.

"You ever hear of anything so crazy?" Artie asked, tossing back an aspirin. "Buying radio spots for a single theater in Mobile?"

Maria took a seat in one of the office chairs, eager to hear the details of the Eastern National deal. Artie sat behind the walnut desk he had lofted on a platform several years ago. It gave him the looming air of a small-claims-court judge seasoned by cheap hustle and swift verdict. It was the most carefully curated set on the lot.

He lit a cigarette, looked longingly from the lit match to the towering paperwork, and ruefully dropped the match in the ashtray. "I have good news for a change," he told Maria. "Eastern National came through with the credit line. Practically had to offer my first-born son, who, to be honest, I'd have tossed in for free. Let him piss in someone else's hamper. We put up a third of the company as collateral, in addition to giving up a few board seats. But no matter how things go in Washington, we'll still have jobs."

"That is good news."

"The bad news is that Ned does too. And he's returning to Los Angeles permanently. However, as a gesture of good faith, he's agreed to support *Devil's Bargain* if we get Production Code approval. Speaking of, you have any further thoughts on how we might handle Breen?"

After leaving Vincent at the Vick's, Maria had gone to Mercury's Research Library. In the closet she hung her purse alongside an ape suit anchored at the groin with a sandbag and a ten-gallon bag of snow flurries made from whitewashed cornflakes. Working as a research librarian at a studio that pioneered new frontiers of historical inaccuracy seemed a Dantean punishment, but Mr. Simmons, a jolly, jowly Quaker going white at the temples, had transformed the Research Library into a sanctuary of fact in a studio besieged by fiction. Across its pinewood shelves stretched thousands of volumes: encyclopedias, atlases, histories, binders of newspaper clippings and articles tagged by date and subject. The Research Library serviced the actualization of a screenplay as much as its inception. Art directors, costume designers, prop men, and set decorators depended on its cataloging of local color and arcana. Alongside the collected works of Shakespeare and the *Britannica*, you'd find thirty inches of collated menus from four continents, five hundred pages of interesting reptile facts, a folio of filling station signage in the upper Midwest, eighty years of mail-order fashions, a rogues' gallery of novelty coffee mugs. The tree of knowledge excavated to the tiniest roots of primal minutiae. A mania of human triviality cross-referenced on ten thousand little white index cards.

Mr. Simmons rose when Maria entered. He was an affable fellow, saner than his taxonomic curation of everything might suggest. He smiled genially, half-moon specs on the tip of his nose.

"Miss Lagana," he said. "How may I be of service?"

"This morning Joe Breen kiboshed a script Artie has a lot riding on. I wanted to see if you had anything I can use as leverage when I negotiate with the Production Code Administration."

"What's the picture about?"

"An artsy filmmaker in Berlin agrees to make indoctrination movies in exchange for the funding to finish shooting his masterwork. It rather strongly suggests that the senators behind next week's hearings in Washington have themselves been bamboozled by this Faustian fella's propaganda."

Mr. Simmons tapped his pursed lips with his index finger. "Last year, I read a story about the German consul's effort to receive Production Code approval for *Victory in the East,* an indoctrination picture by a director named Hasso Beck."

"Hasso Beck? Haven't heard of him."

Mr. Simmons crossed his spindly legs. "In the twenties, he made a number of well-regarded expressionist pictures for UFA. When Hitler came to power, he agreed to make movies for Goebbels."

"No kidding."

"His ex-wife works here. Anna Weber, the miniature maker."

"About this *Victory in the East* movie—I assume Breen's silence was deafening?"

"On the contrary." Mr. Simmons smiled. "Mr. Breen had a great deal to say."

The three-paragraph statement issued on Production Code letterhead was a listless denouncement of the threat hateful ideologies posed to democratic values. It was boilerplate. It was perfect. It was one thing for Joseph Breen to condemn a script to death by a thousand cuts; quite another for him to censor his own words.

"I'd suggest using Breen's statement as a prologue to *Devil's Bar-*

gain," Maria told Artie. "If we frame the entire picture as a cautionary tale dramatizing Breen's own admonishment on the dangers of propaganda, maybe he'll feel pressured to approve the picture. Particularly if he knows you'll take out full-page ads accusing him of hypocrisy if he nixes it."

The thought of publicly pantsing Joseph Breen like that made Artie wonder if the cosmos was not as cruel and indifferent as he suspected.

"It almost makes me hope he does," Artie admitted.

"Win-win."

Beaming, Artie said, "Have I ever told you you're the brother I've never had?"

Her boss could pay her no higher compliment. "I take it you and Ned aren't seeing eye to eye on this one?"

"If my patriotic duty gives Ned an ulcer, it's a sacrifice I'm willing to make."

They discussed various other fires they needed to put out. It turned out that the leading candidate to play a wholesome Andy Hardy–like teenager in *Family First* had three illegitimate children and a voracious drug habit. *The Breaking of the Day,* a portentous melodrama Ned had lobbied for, was already three days behind schedule and fifteen thousand dollars over budget. Contract negotiations with a loaner director from Columbia were going down the toilet. *Unanticipated Descents* had flopped domestically but had done well enough in South America that the Mercury's Rio office was clamoring for a sequel. Finally, there was the Senate.

"Vedette got me on your flight to Washington," Maria said. "What do you think of having a few of our screenwriters draft your opening statement?"

"No, I'll handle it myself," Artie said.

"You sure? We have a couple who went to Yale."

"So they can read snob in the original. Good for them." Artie sank back in his chair and with one hand gently stroked the ridge where the Mephistopheles met his real hair. "I'll write my own opening statement. These senators will rue the day they called me to the witness table."

Maria studied Artie, curious what had changed since that morning, then thought she understood: at heart, Art Feldman was a carnival barker, and the US Senate was handing him a microphone.

"We're showmen, Maria. And showmen don't lose show trials."

3

AS MARIA PASSED VICK'S DRUGSTORE ON HER WAY HOME THAT NIGHT, she noticed Vincent was still sitting in the same stool, nursing the same cup of coffee he'd been served five hours earlier. Against her better judgment, she shouldered open the drugstore door and tapped his shoulder.

"Let me show you something."

It took Vincent three and a half years to travel from Italy to Los Angeles but only five minutes to return. He followed Maria past the Jungle Forest into a piazza paved in ersatz travertine that held the cream-colored haloes of streetlamps. He felt like an explorer stumbling into the magnificent ruins of a lost civilization rearing up from the wilderness. Curated storefronts displayed an assortment of unseasonable dresses and inaccurately priced shoes. Italian-language signage emblazoned the window glass in boldface fonts. Mounted to the clay-tiled roofs, a hidden scaffolding held immense blackout screens that rolled out to allow day-for-night shooting. Café tables sat empty under a white-and-yellow awning, a chair leg steadied by a matchbook, a stack of menus at the maître d's stand. Unadorned by posters or sloganeering or Mussolini's watchful gaze, the piazza recreated no Italy he recognized. Perhaps these inaccuracies were a form of flawlessness, Vincent thought, not errors but imprints of possibility. Perhaps that accounted for the sense of homecoming he encountered in this distant suburb of his extinct world.

"We built it for a screwball comedy set in Rome," Maria was saying. "An American heiress falls in love with a struggling opera singer. Misunderstandings ensue. It was a real piece-of-shit picture, but for sentimental reasons, it's my favorite set."

"It's beautiful," he admitted.

She opened the door of one of the false fronts. They walked down the narrow plywood corridor running behind the façades to provide passage for set dressers. At the end of the corridor, there was a little room with bare walls, a secretary desk, and a stopped clock.

"This was my first office," Maria said. Years ago, when she lobbied for an office of her own, one of Artie's underlings had given her this hideaway that crews used for poker games, naps, and assignations. It had been furnished with a card table, a couch, and a couple thousand peanut shells. Cheesecake pinups plastered every inch of wall, running ten, twenty deep. A geology of bared legs and pouty lip. No matter that she was the first in, last out, and least paid, no matter her industry or talent, to the front-office boys club this was her place, this grubby room where middle-aged louts graded the busts of teenagers. Maria had considered quitting then and there. Instead, she came in alone one weekend to renovate the bachelor's pad. She borrowed a paint scraper from the carpentry shop and peeled the strata of sleaze until she reached bare wall. She swept and scoured the floorboards. Shook salt in the corners to dispel the evil spirits. Helped herself to the desk chair, wall clock, and liquor cabinet of the flunky who'd assigned her this "office." She made the room her own and then padlocked the door in case the prior tenants were tempted to return. Even now that she had a legitimate office, this remained the only space in the studio she imagined was hers.

"I assume you don't have anywhere to stay tonight?"

"I'll be fine."

"Come on," Maria said. "My better half runs a hotel."

Eddie Lu was manning the front desk of the Montclair when Maria walked in. A saxophone melody wandered its way from the wireless. In the wastebasket, a golden banana peel was splayed over brochures for a faith-healing sect.

"You're home early." Eddie unraveled a shroud of cigar smoke with a wave of his well-read copy of *Uncle Vanya* and peered balefully at the man in the cheap suit following her in. "Hey. You. Scram. This is a respectable establishment."

"The Montclair is famous for its hospitality," Maria told Vincent.

"You know this bum?"

"It's a long story. He just needs a room for tonight."

Hearing the note of warning in Maria's voice, Eddie filled out the hotel registration, asking for Vincent's full name and date of birth. "And as for profession . . . I assume bum isn't the preferred term?"

"Is that the Central Pacific?" Vincent was staring at the small sepia-toned photograph of a locomotive Eddie had pinned to the wall. "I've spent a lot of time riding it."

"It's the finest railroad ever built," Eddie said with an authority belied by the fact he had never left Los Angeles County. Of late, Eddie's most regular acting work was recording bodily noises for a phonograph company that pressed sound-effect shellac for broadcast in radio dramas. As Maria led Vincent upstairs, Eddie began rehearsing. Even his fake farts thundered with the doleful resonance of a tragedian.

On the third floor, they passed pinewood doors kicked in by innumerable police boots over the years. In 3E a dwarf who served as Shirley Temple's stunt double and had unsuccessfully run for several state offices stroked tender notes from his ukulele. In 3F a family of Slovakian refugees spoke in beguiling whispers. The resident of 3D was a barfly whose daily ambitions went no higher than the blood-alcohol needed to profess love to a roomful of strangers. Not unlike Mercury itself, the Montclair was a pit stop on the downward trajectory, the penultimate station before prison, morgue, or oblivion.

"I nearly forgot. I have something for you." Vincent dropped to a knee and pulled a rectangular package wrapped in a handkerchief from his carpetbag. "From your father."

It was a red-and-white cigar box. The seal was broken. Maria could barely breathe.

"What is this?" she said softly.

"I don't know."

"You spent three years crossing the country to give it to me."

"Three and a half," he said. "But it wasn't mine to open."

After a long silence, Maria tucked the cigar box under her arm. She wanted to be alone when she opened it.

"Listen," she said, "I have to be at the airport early in the morning, so my secretary will meet you at the front gate and show you to the still photography department. I put out a casting call for brides—a hundred gals in wedding dresses will be waiting for you. By afternoon, you should have enough portraits to convince anyone up north that you've been photographing weddings for years."

"Thank you, Maria. I'll send you a postcard from San Francisco."

"If you want to thank me," she said, "don't come back."

In her room one floor below, Maria unwound the cigar box's red string-tie and lifted the lid.

From her mother Maria learned that expressed emotion was wasted warmth. It was better to keep your gaze iced over lest anyone glimpse what blazes in you. And so Annunziata would have been the first to understand, from the heat in her daughter's eyes, that the cigar box did not contain cigars at all.

Instead, there were hundreds of strips of paper: all those extracts missing from her father's letters, all those words excised by the San Lorenzo censor's straight edge. Maria felt deboned, barely vertebrate, as she sifted through these fragments of her father's meticulous handwriting. Some were no longer than a sentence. Some were simply a single yearned-for word. She took a deep breath, slipped the box into her purse, and crossed the room to her dresser. From the top drawer she withdrew the bundle of censored letters she'd received over the years. It was half past ten and she had work to do.

Later that evening, as he passed through the piazza set on his rounds, Mercury's night watchman saw a light left on in one of the false front's windows. He wandered over, thinking he should turn it off. The night watchman had fled Poland a year and a half earlier and was living on the sofa of the cousin in Boyle Heights who found him this job. He took off his cap and pressed his face to the glass. There was a woman inside the little room with bare walls.

If he remembered anything about that evening—and he would try to remember little from this time in his life—he would remember the deliberateness with which the woman in the false front withdrew letters from their envelopes and pinned them to the empty walls. She moved from left to right, top to bottom. When one wall was covered, she moved to the next, filling them with dozens and dozens of letters. Blocks of text were missing from the letters, rectangular voids venting the plywood grain below. When the letters papered every inch of wall, the woman patched in the holes with handwritten strips she pulled from a cigar box. The watchman stood too far away to read the pieced-together letters. He didn't know who they were from, what they said, or if they had arrived too late. But from the relief on their recipient's face, it was clear they brought welcome news. What the watchman would remember, if he remembered anything, was how at home the woman looked in that room of reconstructed paper she had built herself. It was a long time since he felt at home anywhere.

Years earlier he'd seen a picture about a monster who escaped evil men and came upon a little house in the woods just like this. The monster peered through the lighted window, without malice, simply trying to imagine how the people inside had learned to live there. The watchman couldn't recall how the movie ended. It would depend, he supposed, on who was the monster and who was inside. He checked his pocket watch. If he didn't leave now, he'd have to work through his supper. And yet he lingered at the window a moment more.

PART II

THE PEOPLE VS. ART FELDMAN

1

FOUR MONTHS LATER, ON A SATURDAY EVENING IN DECEMBER 1941, *Devil's Bargain* premiered at the Mercury, the studio's eponymous Los Angeles theater.

A white cruise liner of a limousine docked at the red carpet rented from the Brazilian consulate for the evening. Ned debarked, offered his arm to his date, and together they faced the firing squad of press photographers.

"I can't decide who's worse," Mildred Feldman said, observing the scene from the following limousine. "The loathsome man or the woman who finds the loathsome man attractive?"

Mildred wore a knee-length fur coat that looked like what an overly confident mountaineer was last seen wearing. Appropriate, Artie supposed: Beverly Hills was the Himalayas of social climbing and Mildred was still pushing for the summit.

"Ned's worse," he decided. "His date just wants to become the next former Mrs. Ned Feldman. Knowing she's in it for the alimony excuses her for wanting to marry him. Like a crime committed in self-defense."

The tinted windows leached the red carpet of its vivaciousness and blare.

"If greed justifies bad behavior, then we are all innocents," Mildred said with a sublime blitheness that, after two decades of marriage, still left Artie thunderstruck with lust. "Speaking of innocent, I wonder how Edith's dinner party is going. I am sorry to miss it."

"Of course you are," Artie said drily. "Edith is your dear friend."

Mildred craned her neck, wondering what the holdup was. "I suppose the most enjoyable part of her dinner parties is the next day anyway, when you call the other guests to discuss how awful it all was. That's why I avoid hosting dinner parties more than once a season. Why invite your enemies into your home and arm them with knives?"

Artie smiled. Some of his most ruthless business stratagems were inspired by his wife's hospitality.

Photoflashes detonated across the tinted windows as if flung. The dazzling bursts and plunging darkness gave the growing crowd a stop-motion unreality.

There were more people than Maria had arranged, weren't there? Artie had previously hired fans from Central Casting but recently switched to an entrepreneurial high-school student who managed a rentable network of adolescent autograph hounds and applauders that never failed to punch up a premiere or raise an ingenue's profile. Dollar for dollar, premeditated spontaneity bought better publicity than national advertising campaigns. There were more pressmen in Hollywood than anywhere outside of Manhattan; even the Vatican kept a full-time correspondent here. If the wire services picked up his well-orchestrated hoo-ha, he might triple a picture's rentals overnight. Last year Louella Parsons wrote a glowing profile of him after he arranged for the villain of *The Highwayman* to ride onto Melrose Avenue on horseback to hold up Hedda Hopper's car. But the sensationalism that made the best publicity easily escalated into the scandal that incited boycotts and protests, as the scene outside was beginning to illustrate.

He drained the last inch of liquor from his crystal tumbler. In his white dinner jacket, golden cuff links, and formal toupee, he felt as fraudulent as when frog-marched into holding opinions on nine-irons by the husbands of Mildred's friends. The cinched black tie accentuated his jowls. Two tumblers of bourbon administered from the limousine bar left him with flammable halitosis. According to one early notice, insobriety was the only excuse for buying a ticket to *Devil's Bargain.*

All week Artie had treated Mildred to dramatic readings from the audience cards harvested from a San Pedro preview. When trying to recount the picture's plot, one audience member sounded like a mariner in need of new ways to describe fog. Awfully snobbish, Mildred had thought, for San Pedro. Offending his conservative critics usually gave Artie a perverse thrill. It was worrisome, then, to watch him dissect the trade notices for portents like an augur wrist deep in waterfowl.

Ned's limousine peeled from the curb.

Artie's driver inched through the throng.

"Maybe the San Pedro intelligentsia are wrong, Art. It's a rather large crowd, isn't it?"

It was far larger than Artie had laid out for and yet he would, in one currency or another, pay for it. As the limousine reached the red carpet, he saw isolationist picket signs skate like dorsal fins over the roiling sea of protest: *Peace with Hitler Means Peace for America* and *Keep Americans Out of Europe and Europeans Out of America* and *Smash the Hollywood War Propaganda Machine.* Pressing his nose to the window glass, he felt his heart pare to a throbbing nub of dread. It was one thing to stoke controversy to generate a bit of free publicity. Quite another to step into an enraged mob held back by a few velvet ropes.

"Shall we get out?" Mildred asked, unfazed by the crowd demanding her husband's head. "Or shall we see what's playing at the Orpheum instead?"

"We're getting out." But Artie was immobilized, darned directly to the leather limousine seating. It must be the liquor. Clearly, he hadn't drunk enough. The trouble was "enough" only came into view long after it passed. Only *after* losing seven thousand dollars at the poker table, or regaining consciousness following a three-day bender, or inciting bankruptcy-inducing boycotts, could he glimpse the point where he should have stopped. The horror of quitting too soon exceeded the shame of going too far. That's what Mildred and Ned didn't understand. The behaviors they considered self-destructive, he considered self-preservation: Artie converted his horror into shame to survive it.

The past year provided much raw material for his furnaces. The London Blitz, the spreading German occupation, the collapsing Soviet defenses, still no word from Ada. In Warsaw the SS paraded gallows strung with the corpses of theater owners judged guilty of exhibiting degenerate pictures. Several of Mercury's movies had been listed among the offending titles. The question consuming Artie was how to act morally when moral action incites egregious immorality in response. That his thoughts remained this lucid suggested he still had a way to go before the horror subsided and the shame seeped in.

"What's wrong with you?" Mildred asked. She was so inured to her husband's moodiness that only the morbidly wrong earned her comment.

"What's wrong with me? That guy's sign says *Joseph Stalin Gives* Devil's Bargain *Five Red Stars.*"

"Honestly, Art. I'm sure Stalin has better things to do than review your movie," Mildred said. Edith had told her in strict confidence that she would have found a mistress for her husband had he not already taken the initiative, and Mildred sympathized with the feeling. Artie's recent bouts of moroseness made her pine for Betty Ludlow's phantom presence. God knew her husband wasn't known for his tact, but Mildred could count on him to keep his liaisons quiet. Discretion in adultery passed as chivalry among their social set. It was nearly romantic, she supposed, the lengths Artie went to deceive her.

Looking outside, Artie says, "This is about as festive as a funeral, isn't it?"

"Don't be melodramatic. It's a movie premiere. It won't be anything like that."

"How do you know?"

"For one, your funeral would end in applause."

Artie laughed. There was no one on God's green earth he loved more than her. "You think?"

"I'd be the first on my feet."

"Be sure to have David Selznick produce it."

"He only works with bigwigs."

"What the hell am I?"

"A big wig." Mildred took Artie's hand, and together they stepped into the point-blank range of jockeying publicity photographers.

Later, Artie would struggle to describe the sensory onslaught of those first moments: burnt magnesium leaked from smashed flashbulbs; reporters with press cards tilting from hatbands shouted inaudibly; the shaft of a rented searchlight swiped the sky; the street seethed with the hostility of the six-hundred-strong crowd.

"Christ, Art," Mildred said. "The hell did you do?"

What *had* he done? To his left, a blizzard of photoflashes blanketed picketers. The America First Committee—the flagship isolationist lobby, a marriage of convenience between the self-serving and the easily fooled—had supplied the membership of several local chapters with plywood picket signs: *STOP Foreign Hollywood Money Lords Who Sell War for Profit* and *Art Feldman Is an Un-American Alien Communist Menace* and *Don't Let OUR Boys Die for THERES.*

On the other side of the red carpet, Popular Front activists, Roosevelt supporters, and insufferable do-gooders flew banners that matched their enemies' self-righteousness, if not their free-spirited spelling: *Labor Unites Against Fascism* and *Don't Let England Stand Alone INCREASE British Aid* and *Cursed Is Anyone Who Withholds Justice from the Foreigner—Deuteronomy 27:19.*

The policemen on either side of the red carpet gripped billy clubs with the eagerness of alcoholics clutching bottles they swear they won't drink. Across the street, G-men bedecked in the killjoy couture of Bible salesmen wrote down plate numbers. An aproned vendor hawked franks and ice-cold cola. Down the block the crowd thinned into goggle-eyed snoops and stalled passersby waiting for the mob to justify their interest.

Ned took his arm. "Please tell me you're behind this."

"No," Artie said, shakily. "Only in the midst of it."

Beside him, Mildred endured the press photographers' indifference. She scavenged the crowd for a detail or two she might leaven into a dinner party anecdote. Presently her most interesting anecdotes were about other dinner parties.

"They'll have to let us go to the Oscars after this," she said.

"I'm more concerned with going to prison," Artie said. "Or the morgue."

Mildred sympathized with the protesters inveighing against her husband's character, but she approved of his talent for seizing attention.

"When you win one, I expect to be thanked first in your acceptance speech."

Her confidence was so unmerited Artie mistook it for sarcasm.

"Mildy, if this does well enough to win an Oscar, I'll be thanking my divorce lawyer first."

A press photographer did capture the aftermath of this remark: Mildred's handprint on Artie's cheek. In 1982 the Feldmans' surviving children would find the photograph among their mother's effects after they moved her to a Glendale nursing home. "To my magnificent Mildy," their father had written on the back, "who after all these years still makes me glow." Artie had passed years earlier, and Alzheimer's, that merciless censor, had stripped Mildred's stray utterances of context and clarity. But when they showed her the photograph, she said, "My big wig." Her children shared a look. It was unclear whom in the photograph she referred to when she added, "Where have you gone? Where *have* you gone?"

The two dozen photographers stood behind the phalanx of policemen. Several Artie recognized. Several more he employed. He liked his publicity shots to capture the mechanics of celebrity itself—a star swarmed on all sides by cameras—and always sent a few stillmen to fill out the photographic press corps.

Maria jostled through the pack, asking where he'd been.

"It took us an hour to drive the last two blocks," Artie said. "Why haven't they opened the doors?"

A stout man with a severe haircut stood decisively at the lobby doors. "The sergeant wants to let the crowd thin out before opening," Maria said. "He's afraid they might charge inside."

The encircling demonstrators blocked the road. As the precariousness of the situation began to sink in, Artie noticed a sandy-haired man climbing onto the hood of a parked car to speechify to the picketers. The man was a failed gubernatorial candidate and America First apologist, and like most California Republicans, his politics were prejudices in search of policies.

"I donated to his last campaign," Ned said with dismay. To prove his loyalty to his adoptive country, Ned regularly aligned himself with politicians who would deny his place in it. Artie would have found this contemptible had he not understood the fear that inspired it. What was more natural than collaborating with those who affirm your most dearly held beliefs? And what article of faith do you cling to more tenaciously than your own illegitimacy?

"You should've donated more. He'd do less harm from the governor's mansion than from the soapbox," and as Artie was saying this a speedy streak of color drove through his vision. The object hurled by one of the counterdemonstrators moved too fast for Artie to identify. A spinning smear of red, a brick maybe, arcing over the crowd. It exploded on the failed gubernatorial candidate's face. A gasp plunged through the crowd. The politician was fine, it turned out, hit in the kisser with a ripe tomato, but it was already too late, because this is what the crowd came for, wasn't it? An excuse.

Shoe leather slapped on concrete as the protesters reared up, stampeding through the police line and into one another with the muffled pummel of overcoats and spittle and the berserker battle-ax swipes of picket signs. Trampled fedoras paved the street in heel-marked felt. Ned's date spiked an assailant with one of her high heels. Below the marquee, bodies jammed into a few squares of livid sidewalk, arms pinned, scuffing the shine from one another's shoes. The pent-up charge of wool-on-wool zapped through pressed noses. Artie watched the crowd devour its signage, wasting the very language that had veneered the violence with thought.

Those sheared from the circumference of the crowd stood down the block, unable to tear themselves from the spectacle.

Mildred mitted her hand in his and he threw his hips against the crowd's shapeless pressure and pulled her through the swift-sealing rift. Her mouth was an inch from his ear but he couldn't make out what she said amid the pandemonium. The force of the crowd popped the lock on the lobby door and as they spilled inside, Artie saw the pillbox hats of cigarette girls bobbing on the tide.

Then the lobby tipped over. The ceiling somersaulted beneath his feet and now the chandelier bloomed brilliantly from the floor. Who had planted it there? As the sunroofs closed over Artie's eyes, he saw chandelier crystals petaled in red siren light.

2

THE EVENTS LEADING TO THE RIOT BEGAN MONTHS EARLIER, IN A MAPLE-paneled Capitol Hill hearing room, where the Senate Investigation into Motion Picture War Propaganda had summoned the heads of the Hollywood studios. The hearing began with the testimony of Senator Gerald Nye. Senator Nye, the sponsor of the resolution approving the investigation and the most vocally anti-Semitic of the chamber's isolationists, began the proceedings by accusing the moguls of promulgating "the most vicious propaganda that has ever been unloosed upon a civilized people."

The moguls came prepared. Hiring as their counsel Wendell Willkie, the previous year's Republican presidential nominee, helped nullify the charge that they were Roosevelt shills, and over a week of testimony, the moguls didn't defend their pictures so much as the democratic ideals their underdog lives bore out.

From her seat in the public gallery, Maria watched Harry Warner, Nick Schenck, and Darryl Zanuck ballyhoo the freedoms the senators insisted on discrediting. The Senate investigators were visibly unsettled to have their monopoly on indignation challenged. On the eighth day, Artie was called to testify. Unrecognizably color-coordinated in a conservative gray suit and navy tie, he disarmed Senator Nye's accusations with an aw-shucks everyman persona utterly leached of his genuine personality. Finally, he requested permission to read from a fan letter the studio had received several years earlier.

There was a touch of vaudeville in the way Artie patted his pockets for his reading glasses before realizing they were on the witness table. He futzed about with his spectacles, then with the envelope, until he heard the signet ring of the subcommittee chairman tap restlessly on the rostrum. "You're testing our patience, Mr. Feldman."

"Apologies, gentlemen," Artie said. "My brother and I would like to use the following to testify to our character and the character of our motion pictures. I quote, 'I am a great admirer of the entertaining and edifying movies your studio has produced, and even more, of your commitment to the foundational values of this nation we both cherish. It gives me great pride to count you among my supporters, and I hope you will count me among yours.'" Refolding the letter, he added, "That's all."

"And who authored this . . . tribute?" the subcommittee chairman asked.

"I wouldn't want to cause embarrassment to the sender. He's a man of some public prominence."

In the gallery, Nye tamped his exhilaration into an appropriately disapproving scowl. Conquest's primal intoxicant flushed through him. He would ask his chief-of-staff to write him a statement for the front page of tomorrow's paper: "It is with neither delight nor triumph to learn that the investigation I set into motion has exposed yet another member of the cabal of . . ." Like that, only more so.

"Mr. Feldman, may I remind you that you are under oath."

"If you insist, Senator."

"I do, Mr. Feldman. I do."

The witness slipped on his spectacles—and what was this? Was the witness grinning?

"This *is* embarrassing," Artie said. "It appears this letter of praise and commendation was written by Senator Gerald Nye."

Gasps and sighs, as if the very foundations of the Capitol had sprung leaks. The chairman smashed his gavel but it was too late to maintain order. Mr. Feldman turned to the press gallery and a showboating impresario soared out of the meek supplicant in reading glasses.

"Senator Nye has inoculated himself against charges of hypocrisy by believing in nothing at all."

As the laughter boomed and the cameras blazed, Nye knew he would indeed make tomorrow's front page.

"My brother, Ned, is something of an autograph hound," Artie continued, brandishing the letter jubilantly. "He keeps correspondence from illustrious figures such as the senator here. A few years ago, he cut a twenty-five-dollar check to Senator Nye's reelection campaign and the senator responded with this fulsome letter of praise whose sentiments I wholeheartedly endorse. However"—here Artie turned to directly address Nye, who had slumped so low in his seat he was nearly supine—"you really should raise your rates, Senator. It would cost me a great deal more than twenty-five dollars to buy a review this good from the *New York Daily News.*"

The senator's insistence that the letter had been composed by his chief-of-staff and signed unread was lost amid the general ridicule.

By the time the TWA flight landed back in Los Angeles, Artie was more famous than the actors he employed. Walter Winchell, the celebrity gossip columnist and broadcaster whose weekly audience comprised a third of the country, and who, due to his allegiance to FDR and lambasting of the America First Committee, had become the bête noire of the isolationist movement, praised Artie in print, on air, and in person. Artie's critics had also risen in stature. Charles Lindbergh, the aviation hero turned America First spokesman, referred to him as "the grubby little jester" whose "antics demonstrated that the loyalties of his kind can, should, and must be questioned." Awfully bold from a guy who had been decorated by Hermann Goering.

"You make an ass out of one lousy senator," Artie observed in the taxi back from the airport, still mystified by the whirlwinds of public opinion he had unleashed on himself. "I'm in the wrong business. I should've been a revolutionary."

The idea of her boss storming the ramparts in an obnoxious hairpiece and plaid sports coat amused Maria. "I'm glad you're not letting the attention go to your head."

"Speaking of overinflated egos, any word on how Rudi Bloch has fared with his *Devil's Bargain* rewrites?"

"They should be on my desk," Maria said. "I'll resubmit to Joe Breen tomorrow."

The taxi dropped her at the Montclair Hotel at nearly midnight. From the street she saw the light on in Eddie's window. No matter what time she came home, he stayed up to fall asleep with her. They had gotten to know each other two years earlier on the set of *Shanghaied in Shanghai,* an embarrassing entry in the East Asian detective canon in which Eddie played a sidekick prone to malapropism and mispronunciation. The screenplay was a masterpiece of narrative ineptitude cranked out by a failed newsman and a successful alcoholic between hands of pinochle. One day, Maria was passing through the soundstage where the film was shooting when she heard Artie's voice. This was rather peculiar given that Artie was in New York that week. The crew had gathered around Eddie. He was doing witheringly exact impersonations of the front office bosses, stretching between takes the dramatic range pinioned by stereotype when the camera rolled.

When he got to Maria, she heard the faint burr on her *R*'s, the Italianate lilt that still bobbled her sentences when she spoke quickly. She could hear in his impersonation the hours of self-taught elocution lessons with KNX's live program of murder trials as her textbook. Maria supposed she should be insulted, but the texture of her voice on this stranger's tongue instead felt exhilaratingly intimate.

To date, Maria had produced enough original scholarship on her reluctance to say "I love you too" to satisfy a semantics dissertation. Given that her great-aunts had spent much of her childhood trying to marry her off, she felt entitled to enjoy adulthood unwed. Part of what attracted her to Eddie was that their relationship was without the expectation of long-term commitment that would doom it from the beginning. It was a relationship terminally afflicted by state law. True, they could drive to Mexico for a church wedding, but to the state of California a Tijuana marriage between an Italian American woman and Chinese American man was as legally fictitious as the ceremonies set in the final frames of MGM romances.

Much to her surprise, the anticipation of demise helped to defer it. When Maria grew fed up with Eddie's unsolicited advice, devil-may-care bed making, and refusal to concede an argument, she ignored his shortcomings rather than give him the opportunity to augment them. In turn, Eddie overlooked the broken dates, the supremacy of her career, her reluctance to ever say what she really felt. The practice of forestallment resulted in the most durable relationship of both their lives. When Maria's neighbor in 2C had moved out the previous summer, Eddie moved in. Adjacent rooms were as close as they would come to living together.

She let herself into his room, dropped her suitcase on the floor, and flopped on the unmade bed. The bathroom door opened and Eddie stepped out with a towel wrapped around his waist. The lamplight gilded steam that vanished as it rose.

"Make yourself at home, why don't you," Eddie said offhandedly. He was most comfortable expressing affection in a register of plausible deniability. Maria liked that he was most credible at his least sincere.

"You should try making yourself at home," Maria countered. "You live here."

"Hey, we all make mistakes." Eddie sat beside her and put his hand on the ribbed stocking band where her dress had ridden up. A gesture of comfort that might rise to a request for permission. "How was the hearing?"

"It was a circus."

"I know. I read about it in the papers."

"You should have seen Artie. I mean, Jesus, who would have thought Art Feldman would become a voice of conscience?"

"He know what he's doing? It sounds like he's pissing off some powerful people."

"I don't know. I honestly can't tell if he's gamed this out or if he's just running on pure outrage and self-absorption."

Maria took Eddie's hand from her thigh and pulled him a few inches nearer. The heat of the shower left a steamy glow on his intolerably flawless complexion. Every morning, she daubed and powdered her face with the precision of an Ottoman miniaturist, subjecting her skin to emollients and cold creams and ointments that pledged the life-changing potential of regular application. Meanwhile, Eddie achieved better results with hotel soap.

"Be careful, okay?" he said. "I've dealt with these nativists my whole life. Anyone whose ancestors didn't climb off the *Mayflower* they consider fresh off the boat."

Eddie was the only person whom Maria allowed to worry for her welfare. At first, she'd felt smothered by his solicitude, which was meager by any conventional standard. She was aware that the upheavals of her childhood—the guilt surrounding her father's arrest, the precariousness of exile, her mother's withheld affection—inspired her craving for self-reliance but also left her vulnerable to emotional dependence. Psychoanalysis was the latest fad among picture people and for several years she dutifully submitted herself to an Austrian analyst's weekly interrogation, but the ability to identify the crosscurrents of contradictory desire that doomed her relationships did not give her power to quell them. Settling the shrink's weekly bill felt like bribing a meteorologist to stop the storm. What made Eddie different from other men she'd dated was that he had nothing to hold over her, nothing to tempt her, nothing to offer her but himself; he did not expect her to fix him a cocktail or cook his dinner; he did not want to improve or change her. She made more in a week than he made in a month, could afford far nicer accommodations than a room in the Montclair, could leave at any time. She knew Eddie was self-conscious that he could give her so little, but the little he could give her was as much as she wanted.

"I'm never taking a boat again," Maria said. "From now on, I'm only taking the plane."

"Oh, you're a real hotshot, aren't you?"

"I'm a very important person, Eddie."

"I'm starstruck."

"As you should be."

"What was the plane like?"

"Terrifying," Maria admitted. "The engine makes a dreadful racket, the wings shudder as the plane takes off, and then the earth just peels away. Everything below becomes so small so fast. It's incredible. You have to try it someday."

"No, thank you. I'm a land mammal. I'll stick to trains."

Maria knew that outside of the Pacific Electric Red Cars, Eddie had never even been on a train. Once, he admitted he'd never left Los Angeles County, and it never ceased to impress her, the worldliness Eddie had extracted from the couple square miles where he had spent his entire life. A few times she'd suggested they take a vacation, but Eddie never had any money and he was too proud to let her pay for him.

"I wish you'd come with me," she said.

"I had business here."

Maria brought her hand to her mouth, mortified that she'd forgotten Eddie's audition for the Chekhov play. He'd been practicing his lines every night for weeks. "How did it go?"

Eddie shook his head. "They were very apologetic." There wasn't a trace of surprise, anger, or bitterness in his voice, just the simple statement of fact. When faced with disappointment, Eddie retreated so far into himself that his resignation was easily mistaken for acceptance. Maria—who routinely felt unfastened by all the psychological shortcomings her mother had passed down, along with the emotional repression necessary to manage them—found Eddie's mastery over his darker moods mesmerizing. Only in character would he risk uncorking the furies he kept bottled up. The first time Maria heard him perform a Shakespearean soliloquy, she understood why Eddie needed a vessel as capacious as Othello or Lear to pour himself into. The man offstage was the dramatis persona whereas the man under the lights, spitting life into four-hundred-year-old English words, was the real Eddie Lu.

"I'm sorry, honey," she said. "I know how much you wanted this one."

"What can you do?" Eddie kissed her forehead, pulled on an undershirt and briefs, and came back to bed.

"Did Vincent get off to San Francisco okay?" she asked.

"Nope. He's still here."

Maria sat up, beset by an inarticulate unease. "Why?"

"Apparently, the still photography department is short-staffed. When they saw him using the facilities, they offered him a job."

Maria was deeply annoyed. All she intended was to give Vincent the opportunity to augment his black album of emigrants with a few photos of extras in wedding dresses, something to impress the brides of San Francisco, to ensure the success of his venture so he wouldn't come calling on her again. What she hadn't intended, what she hadn't at all wanted, was for him to remain in Los Angeles, much less at the one place where she could reliably forget her past.

"I'll have to have him fired," she said.

"Why?" asked Eddie, taken aback by the vehemence in her voice. Maria could be hard-nosed, but she wasn't cruel. "He seems harmless enough."

"He's an asshole."

"He's also an insomniac. Keeps me company when I'm working nights. We play cards."

"My father is still in San Lorenzo because of him."

"From what you said, it didn't sound like he had much of a choice."

"Vincent betrayed him," Maria insisted. "He abandoned him. If my father is even still alive, he's languishing in that godforsaken place because of Vincent. And it took him three and a half years to come out here and tell me? Set aside my father: he betrayed *me*. No, fuck him. First thing tomorrow, I'm telling the boys in the gatehouse he's barred from the studio lot."

"That's a bit harsh, isn't it? He also brought you the censored snippets of your father's letters."

The relief Maria experienced while piecing together her father's letters was intense but short-lived. The diminishing returns of repeated readings made clear that the rifts in her family were too vast to paper over with little slips of paper. She did not accept her father's forgiveness. How could she? How could she accept his forgiveness when she couldn't separate her sense of guilt from her ability to love?

"Tell me what's wrong," Eddie said.

The exhilaration of the previous two weeks in Washington, the exhaustion of crossing a continent in a day, the soapy scent on Eddie's skin, it all primed her for a lapse in judgment. Lying back in his bed, staring at blistered ceiling paint, she told him about the testimony her father compiled from the families of political prisoners; the burnt-down cinema; the protectiveness and outrage she felt while bringing her father's papers to the alley; the toothpaste leaking from the corners of his lips.

"Jesus, Maria." Eddie sat up, knowing Maria least wanted comfort when comfort was what she most needed. "I had no idea."

"If you start feeling sorry for me, I'm sleeping in my room," she warned. "I mean it."

"I *am* sorry. That's a terrible thing to have happened to you."

"I'm tired. Let's go to bed."

"Just one question: Why tell me now?"

Maria was beginning to regret she had said anything at all. Avoidance might not be the ideal solution, but it was more constructive than confession. Cleansing the mind by revealing its most putrid parts felt as excruciating and ineffective as purifying the soul with a flagellant's whip.

"Because I wanted to end this conversation, not prolong it."

"We've been together for two years. You could have told me this anytime. Why now?"

"I'm not an idiot, Eddie. Too little self-awareness isn't among my shortcomings."

"Too much of it might be."

"I realize I'd feel sympathetic to Vincent if I didn't hate him for the same reason I hate myself, okay?"

"Maybe that's the very reason he deserves your mercy."

Eddie's pushy insistence that she was more decent than she knew herself to be was exasperating. "Mercy? I'm sorry, Eddie, but I have no idea how to do that."

"In my limited experience, mercy is what we choose *not* to do."

"Like me choosing not to clobber you right now?"

Eddie smiled. "A very apt example."

"If you'll drop this, I won't have Vincent dragged off the studio lot tomorrow. At least not first thing."

"That's a start."

"Why do you care about him?"

"Oh, Maria. I don't care about him at all." Eddie ironed the creases from her forehead with tender strokes. "I care about you."

Maria's lashes were long and gritty with mascara, and sometimes, looking down at her like this, Eddie felt himself slowly sifted into her eyes. She blinked and he watched his reflection reemerge in her swept-clean gaze. He sat beside her until she fell asleep.

He stayed up thumbing through the compendium of Chekhov he kept on his nightstand, beneath a bottle of scotch, where a forsaken believer might stow his Bible. A pity about the audition. He'd have loved to perform Chekhov. In plays like *The Seagull* and *The Cherry Orchard,* even the nobodies were somebodies to themselves, and Eddie would have happily spent his career as a bit player if he only performed Chekhov.

These days, when he received any work at all, it was playing a servile houseboy, a white slaver issuing risible pidgin, a pigtailed opium peddler foiled by a junior reporter and a plucky blonde in a tight sweater. Characters either entirely emasculated or entirely predatory, living at the lurid limits of deviancy.

Once, just once, he wanted to play a character of eponymous substance: Doctor Faustus, Uncle Vanya, Macbeth. He'd settle for

Charlie Chan or Mr. Moto but honorable East Asian sleuths usually went to European Jews in eyelid tape, permitted to inhabit any ethnicity but their own. Of course, he was happy to war-paint his cheeks to play Apaches in Republic's Westerns, so perhaps he was a flawed messenger of his own disenfranchisement. Or perhaps racism demonstrates its tenacity by making hypocrites of even its victims.

Outside, an open-top bus heavyset with Midwesterners came to a stop. Neon tubes running along the side blazed *See the Stars by Starlight.* Up front a tour guide backfilled the biographies of marquee players with colorfully erroneous anecdotes. The more implausibly detailed, the more confidently believed.

Eddie remembered when horse-drawn tourist buses trundled through Chinatown—not the new Chinatown based around Central Plaza, but the earlier iteration razed to make way for Union Station, where his grandfather settled after completing work on the Central Pacific Railroad. Come winter the invalided and retired traveled west on tracks his grandfather had lain. Popular on any itinerary was a safari through Chinatown in omnibuses pulled by dray horses and tiered in theater seating. Bellowing through megaphones, the guides recounted local histories as spurious as those presently dispensed on the street below. In their telling, every teahouse was an opium den, every well-dressed man a tong gangster. No Chinatown resident—no matter how respectable—escaped the leveling force of the megaphone man's typecasting. As a boy Eddie was incentivized to comport himself accordingly because those rubbernecking tourists who believed anything would toss pennies and nickels, once even a silver dollar.

On some soundstages it felt no different: he was a Chinatown nobody working for change while a white man behind a megaphone told him how to act.

His grandfather, a world-class bullshitter, used to claim he came to California on a block of ice. It had been an afternoon some seventy years past, out working on the Central Pacific in a stark desert where the only vegetation was barbed and forked like gladiatorial weaponry. The kind of heat conducive to mirage. His grandfather heard the low hum of an approaching train shimmer through the rails. The train wheezed to a halt right in front of him. Through the slatted wooden freight cars, his grandfather saw a glossy dazzling blueness. Two-ton blocks of ice cut from Lake Erie, the engineer said, destined for California and then overseas to Shanghai. The ice trapped the sunlight slicing through the slatted cars. His grandfather could see the millions of little white fractures threading the blocks.

"And what did you do?" Eddie, six years old, had asked.

"I climbed aboard and rode the ice floe until the desert ended."

In bed, Maria had fallen asleep in her clothes. Eddie carefully extracted her earrings from her earlobes, set them on the nightstand, and pulled the blanket to her chin. He was thirty-five years old with nothing but a string of bit parts to his name and a job as the night manager of the crummiest hotel in Hollywood, but as he sat there watching the woman he loved sleep in his bed, he was startled with gratitude for how his life had turned out.

At one in the morning, he figured he should head back down to the front desk. He wondered if Vincent was still up and if he fancied a hand of cards.

VINCENT HADN'T INTENDED TO REMAIN in Los Angeles for more than one night, but when he showed up to photograph the dozens of extras in wedding dresses, Mr. Jacobs, the wry, bespectacled head of the still photography department, looked him up and down and said, "They sent you over fast."

Vincent explained that he didn't work at Mercury. Mr. Jacobs didn't want to hear about his personnel problems; he had problems enough with all these brides wandering about, to say nothing of being short-staffed. One of the department's portrait men, an incurable drunk working in a medium that demanded steady hands and single vision, had been sent home a half hour earlier with a case of the shakes. After checking Vincent's breath for booze and sending the brides to the casting office, Mr. Jacobs explained the day's agenda: photographing an actress in low-cut costumes for Production Code approval. In the stills submitted to the censors, the actress was photographed from low angles, whereas on set she would be filmed from higher angles, thus excavating an extra inch of verboten cleavage from the neckline. Impressed with his sobriety, if not his work, Mr. Jacobs began to call Vincent in whenever his usual portrait man was out on a bender. Vincent performed photographic tests of actresses Mercury was considering putting under contract. The prints were shipped off to the executive offices where dumpy men in bad suits decided on the program of electrolysis, dental work, cosmetic surgery, crash diets, and posture coaching the starlet would be subjected to. What imperfections these grisly regimens failed to remedy were airbrushed out by the still photography department's full-time retoucher.

After three and a half years living on the road, his early days in Los Angeles proceeded as a span of restlessness. He couldn't fall asleep, no matter how he twisted and turned, and standing up to assess the situation, he saw what was wrong with the bed: it was stationary. Months bedding down in boxcars had made it impossible to get comfortable at anything less than thirty-five miles an hour.

After he received his first paycheck, Eddie took him to Bullock's to enliven his wardrobe with a tweedy blazer, bright sports shirt, and khaki slacks. Stout seamstresses prodded him with needles and salesmen pronounced French words as they did in Paris, Texas. The primary colors of California couture took inspiration from the traffic signals. He felt too conspicuous, but Eddie said conspicuousness was the prevailing fashion. Bedecked in a green blazer and yellow sports shirt, he climbed into Eddie's jalopy for a tour of the sights. The "sights" consisted of the Santa Anita and Hollywood Park racetracks, gaudy rings of mud and demolished hope that devoured the unclaimed portions of his paycheck. The race caller's voice fizzed from the PA system and into the crisp morning like cola into an iced glass. The scent of dirt hung in the air after the clods kicked by horse hoof fell and scattered. Bob Hope was said to have been spotted in the grandstand. Vincent wagered his last cent on a pony named Dead Stinking Last.

Whenever Vincent passed Maria in the hallway of the Montclair, he sensed a chilly remoteness behind her civil demeanor. He knew he should go, carry on to San Francisco, no longer inflict himself on a woman who looked at him with barely concealed contempt. But paradoxically, her contempt was what made him stay in Los Angeles. She was the only person for six thousand miles who recognized him for the coward, liar, fugitive, and fraud he was. Who else could level him with a single look? Who else could judge him with the mercilessness he craved if not a woman whose exile from Italy was freighted with as much guilt and remorse as his own? How could he leave the only person in America who knew his real name?

On Eddie's nights off, when there was no one to accompany him through those long insomniac hours, Vincent flipped through the black album of reassembled passport photographs. It was his only possession of any value, a gallery of familiar faces accompanying him across tens of thousands of foreign miles. Only the last entry remained unfinished. Below the torn half of his passport photograph were the words *Nino Picone, Departed: March 15, 1938. Arrived:*_____. He had intended to complete the entry when he reached Paris with Giuseppe, but he had lost the other half of the passport photograph somewhere on his travels.

Through the hotel room window, he could see the city's low-slung sprawl, dappled in the bluish bloom of streetlamps, stretching to the serrated horizon where the Santa Monica Mountains cut into the cosmos. He could see lustrous arches rising from nocturnal lawn sprinklers. Taillights dragged jots of color behind wedged headlamps. He wished Giuseppe were here.

There was no word from San Lorenzo. Transatlantic mail had ceased. Only rumor was ejected from the event horizon beyond which Europe vanished into blackness. Though the absence of news was maddening, it lulled him into states of suspended disbelief. Perhaps Giuseppe had made it over the Pyrenees? He could wait out the war in Lisbon, or sail to England. Perhaps he'd found passage through one of the French resort towns—Marseilles, Nice, Toulon—where Europe's refugees had honeymooned when their lives had still lain ahead of them. Worse than the obscurity of Giuseppe's fate was the certainty of Concetta's. He could see her at the table with her basket packed, waiting for her son to come home.

His nightmares never featured Gallo or Ferrando or Himmler, only Concetta Cortese. What relief did waking offer when the nightmare's monster was the dreamer himself? He had deceived her, preyed upon her hope, stolen her son's death from her. Was unworthiness the waste heat of survival? Did all émigrés see themselves in a similar haze? Or was his unworthiness rooted in the specific history of his stolen name?

If he was lucky, he would fall asleep before dawn.

BY EARLY AUTUMN 1941, SOME ten thousand German-speaking exiles had settled in Los Angeles. Several dozen found employment at Mercury under the aegis of the European Film Fund, which provided work to Jewish and dissident refugees. As morally enthusiastic if financially tepid supporters of the organization, the Feldmans had expected to land Ernst Lubitsch–level talent. Or at least a few $4000/week directors willing to work for $500 and free lunch. Instead, the majors skimmed the cream, leaving Mercury a backwash of modernist poets posing as story editors, avant-garde painters passing as art directors, and twelve-tone geniuses incapable of composing a hummable major-key melody. Sublime Weimar playwrights, transcribers of the most complex psychologies, fumbled with the gears and levers of English grammar, unable to sleeve more than a few words into a simple sentence. Only in the commissary would an exile risk unsealing his native language from its diplomatic pouch.

Vincent gradually became conversational in the patois of German, Hungarian, French, Polish, Yiddish, Italian, Czech, English,

Esperanto, sign language, pictograms, and charades through which Mercury's émigrés relayed studio gossip and war news. Outside of Eddie, they were his only friends in Los Angeles, an assortment of imposters and pessimists in whose company he felt at ease.

"Vincent, have some champagne," said Otto Hatszeghy, a German Jew with a Hungarian surname who converted to Lutheranism in an Austrian church in 1924 and reconverted to Judaism in a Lisbon synagogue in 1939. No one was simple.

Vincent took a seat. Across the table sat two adversaries who had been at each other's throats for nearly as long as they'd been in each other's beds: Rudi Bloch—the screenwriter of *Devil's Bargain*—a portly Vienna-born playwright suffering late-stage megalomania, and Anna Weber, the miniaturist from Berlin who had designed the scale model of the Mercury studio lot that sat outside Artie's office.

Anna was seventeen years older, four inches taller, and a few thousand English words more articulate than Vincent. Self-conscious about her accent and little else. She lived with Rudi in a Santa Monica bungalow and the twenty minutes it added to their daily commute was worth the additional mileage between them and Germany. She wore a locket in which she kept the strand of Beethoven's hair she'd stolen from the grizzled lock Alma Mahler allowed dinner guests to view while coffee was served. She had a pet tortoise bedazzled in rhinestones in her office—her sole concession to the eccentricity Mercury's set designers were known for—and always ordered it a side salad at lunch. She was a militant cynic, an ex-wife twice over, and a mean bastard. The ruthlessness with which she dealt with fools reminded Vincent of Concetta.

"Today Joseph Breen resigned from the Production Code to become the newest chief executive to run RKO into the ground," Anna said, dumping Vincent's water glass into the potted ficus and refilling it with champagne. "Guess what was the last script he approved on his way out the door?"

Vincent gave Rudi his congratulations.

"Please, Rudi doesn't need help celebrating himself," she said.

"It's Otto we're toasting. He's been offered the part of the Goebbels-like Mephisto."

"Given the scarcity of roles for émigrés with accents," Otto said, "I know I should be grateful for the opportunity, but I still have reservations."

"You're afraid you can't do justice to my script," Rudi suggested.

"Um, well, not exactly," Otto said, moving around Rudi's wounded pride with the care of a hunter sidestepping an elephant with an arrow in its ear. Staring at the little leaping bubbles of champagne, Otto said, "It just seems a dreadful irony that to survive in exile one must embody the very persecutors one flees. And then there are the practical risks. My parents are still in Europe and Hatszeghy isn't the most common name. What if the Germans decide to make life even more difficult for my family?"

"Use a false name in the credits," Vincent suggested. "Ask Artie to credit you as John Doe."

Otto stroked his pencil mustache. "I suppose that could work," he admitted.

"I'd never stoop to using a false name," Rudi declared. Declaration was his preferred mode of discourse after denial.

Anna gave Rudi a warning look. "Don't be unsocial."

"'A high degree of intellect tends to make a man unsocial,' as Schopenhauer wisely counsels," Rudi said.

"You're nothing if not intellectual," Otto agreed, by which he meant Rudi could quote people smarter than him. Otto turned to Anna, who, aside from romantic partners, had excellent taste. "What do you think of *Devil's Bargain*?"

Anna thought little of it, mainly because Rudi had drawn his inspiration from her life. Before becoming a successful movie miniaturist, she had been an unsuccessful architect. After the Nazis came to power, she was offered the opportunity to put her signature on the city she loved with a commission to design several projects for the Berlin Olympics. She had said no. Rudi had first envisioned *Devil's Bargain* as an alternate history of that decision, one in which she had said yes. And in truth, Anna wished she had. Turning the devil down was her greatest regret. Her first husband, Hasso, had been wise enough to accept.

"I found the premise a bit dreary," Anna told Otto. Pinching Rudi's cheek, she added, "Much like its author, it's too serious to take seriously."

Rudi bristled at the insinuation. "From where I sit at the head of this table—"

"You aren't sitting at the head of the table," Anna observed with what Rudi considered a pitiful adherence to the literal.

"My dear Anna, the head of the table is wher*ever* I sit." Rudi held up his hand to silence the others. Vincent thought Rudi was asking for the mustard. Now Rudi was a pompous man with a condiment bottle. Once he'd been Bertolt Brecht's peer.

Anna looked away as Rudi shuffled through the same dozen quotations that had replaced his capacity for coherent argument. Scanning the commissary, she found it strange that hierarchies here should be as rigidly stratified as any outside Prussian military mess halls or middle school cafeterias. Directors sat with directors, actors with actors, screenwriters with screenwriters. The divisions were further refined by salary: a $500/week screenwriter would never sit with a $300/week scribe. Slicing status into such thin gradations ensured that everyone felt utterly alone, even when surrounded by two hundred others. The exception was the table where the émigrés ate together. Naturally, Anna thought, it was farthest from the food and nearest to the exit.

Rudi prattled on: ". . . my goal is to dramatize Karl Kraus's maxim: 'The devil is an optimist if he thinks he can make people worse than they are.' "

Can one feel schadenfreude for oneself? Anna assumed this was the only explanation for why she submitted to Rudi's lobotomizing lecturing when she could have brought a bagged lunch and eaten alone in her office while listening to the BBC on the shortwave. Then again, she knew that conversation in the movie colony was performed in two keys—gushing enthusiasm and unvarnished contempt—depending on whether its subject could overhear you, and thus, for the sake of her reputation, she tried not to stray out of earshot of the exiles' table. She felt her mind dull under the hammering banality of Rudi's "thoughts" on the transformative power of storytelling, which made clear that storytelling only had the power to transform its worshippers into insufferable morons.

It astonished her that she and Rudi had been sleeping together—occasionally between, more often during—their various marriages for going on twenty years now. They could only maintain a healthy relationship with each other so long as they were in unhealthy marriages to other people. They'd met when Rudi was even more of a nobody than he was now, a taxi dancer employed by various Berlin hotel ballrooms to dance with unaccompanied ladies. Rudi used to be such a gentleman, but his self-esteem surged as his stature plummeted, leaving him psychologically lopsided and easily lampooned. And yet he was still the most marvelous dancer. The cantankerous vanity, the bullying sanctimony, the wounded pride, everything that might be described as Rudi's personality, it all vanished when he stepped onto the dance floor at Ciro's or the Beverly Wilshire. No matter what the orchestra was playing, Rudi would hum a Viennese waltz in Anna's ear. Taking her into a turn, he seemed to glide out of himself and into the ethereal, his body erect, his hand riding high on her shoulder blade, off tempo with the music crooning from the bandstand but in perfect harmony with the Strauss waltz he hummed, and the seesawing swell of their steps left Anna wordless with warmth for the strangeness of people because who was a less likely vessel for grace than Rudi Bloch?

"'Evil is whatever distracts,' as Kafka reminds us," Rudi was telling the table.

Dear Lord, Anna thought, *has he already come to Kafka?* Rudi's compulsion to memorize the great works of German literature was the product of detention camps and consulate waiting rooms, a means of increasing your net worth when you owned only what you smuggled between your ears, a reminder that the language now dedicated to your dehumanization had once been sublime. ("In the face of unspeakable silence, we must reach for the poets," Rudi once said while reaching for an egg salad sandwich. "Please. Your poets are just drunks in scarves," Anna had replied.) Anna wasn't surprised that Rudi's need to recite the plays of Goethe and the poems of Rilke grew as his ability to express himself in German diminished. German was the language Anna thought, counted, dreamed, prayed, and cursed in; it was lovely to remember that it could be beautiful, even if she knew Germany too well to ever speak German beautifully again.

". . . and Schiller cautions: 'Live with your century, but do not be its creature.'"

"For fuck's sake, Rudi," Anna said. "You sound like a *Bartlett's* with the trots."

Failing to find an open seat in his salary range, an actor carried his tray from the commissary.

"So a thousand-dollar-a-week actor eats lunch in a toilet stall to avoid the embarrassment of sitting next to a nine-hundred-dollar-a-week actor?" Vincent asked Anna.

The short, wiry Italian portrait photographer was a few years older than her son Kurt, and his fumbling attempts to compose repartee at the speed of conversation in a language he barely spoke roused Anna's maternal sympathies. The poor fellow hadn't yet learned that saying nothing eloquently wasn't a skill to hone but a pathology to cure. Kurt had been like that, so eager to impress his elders. She remembered when—

Anna noticed Vincent was looking at her expectantly. "I'm sorry, what did you say?"

"It doesn't make much sense, does it?" Vincent repeated. "The dining hall customs."

Anna sighed. The Italian mistook pointing out the abundantly obvious for clever conversation; he'd fit right in in Hollywood. She said, "Only an anthropologist with field experience among cannibal tribes could decipher the taboos of the Hollywood commissary."

Vedette Clement—Maria Lagana's secretary—approached the exiles' table. Conversations with Vedette left Anna in need of an aspirin and a dark room. Vedette bombarded the senses with loud blouses and percussive jewelry, laboring to make a statement with great volume and limited vocabulary, succeeding in leaving a distinct impression though never the one she intended.

"Word's come from on high," Vedette told the table. "Production begins next Monday."

Otto said, "I must have a word with Mr. Feldman."

AT FIRST, IT ALL SEEMED to go wrong exactly right. Shortly after the commencement of the long-delayed production was reported in the trades, the hate mail came in from the America First Committee membership. Three the first day. Eighty-seven the second. The conspiracies they laid out implied a pitiful hunger for explanation, no matter how malicious or unlikely. On the third day Artie gathered the letters in his metal wastebasket and invited Maria in to strike the match. This wasn't their first rodeo. The ceremonial burning of hate mail was to a Mercury picture what the lighting of the torch was to the Olympic Games. But rather than drop the match, Maria said, "Why don't we use these too?"

Artie began publishing them in weekly advertisements in *The Hollywood Reporter* to stoke interest among the critics and gossip columnists. He hired private investigators to perform background checks on all studio employees. After discovering that one of the janitors was a member of the Silver Shirts, he put it out to the papers that he foiled a German attempt to infiltrate his studio. That German agents likely had more urgent espionage than spying on Mercury Pictures International was a possibility the newspapermen happily ignored. He stationed armed guards outside his office, kept the shooting schedule under lock and key, and doled out aliases to all cast and crew. Naturally, he trumpeted these security protocols to reporters with all the restraint of a catchpenny boxing promoter.

Artie was so focused on publicity that he left the day-to-day oversight of production to Maria. She managed budgets, office politics, celebrity personalities, city permits, demands from the insurer, demands from the agents, demands from the lawyers, demands from the Production Code, demands from each of Mercury's thirty-two departments, fire-code violations, contract disputes, above-the-line costs, below-the-line costs, payroll, script breakdowns, vendor invoices, memoranda, shooting schedules, production delays, daily logs, overages . . . in short, the invisible and unglamorous bureaucratic apparatus that made a picture possible.

All this Maria accomplished with minimal input from Artie, so when she saw him unveil the mockup poster the advertising department had sent over, she was furious. The poster had been inked by a freelancer in Long Beach whose principal trade was tattooing cheesecake pinups on sailorly biceps. Of late his most common commissions were the names, Social Security numbers, and blood types of Navy draftees. Maria wasn't concerned with the poster itself, a mélange of expressionism and pulp as envisioned by an eye practiced in memorializing errors of judgment on skin. No, what bothered Maria were the credits. Everyone was listed as John Doe. Even her.

"It's brilliant, isn't it?" Artie said. "One of the actors asked to be credited as John Doe, over concerns that his involvement in this picture might imperil his folks back in Europe. It occurred to me that crediting everyone as John Doe could be a publicity coup."

"Art, you gave me your word I'd receive the producer's credit on this."

"Anyone who matters will know who produced this," Artie said, dismissing her concerns with a wave of his hand. "Irving Thalberg was the greatest producer in history and he insisted his name not appear in the credits of his pictures. He thought it wasn't classy."

Surprisingly, being lectured on class by a man who had named his toupees failed to cheer her. She accepted that the anonymized credits were a sensible policy to protect relatives marooned in Europe—including her father, if he was still alive—and she even accepted they were a clever marketing ploy. What she found unacceptable was remaining nameless.

"The whole point is to telegraph to the press that *Devil's Bargain* is so sensational that for their own protection everyone involved needs a pseudonym. Everyone is getting one, no exceptions. But here, I have an idea." In the lower right corner, under the *Produced by* credit, Artie crossed out the *John* in *John Doe* and wrote *Jane*. "Jane Doe. No one, and I mean no one, will have any doubt who Jane Doe really is. Satisfied?"

Maria might have been had she not noticed the one non-anonymized name on the poster. It appeared right above the title, in small but legible cursive: *Art Feldman and Mercury Pictures Presents . . .*

3

IT TOOK TWO HOURS TO DISPERSE THE CROWD, FERRY THE INJURED TO the hospital, and arrest the stragglers who stormed the Mercury at the premiere of *Devil's Bargain.* Thirteen cuffed men squatted on the curb, ties crooked, shirt flaps out, partially disrobed by the violence that had sprung from them. The uniformed officer walking down the line plopped fedoras on their heads at random. These defused men turned from the press cameras as if *now* they remembered to feel shame, when a pressman photographed them in a hat that didn't fit.

Maria stepped back into the lobby. Despite Ned Feldman's frequent urgings to invest in exhibition, the Mercury was the studio's only theatrical holding, a Pacific-themed muddle of travertine and turquoise. Along the walls papier-mâché palm trees bowed defeatedly. Broken mirror glass reflected specks of ceiling on the floor. A sconce dangled from its electrical wire like a tooth from its nerve.

The auditorium fared no better. Springs corkscrewed from ripped seats. Entire rows had been ripped out and regurgitated in feathery spews. Artie surveyed the wreckage, his tuxedo shirt stamped in dirty footprints, a lump budding from his left temple. The whites of his eyes were red. He'd peeled the trampled roadkill of his toupee from the floor, dropped a couple ice cubes in it, and held it to his head.

"Don't clean that up," he barked at a ticket clerk who'd begun sweeping up broken glass. "Nothing gets tidied up until the newsmen get their photos."

Maria walked over.

"You okay?" he asked.

Maria nodded. "You?"

"Peachy. How many newsmen are outside?"

"I counted over fifty."

"I'm sure more are on their way. This will make the front pages."

"What do you want me to tell them?" Maria asked.

"Tell them to bring their cameras."

There wasn't enough undamaged seating to accommodate the newsmen who crowded in: wire service reporters, trade hacks, gossip columnists, the correspondents from forty-two dailies and sixteen foreign news bureaus. Even the Vatican's pressman came to see the picture that caused a riot.

Artie addressed the newsmen cramming the aisles.

"This wasn't what I had in mind when I hoped for standing room only," he joked feebly. His smile was a pain-packed grimace. "I intended to make a few remarks, but maybe tonight's already remarkable enough. Here's what all the fuss is about."

The house lights dimmed and a strident score piped through the speakers. As the projectionist brought the opening credits into focus, a rustling surprise spread from the front row to the balcony heights. John and Jane Does all the way down, the picture's cast and crew as anonymized as its audience.

Maria slipped from the theater to the backstage door. The proscenium arch lay panther pelts of shadow across the stage. She pulled back the curtain a few inches, and for the next ninety-five minutes, while the audience watched the picture, she watched the audience. The newspapermen crammed into the aisles jotted notes in a dozen different languages. Soon, they stopped scribbling and let the picture wash over their eyes unmediated by critique or comment. When the last frame faded to black, a great applause rose from the ruined theater. In the backstage shadows, Maria Lagana bowed.

• • •

IN THE MORNING MILDRED SAID, "Have you heard of Pearl Harbor?"

"Who's producing it?" Artie asked.

"On the radio, they . . ." Mildred shook her head. "It's probably just Orson Welles causing a panic again."

BLACKOUT

1

ON DECEMBER 11, 1941, ONCE WORD CAME OVER THE WIRELESS THAT Italy, following Germany's lead, had declared war on America, Annunziata walked out to her garden. It rained the previous night and a sour mugginess steamed off the winter vegetables. Her heels dented the dirt as she crouched to inspect the garlic, cabbage, and onions that grew in California's temperate winter.

What would her grandparents have thought if they could see her? They'd been sharecroppers tilling arable plots smattering Calabria's highlands. Most were no larger than this backyard garden, hemmed in by rock and clay, green stalks spearing the sepia bleakness. Annunziata's backyard had the bagged mulch and fertilizer and plentiful hose water that her grandparents would have seen as the conditions of paradise itself. More importantly, the land was hers. Perhaps this explained the popularity of vegetable gardens in Lincoln Heights: you were answering your ancestors' prayers.

The fava beans would have been lovely, Annunziata thought as she ripped out the rows. She uprooted garlic, broccoli, and kale.

Veiny roots clasped the soil as she grubbed out the artichoke and exhumed bone-white celery stalks. She pulled the Old Crow from the watering can and drank straight from the bottle.

Rumors circulated that the police had already rounded up Japanese gardeners on the theory they had planted messages to bombers in their crops. As if airplanes needed directions sown in gardens to find the largest metropolis on the West Coast. What would her grandparents say if they could see her ripping out the carefully tended produce? She thought they would have understood. Bureaucratic folly was as fearsome a peril in the Mezzogiorno as any drought, pestilence, or earthquake. The only promise to its citizens the state kept. Her grandparents wouldn't have expected it to be any different here.

She uprooted it all, took a final pull of Old Crow, and went inside.

"You believe this?" At the kitchen table Ciccio was showing Mimi the tin whistle the Office of Civilian Defense supplied him with when he volunteered as an air raid spotter. Its embossed provenance: *Made in Japan.*

"So what?" Mimi said. "You were made in Sicily and you work well enough."

"Lies," Lala said.

Annunziata walked past without saying a word. She was fifty-one years old and still lived in the same room she moved into with Maria when they came to Los Angeles fifteen years earlier. Now that her aunts were getting older, she'd taken over the day-to-day operation of the restaurant. The scent of cooking oil and garlic clung to her hair and hands no matter which brand of bath soap she used. Long ago she'd sold the few evening gowns she brought with her from Rome. What would her life look like if, on one of her trips to the La Grande departures hall, she had purchased a ticket and boarded a train? She doubted she would be any happier, but at least her disappointments would be new. Novel disappointment sounded awfully fulfilling right about now. Last week she took one of Pep's shapeless dresses off the laundry line and wore it the entire morning before realizing it wasn't hers. Hard to see her life as anything but a failure.

She changed out of her gardening clothes and tossed her dirt-stained overalls into the hamper. Brittle stacks of *L'Italo Americano,* one of the city's two Italian-language newspapers, loomed in the back of her closet: one copy of every edition to feature a review of the movies Maria worked on, and several dozen copies of the September 17, 1940, edition. In addition to its extensive obituary coverage, *L'Italo Americano* often featured profiles highlighting the contributions Italian immigrants had made to Los Angeles. On September 17, 1940, the paper ran a piece on Maria's work in the movies, calling her a "credit to her people," like Saint Francis or Jimmy Durante. Annunziata had driven around Lincoln Heights, buying out the stock of every newsstand and corner store she came across. She left one copy strategically opened on the parlor coffee table for several months. The rest she kept in the closet. The collection was her most cherished valuable, the first thing she would save from the fire.

In the kitchen, Ciccio was incessantly blowing the tin whistle to see if the Japanese had sabotaged it. Annunziata restrained the urge to walk in there and shove the whistle up his nose. Should she call Maria? Wasn't that what a good mother would do? It had been months since they last spoke. They weren't estranged so much as exhausted by the effort it took to steer conversation past all that they couldn't manage to say. It was safer to stay on separate shores than to navigate an ocean cluttered with icebergs. Strange, then, that Annunziata found herself crossing to the parlor. The telephone line had been put in a few years earlier, after Mimi, who for years insisted the voices coming through the telephone were spirits trapped in purgatory, had relented. Before she could talk herself out of it, Annunziata lifted the receiver from the cradle and called.

"Yeah?" Maria said by way of greeting.

"It's me."

"What's wrong?"

"That's a short question with a very long answer."

"No," Maria said, "I mean, are you in the hospital?"

"Why would I be in the hospital?"

"Why else would you be calling?" Maria said, casually breaking her mother's heart.

Annunziata closed her eyes. "I just wanted to make sure you heard the news."

"Yeah, I heard it. Not surprising, but it still knocked the wind out of me."

"We've been listening to the news since dawn. I didn't know listening to the radio could be such hard work."

"The psychiatrists have a term for that: radio fatigue."

"Radio fatigue," Annunziata repeated. "That sounds about right. You think they'll stop playing Caruso on KFAC?"

Annunziata could hear the smile in Maria's voice. "I don't know, Mamma."

"They'd call Caruso an enemy alien now too, if you can believe it. Caruso, the Man with the Orchid-Lined Voice, an enemy alien! What a disgrace. I'm glad he's not alive to see it."

Last month Annunziata, Mimi, Lala, Pep, and Ciccio went to the police station to register as resident aliens. The desk sergeant who fingerprinted and photographed them halted the line here and there to book an arrested criminal. Lost on no one was the bleak irony of these parallel procedures. By midday, the immigrants complying with the law and the native born who violated it shared the same line.

"Pep is sitting on the porch with a butcher's knife. She says the police will never take her alive."

"Mamma, you've got to tell her this isn't the old country. She can't go around stabbing policemen anymore."

"Feisty old gal, isn't she?" Annunziata said, peering out the window to where Pep sat sentry. "I hope I have the energy to be as paranoid as my aunts when I'm their age."

"I'm serious, Mamma. God knows we'll be under enough suspicion as enemy aliens without Pep actively trying to kill policemen."

"Come home, Maria."

"To that madhouse? No, thank you."

"Please. I miss you, my dear."

2

BROWNS AND GREENS BLOTCHED THE DISTANT HILLS WHERE THE WHITE-lettered *Hollywoodland* sign was stamped on Mount Lee, a subtitle translating the gorgeous vacuity of the cloudless sky.

What a sight, thought Artie, who stood at the window whistling with the early-bird brio of an orange juice jingle. He felt invigorated with morbid cheer. The country's entry into the war had reversed his fortunes with dizzying speed. He went to bed on the evening of December 6 a pariah and woke on the morning of December 7 a prophet. Over the following days, he watched his enemies recant their prior beliefs. The America First Committee disbanded. All of Artie's inquisitors at the Senate Investigation into Motion Picture War Propaganda voted for the declaration of war. Charles Lindbergh, who weeks earlier had publicly questioned Artie's allegiances, was denied a commission in the Air Force over concerns about his divided loyalties. The advice Artie delivered to his kitchen radio for months had been elevated into federal policy. *Daily Variety* heralded the disastrous premiere—a touch tasteless, even to Artie—as Hollywood's Pearl Harbor. Most remarkable was the phone call he just received.

A knock at the door. His mid-morning meeting attendees filed in. Maria took one of the upholstered chairs ringing the coffee table. Ned nodded his greetings. Vedette scratched notes on her secretarial pad. Ernst Rosner flopped onto the settee, shedding dandruff across the cushion.

"I just got off the horn with the brass hats at the War Department," Artie told them. He realized he was still holding the receiver in his hand. He returned it to the cradle. "They want to hire us."

"The Army must be in a bad way if they're trying to get a bunch of fifty-year-olds with bad backs to enlist," Ned said.

"They're not asking us to enlist. They're asking us to make pictures, to fill the gap until they get their own in-house outfit up and running. In addition to our usual production schedule, we'd be making training and indoctrination films for new conscripts to explain the stakes of the war and why we've entered it and so on." Artie looked pointedly at Ned. "In other words, propaganda."

"With respect, Art, why on earth would they entrust you with that?"

Artie shook his head, too bemused by how fast his luck had U-turned to even feign offense. "Senator Nye spent the last six months denouncing me as a crackerjack propagandist. Apparently, President Roosevelt was listening. He personally directed the War Department to reach out to us. You feeling okay, Ned? You look a little pale."

"It's your shirt." Ned nodded to the plaid button-down composed of a dozen mismatching pastels. "It's giving me vertigo."

"Vedette, would you mind getting my brother some water? He's feeling a bit faint. Now, I should receive more guidance from the War Department in the coming days, but for the moment I want department heads to think about who they can lend to this while keeping in mind we're looking at losing around a third of our workforce to the draft." Artie turned to the next item on the morning's agenda. "I spoke with Warners and in light of recent events, they not only want to distribute *Devil's Bargain,* but bump it to the top of the double bill. Publicity really needs to sell the patriotic angle, okay? Let's make people feel it's their duty to watch this picture, that they'll leave the theater being able to see through enemy misinformation campaigns, et cetera. Maria, find out if we can get Army and Navy recruiters down to the theaters—anyone who enlists gets in free, that sort of thing. We play it right and this could be our biggest earner since *Husband.*"

To date Mercury's highest grossing movie was *What My Husband Gave Me,* an "educational" film on the dangers of syphilis. Nine years after its initial release it was still wildly popular in Florida.

Maria broached the subject of screen credits. If the country was already at war, then surely they could dispense with the pseudonyms?

"Hardly the time for selfishness, Jane Doe," Ernst said, helping himself to a sixth cookie from the communal tray.

"It's too late anyway," Artie added. "More prints are already being struck and the publicity materials are out the door."

The indifference with which her concerns were disregarded exasperated Maria. Screen credit was the coin of the realm, the only marker of past success and guarantor of future employment. Why should she feel selfish for requesting this barest acknowledgment: her name on her work.

The conversation shifted to concerns that Japanese bombers would mistake studio soundstages for aviation plant hangars.

"Jack Warner told me he painted a great big arrow on his roof that says *Lockheed That-a-Way!*" Artie said.

They decided instead to see if any swimming pool diggers were doing bomb shelters.

More pressing was the question of how wartime shortages would affect pictures already in the pipeline. Rubber, electricity, paper, petroleum, wood, paint, metal . . . everything from the boiled sugar in breakaway windows to the cardboard in ticket stubs was subject to rationing and requisition. Most troubling was the rationing of film.

"Nitrocellulose," Ernst said, ladling his paw into Artie's fishbowl of jelly beans. "The principal chemical in film stock is also the principal component in gunpowder."

Finishing his presentation on the economics of rationing, Ernst folded his spectacles and seated them in his breast pocket. His unshielded irises were a vivid muddle of wet-grass greens, mahogany browns, the golden glow of smeared firefly. All his guile seemed compressed into those colored coins hole-punched by pupils. As the keeper of Mercury's finances, he was the most despised figure on the lot, and it wearied him, depleted him, and most mornings he woke astonished that his spirit remained barnacled to his body. He no longer bothered hiding the hemorrhoid donut that hung at the ready, on his office wall, like a bedraggled lifesaver. If he had stayed at his comfortable perch at Goodyear, he'd have died from boredom. What a blissful way to go.

ACROSS THE ROOM, NED SWISHED lukewarm coffee and waited for his opening. He'd been caught as unaware as anyone by Pearl Harbor and was still gauging how to position himself in this altered landscape. He'd been convinced—absolutely *convinced*—that *Devil's Bargain* was the sort of flopperoo he could cite as evidence of his brother's diminished judgment when making his case to the board for putting Artie out to pasture. He'd gone to sleep on December 6 confident he'd given his brother enough rope to hang himself. Now? Now the board thought Artie was goddamned Nostradamus.

Which made the previous day's phone call with the Eastern National banker particularly interesting. To begin with, the memo scheduling the call suggested Ned take it at home given the time difference between coasts. An innocuous enough explanation, if he wanted to believe it. The banker forecasted boom times for Hollywood: the ramped-up war economy would put disposable income into consumer pockets just as rationing put sharp limits on how it could be spent. You couldn't engineer a better environment for a studio like Mercury to return to its former glory. The banker couched his overture in the hypothetical and plausibly denied, but Ned could read the signals: the events of the last week had made Eastern National *more* interested in taking over Mercury. The offer, made through implication and ellipsis, was that if he delivered them the necessary board seats, they would cut Artie loose and put Ned in control of a fully capitalized major studio. Was Ned prepared to do that? No, he couldn't, but there must have been a noncommittal waver in his voice, because the banker suggested Ned take time to think it over.

Now Artie was saying the proceeds from Warners should go to paying down their debt.

"I'm surprised to hear you say that, Art."

"You're surprised I don't want my nuts hanging over a bear trap longer than necessary?"

"Given how our stock is trading, I figured you'd want to ask Eastern National to double, triple our credit line. The war's going to have us doing gangbusters. It's a once-in-a-lifetime opportunity. It's not like you to surrender."

Ned's arguments slipped into his brother's insecurities like needles into inflamed nerves.

"These restrictions will hit the majors far harder than us. I mean, c'mon, Art. Ever since the onset of the Depression, you've learned to ration, make do, live without. It's the rest of the business that's struggling to catch up."

Artie found himself in the unpleasant position of agreeing with his brother. He looked at Ernst, hoping to elicit a conflicting opinion.

"I concur," Ernst said. "Eastern National will probably ask for a couple board seats, but if you can stomach that, a more robust credit line makes perfect sense from where I sit."

Still smarting from the snub, Maria ignored the SOS's Artie was blinking at her. "I agree," she said. "It takes the majors six months of intra-office memoranda to set up a meeting. Meanwhile, we can rush a picture from script to screen in half that time."

"We'll have the market largely to ourselves until summer," Ned said. "But Art, I know you're wary of giving up any more board seats, so it's your call. Whatever you decide, I fully support."

On the sidewalk a queue fed a blood drive's vampiric appetites.

"Fuck it. In for a penny." Artie tapped the next illegible scribble on his agenda. "Alongside whatever government propaganda work we do, we'll obviously want to exploit the war in our dramatic features as well. We have a topical script kicking around called *Tell 'Em in Tokyo*. Piece of shit spy picture. Any objections?"

Ernst raised a finger. "Among the shortages we face is the scarcity of actors who can play Japanese villains. There are only a couple Japanese actors in the entire Screen Actors Guild and none are particularly eager to play Tojo's minions."

Cream spiraled in Ned's freshly poured coffee. "I'm not sure we'd want them to. This talk of evacuations and relocations . . . I don't believe it, but we ought to plan for the worst in case the Henry McLemores of the world have their way: What happens if we're halfway through shooting and our lead villain is interned? Senator Nye is already claiming Japanese fifth columnists aided the attack on Pearl Harbor."

Artie blew a raspberry. "Anything that cuckoo believes is ipso fatso false."

Vedette glanced up from her dictation pad. "I hear Jap farmers are lacing the lima beans with arsenic."

It wasn't Vedette's easy slide into prejudice that unsettled Maria so much as the suspension of disbelief it suggested, as if reality took the crooked shape of the mind into which it was poured. What gave conspiracy the credibility reasonable explanation lacked? What hunger for order, even diabolical order, did it satisfy?

Ernst turned to Vedette. "I say this as your friend: You are a moron. Japanese farmers own about two iotas of California's farmland, but grow most of its crops. Guess who's ginning up these rumors? The trade associations representing white farmers. Relocation is competition elimination, pure and simple. There's your conspiracy."

Vedette's smile shriveled to a stern lump of lipstick. Her mother had warned her about working for these people.

They tossed around possible Chinese and Korean actors to cast as a leading villain. Keye Luke? Chester Gan? Philip Ahn? Did they know any others? *Were* there any others? Peter Lorre?

Artie brushed crumbs from his shirtfront. "A Hungarian Jew may not satisfy the realism the moment demands."

"*The Good Earth* looked like it was cast from a Leopoldstadt streetcar," Ned said, "and that was a smasheroo."

Artie heard producers had gotten so desperate they were signing their bartenders and laundrymen to $1000/week contracts, asking themselves why there were so few Asian actors, wondering whom they should blame.

"May I make a suggestion," Maria said. "Eddie Lu."

Ned nodded. "He was great in *Shanghaied in Shanghai.* What agency is he with?"

Eddie was represented by a Boyle Heights hustler who had three hundred clients and was barely getting by. Presently his most successful actor was a horse. "A boutique outfit," Maria said.

"What will he cost us?" Artie asked.

For her entire career, she had been loyal to Artie. But if he was going to withhold her producer's credit, she saw no reason to choose his interests over Eddie's.

"As you can imagine, he's been getting a lot of offers over the last couple days," she said. In fact, he'd received only one, for $150 a week. "You'll have to go in with a strong bid. I'd say nothing less than two thousand a week."

Artie snorted, incredulous. "That'll make him the highest-paid actor on the lot!"

Mustering all her innocence, Maria said, "Will it?"

"There's one final item we need to address," Ernst said, sifting through his notes. "I have it on good authority that due to concerns over espionage, the Department of Justice will mandate restrictions on the employment of enemy aliens in certain jobs . . ."

Maria shifted uncomfortably in her seat.

". . . these restrictions mostly affect the maritime, aviation, radio, and munitions fields, but there is one area of concern for us: photography. The DOJ doesn't want enemy aliens around cameras for fear they could be used for spying or surveillance."

"You're joking," Maria said, knowing full well keeping Mercury solvent left Ernst Rosner far too depressed to joke.

"You try reasoning with these pencil pushers. It's like challenging a helmet to a headbutting contest." Ernst tossed a few more jelly beans into the multicolored mush coating his tongue. "The good news is that only four employees will be affected. We have three German nationals in the camera department. And there's one Italian national working part-time in the still photography department."

"Can we fight this?" Artie asked. "I mean, Christ, Ernst—Hitler and Mussolini chased these poor bastards out of Europe and the DOJ thinks they'll turn around and spy for their persecutors?"

"If they are nationals of an enemy nation, the DOJ will treat them as enemies. My advice? It's not worth jeopardizing a War Department propaganda deal for the sake of four employees."

Artie knew Ernst was right, of course. This was a business, not a civil liberties organization. Nonetheless, the faintest doubt rippled through his certainty: For the past few years he'd produced movies to stoke fears of enemy spies living among us. He'd believed he was on the side of the angels, but devils must tell themselves they're angels too.

"Pay them through the end of the month," Artie told Maria. "But fire them tomorrow."

3

THE BLACKOUT BEGAN AT DUSK. THE CITY CUT THE POWER TO streetlamps and traffic lights, ordered all businesses and residences to go dark, and when Maria left the office at six, it could have been midnight on the moon.

Instead of walking to her car, she wandered through the back lot while trying to ignore the anxiety tightening her stomach. It was all very foolish: On the day her country of residence declared war on her country of birth, she was most preoccupied with her return to Lincoln Heights. When had she last seen her mother? A year ago, at least. There had been no big fight, no outburst of recriminations, just a gradual acceptance that her mother was constitutionally incapable of facing the role Maria had played in her father's arrest and their subsequent exile, and that this poisoned their relationship with distrust, embitterment, and passive aggression. That this wasn't true did not diminish the intensity with which she believed it. Maria could believe the neatness of the stories she told herself about her mother so long as their integrity was not compromised by reality. It was easier to believe her mother, the most confrontational personality Maria had ever known, would refuse to confront Maria out of weakness or pride than out of a desire to shield her daughter from the damage her actions had caused.

The cold wind barreling down the studio alley sprayed sand from

Wild West Row across the blacktop. The streetlamps were gloomy globes of dark glass. A door swung closed in the music department, lopping off the last bars of "Chattanooga Choo Choo." Ahead, where shadows stretched in a sheet of carbon gray across the Italian Piazza, Maria saw a solitary figure walking along the perimeter. Who else would she find here on the day Italy and America declared war on each other?

Maria fell into step beside Vincent. Neither spoke and their footsteps were the only dialogue of the two-person passeggiata. They hadn't exchanged more than a few hundred words—all perfectly polite, perfectly meaningless—since Maria had returned from Washington months ago.

Finally, Maria asked Vincent how he was holding up under the day's news.

"I'm fine," he said, expressionless, sealed in, conceding nothing.

"I'm not sure whether to feel relieved or terrified," Maria admitted.

"Those aren't incompatible reactions, given our position."

Our position. The possessive plural was now unsettlingly accurate. In a studio that divided its employees by the finest gradations of stature, there was no gap quite as gaping as what lay between her and Vincent. But on paper, they were both enemy aliens now.

They took another lap around the piazza. As her thoughts spilled uncontrollably into the night ahead, it occurred to Maria that while living with her father, Vincent might have gleaned the context to explain some of her mother's neuroses, fixations, and avoidances. Why Maria demanded her mother's mind be a grid while accepting that her own was a maze was a hypocrisy she tried not to dwell on. Three years of psychoanalysis had taught her the mind was so inscrutable it reduced an otherwise practical woman to a conspiracy theorist searching for the hidden forces governing her demons within the symmetries of inkblots.

"Did he ever talk about my mother?" she asked.

"Your father? He was a broken record where Signora Lagana was concerned. I must've heard the same dozen stories a thousand times: the trip to Ischia, the umbrella incident, how they met."

"How did they meet?" Maria felt divided by the desire to understand her parents and the conviction that she never could, wanting to know how they met if only to more accurately wish that they never had, longing for clarity and expecting more noise.

"She crashed into him on her bicycle. Then he took her out to lunch."

Maria was unaware her mother even knew how to ride a bicycle. She felt envious of this interloper who was more familiar with her parents' history than she was. Perhaps she had broached the subject not to gain perspective on the night ahead, but to strengthen her resolve for the morning to come.

"I have to fire you tomorrow," she said. "The Department of Justice plans to prohibit enemy aliens from using cameras."

"Why?"

"They're worried about spies."

Vincent absorbed the news with a glum nod. "I've overstayed my welcome in any case. I'd hoped . . ." He trailed off, unable or unwilling to recall what he had ever hoped to receive from Maria Lagana. "Tomorrow morning I'll do what I should have done the day I arrived."

"What?"

"Leave."

"I'm afraid you can't do that either. The DOJ is prohibiting enemy aliens from traveling more than a couple miles from their place of residence."

Vincent gazed uneasily across the back-lot set as the borders cinched around him. "You travel halfway around the world just to end up in confino again," he said, shaking his head. "How does an itinerant photographer make a living if he's prohibited from being an itinerant and a photographer?"

The constellations shined a few watts brighter over the blacked-out city. Perhaps the impending reunion with her family had left Maria susceptible to the idea that she could change; perhaps she was depleted by the sustained ferocity of her self-loathing; perhaps it was just the sight of a lost Calabrian walking circles around a fake piazza beneath a velvet night begemmed in starlight. All Maria knew with certainty was that she wanted to make peace with the ghosts of her homeland on the day America declared war on it.

"Come on," she said. "I might have something to tide you over until you find another job."

THE FILM LIBRARY WAS A two-story structure of fire-retardant cinder block just beyond the camera department. Cost cutting made Mercury reliant on stock footage, and their cheaper pictures were created here as much as on the soundstages. Maria heaved open the heavy steel door. Every few feet violently illustrated no-smoking signs depicted the fate awaiting those who failed to respect the incendiary qualities of nitrate film.

In the screening room, Maria fed a reel from *Triumph of the Will* into the projector. She'd seen the picture for the first time in November '38, when Leni Riefenstahl had visited Hollywood on a goodwill tour. Generating goodwill in an industry founded by Jews would have been an uphill climb, even if her visit hadn't coincided with Kristallnacht. Riefenstahl dismissed the news with claims of ignorance that would prove progressively unsteady the more she leaned on them in the coming years. The Hollywood Anti-Nazi League organized boycotts, and outside of Walt Disney and Hal Roach, the Führeress received a frosty welcome. Out of morbid curiosity, Maria attended one of the screenings. Aside from Dorothy Arzner, she had never seen a female director before.

Watching the Party faithful march through Nuremberg rally grounds with the rigorous geometry of Busby Berkeley chorus lines, Maria was unnerved by her inability to dismiss Riefenstahl as a mere propagandist. What troubled Maria—as much as anything else—was the spectacle of a filmmaker pressing her undeniably singular vision into the service of a picture that denied the singularity of individual experience. Riefenstahl marshaled hundreds of thousands of participants without betraying the slightest curiosity in human beings. The resulting picture was a feat of engineering, as precise and soulless as a munitions production line. No wonder German consuls screened the picture for foreign governments to weaken resistance in the run-up to invasion. Maria had left the theater overrun and defeated.

Now, in the Film Library's projection room, *Triumph of the Will* again transfused its dread into the pit of Maria's stomach. What were Hollywood's valentines against this opus of domination? How could a film industry historically prohibited from propaganda compete with a film industry created to single-mindedly pursue the goal?

She went to the RCA Victor in the corner. A phonograph with several jolly fellows in lederhosen on the cover sat on the table. She unsleeved the polka record and set it on the turntable. The shellac hissed like something slick tossed on the griddle. Tubas burst through the flared amplifying horn.

She started the movie reel from the beginning but played it at double speed. At this faster tempo the procession of stormtroopers transformed from an invincible army of death into a prancing troupe with only the love of oompah in their hearts. Their legs shot up and down in brisk showgirl strides. They progressed with a sort of spirited unwieldiness, as if attached by strings to the hands of an eager but inexperienced puppeteer. Simply changing the projection speed and musical accompaniment subverted what Riefenstahl needed thirty cameras and a cast of thousands to achieve. Riefenstahl couldn't be outdone, Maria decided, only undone.

"A couple boys from the War Department dropped these off today," Maria said, opening the door to a storage room. "There must be a few hundred hours of German, Italian, and Japanese propaganda reels in here. Watch each one and write scene-by-scene summaries for the unit working on the War Department films. It'll be mind-numbingly, soul-crushingly dull—everyone else whom I offered this commission had the good sense to turn it down—but at forty dollars a week it beats the bread line."

Vincent frowned at the thousands of stacked film canisters. "It hadn't occurred to me that I'd have to submit to a program of fascist indoctrination in Los Angeles," he said.

"Life is full of surprises, isn't it? Rudi Bloch will oversee the Propaganda Unit. You can leave your summaries with his secretary."

"Maria?" he called after her. "Thank you for this."

Someday she would ask Vincent about what her father, in his letters, had been unable or unwilling to tell her, about his life, his suffering, its meaning, her role in it, and what stories he told when he spoke of her. But she was already late for dinner and had to drive across town.

MARIA FOLLOWED THE FAINT GLOW of taped-over taillights through inching traffic. Frazzled cops directed her through intersections where streetcars spidered blindly beneath clanging wires.

Without headlights, streetlamps, or stoplights, cars coasted into one another, and the double-parked wreckage barricaded all but the major east-west arteries. Steam parachuted from popped hoods, sheet metal cymballed in the distance, and the Santa Ana winds carried the industrial tang of burned rubber. *What a fucking mess,* Maria thought. Why would the Japanese bother bombing a city so determined to demolish itself?

At Figueroa, where traffic backed to a standstill, drivers climbed onto the hoods of their cars to stare down the congestion while the KNX broadcast said the police had blocked off 3rd Street to the rubberneckers cruising Little Tokyo.

Crowds prowled through the stalled cars. Waitresses and gas jockeys among the self-deputized vigilantes, bunions in aching work shoes, a whole day on your feet and then moonlighting as patrolmen. Bankers and society ladies with beachfront property depreciating as the threat of invasion rose, a good investment, they'd been assured, with patios opening onto the Pacific, your nearest westerly neighbor an ocean away. Reformed reprobates flexing the muscle memory for trouble. All of them whipped into a frenzy, descending on storefronts flouting the blackout, smashing neon tubes advertising tiki drinks and fresh coffee, flipping off lobby lights with swung baseball bats, these grease-streaked mechanics and crew-cut office clerks and housewives who had six shapes of Jell-O mold and the most wonderful bean casserole recipe.

Ahead they thronged the base of City Hall. A lone light had been left burning on the twentieth floor. Maria could feel the primal frustration course through the mob as they glared at those taunting heights. How a sixty-watt bulb a few hundred feet up illuminates the vanity of your hopes, the futility of your efforts. Bright as a lighthouse guiding distant ships to your shores.

Lobbed soda bottles and stones shot out of the crowd, bending in useless arcs toward the City Hall tower. Then some genius pulled out a revolver. The concrete façades multiplied the single gunshot to an echoing fusillade. Arrowheads of glass rained on the crowd. The lightbulb kept burning.

The fleeing cavalcade made Maria think of old country worship, the processions of flagellants, the spirit purified through rites of bodily anguish, or the body brutalized to match the ruined dimensions of the soul. She gripped the steering wheel. She turned left.

On a typical Thursday Broadway's blade signs shed thrumming color, but now the city's busiest street was lit only by cigarettes. Stupefied by darkness, pedestrians lurched in outstretched zombie shuffles. Now and then two people walked right into each other's arms, and before pulling away, apologizing, and returning to the unlit anonymity, they might laugh, or swear, or stare in bewitchment at having walked through miles of night to find themselves in a stranger's embrace.

A blind man blithely tapped his cane, nothing in his world amiss.

No one could figure out how to kill the power to the billboard atop the tourist board's office. Its blazing neon lights proclaimed *Welcome to Los Angeles.*

Maria drove north through Chinatown, crooking east on Broadway where the light of votive candles writhed in the stained glass of St. Peter's, the saints robed in lurid reds and violets, the votives still burning because even in the blackout the priest would not puff out the prayers his hundreds of Italian congregants had attached to candlewicks that day.

". . . A NOTICE FROM CITY sanitation. There's some kind of intestinal parasite in the tap water. I'm going to bottle and sell it as Dr. Charles Scarborough's patented laxative," Ciccio said. And if there was no market for that, he would peddle it as "fire-retardant water" to Valley homeowners convinced their suburban bungalow was Tojo's next target. He'd read the papers. It was a matter of civic pride to think your town was next. No one wanted to believe themselves unworthy of gruesome aerial death.

"My husband," Mimi said from the kitchen, a two-word verdict, slur, regret.

"I warned her," Lala said. "*Never buy a cat in a bag,* I said. But does she listen?"

"You hear they installed a new air-raid siren at Italian Hall?" Ciccio told Maria at the table. "The Army developed it as a battlefield weapon. It'll pop the enemy's eardrums at a hundred yards."

"What good's an air-raid siren you can only hear once?" Maria asked.

"What?"

Pep sawed thick hunks of semolina bread. All the lights in the house were out. Annunziata ladled vegetable stew into bowls and Maria felt tied into her body, into this room, into the world itself by those fragrant twists of steam.

They gathered at the table, these incorporeal voices blurting through blackness.

Annunziata said, "You hear the two Esposito boys got called up?"

Mimi was aghast. "They drafted the younger one? With his eyes?"

Maria didn't recall the younger Esposito boy ever wearing glasses. "What's wrong with his eyes?"

"He has a hypocrite's eyes."

"I don't think that qualifies him for a medical deferment."

"At least they won't take the older Esposito boy," Lala said. "He's a cuckold."

Ciccio refilled his wineglass. "The recruiters won't know that."

"Of course they will. He's famous for it. Ask anyone."

"I'm pretty sure the War Department doesn't keep tabs on that sort of thing," Maria agreed.

Pep slurped soup. "Someone has to tell Roosevelt what the hell is going on."

Mimi sighed. "They expect to win a war with an army of hypocrites and cuckolds? I'll have to go to church twice this Sunday. Twice."

"God doesn't like you," Pep said. "Never has. Me? I don't blame Him."

"Oh, that's rich, coming from the likes of you," Mimi said. "Unlike some of us, *I* actually read the Holy Bible."

"Sure, but only the bit about the Sodomites." Lala crossed herself. "To put Ciccio in the mood. I can hear them through the wall. First, it's a few passages of fire and brimstone and then . . ."

"And then . . ."

". . . like a couple Irish jackrabbits." Lala crossed herself again.

"They're not young." Broth drizzled from Pep's dunked bread. "How I worry for their hips."

Annunziata's chair creaked. "If you want to know the truth, I'm surprised a bit of brimstone hasn't come through *our* roof."

"We're roofed in Johns Manville asbestos shingles," Ciccio said with pride. "Thirty-year warranty *including* acts of God."

"Oh, sure. And you're an expert."

Ciccio's spoon clinked on his bowl. "You want to hear about an act of God? Last month I lost seven games of tic-tac-toe to a chicken. One game, sure, okay, I'll give you that. Two or three even. But seven in a row? No, signora. No, no, no. *That* is something else. *That* is a miracle chicken."

"Your husband, Mimi," Lala said. "Outwitted by poultry."

Maria laughed, a little surprised that on the evening she became an enemy alien she would find such comfort in a blacked-out bungalow teeming with the lunatics and doom mongers that comprised her family. Her voice slipped into Italian and Calabrian dialect like a stylus dropping on a record's groove, and at home in her first languages, she no longer felt at a loss for words.

Through the window, she saw the silhouettes of neighbors sitting down in darkness to their own stews made from uprooted vegetable gardens. Her great-aunts' black dresses blew wraithlike on the backyard laundry line.

Wordlessly, she went into the yard, collected the dresses from the line, and came back inside. She climbed on a chair and arranged them over the kitchen windows.

"Blackout curtains," she said, but she didn't turn on the light, not just yet.

MARIA KNOCKED ON HER MOTHER's bedroom door to ask if she could borrow a nightgown. Annunziata was on her knees, pulling stacks of newspapers from the closet.

"What's all this?"

"Just clearing out some old junk," Annunziata said, standing to block her daughter's path. She was embarrassed by the heap of newspapers, how pitiful it must look, this shrine to her estranged daughter.

Maria sifted through brittle editions of *L'Italo Americano*. "You kept Mercury's reviews."

"Only the good ones."

"Mamma, I hate to break it to you, but our publicity department wrote all these," Maria admitted. "We include pre-composed reviews in our publicity pressbooks for exhibitors to place with their local papers. The local theater gets free publicity and the local paper gets a film review section without having to pay a critic."

"I'd wondered why they were so positive."

Through the wall Maria could hear Ciccio give randy readings from the book of Genesis. There must have been sixty or seventy copies of *L'Italo Americano* heaped on the floor. "What inspired you to clean out your closet tonight?"

A few gray hairs fell over her mother's face as she massaged her temples. "Because the FBI's been all over Lincoln Heights today," her mother said. "They move in pairs, you know. Like heathen Morons."

"Mormons."

"Whomever. They arrested veterans of the Great War, Italian teachers, the publisher of *La Parola*. I watched them arrest poor Signor Greco, the accountant. He tells the G-men that he *fled* Italy, that the Blackshirts chased him out. I couldn't believe my eyes. I really couldn't. In Italy, the antifascists are arrested for crimes they didn't commit, and here? Here they're arrested for crimes they're the victims of."

Her mother exhaled and closed her eyes.

"When I was at the market, Signor Esposito said the editor of *L'Italo Americano* destroyed his entire archive, all the way back to the first issue in 1908. Piled every last paper into an alley and set them on fire. It must've taken hours to burn it all."

"Jesus," Maria said.

"Don't take the Lord's name in vain."

"Why would he do that?"

"I'd have thought you of all people would know the answer."

Maria was reminded why she so rarely returned home: no matter what she did, no matter whom she became, within these walls she remained the twelve-year-old whose recklessness had cost her mother so much.

"The FBI wanted to use the *L'Italo Americano* archive to create arrest lists of prominent Italians." Annunziata opened a paper to an eight-hundred-word puff piece on her daughter, a credit to her people. "Any important or influential Italian in Los Angeles has appeared in these pages. The editor, he wants to protect his community. He wants to protect the people he loves. What's more understandable than that?"

Every daily edition since 1908: thirty-three years of obituaries and marriage announcements and advertisements and headlines. It was more than a newspaper archive. It was the daily history of the small corner of Los Angeles her family had tried to make their home. Maria wondered what irrecoverable testimony had been lost in the flames.

"It's not understandable," Maria said. "It's unforgivable."

Her mother gazed at her, unrecognizable with tenderness. "I once thought so too. Now, tell me about your life? Are you married?"

Maria was surprised her mother had waited so long to ask. "No, not married, but there is someone."

"Please tell me he's not Sicilian. I don't think I could take the shame."

"No, he's not Sicilian."

"Then what is he? He's not Apulian, is he? I couldn't take the shame, Maria, I really couldn't."

Maria shook her head. She was enjoying seeing her mother again and didn't want to contaminate their reunion with the xenophobia that was her mother's sole gesture to assimilating into American culture.

"What's his name, then?"

"Eddie. Edward."

"Edward," her mother repeated, skeptical of the name's Protestant connotations. "He treats you right?"

"He treats me real well, Mamma. What about you?"

"What about me?"

"You have any secret admirers?"

Her mother emitted a single, incredulous laugh. "I'm too old for that."

"Are you?"

"As a matter of fact, I'm ancient."

"Mimi wasn't too old."

"Yeah, and she got herself a real catch, didn't she? A snake-oil man with three teeth and a hearse."

"You miss Papà, don't you?"

"Your father is the worst thing that's ever happened to me," her mother said. "He also happens to be the love of my life."

"He's gone, Mamma. Whether he's alive or dead, he's gone."

"I wish he was, my dear," her mother said, rising to her feet and kissing Maria's forehead.

"Tell me about when you ran him down with your bicycle."

"What a day that was," her mother said, staring past Maria and into a vista of happier times. "Play your cards right and I'll tell you the next time you come over."

MARIA ROSE EARLY THE NEXT morning to buy the final edition of *L'Italo Americano*. It gave top billing to the war declaration, but Maria flipped to the details on the previous night's blackout. She read about antiaircraft guns opening fire on phantom airplanes, the shrapnel and dud ordnance that crashed through bungalow roofs in Long Beach and Santa Monica. The casualties of hundreds of automobile accidents inundated hospitals across the county. In Hermosa Beach a soldier shot a woman for refusing to stop when he waved her down. Her widower said, "We thought he was a hitchhiker." There were stories encouraging you to buy war bonds, donate blood, organize scrap drives, stand for the national anthem, and most importantly, register as an enemy alien. That declaring yourself an enemy was posited as patriotism was an irony Maria did not wish to explore.

Annunziata took the morning's paper from Maria and added it

to the dozens they had hauled from the bungalow and piled in the backyard. The unformed heap sprawled across the dirt where she had uprooted her vegetables the previous day. If the editor of *L'Italo Americano* was willing to destroy his archive, Annunziata could destroy hers. It was the least she could do to protect the daughter she loved so imperfectly.

Annunziata's hands shook as she fumbled with the matches. The first match snapped in half. The second sparked but wouldn't light. She didn't understand why her hands were shaking, why Maria was just standing there like an idiot. She struck the match again and again as despair reared up and overwhelmed her. For so long now she skated across the airy hollow where something precious had been pitted. That precious something was the hope she would ever understand her life. She was tired of pretending she wasn't falling apart.

"Help me," she said.

Maria was stunned. What had those two words cost her mother? Maria would have never imagined two whispered syllables could carry so much pain. She would have never imagined this indomitable woman who survived earthquake and exile would be broken by a matchstick.

"Mamma, I—"

"Just help me."

Maria took the match from her mother's shaking hands, lit it, and passed it back. Annunziata dropped to one knee and ran a hand over the newspapers as if they were the only valuables she hadn't sold, lost, or left behind, as if they were the very last of her earthly treasure.

"You don't need these anymore," Maria said.

"Don't I?"

"You have me."

Shaking her head as if this was the biggest whopper Maria had ever tried to pull over on her, Annunziata brought the match to the base of the heap, hanging little flames on the edge of the broadsheets. The pages curled and withered. Sparks hissed past their ears, and it was uncanny, wasn't it, the volume of smoke a single daily paper contains, this pillar sprouting from a contracting pedestal of ash. The wind peeled pages from the pyre. Soon the air around them beat with incinerating broadsheets. The papers trailed tailfeathers of fire high above the yard where Maria and Annunziata stood with their heads tilted back and their eyes pointed skyward, as they once had on New Year's Eves in Rome, when Giuseppe launched fireworks from the roof of their apartment building. He would let Maria strike the match and the flame would race up the fuse with the crackle of cooking oil. The lurching spray of sparks singed the peach fuzz from the back of her hand. Watching the firework slip skyward atop a wind-socking flame, Maria would lean back against her parents' legs, certain nothing in their lives could ever go wrong.

Now, as the ashes of a few hundred newspapers drifted down across the yard, Maria wrapped her arm around her mother's shoulder.

A square meter of burned grass was all that remained of the mountain of newspapers, and looking at it, Annunziata was amazed the load she and her daughter carried between them had become ribbons of weightless smoke. When the fire burned down, Mimi came out and set potatoes to bake in the coals.

In the weeks ahead, life as an enemy alien takes shape. Fingerprinted and interviewed, subjected to dawn-to-dusk curfews, banned from coastal exclusion zones, provisioned with the enemy alien card you must carry at all times, prohibited from traveling more than five miles from your place of residence. Because Lincoln Heights lies seven miles from the Montclair, you cannot return to your childhood home. This morning, among the wingbeats of burning paper, is the last time, for a long time.

Cameras, radios, flashlights: all become contraband surrendered at the nearest police precinct. Vincent's final portrait is the passport photograph you need for your enemy alien registration card. Of all the passport photographs he's taken—all those torn in half and joined together, all those named, dated, and collected in the black album he hides in his office desk, in case the police search his room at the Montclair—this is the first used to restrict movement. Everywhere he goes, the borders tighten around him; one day, he fears, they will contract to a point too small to stand on, and only his claustrophobia will outlive him. After printing the passport photograph, he relinquishes his camera to the Enemy Aliens Property Board. He feels he is giving up his eyes. The clerk sets down a peanut butter and pickle sandwich, writes out a receipt, and tells him to have a good afternoon now.

Your hair will smell of smoke for days, and when the police searching the bungalow ask about the ashes in the yard, your mother will say, "It was my garden."

4

ON NEW YEAR'S DAY 1942, ANNA WEBER BROUGHT HER TORTILLA soup—a watery revival of the previous day's ghastly chili—to the exiles' table. Over the last three weeks, she had watched the commissary depopulate as military enlistment consumed the studio's workforce. By necessity, this meant those remaining received promotions, including Anna. She supposed she should feel grateful to have been bumped up to overseeing the Propaganda Unit with Rudi, but gratitude was a state of mind she resisted the more adamantly it was expected. For a European émigré with a German accent, the presumption of gratitude was second only to the presumption of guilt. Rather shameless given that the asylum application process consisted of making her feel unwelcome and unworthy at every stage.

These thoughts swarmed at the edge of her mind as she took a seat beside Rudi, who was pretending to listen to Raymond Benoit's story of his flight from France.

". . . still in Paris when Ned cabled me," Raymond Benoit droned on. No one really knew what a French philosopher was doing at Mercury, but he only made $50 a week and was thus too trivial to even gossip about. "Ned heard from a mutual friend that I'd been unable to secure an entry permit, and he promised to arrange for a work visa and a job at Mercury. I felt obliged to tell him I was a philosopher with no experience in the picture business. Do you know what he said? He said that paying someone to think would be a welcome novelty."

Raymond chuckled lightly, as if he hadn't retold this story every week for months. If he couldn't exorcise his demons, perhaps he could bore them to death. Anna wanted no part in confessional sessions that diminished the experience of suffering by insisting it had meaning.

". . . Ned arranged first-class passage and I sailed out of Marseilles a week before the German invasion."

"You must feel grateful," Anna said tartly.

"Immensely," Raymond said as he fortified himself against a scoop of commissary casserole with a precautionary antacid.

Across the table, Vincent Cortese, the unit researcher, was chatting with Polina Rabina, a Russian Jewish costume designer who amplified her bland personality with loud blouses that did not inspire confidence in her professional judgment.

Rudi tapped his coffee mug on the table and called to order the Mercury Propaganda Unit. "As you know," Rudi said, "Art has entrusted us with—"

"He knows we're enemy aliens, doesn't he?" asked a film editor from Bremen.

"Believe it or not, our . . . tenuous legal status is why we've received the job. Art knows he won't lose us to the draft."

Rudi distributed a memo outlining the topics of their various films, which covered everything from potted histories of Germany, Japan, and Italy to lessons on proper sexual hygiene.

"Wherever possible," Vincent read aloud, *"we will highlight not only the values we fight against but those we fight for: due process, equal protection, civil liberties . . ."* He was halfway through the list when he seemed to realize the filmmakers were excluded from the universal rights their pictures promoted.

"Historical accuracy has never before impeded the fantasies this place produces," Anna told him. "Why should it now?"

Aside from Raymond, who would volunteer for any task in a

doomed bid for relevance, Vincent Cortese was the most inconsequential person assigned to the unit. But as the unit researcher, he had access to hundreds of hours of German propaganda. This fact was of great significance to Anna. She decided she would approach him today.

"For the most part," Rudi continued, "we'll make these films in the cutting room rather than the soundstage, but we'll also use a number of impressive miniatures of Berlin that Anna has built in her spare time over the last few years. Anna, would you lead the way?"

The Mill was where Mercury's most questionable ideas came to misbegotten fruition. Set blueprints for upcoming productions hung from pushpins across the far walls. Racked lumber awaited carpenters who worked with such economy it was said they could carve a regulation-length billiard cue from a toothpick. Across hundreds of feet of shelving were tins of putty, acetone, acrylics, mortician's wax. Featherweight cinder blocks fashioned from upholstered felt. Taxidermal squirrels and armadillos ready to carpet highway shoulders. Chalk nubs slingshot to produce zinging bullet ricochets. Cobwebs conjured by reeling rubber cement through a desk fan. And, of course, the endlessly versatile rubber condom, brimming with chicken blood and exploded by squib in the gunned-down-in-the-gutter climax to *My Overcoat Is a Casket,* or swollen with water and dropped from the ceiling to become those wondrous, wobbly raindrops in *The Lives of Ants*.

The Mill had already been converted to serve the war effort. The Army Quartermaster Corps had raided the studio's prop department for its real rifles, and the carpentry staff busily manufactured wooden replicas. To camouflage its Santa Monica aviation plant from aerial attack, Douglas Aircraft enlisted Mercury's set designers to erect a residential neighborhood of false fronts on the roofs of its factories and hangars. A hundred feet in the air actors culled from Central Casting lived in a floating subdivision. Emerging from plywood houses, the actors watered shrubs leafed in dyed chicken feathers, walked dogs past smokestacks disguised as telephone poles, watched inflatable cars move by wires across painted-on streets. There was a functioning postal system, a morning milkman, kids playing catch, and housewives laying laundry on the line. Life on the roofs of Douglas Aircraft was as idyllic as a Norman Rockwell painting. The residents of those placid heights were perhaps the only Angelenos untouched by the war.

A tortoise bedazzled in rhinestones lumbered toward Anna. She unwrapped the side salad she ordered from the commissary and waited for the tortoise to tuck in before moving on.

"Over here." Anna led them to the far end of the room where a scale model of a Berlin neighborhood rose in miniature across several steel-framed tables. The model represented perhaps a square kilometer of the city circa 1928, from the grand hotels and department stores in Potsdamer Platz to the tenement slums of Kreuzberg.

Why this urge to re-create the places she'd fled? The deeper into banishment Anna journeyed, the more vivid her recall of the city she left behind. She felt lofted into an omniscient altitude from which she peered down upon streetcars and cafés and slums. Everywhere human bustle blighted her model's architectural precision—the prim hausfrau averting her eyes from a legless veteran, the brawl between brownshirts and Red Front Fighters spilling from a biergarten, a couple policemen fishing a body from the Landwehr Canal—imbuing the miniature with the festive depravity of Hieronymus Bosch's hell.

"It's good," Polina conceded. "It's very good."

Stroking his push-broom mustache, Raymond searched the streets south of the Anhalter Bahnhof until he found the restaurant he'd frequented every Tuesday during his student years. "It's magnificent, Anna."

Anna accepted their compliments as statements of obvious fact. Ribbons of smoke unwound from her cigarette and marbled her pale complexion. Her hair was the color of burnt wick, streaked in the silver light of the overhanging lamp and a few dozen strands of undyed grays. She felt no pride in her accomplishment, only a profound sadness that she could only return to Berlin in a few square meters of model miniature. Nor did she take pleasure in the admiration of her colleagues, whom she regarded as failures, frauds, and fools. Despite her chosen medium, Anna Weber had no doubt she was a giant.

The wires holding B-17s, sponged with blue paint, blended into the matte sky.

The overhead lights suffused the spun-glass clouds with warmth.

Anna reached up, flicked one of the bombers, and its shadow careened over Kreuzberg.

She turned to the six other émigrés. "We shall begin, yes?" she said.

Because the War Production Board was putting a $5,000 per picture cap on all new sets, the Propaganda Unit would use in-camera effects to integrate individual actors into miniatures. If the strategy succeeded, it could be replicated in Mercury's dramatic films. The most promising effect had been devised by Eugen Schüfftan, one of Anna's colleagues at the Berlin studio UFA, to combine crowd scenes with the models she made for *Metropolis,* using a series of mirrors and transparent panes.

By late afternoon, Anna had finished working on the mirror, Raymond had mounted it on a Century stand, and Vincent had positioned it beside the model. Everyone still looked depleted from last night's New Year's Eve boozing and Rudi suggested they break for the day. As the rest of the unit filed to the door, Anna asked Vincent if he would stay to help her clean up. Rudi told her he would see her at home that night.

"He's oddly less tyrannical now that he actually has a bit of power," Vincent observed as Rudi shuffled down the hall.

"Aside from his delusions of grandeur, he's harmless. He just thinks he was a St. Bernard."

"I'm sorry?"

"It's a German émigré joke. Two dachshunds meet at the corner of Hollywood and Highland. One looks to the other and says, 'You must have been a St. Bernard too.'"

Vincent smiled. "Were you two married?"

"Multiple times, though strangely never to each other. I've known Rudi for—God, about two decades now. It's both far too long and not nearly long enough."

"I know that feeling."

"You can't begin to imagine that feeling, I assure you. I can remember what Rudi looked like when he was thirty pounds lighter, and he can remember how my legs looked when *I* was your age. I suppose we return to each other's beds with the same exhilaration murderers must feel when returning to the scenes of their crimes."

"And they say romance is dead," Vincent said, picking up a broom to sweep the floor.

"How have the indoctrination sessions been going?"

"Down in the Film Library?"

"Yes," she said, hoping to receive what she wanted without revealing what it was.

"Goose-stepping and saluting with interludes of the same three sweaty men spitting at microphones. The morally repugnant has never been so drearily monotonous. And I have another three hundred hours of this crap to go." To Anna's annoyance, he changed the subject. Looking at the mirror, he said, "How did you and Schüfftan figure this process out?"

"We're German, obviously."

"Did you like working for Lang?"

"Lang hired me at UFA and on principle I cannot speak ill of him. However, I will speak ill of God and say that He has a Fritz Lang complex. I joke," she said solemnly. "No one had ever seen anything like *Metropolis*. Yes, the story is shit, but visually it is sublime. I'm honored to have had a hand in it, even if it was one of Hitler's favorite movies."

"Really?"

"All those marching automatons, I suppose. One megalomaniac's cautionary tale is another's call to action."

Anna had stepped to the far side of the mirror to double-check the fastener.

"Take a few steps back." Vincent peered through the camera's viewfinder. It was the first camera he'd touched since surrendering his to the Enemy Aliens Property Board. Anna shrank in the mirror until she was the size of the other tiny figures on the Berlin street. "A few more. There."

Monocled in the viewfinder, he saw Anna standing directly beneath 54 Oranienstrasse, a ramshackle tenement block pasted with stamp-sized posters advertising a Communist Party march and a competition for Kreuzberg's best legs. If you limit yourself to what you see in the viewfinder it's as if she never left, as if she's back on that Berlin corner, listening to bombers break open the sky.

"Well?" she asked. "How do I look?"

"Like a St. Bernard."

AS A CHILD ANNA WEBER lived at 54 Oranienstrasse #8, but strike that, Anna did not have a childhood. Or at least her childhood had gone unacknowledged by the adults in 54 Oranienstrasse #8. Devoted members at various times of the Spartacus League, the German Communist Party, and the Red Front Fighters, Comrades Jannik and Elena Weber did not allow the responsibilities of parenthood to interfere with the obligations of politics. Her father was a stout man with gray eyes and a grizzled goatee modeled on Lenin's. Her mother corresponded with Rosa Luxemburg, organized lectures at Pharus Hall, and translated Mayakovsky into German. Both possessed the intellectual hubris and moral adaptability revolution requires. That neither had ever visited Lenin's Russia did not prevent them from correcting the impressions of the Russian émigrés who had escaped it. They evangelized for atheism with a mercilessness Torquemada would have admired. They ran a Marxist press later requisitioned to print billion-mark notes at the height of hyperinflation, an irony from which her father never fully recovered. In the hothouse of revolution that overtook the drafty one-room flat in Kreuzberg, child-rearing was dismissed as a bourgeois preoccupation. Only later did it occur to Anna that her parents were too ill-equipped to raise her, and thus dedicated themselves to an exercise where failure was both foreordained and forgivable: saving the world.

The nearest her father came to abandoning faith in the German Revolution was the day it began in 1918. He watched insurgents fleeing gunfire funnel down the narrow walkway of a public garden because even running for their lives his fellow revolutionaries would not dare disobey signs instructing pedestrians to stay off the Kaiser's grass.

The next morning her father returned to the streets to keep his date with history. Her mother paced the flat, rereading the newspaper accounts of the Kaiser's abdication and glaring at Anna as if *she* were personally hindering the rise of the German proletariat. Finally, she threw on her coat and promised Anna she would return shortly. Anna saw neither of them until they were released from jail six weeks later. The only food in the flat was a pot of horse lung soup and two bruised turnips.

Was it any wonder, then, that the bourgeois conventions her parents dedicated themselves to dismantling became the objects of her fervid craving? When your mother tells you, at the age of nine, that your father hums the opening bars of the "Internationale" while orgasming, what is more seditious, more subversive than the quaint banality of a dollhouse?

Anna's apprenticeship began at H. G. Bergmann's. Across its tall shelves stood open-faced Victorians verisimilitudinous down to tiny teacups in saucers the size of collar buttons. There were Wunderkammern trimmed in lacquered sea turtle shell and filled with exquisitely carved furniture. Dioramas of alpine villages, viewed from aerial aloofness, abounded in human folly. How ordered and understandable the world became when reduced to 1:12 scale.

Herr Bergmann was an ornery, whiskery Prussian who smoked cheap cigars rolled from lettuce soaked in nicotine, a widower who began crafting dollhouses thirty years earlier after losing two daughters to childhood influenza. Like so many miniaturists, Herr Bergmann was uncommonly tall.

Perhaps Anna reminded him of the two daughters whose names he never spoke. Perhaps he recognized his own banishment in the adolescent girl who spent hours peering into little homes where no one lived. He hired her to help around the shop and within two years she was a competent enough craftsman to design and construct dollhouses of her own.

One day, Herr Bergmann called her into his office to tell her that her apprenticeship had run its course. "You are too big for such small houses."

Anna disagreed. Anything larger would overwhelm her.

"You are no dollhouse maker," he insisted, his hazel eyes burnished with a benevolence Anna would only later identify as paternal pride. "You are an architect."

Herr Bergmann helped her get a job as a studio assistant converting the blueprints of a Bauhaus architect into to-scale models. She sat in on workshops in line and color, textiles and ceramics. She admired the pragmatic utopianism of the Bauhaus: that good design was a synthesis of form and function, easily prefabricated and mass producible, that beautifully designed buildings would lead to a more humane society. However, in practice the Bauhaus only reaffirmed that utopias are as corrupted by bias as what they seek to supplant: the school relegated its few female students to weaving workshops, and reserved its architecture courses for men. Berlin was no better. Even in the pre-crash bubble, few of the major architectural firms in Berlin employed women beyond the steno pool, but Anna's talent for miniatures led to a job at UFA, the German film conglomerate.

It was there, in 1923, that she met Hasso Beck, a brash young director with unctuous hair and a fur-collared overcoat who invited her dancing. It wasn't the thrill of seeing herself on the director's arm, nor the satisfaction of feeling chosen over all those aspiring ingénues, but Hasso's malleability, his putty-like capacity to mold himself to the requirements of a situation, that startled her with lust. What was more transgressive than his clear-eyed, coldhearted opportunism? What would her parents have made of this suave arriviste in camel hair and cashmere? Was there any more lethal a repudiation of their values than marrying a director of effete champagne comedies? Hasso was a blunt instrument to break her parents' hearts. That alone made him worthy of hers.

Their son, Kurt, was born the following year. Though the government lurched from crisis to crisis; though political street fights roiled the city; though Hasso was having an affair with a script girl and took as little interest in parenthood as her own father; though she continued to burn her mother's letters unopened, Anna felt more peaceful now than at any point in her life. She told herself her thwarted architectural ambitions were a blessing; few people would have ever entered her houses or apartment blocks, but hundreds of thousands, millions even, had entered her miniature edifices of shadow. Even Hasso's pathological abdication of parental responsibility had a silver lining: Kurt was her son, hers alone, and she would not fail him as her parents had failed her.

"Of course I don't *believe* in any of this blood and soil bullshit," Hasso assured her when he joined the Nazi Party in 1931. Anna didn't doubt his imperviousness to ideology. It was his most attractive quality: he believed in nothing but himself. "It's an insurance policy against democratic failure."

Did Anna rebuke him? Did she warn him that as a student of German literature he should know how Faustian bargains end? Did she remind him that he owed his career to Erich Pommer, UFA's Jewish production boss who glimpsed the ambition in this blond-haired farmer's son? She did not. She said, "I want no part in this," and believed this was a decision she could legitimately make.

After Hindenburg appointed Hitler to the chancellorship in 1933, UFA was folded into the newly established Ministry of Public

Enlightenment and Propaganda. One by one, Anna's colleagues were dismissed: Jews, Communists, Socialists, friends and adversaries, the talented and the mediocre alike.

"They're firing the people responsible for Germany's most reliably profitable export," she said. "It's the thoughtlessness, more than the cruelty, that I can't understand."

Hasso freshened his drink. "Look on the bright side, Anna. There's more room to grow when there's no one above you."

"First-class berths are always available on sinking ships."

Lamplight carouseled in Hasso's beveled tumbler. "Better that than in the sea with the rats. With Goebbels as my patron, I'll be the Reich's Fritz Lang." Hasso's lack of humility vied with his lack of humanity as his personality's overriding feature. "And with me as your patron, Anna, you can be whatever you want."

"I couldn't stand the company."

Hasso let that pass. "Today, I had lunch with a new friend who has been tasked with overseeing construction of the Olympic Village for the summer games. He tells me he's in desperate need of architects. Isn't that what you've wanted? The opportunity to see your miniatures become life-sized?"

Anna sat very still. "In exchange for what?"

"Nothing, just a bit of paperwork. Your signature on a dotted line."

"What kind of paperwork?"

"I'd like you to join the Party. You are my wife. It would reflect well on me."

Anna knew what Hasso was offering and what it would cost her. She did not know that the soul she refused to sign away would soon feel worthless to her. Nor did she know that in the months and years to come, she would look back at this moment of indisputable righteousness as the great error of her life.

"No," she said.

She left the studio, the mansion in Charlottenburg, and the marriage. Several months later she was seated in the Romanisches Café across from Walter Gelb, a short, curly-haired Jewish architect she knew from the Bauhaus. Walter owned a stake in a building firm and his gentile partners decided that a Jewish stakeholder would doom their bids on government contracts. "They want to buy me out but their best offer is a third of what my share is worth in a firm whose reputation rests on *my* work," he said. "And a tenth of what it will be worth if the contracts come through on these Nuremberg commissions."

When Anna suggested it might be safer to accept his partners' offer and move abroad, Walter snapped, "It's easy for you to say that, isn't it? You haven't built anything." Walter knew all about her work at UFA, her early years at H. G. Bergmann's, so was he saying that the twee spaces of the feminized and diminished lacked the integrity of the fully built? Or that her decision to relinquish her career at UFA was so without loss that she couldn't grasp his? That even her failures did not bear comparison to his? She might have pointed out that, though she had always been a more talented architect, the firm ending Walter's career had denied her the opportunity to begin hers. And when she realized she was sitting across the table from a Jewish socialist and felt that *he* was persecuting *her,* her shame made it impossible to reject his proposal.

"My lawyer says I can transfer my holdings to an Aryan spouse," Walter explained. "Strictly a business relationship. I can park my stake in the firm in your name until this madness passes. And you'll no longer need to depend on Hasso for alimony."

When Hasso learned of this, he sued to reopen the custody agreement on the grounds of maternal neglect. That she had remarried a Jew made the hearing a formality, and though Hasso had never demonstrated any interest in Kurt, though he had previously relinquished all rights to Anna without contest and had seen the boy only twice in the last year, he received full custody while Anna's lawyer failed to secure her so much as a monthly visitation.

The morning Kurt disappeared into the backseat of Hasso's chauffeured Opel was one of those autumn days when the Tiergarten quivers in red and gold. Anna walked through the park, then east along the Landwehr Canal toward Kreuzberg. She hadn't seen her parents in over ten years. Estranging herself from them had been among her greatest accomplishments and now she stood outside their apartment block, the rust-colored courtyard canopied in drying laundry, the dogs devouring offal from a tin pail. Did reenacting the failures of her parents prepare her to forgive them? No, she failed Kurt more catastrophically than her parents had ever failed her and she forgave them nothing. Then what led her here? Why was she climbing the bowed wooden stairs to visit the two people she loathed more even than Hasso? Perhaps she wanted to tell someone she had lost her only child and they knew how that went. Perhaps she had taught them long ago what she now needed to learn.

A stranger in a disheveled bathrobe answered at #8 when she knocked. The man had no idea where the previous tenants had gone. Anna went down the hall to that incorrigible busybody Frau Dressler. "Do you have their new address?" Anna asked. With a lively smirk, Frau Dressler said, "The communists? Dachau."

Anna returned home, and for two days, she lay in Kurt's little bed, inhaling the boyish odor. The tortoise bedazzled in rhinestones lumbered brightly through the empty room. She and Kurt had decorated the tortoise shell a few months earlier. Hasso hadn't let the boy take the tortoise with him. Anna promised Kurt she would take care of it.

Kurt lived in Hasso's Wannsee mansion, a beautiful six-bedroom villa appropriated from a Jewish family. Anna walked past once but couldn't bring herself to peer through the barred gate. However, Anna still saw Kurt. All of Germany did. Hasso cast the child in propaganda pictures that brought Goebbels to his feet in applause. Anna lined up at the box office, bought a ticket, and in a theater crowded in Hitler Youth, struggled to breathe. Her Kurt, who once gaped up at the long-lashed eyes of zoo giraffes, now towered on two-story cinema screens.

It isn't him, she told herself. He's only acting. But if that wasn't her Kurt then why did she attend multiple screenings a day? If he was only acting then why her certainty that the role he performed was the person he was becoming?

In 1938, Walter Gelb was arrested and sent to Flossenbürg, the Bavarian concentration camp Himmler established to quarry granite for Albert Speer's architectural projects. Within the year he was dead. Anna had to leave. She went to the offices of Walter's firm, prepared to sell his stake.

"We were sorry to hear about Walter. He deserved much better." It was as close as his partners came to an admission of guilt.

Their offer to Anna was a fraction of the offer they had made Walter, despite the firm tripling its revenues in the intervening years. Not that it mattered. Legislation prohibiting émigrés from taking more than a few marks from Germany made it all but impossible to move wealth across borders. Checkpoint guards ransacked suitcases, strip-searched travelers, ensured refugees left with nothing but their lives.

"I want the payment made in diamonds."

"You're in luck," the partners said. "It's a buyer's market for diamonds."

When Anna reached the French frontier two weeks later, German border guards searched her belongings with a zeal that rendered half her wardrobe unwearable. Only one, hardly more than a boy himself, paid the slightest attention to the tortoise shell festooned in rhinestones. Strange people, these Berliners, the guard thought, handing the tortoise back and glancing to the next refugee in line. Anna didn't pry the diamonds from the tortoise until she reached Marseilles.

For months she lived in consulate waiting rooms, train station terminals, and dingy hotels. Her passport became a slender Book of Babel, inscribed with restrictions, expirations, and denials in five alphabets. She completed affidavits attesting to her solvency, produced guarantors in the form of second cousins in Washington Heights, endured interviews with American consular officers dubious of her value.

When her second cousins in Washington Heights secured her visa, she wanted to write *stet* beside her name. Her relief was without thankfulness. She wouldn't thank a country that made her beg for her life, nor one whose parsimoniousness ensured that many with whom she traversed the archipelago of consulate waiting rooms would one day have their identities reduced to numbers on the forearm.

On a cold spring morning in 1940, she stood at the stern of an ocean liner and watched the waterfront compress to a beige blip of coastline slipping off the edge of the planet. Milky coils of seawater churned on the propellers. The wind unraveled warmth from her neck like a long scarf. Out here in regions of the ocean represented by kraken and hydras on medieval maps, this hinterland of creation where reason ends and monsters reign, Anna felt gripped by the idea that if she could only rebuild Berlin, in all its detail and depth, she would find her son waiting there for her to come home.

SHE REVEALED ONLY A SMALL part of this to Vincent on New Year's Day and her reasons for telling him even that much were entirely practical: she wanted to see Kurt, if only in the impounded German propaganda pictures Vincent had access to.

Vincent was unnerved by her request. Then he thought of what he owed Concetta, and said, "Yes, of course. We can look now."

They stopped short outside and stared at the fleecy whiteness layering the streets and rooftops. Fat flurries wandered through the air and clumped on Anna's eyelashes. For a moment, she was sure she had wandered into an outdoor winter set, and she marveled at the production values, how real it all looked.

"What are they shooting here?" she asked.

"I don't think they're shooting anything."

Concerned that Axis spies would use weather reports to plan aerial attacks, the government had banned public meteorological forecasts. No one could have known that on New Year's Day 1942, for the first time in a decade, it would snow in Los Angeles.

Watching flurries pile high in the palm trees, Anna experienced a quiet moment of gratitude.

THE FALSE FRONT

1

FROM THE MOMENT EDDIE READ THE SCRIPT FOR *TELL 'EM IN TOKYO*—AN espionage drama in which he starred as a nefarious Japanese spymaster—he knew he would regret accepting the role. He knew with equal certainty he would not turn it down. The contract was $2000/ week. More than enough to buy back later the scruples he pawned now.

But as production ramped up in January, he grew increasingly uneasy with the role. His character existed as little more than a constellation of crudely joined stereotypes and paranoid fantasies. How could he bring to life a part written to remain lifeless? The director rebuffed his efforts to invest the caricature with character. "You weren't hired to act," the director told him bluntly. "You were hired to be hated."

Eddie asked Maria—who had taken a supervisory role over Mercury's dramatic production slate while Artie focused on War Department propaganda—to intercede with the director. Perhaps he had been too confrontational, or perhaps Maria, overworked and underappreciated, was tired of tending to the professional problems of the men in her life. She suggested that nepotism had limits, that he could sort this out himself. He suggested that she cared about Mercury's bottom line more than his welfare. She reminded him that he was earning roughly fifteen times his market value *because* he meant more to her than the studio's bottom line. He felt belittled; she felt taken for granted; they slept in different beds.

It wasn't until after *Tell 'Em in Tokyo* finished shooting in mid-February that the static between them began to clear, and on February 24, 1942, they attended the costume party the Feldman brothers were throwing to celebrate Mercury's twentieth birthday.

In a satin-lined cape and plaster mask, Eddie made a decent Phantom of the Opera. Maria, however, upstaged him. Bewigged in a headdress that was part Nefertiti, part thunderbolt, with flared eyebrows shooting toward her temples, she was a dead ringer for Elsa Lanchester's Bride of Frankenstein. It took her an hour to paint the complex stitching suturing her head to her neck. When Eddie tried to kiss her, she threatened to kill him. He watched her paint Leg Silque Liquid Stockings on her shins. Now that silk and nylon hosiery had been sacrificed to the war effort, the market for painted-on stockings was surging.

"Let me get the back of your legs," Eddie said. She looked at him skeptically. "What? You might miss a spot."

Eddie brought the brush to the back of her calves. He was of the opinion that, whatever its merits, the peeling off of silk hosiery didn't hold a candle to the painting on of Leg Silque. He painted the liquid stockings on in long brushstrokes, blowing on the wet paint until it hardened to a caramel-colored varnish. From more than six inches away, you wouldn't know Maria wasn't wearing silk. The brush licked the soft divot between the tendons on the back of her knees, and she leaned into him as he slowly pulled the bristles up her thigh. To draw on the stocking seam, he pressed a yardstick to the back of her legs. He dragged an eyebrow pencil along the yardstick to ensure a straight, steady line. She reached around, grabbed a fistful of his hair, and as her grip tightened, the drawn-on seam veered off course. He dropped the eyebrow pencil, slipped his hand between her legs, and, mindful of Maria's death threat, took care not to smear her makeup as he kissed her.

It was another forty-five minutes before they finally left the Montclair and walked through the cool February evening to Eddie's car. Eddie was pleased to note his month-old Cadillac still smelled of fresh car when he unfolded the droptop to accommodate Maria's wig. To discourage the tire theft that ran rampant since rationing began, the dealer had seared Eddie's initials into the rubber with a branding iron.

He turned the key in the ignition and listened to the engine's pent-up velocity purr through its valves and shafts. Eddie Lu, Cadillac owner. He couldn't get his mind around it, any of it. The swiftness with which his personal, professional, and civic circumstances had shifted since the outbreak of war still unsettled Eddie. The Chinese Nationalists who fought against Japanese occupation for a full decade before Pearl Harbor had become America's most important ally in the Pacific Theater. In radio addresses, politicians took pains to affirm the country's alliance with China, reminding listeners that its people were the war's first victims. *Time* ran a piece titled "How to Tell Your Friends from the Japs." Its suggestions included "most Chinese avoid horn-rimmed spectacles" and "Chinese, not as hairy as Japanese, seldom grow impressive mustaches" and "Japanese are hesitant, nervous in conversation, laugh loudly at the wrong time." It attached the caveat that "even an anthropologist, with calipers and plenty of time to measure heads, noses, shoulders, hips, is sometimes stumped."

Wherever he went, the eyes of amateur phrenologists followed him. He always wore his "I Am a Chinese American" button in public. Except for tonight. Tonight, he pulled his phantom mask over his face, left his button in the car, and offered Maria his arm. A waitress from Vick's Drugstore, accustomed to serving costumed oddities on her daily shift, didn't glance twice as they passed. Eddie tried to remember when in the last two months someone passed him on the street without looking back. If he was less conspicuous inside a monster's mask, it said more about the faces he blended into than the one he hid.

They walked into the commissary, where patriotic bunting gave the party the atmosphere of a jingoism-themed junior prom. On the bandstand, brisk melodies shaped by hot breath burst from trumpets. Backslapping producers with blazing teeth and wobbly jowls traded bons mots. One starlet wore a quivering dress sewn from one-dollar bills; to judge by its scant coverage, she was nearly broke. Another was costumed as the concept of skin.

Maria said, "I seem to have taken the invitation to dress up too literally."

"It looks like Artie's complex has really progressed," Eddie said, staring at the figure in grenadier uniform, red sash, and bicorne hat.

"Oh God. Did he come as Napoleon?"

"Go say bonjour," Eddie said. "I'll get some drinks."

Eddie waited at the bar beside Harold Chandler and Gerald Flann, a pair of bit players who held the unofficial world record for on-screen deaths, having been killed off in over four hundred separate productions. The daily enactment of their demise had left them with a come-what-may serenity and the pale complexion of the posthumous. They were dressed up in combat fatigues.

"You know, I was in the trenches with the German Army in the Great War," Harold was telling Gerald. "Darkest days of my life."

"I didn't know you served in the German Army."

"I was in *All Quiet on the Western Front*. It was hell, Gerald. Absolute hell."

"That might have been a Great War, but the *greatest* war?" Gerald expounded. "Greco-Persian, old boy. Why, I can still remember the speech Leonidas gave us at Thermopylae. Sent a shiver down my spine."

"I don't remember seeing you at Thermopylae, Gerald. You should've said hello."

"I was Slain Spartan #37. You couldn't miss me, Harold. There was a Persian scimitar in my head. Brutal day we had at Thermopylae, wasn't it? They ran out of coffee before noon. But we held the Persians off, didn't we?"

"Every time I pass a Greek diner, Gerald, my heart sings with pride."

Still eavesdropping, Eddie flagged the bartender and ordered two scotch and sodas.

"Slain Spartan #37, now *that,* Harold, was a role worthy of my dramatic range. Not like these travesties I've had to take recently: Bayonetted Redcoat #12, Tomahawked Cavalryman #25, Speared Crusader #6."

"Say, Gerald, now that I consider our service record, I'm beginning to have doubts about joining up with you . . ."

"Our luck's bound to turn, old boy. I can feel it in my bones. Our big break is around the corner." Arm in arm, they raised their glasses to the dead men they had been, and then left to enlist in the US Navy. "I think this war will work out for us, Harold. I really do."

Drinks in hand, Eddie pushed back through the crowd. The thunking heels of lindy-hopping couples dimpled the boozy air. Some weisenheimer made a crack and the offended gasp hissed like a harpoon hitting its mark. Eddie wondered if adults in New York or London felt the need to dress up as their first pet or favorite fruit or whatever just to have a cocktail with other adults. Perhaps requesting that movie people come in character relieved them of fears of their own inauthenticity. Or perhaps it just encouraged guests to pretend they didn't despise one another.

Sigmund Freud was hoping to get Jane Russell on his couch. "It's your mind I'm attracted to," he insisted.

One of the Wall Street bankers watched a guy in a Tarzan leotard teach a chimpanzee to smoke cigars while his colleague made a list of who to fire if Eastern National acquired Mercury.

Across the room, Artie was examining Maria's wig with scholarly interest. "That's a hell of a hairpiece. What's its name?"

"It doesn't have a name."

"Have I taught you nothing?"

Maria considered her options: The Bambina . . . The Beaut . . .

". . . The Boss, boss," she said. "The Boss."

After they downed their drinks, Eddie pulled Maria to the dance floor. This surprised her because even in the movie colony's permissive milieu Eddie was reluctant to advertise their relationship. They didn't kiss or hold hands in public, but if Maria's grandfather had told her stories of lynch mobs descending on the old Chinatown, she'd be wary too. They'd go to the Cocoanut Grove, and maybe toward the end of the evening, when the crowd thinned, he'd take her for a spin among the last lingerers too stinko to see straight, but in public it was always there, the membrane history interposed between them.

The big band started up on a groggy number and Eddie drew Maria into his arms.

"My girl," he said, and behind the phantom mask he was smiling. Maria leaned up and kissed him. The mask's plaster lips were chapped and chalky. The painted gypsum flaking into her mouth dissolved on her tongue and caulked her molars. Maria didn't care that she was mussing up her makeup. She had never felt more erotically dazzled than when kissing a fifty-cent plaster mask on a crowded dance floor while Eddie traced the seam he had drawn on the back of her thigh.

They left early to get Maria home before the enemy alien curfew but carried on dancing in the Montclair lobby. Exhausted by sex and alcohol, they collapsed into bed at two in the morning. It would have been a perfect evening had the mournful wail of air-raid sirens not awoken them an hour later. Eddie jolted out of bed and stumbled to the window. Searchlights swiped the clouds. The neon pulses of tracer rounds stitched across the sky. "Get in the bathtub," Eddie said. On the street below, a white-helmeted air-raid warden ran through the street screaming, "The Japs are invading!" A stuntman Eddie knew from Republic Westerns emptied his six-shooters at the airplanes he swore he could see. The shells of antiaircraft guns jacked into the sky fell back to earth, thudding across the city.

Before Eddie climbed into the bathtub with Maria, he glimpsed an elderly woman walking down the street. Peering into the sky, skeptical, she shook her head and continued on her stately way. Eddie would remember her as the greatest hero of the war, the only person in Los Angeles County who hadn't lost her fucking mind. Even before the smoke cleared, the county sheriff had begun arresting Japanese Americans for coordinating the air raid, which proved inconvenient the following morning when it became clear there had been no air raid, no invasion, the city's defense force had been fighting a fleet of phantoms, waging war on shadows. Eddie experienced the municipal disappointment following the Secretary of the Navy's announcement that it was all a false alarm, a case of war jitters. What inspired this craving to live under the shadow of unreal threat? What dark yearnings did besiegement relieve?

In the end, it hadn't mattered that it was a false alarm: Roosevelt had already issued the executive order approving the construction of internment camps. For a while, the money pouring into Eddie's bank account papered over his moral qualms, but following the forced evacuation of Little Tokyo, he had grown increasingly uneasy with the fifth-columnist roles he'd been assigned, which offered in grotesque fantasy the evidence of treason the public hungered for, if only to justify what they inflicted on their fellow citizens.

THREE MONTHS LATER, ON AN afternoon in May, Eddie found himself thinking of that night while waiting for a matinee screening of *Tell 'Em in Tokyo* to begin. He waited for the houselights to dim before taking a seat alongside the last-row residents, those day drunks and adolescent canoodlers who went to the pictures to vanish from sight. The anonymity of air-conditioned darkness was among the more forgivable reasons for voluntarily submitting to the intellectual battering of *Tell 'Em in Tokyo.* Farther down the row he saw a few Navy seamen out on day passes, sharing a brown-bagged bottle of Wild Turkey, their evening beginning at three in the afternoon. Eddie slid another inch into his slouch. He yanked down his hat brim. Paranoia prickled across his exposed skin. This, as much as anything, made him an Angeleno.

Twenty minutes into the picture, one of the sailors whispered, "It's him."

Without looking over, Eddie could feel the hard heat of eyes on him.

"It can't be," said the second sailor, swigging the bottle.

"Look." The first sailor pointed ahead. A closeup of Eddie Lu filled the screen. "It's *him*."

Eddie tried to shield his face with his hand. He was mortified. Even in a profession that encouraged narcissism, being seen at a matinee showing of your own picture was like getting caught in a depraved act, insofar as it revealed the dimensions of your craving and need. He hunched over, jostled past crowded knees, and as he hurried from the auditorium, he heard one of the sailors say, "C'mon, he's getting away."

He'd reached the lobby when one of the sailors seized his shoulder and roughly spun him around. "See? What did I tell you? It's him."

Eddie glanced to the ushers, worried they would notice.

"Listen, fellas," he said, trying to shrug off the sailor's grip. "I'm happy to give you an autograph, but don't cause a scene, okay?"

The sailors weren't listening. "Should we call the police?" the third one asked.

"Call the police? You should be ashamed of yourself," the second one said. "We're shipping out next week and you're afraid of dealing with one lousy Jap spy yourself?"

If it took Eddie another beat to catch up with the sailors' deliberations, it was because he still retained some unwarranted trust in human rationality. Whether it was the documentary realism *Tell 'Em in Tokyo* employed, or the vividness of Eddie's on-screen performance, or simply the considerable volume of alcohol rushing through their veins, the three Navy seamen up from Long Beach on day passes thought they had singlehandedly apprehended the villain of the picture they had been watching.

For portions of his career, Eddie Lu had worked alongside stuntmen—ex-boxers, rodeo clowns, acrobats, and the incurably drunk—who threw themselves from buildings, somersaulted down stairwells, tobogganed from truck bumpers, hard men who in the air moved with the easy grace of eagles and broke bones so often they could set them themselves, and even though the bones never healed right they displayed their misshapenness as medals of honor in their war against death. From them, Eddie learned how to absorb a punch and a fall, but the most important lesson passed down from those who worked in burning buildings was knowing how long you could stay in the fire before you had to run.

He rammed his shoulder into the first sailor's chest and pivoted from the collision, a neat two-step that smeared lobby light across his eyes, and then he was ducking beneath the second sailor's outstretched arms, barreling toward the glass doors and into the afternoon air. The sailors chased him for three blocks, their footfall slapping the sidewalk, their shouts roaring in his ears. He popped into an alleyway where a couple Hooverville hobos roasted pigeons over an oil drum barbecue. He was drenched in sweat. His hands shook in his pockets. He waited until the sailors had given up their pursuit but still couldn't wake himself from the nightmare.

It was early evening. He found a diner, ordered a banana split, ate two bites, then circled back to his Cadillac.

At a red light on Alameda, he spied a Bela Lugosi lookalike sitting at a bus stop between Judy Garland and Clark Gable impersonators. Lookalikes were most convincing when off duty, hunched up to elude notice, disguising the impersonated celebrity beneath a steeply pitched hat and dark glasses. The public grasped at fame while the famous reached for anonymity, and where was the interchange more overt than in the low-profile lookalike bussing home from a job?

But no: the slouched figure in funereal black between the Judy Garland and Clark Gable impersonators was *the* Bela Lugosi.

Eddie rolled down his window and called out.

Bela's cool-eyed caution conveyed a history of evading autograph hounds, picture-happy tourists, and process servers. Five months shy of his sixtieth and the hand of mortality had begun to hover over the Immortal Count. No longer the svelte figure of ice-blooded seduction, Bela Lugosi needed a fresh cladding of pancake makeup, a costume change, a more forgiving light. His fingers scissored an unlit cigar and creases rayed from his pouched lids as he frowned at the Cadillac. A millimeter of white roots showed at his temples. Five inches of Jockeys showed at his undone fly.

"Edvard!" The untrammeled eyebrows—always Bela's most expressive feature—hoisted his whole face in levitating delight. "You owe me ten bucks!"

The two had met years earlier on the set of *The Mysterious Mr. Wong,* a lifeless Monogram programmer exploiting the popularity of Fu Manchu villainy. Bela's turn in the eponymous role affirmed his commitment to professional ruin. Though Eddie received a supporting role to lend an atmosphere of authenticity to the proceedings, no amount of atmosphere could authenticate a heavily accented Hungarian with rubber-cemented eyelids. Their friendship was founded on disdain for their employer and shared experience treading the career quicksand of typecasting.

Eddie offered him a lift. Maria was still at work, and he craved the company of a friend who knew exactly who he was. Bela, however, demurred. "I couldn't put you to any trouble. The bus will arrive momentarily."

"You're still in North Hollywood, right? This bus doesn't go there."

Bela's left eyebrow arm-wrestled his right, then he sighed, stood, and bid his companions farewell. "Edna. Harris." He tipped his hat at the Judy Garland and Clark Gable lookalikes. "Until we meet once more."

"Take care, Bruce," the Judy Garland said, trading her ruby slippers for a more practical pair of dark pumps.

Bela sunk into the seat cushion with a bleat of approval.

"Bruce?" Eddie asked.

Ignoring the question, Bela pinched the cushion, testing its ripeness. "This is a beautiful automobile," he declared.

"I'm considering selling it."

"Why?"

"I've nearly paid more in speeding tickets than I paid for the car."

"It's a fast machine."

"Even while it's parked?" It wasn't only traffic violations. His rearview regularly lit up with the spinning sirens of police who assumed the car stolen. Only a chauffeur's cap would mollify a patrolman's suspicions. He asked what brought Bela to the bus bench on that warm May evening.

"Let us say a series of mistakes."

Eddie put the Cadillac into gear, felt the engine thrum through the steering wheel. "How about that. We came the same way."

WHAT BROUGHT EDDIE DOWNTOWN BEGAN the previous day, when Gerhard Stahl, the director of *Tell 'Em in Tokyo* and its follow-up, *On a December Sunday,* stopped by Eddie's dressing room to tell him he needed to work with a vocal coach.

"Art saw the rushes," Gerhard said, leaning against the vanity counter. "He thinks you need help with your English."

"I speak it just fine."

"You speak it like you were born here."

"I *was* born here," Eddie said.

"That's the problem, accent-wise."

"Don't say it's Earl Chesterfield."

"It's Earl Chesterfield," Gerhard said. Life in Germany as a Jew—and in America as a German—had sensitized Gerhard to plausibly denied bigotry. The look lingering a beat too long, the open seat beside you on a crowded streetcar, the language of insinuation its orators pretend to be deaf to. And how it stresses your sanity to recognize what everyone dismisses. Gerhard was not unsympathetic.

"It's only a role you play," he continued. "It's a job. You're paid to be someone else. That's all. Tell me we're okay, Ed."

Eddie saw the director was stricken with the neediness of the well-meaning, the doe-eyed gaze that says *forgive me so I don't have to change.* Five years in America and Gerhard had fully assimilated into the custom of causing offense while demanding courtesy. "You can't get mad," he called as Eddie walked out. "You're paid too goddamn much!"

Eddie made it six blocks down Sunset when revolving reds lit up his rearview. The patrolman swaggered with a thickset leisureliness, his hair steepled in a sleek high-and-tight, his bull-necked volume streamlined for speeds it would never attain. He scanned Eddie's license and registration.

"Have I arrested you?" the patrolman asked. The current of a Cork County brogue rippled his *R*'s. Irish policemen always gave Eddie trouble, as if shoring up their tenuous citizenship depended on demeaning his.

"No, sir."

"We've never run into each other?"

"I don't believe so, sir."

"I know." The patrolman snapped his fingers. "You're an actor, aren't you? I've enjoyed your pictures, sir. I've enjoyed them mightily."

The patrolman's merriment allayed Eddie's misgivings. Now and then your worst suspicions proved wrong. "Thank you, Officer. I appreciate that."

"You were brilliant in that one with Anna May Wong. What was it called?"

Gerhard's words still rang in Eddie's ears: *It's a role you play*. His smile tightened cheerlessly. *"Daughter of Shanghai,"* he said.

Anna May Wong, the only Chinese star in the Hollywood firmament, had grown up on the outskirts of Chinatown, not far from Eddie. Following MGM's adaptation of *The Good Earth,* Paramount wanted to relaunch Anna May as the Marlene of the Orient in 1937's *Daughter of Shanghai.* Joseph Breen's prohibition on miscegenation meant that a Caucasian in yellowface could not play her love interest; a leading man of actual Asian heritage was required. Eddie's name was floated but the part went to Philip Ahn. Not even professional envy dimmed Eddie's admiration for Philip Ahn's performance as an FBI agent investigating human trafficking. From his first frame, Ahn played the part with a high-toned urbanity that would render Cary Grant romantically inert. Watching the first male Asian romantic lead since the advent of sound gave Eddie what the medium had long withheld: the opportunity to witness his desires brought to life. Though Eddie had appeared on-screen in dozens of pictures, he had never seen himself more clearly than in Philip Ahn's performance. Anna May Wong soon returned to her usual run of Madame Butterfly and dragon lady roles, and Paramount would squander Philip Ahn's talents on garish Japanese heavies, but on a December evening in 1937, Eddie was possessed by their powerful shadows, this fluke he mistook for the future.

"*Daughter of Shanghai,* a wonderful picture," the patrolman went on. "Say, would you sign a few autographs for the switchboard girls?"

Back on the road, gripping the wheel, Eddie's hand still shook with the jagged flourishes of Philip Ahn's autograph.

The following afternoon—six hours before he offered Bela Lugosi a ride home—Eddie found a small man in a moss-colored velvet blazer waiting in his dressing room.

"I'm Eddie Lu. It's nice to meet you, Mr. Chesterfield." Eddie mired his hand in the linguist's moist grip.

"*Dr.* Chesterfield. I did my PhD at Cornell." Like a Russian count holding fast to the noble address of his liquidated class, the independent scholar insisting on academic titles evoked banishment, destitution, an indignant refusal of reality. "And it's a pleasure to meet you, Mr. Ru."

Even before *Dr.* Chesterfield mispronounced his name, Eddie wasn't inclined to look on him kindly. Chesterfield had written his dissertation on American dialects, and after being denied tenure at a Big Ten university that regularly graduated illiterate linebackers, he decamped to Hollywood to teach white actors portraying ethnic minorities how to speak—and this was the word he used, Eddie would not forget it—*naturally*.

"Naturally?"

"In keeping with the audience's expectations, Mr. Ru," Chesterfield said gamely.

"And, what, the audience expects me to mispronounce my own name?"

"I don't need to tell you that we live in a bigoted and uninformed society. Without certain conventions, the average moviegoer would get confused. They wouldn't know who to root for or against. They expect pictures to affirm what they already believe." Chesterfield gave a little shrug, as if he were merely a messenger from that vast and mysterious kingdom of public opinion, wholly innocent of the news he related. "If you speak like Laurence Olivier, the audience wouldn't understand you, any more than they would understand Olivier speaking pidgin. Adhering to stereotype is the only way a screen actor makes himself intelligible to an unintelligent audience."

As with proctologists, electric chair administrators, and IRS auditors, sadism easily passed for thoroughness in *Dr.* Chesterfield's line of work. He gave Eddie a well-thumbed book of tongue twisters. It was dog-eared on *Larry's load rolls readily on the lonely road.*

"Your character transposes his *L*'s and *R*'s," Chesterfield said. "Now, let's practice together, shall we?"

Someone opened the soundstage door and the air pressure unsealed, a sibilant hiss that reminded Eddie of the Frigidaire unlatching on a summer afternoon, the frosty glow of ice, misting, otherworldly.

"Or we could begin with something simpler. Introductions, the first lesson when learning any new language. My name is Dr. Chesterfield. What's yours?"

A couple of overalled workmen decorated a Japanese restaurant set with signs from a Chinatown noodle shop.

"My name is Eddie Lu."

"Come on, Mr. Ru. You must try harder. What's your family name?"

Once a freight train crossed arid wilderness bearing precious cargo: blue blocks carved from Lake Erie, rimed in frost and insulated in sawdust. Fog vented through the boxcar slats as his grandfather swung aboard to ride the four-thousand-pound glacier across infernal deserts and into California.

When the lesson ended, Eddie drove downtown and bought a ticket to the first showing of *Tell 'Em in Tokyo*.

He wanted to read his family name written in blazing light.

"DR. CHESTERFIELD," BELA SAID WITH a commiserating smile. "I see him every few months for a tune-up."

"A tune-up?"

"In case I lose my accent. I have a recurring nightmare I'll wake up speaking like Jimmy Stewart. Then where would I be? I'm hanging on to my career by my accent and my eyebrows."

"You still have the best eyebrows in the business."

"That's kind of you to say, Edvard. You heard about *Son of Dracula*?"

Eddie had heard Universal planned to resurrect Bela's famous role. He'd also heard Bela had been passed over for the part.

"I called the producer this morning to demand an explanation and he said he was so happy to hear from me."

"That's promising," Eddie said.

"Do you know why he was so happy? Because he thought I was dead."

"On the bright side, he was mistaken."

"Don't be so sure."

Bela unscrewed a flask and took a swig of asparagus juice to soothe the sciatica that booby-trapped his lower joints. What Eddie wanted to know, what he hoped to draw from Bela's example, was how to survive in this business as a perpetual villain and permanent outsider. Could you outrun the monsters you embodied, or were they forever your face?

He slowed at a stoplight in what a few weeks earlier had been Little Tokyo. *For Rent* signs filled the desolate shopfronts. The detritus of hasty departure littered alleyways that lay in the shadow of City Hall. Parking was abundant in this ghost town transplanted to the heart of Los Angeles. It brought back memories of when the city demolished Chinatown to build Union Station. He'd been given a few weeks to leave the home where he'd lived his entire life.

Already the first new tenants had arrived in Little Tokyo: Black families migrating from the south to search for work at the aviation plants and shipyards. In the lot across the street, schoolboys divvied themselves into a game of GIs and Japanese.

The light flipped green, but Eddie stayed to watch them hash out allies and enemies in the late-day light. He rolled down his window to make sure he heard right: the boys on the blacktop all wanted to be the Japanese, and if refugee children from the Jim Crow South rooted for them, whose fault was that?

BELA UNLOCKED THE DOOR TO his three-bedroom bungalow. Electrical appliances and pastel linoleum outfitted the bright airy kitchen. The living room was appointed in mail-order homeyness, imbued with a pushy faith in coordinated color schemes.

"Dreadful, isn't it?" Bela said, setting his fedora on the coffee table. "I live in a Montgomery Ward catalog."

Eddie thought the well-lit aesthetic of showroom optimism might benefit an actor fleeing the vampire's curse.

"I had to give away my panther. The landlord doesn't allow pets."

Notwithstanding this, out on the porch, a dozen squirrels convalesced in a wire enclosure. Bela explained that a neighborhood boy with a BB gun was waging war on the local fauna, pretending pigeons and squirrels were Zeros and Panzers. Bela collected the casualties on his evening walks and nursed them to health.

"Last week I found the little barbarian marching with his air rifle and I asked to borrow it."

"And?"

Bela took a chug of asparagus juice. "And I shot him."

"You what?"

"Don't worry, Edvard. It was only a flesh wound."

"Bela, there are laws against that."

"I'm not a madman. I made sure he didn't know who I was before I gave him a dose of what he had coming."

"You're the most iconic figure to climb from a coffin since Jesus."

"The little shit thought I was Boris Karloff."

Eddie laughed. More likely Bela shot the boy for having the temerity to mistake him for his nemesis. After *Dracula* catapulted him to international celebrity in 1931, Universal offered Bela the role of the Creature in *Frankenstein.* He declined on the grounds that lurching between a pair of neck bolts wouldn't advance his ambitions to become a romantic lead. Apparently, he'd been a heartthrob of the Budapest stage. A lot of funny-looking fellas in Hungary, Eddie figured. By rejecting the role, Bela created the monster that tormented him for the rest of his career. Boris Karloff supplanted Bela Lugosi at Universal, and one year after its inception, Bela became a has-been in the genre he forged. Hard not to pity him for thinking he was more than his most famous monster.

"I ask you, Edvard, what's the point of being forgotten if you cannot teach a child murderer a lesson? Now, do you want a beer or not?"

The Coors appeared in a lukewarm bottle. Eddie had forgotten Bela drank his beer at room temperature. He set the bottle on a wooden coaster and examined the bookcase.

"I'll put my Oscar on the top shelf," Bela said, a trace of vanished sincerity in his deadpan tone, as if he'd been saying this for years, unaware or indifferent to all that had ground the expectation to irony. For now, however, the shelf housed only a voluminous and pricey Hungarian stamp collection. Why Bela considered obscure European postage a sounder investment than a mortgage was a question Eddie was too polite to ask.

Instead, he said, "So, who's Bruce?"

Bela peered into the lawn-clipping dregs of his asparagus juice. "Bruce Lancaster is a Bela Lugosi impersonator I play from time to time."

"Excuse me?"

"As you can see, I'm not riding as high as I once was, but I make decent money impersonating myself."

"Why the intermediary character?" Eddie asked. "Why not just be yourself?"

"Imagine if it gets around that the great Bela Lugosi is doing birthday parties? Besides, I'm far too principled to prostitute myself."

"But Bruce Lancaster is more pragmatic," Eddie said.

"Bruce Lancaster is downright mercenary."

"But the Judy Garland and the Clark Gable lookalikes, they must know who you are."

"Edna and Harris? Never. They think Bruce Lancaster is devoted to his character."

Bela looked frazzled from the heavy traffic of personas commuting through him. He excused himself and as his footsteps padded across the carpeted hall, Eddie pulled one of the stamp binders from the shelf. He was still thumbing through it when he heard the percussive thuds of kneecaps, elbows, and skull on tile. He hoofed it to the bathroom.

"Bela? You okay in there?"

Eddie jiggled the locked knob. His time working the front desk of the Montclair had bequeathed him an eccentric but undeniably useful skill set, among which was a familiarity with busting down locked bathroom doors. Contrary to popular opinion, one doesn't kick it down. Better instead to use a heavy object, such as a leather-bound stamp album, raise it overhead, plow it through the knob, and when the door swings open you might find a ceiling pasted in gray matter, a bathtub dyed in four quarts of blood, or an actor splayed across the bathmat beside the empty vial that slaked his vampiric thirst.

Eddie searched the folds of Bela's jawline for the sluggish cadence of a pulse.

At the Montclair he'd dealt with overdoses by firing up the vacancy sign and phoning the police, but public knowledge of Bela's morphine habit would render his pictures uninsurable. What Eddie euphemistically called Bela's career would expire before the ambulance arrived.

Bela's pupils tightened to pinpoints. A ripe funk wafted from his armpits, some luscious bite of decay. Eddie wiped his face with a cold towel, and even when Bela regained consciousness, the dreamy rapture clouded his gaze. Outside the night was falling everywhere.

"The asparagus juice wasn't cutting it," Bela finally said.

Eddie helped him to his bedroom and after some time passed asked if he could do anything.

"Make sure they bury me in my cape."

"Still a ham, I see."

"Filet, Edvard. I've always been filet."

"Tell me, you regret turning down *Frankenstein*?" This was the great unmentionable in Bela's life, and had Eddie not just peeled him from the bathroom floor, he never would have broached it. "I ask because I'm tired of playing these stock villains, Bela. I know Chekhov, Ibsen, and O'Neill inside and out. I know the soliloquies from every Shakespeare tragedy. I know what I can do as an actor. And I know when they offer you a part, what they're really doing is telling you what you are."

The sky was velvety black and the light of a passing car skated across Bela's eyes. Eddie looked away. He didn't know why he was more comfortable boasting his embarrassments than confessing his aspirations.

"At the National Theatre in Budapest, I was in *Hamlet.*"

"You played Hamlet?"

"Rosencrantz," Bela said glumly. "How much are you making playing Jap heavies?"

"Two thousand a week."

Bela shook his head in wonderment. "I made five hundred a week for *Dracula.* What I'd give for Roosevelt to declare war on middle-aged Hungarians who can't pronounce *W*'s. Listen, it's better to succeed as a villain than fail as a hero. Turning down *Frankenstein* is my biggest regret, and believe me, it's had competition. My advice? Cash the checks promptly and don't invest in stamps."

A half century later, from his retirement community in Florida, Eddie watched Martin Landau receive an Academy Award for his portrayal of Bela in *Ed Wood.* He wondered what Bela would have made of his life turning into an Oscar-winning role. "Bruce Lancaster played it better," he imagined Bela saying. A few years after that, the US Postal Service issued a stamp in Bela's honor, a tribute that would have brought the philatelist considerable satisfaction until he learned the USPS issued *two* Boris Karloff stamps. Eddie was among the mourners at Bela's interment in Holy Cross Cemetery in 1956. He was buried in his cape.

As he left the apartment, Eddie set his Cadillac key on the coffee table with a note telling Bela to return it when he could. Outside, the air had cooled. Eddie searched for the bus stop. The sidewalk tunneled beneath eucalyptus boughs, and palliative scents layered and peeled from his face. The thrum of summer insects and pigeon flight rustled in the foliage above. Passing headlights gilded the downcast leaves and in that canopy of dripping gold the air was minty, crisp, and cleansing.

Sitting at the bus stop, he heard rubber gasp on asphalt. A boy, maybe ten or eleven, sat in the saddle of his bicycle and pointed an air rifle at him.

"I thought you were someone else," the boy said, lowering the rifle a few discontented inches.

Eddie watched streetlights scatter shadows across the bus window as the city rolled by. In a playground the children of aviation workers waited for their parents to get off work. They busied themselves with more rounds of GIs and Japanese. And it was probably nothing, just the way street noise narrates your garbled wants at the end of a weary day, but as the boys argued over who played who, he was sure he heard one saying, "I'm Eddie Lu! I'm Eddie Lu!"

2

ARTIE USUALLY DEALT WITH HIS DOUBTS BY HIRING MORE SYCOPHANTS, but by summer 1942, no number of yes-men could quell his unease.

The malaise had descended on him during a swing-shift showing of *Little Tokyo, U.S.A.* After years plundering the intellectual property of better capitalized studios, he felt downright honored to learn the Twentieth Century–Fox production had ripped off the documentary style of *Tell 'Em in Tokyo.* He fondly remembered those freebooting days when he bribed secretaries at rival studios for the scripts to their biggest forthcoming productions. He liked to time his knockoffs to open a month or so before the originals. Thus, he could hijack a major studio's publicity campaign, while also claiming that it had ripped off *him.* Among the great thrills of his professional life had been accusing *Gone With the Wind* of cribbing from Mercury's three-hanky Civil War weepy *The Breeze Blew Them Away.*

But from the first frames of *Little Tokyo, U.S.A.*, he felt queasy.

"For more than a decade," the voiceover intoned, "Japanese mass espionage was carried out in the United States and her territorial outposts while a complacent America literally slept at the switch."

Over sixty-four dismaying minutes, *Little Tokyo, U.S.A.* made the case that Los Angeles was home to twenty-five thousand Japanese saboteurs whose treachery not only excused but required wholesale internment. Particularly disturbing to Artie was the realization that parts of the movie had been filmed on location, amid the evacuation itself, casting Japanese internees as unwilling extras in a movie justifying their relocation.

As he watched, Artie felt cored by contradiction. Conspiracy was one of Hollywood's most reliable plot engines, but by encouraging audiences to accept the plausibility of conspiracies in peacetime, had Artie primed audiences to see enemies everywhere in war? Weren't these stab-in-the-back fantasies as perverse as any found in German propaganda reels? And weren't fears of fascism coming to America borne out by the concentration camps going up in the California desert?

He tried to read the mood of the audience. Were they put off or persuaded? From what he could tell, they were convinced. Less by the lurid conniving at the heart of *Little Tokyo* than by the fact of internment itself. The severity of the sentence was the most compelling evidence of guilt, because otherwise how could you trust the legitimacy of your institutions and the righteousness of your ideals? Otherwise, how could you believe yourself better than what you hate?

He was still thinking about this the next afternoon when his secretary knocked on the door. "Major Greene's on the horn for you," she said.

The major told Artie the War Department was pleased with Mercury's propaganda films and wanted to order another dozen.

"Our accounting department will be thrilled."

"I'm sure," the major said. "However, we do have one significant concern. Until now, we've been using these to indoctrinate enlisted men, but we'd like to begin releasing them in theaters to educate the public. We've tested a few over the last several weeks, and the audience feedback has been positive with one glaring exception: they think the scenes depicting combat are fake. Apparently, our combat footage isn't as realistic as what they're used to seeing in the movies."

"Hey, we're doing the best we can with what the Signal Corps provides us," Artie said. "But to be perfectly honest—and I doubt I'm telling you anything you don't already know—their footage is very amateurish."

The major sighed. "Yes, I'm aware of that. What would you suggest?"

"To begin with, I'd enlist professional cameramen who understand film grammar, who know how to build a series of shots into a coherent scene. Then I'd shoot reenactments."

"That's a no go. We have a strict policy against reenactments."

"On a soundstage, in the most controlled conditions possible, a filmmaker needs multiple takes to get the right shot. The idea that you're going to send a couple guys into a foxhole with a camera and expect to compete with Hollywood just isn't feasible. If you want the war to look real on-screen, you'll have to fake it. But what do I know? I've only been doing this my entire career."

The major said he'd run Artie's thoughts up the flagpole. They discussed a few other matters before the major turned the conversation in a troubling direction. "In order to avoid production delays, you should know you'll have to find a new miniaturist."

"Anna Weber? You have a problem with her work?"

"A few boys from the Chemical Warfare Corps are coming to LA on Monday to have a word with her."

Artie frowned. He'd never heard of the Chemical Warfare Corps. "I'm sorry, sir, but what the hell do they want with my miniaturist?"

The major ignored the question. "I just wanted to let you know so you have time to line up a replacement."

The phone call troubled Artie, and though he should have gone to watch the rushes, or read the daily logs from the three pictures currently shooting, or review that quarter's revenue targets, he instead sat lost in thought until Maria came in.

"What are you doing here?" he asked. It was quarter past seven in the evening, and Maria, like a sizable percentage of his employees, was subject to the enemy alien curfew. A few times a week, she had to bed down in the studio bomb shelter after overseeing the production of pictures that championed rights and freedoms she no longer enjoyed.

"Heading out soon." Maria passed him a manila envelope with screen test expenditures awaiting his signature. Usually, he would have paid closer attention to the unexpected overages, but the strange call with the major still preoccupied him, and he barely glanced at the paperwork he autographed. He didn't notice her slight smile of satisfaction as he handed back the expense sheets without asking what they were for.

Maria nodded to the white dinner jacket hanging on the door. "Big night?"

"Ned's wife is throwing a dinner party. God help us."

Ned had married Abigail Grafton in a quiet ceremony that spring. Mildred had made a point to introduce Abigail to Hollywood society, particularly its lawyers. That Mildred was so keen to make the newest Mrs. Ned Feldman the newest ex–Mrs. Ned Feldman was among the innumerable reasons Artie loved her. She was a romantic. If Abigail got a piece of Ned's company stock during a divorce settlement, and if Mildred could sway her to vote with Artie, he might shore up the leverage he was losing to the Eastern National bankers.

Artie said, "Ned invited a few more big fish to spear."

"More investors?"

"He won't rest until every Mephisto with a brokerage license has a piece of my soul." Artie stared at the bare wall over his settee. "You know, I should really do something with that wall."

"Get a painting. It might calm your agita to have a pretty view."

"Maybe something classical."

"Classical is good."

"Cain and Abel, say. Or Romulus and Remus."

"I'm glad you and your brother are getting along."

"My sister was something of a painter, I ever tell you that?" he said. "She painted little scenes on horse blinders. She'd paint the first half of a story on the right blinder and the second half on the left blinder. She had a real knack for it." Artie looked at Maria. "I don't want to pry, but your father—can I ask how you made peace with not knowing what happened to him?"

"Oh, Art." She smiled unhappily. "I haven't."

Artie was disappointed to hear this. He'd hoped Maria managed loss with the same brisk efficiency she brought to all her tasks.

"Mildred wants me to see a shrink," Artie admitted. "There's a guy we took Billy to during his Laundry Hamper Period. Seemed to know what he was doing."

"I'm sure your Famous Fratricides decorative theme will provide much to analyze."

"Mildred's trying to sell me on acceptance. She says it's the bedrock of all the great religions, but given her refusal to accept the current square footage of our house, I can't say I'm convinced."

"Acceptance has always sounded like a euphemism for surrender to me."

"Exactly," Artie said, nodding gratefully. "That's exactly it. Accepting the unacceptable is acquiescence. But where does that leave me? Contemptuous, indignant, and alone, with my mind spiraling into itself, wondering if Ada's okay and what happened to her and why I didn't do more when there was still time. I mean, Christ, how do you learn to live with yourself?"

"I'm sorry, Art," she said, reaching over to squeeze his hand. "I don't know how."

"Thanks for hearing me out," he said, and he meant it. It was nice to talk about Ada with someone who saw incomprehension as a reasonable response to the incomprehensible.

"One more thing," he said, and jotted down a note about his phone call with the major. "Would you leave this on Anna Weber's desk on your way out?"

DESPITE WHAT SHE TOLD ARTIE, Maria had no intention of going home tonight. Down at the Stage 3 elephant door, her crew for the night shoot was waiting. A few more minutes and they would all be landlocked on the studio lot until morning.

A gaffer threw his cigarette on the pavement. "Well?" he asked. "Are we getting overtime?"

Maria tapped her purse. "Art just signed off on the expenses. I have your checks right here."

She was using the accounting practice of last resort, which Ernst Rosner had perfected over his many years keeping Mercury solvent: pay the Los Angeles bills with checks cut from the New York bank and the New York bills with checks cut from the Los Angeles bank. By the time the accounting department learned about the "screen test" expenses, she'd have a cut of the night's work to show Artie. Ever since he reneged on his promise to give her the producer's credit on *Devil's Bargain,* Maria had searched for the movie she wanted her name on. This was it.

"All right, then," the gaffer said. "*The False Front* begins."

IN FACT, IT HAD BEGUN two months earlier when Eddie climbed off the bus that May evening, walked the final four blocks home, and cocooned himself in the bedspread alongside her. His adventure with Bela had delayed the aftershock of the *Tell 'Em in Tokyo* incident, but alone in the dark with her, it shuddered out of him. His breath huffed across her face in viscous whooshes. The bedsprings creaked. No business conducted in bed had ever inspired him to turn off the lights—naked, he was without self-consciousness, but now, still clothed in his suit and tie, he couldn't bear for her to see him. He pulled the sheets over his head, as if the thin cotton, still scented in lemony laundry suds, provided any protection at all. Together they burrowed into the dank air and she told him she loved him, again and again, until the words ceased to represent anything but the steadiness of her presence. She didn't know what to say or not say to comfort this man whose contempt for sympathy was limitless. His mastery over emotion had always fascinated her. He could cry on cue in front of a camera, and then, when the director called print, he'd be back to telling dirty limericks. And now he was skidding out of control in their double bed. "I'm here," she said, and kept saying it, stating what was plain to see, what he already knew, telling him that he didn't have to face himself on his own.

Over the following days, Maria kept returning to the image of Eddie running. It was an open question whom he was more desperate to outpace: the sailors, or the character they mistook him for. Maria wanted to *do* something. The problem was that what she *did* was manage the production of the very pictures Eddie deplored. What she did wasn't very good, but she was very good at doing it.

Eddie's frustrations with Mercury fueled Maria's own growing doubts about her place at the studio. Since January, she had done the work that used to be divvied between her and two other associate producers now serving in the Navy. She did so without complaint, under the expectation that Artie would name her Executive Producer of Mercury Pictures. The months passed and the promotion never came. If she brought it up, Artie would say, "You just need a little more seasoning." Or: "Now's not the right time." Or: "You know how much I rely on you." Or: "Let's just wait and see."

Well, Maria had waited and what she saw was this: The draft had hollowed out the manpower of every studio in town. It presented a once-in-a-lifetime opportunity for a woman to rise. And it wouldn't last.

"I was thinking I'd put out feelers to Columbia," Maria said. "See what's available there."

"You should," Eddie said. "Just working for someone who doesn't talk to his toupees would be a step up the sanity staircase."

"Eleven years I've worked here," she said. "It's time for a change."

Before she could think of leaving Mercury, she wanted to produce a movie both she and Eddie could feel proud to put their names on.

For weeks, she rooted through the story department for a piece of intellectual property not yet drained of its intelligence by the studio's contract writers. She jotted ideas at Vick's Formica counter while Eddie voiced skepticism for the fare of a diner that sold stool softener by the pound. She found a short story about a Chinese railway worker who becomes a vigilante, righting the wrongs committed by a rapacious railroad magnate, but its potential for appalling publicity copy—*This year's most thrilling Western is an Eastern!*—made her shelve it.

Nothing was right. Nothing felt real.

THE STORY DEPARTMENT SHARED THE floor with the editing suite where Vincent carried on the godforsaken work of Propaganda Unit researcher. One afternoon, after another fruitless forage for adaptable material, Maria dropped in to see him. After being shunned by Maria for most of his time at Mercury and then compelled into cataloging every unwatchable minute of disinformation to emerge from Italy and Germany over the last decade, Vincent was understandably wary of her.

She disarmed his suspicions by showing him the bundle of her father's reassembled letters. There was so much context missing, so much hovering outside the margins that he might cast light on.

"Madonna," Vincent murmured when he recognized the handwriting. He noted the care with which Maria had fitted the censored strips into the letters' lacunae and thought of the passport photographs his mother once pieced together. "These were in the cigar box?" he asked.

She nodded. "He wrote about you a lot, didn't he?" she said as he read through the letters.

"I didn't know he wrote about me at all."

"We were both his children."

"He was very kind to me," Vincent said, "but Maria, you were his only child."

Over the course of many afternoons in the cutting room, Vincent added detail and texture to her father's letters, telling her about how he liked sticking it to the local government by helping peasants evade their taxes, how he loved candied bergamot peel, how after a few glasses of wine he would begin reciting from memory old courtroom orations that long ago convinced skeptical judges to overturn guilty verdicts. Vincent had no grand revelations to offer, only the successive accretion of detail that constitutes a life. Maria wished she had shown these letters to Vincent sooner, but until now what he couldn't tell her had seemed so much more important than what he could.

One afternoon, she found Vincent hunched over the viewing window of the Moviola, marking footage for the latest propaganda documentary, *Axis Enemy: Germany*.

"When I was over at the Warner film library, I stopped by the set of that *Algiers* knockoff they're making," he told her.

"I heard about that one. With all the émigrés. 'Marrakesh'?"

"Casablanca."

"How'd it look?"

"The picture? Pure schmaltz," he said, not without admiration.

Maria noticed a cigarette burn at the center of his palm.

"It's nothing," he said, stuffing his hand painfully into his pocket. "I touched a hot stove."

Maria let that go and peered into the Moviola. She was somewhat surprised to see Gary Cooper staring back at her.

"I know, I know, I know," Vincent preempted.

Nonetheless, Maria felt obliged to state the obvious. "This is *Sergeant York.*" Even she thought passing it off as a documentary was a bit much.

"Rudi wants combat footage and I haven't found anything better than *Sergeant York.* The best the Signal Corps makes available is merely unusable. More often, it's indecipherable: jumpy blurs of smoke and unfocused shaking. Soundstage skirmishes look more realistic than the real ones."

"Artie was telling me about this. It's only now dawning on the brass hats that it's easier to train a photographer to shoot a gun than train a soldier to shoot a camera."

Vincent was quiet for a long moment, then said, "I know enemy aliens are barred from joining the Army, but could Artie pull any strings with the Signal Corps? The Americans will invade Italy sooner or later. I'd like to be there, maybe even to photograph the liberation of San Lorenzo."

"After everything that's happened, why on earth would you want to go back?"

He looked away and said nothing.

Given that the War Department trusted Artie enough to commission him to produce indoctrination films, he probably could pull a few strings for Vincent. But Maria shook her head. Vincent was her only real connection to the last sixteen years of her father's life. There was still more he could tell her, more she wanted to hear. The stray details lodged in the brain of a passport photographer comprised her father's afterlife. After spending the past year wishing Vincent would leave, Maria now felt unwilling to let him go.

"If they think it's too dangerous to let an enemy alien keep a camera on the home front, you really think they'll let an enemy alien have one on the front line?"

"They let Robert Capa," he said.

"I hate to break it to you, but you're not Robert Capa."

"I'm not Vincent Cortese either."

Maria didn't know what to say, so she just nudged him aside to study the footage cut for *Axis Enemy: Germany*.

By now, Mercury's war documentaries had developed a house style of appropriating enemy propaganda and splicing it with footage from dramatic pictures, stock film, and reenactments. They were movies made of other movies, and thus represented the zenith of Hollywood's production practices. Watching the reel unfurl in the Moviola, you could see the war collapse the distinctions between the documentary and the entertainment film: documentarians staged reenactments and looped in footage from studio dramas while Hollywood directors gave back-lot fantasies an air of gritty authenticity by shooting them newsreel-style. Everywhere there was a pent-up hunger for what resembled reality. And with that thought, Maria knew only one role was worthy of Eddie's talents.

"YOU WANT TO MAKE IT about *me*?" Eddie asked that evening over roast beef at Al Levy's Tavern. No one but her mother could wring more skepticism from a monosyllable.

She set down her fork and sketched out the beats. It opens with Eddie at the movie theater, watching himself in *Tell 'Em in Tokyo*. Following the showing, several patrons mistake him for the spy he portrayed in the picture, he runs, and a manhunt ensues; throw in a little backstory and culminate with a suspenseful chase through the maze of Mercury's back lot. Sure, it followed the usual contours of the mistaken-identity/innocent-man-on-the-run thrillers every studio pumped out, but what better dramatized the nightmare the war had thrust on Eddie, as well as Mercury's exiles? Besieged by suspicion, your loyalties doubted, your treachery presumed. The dread that you will pay for the crimes of the character foisted upon you. These anxieties were not unfamiliar to Maria.

Eddie bobbed his head from side to side as he sliced his roast beef. "Art might find it . . . *cerebral*," he said, using the word Artie deployed to gently dismiss idiocy.

"This from a guy who reads Shakespeare for fun. What's that one you read me, with the play within the play and the actors playing actors—'A Summertime Snooze'?"

"Please tell me you're not referring to *A Midsummer Night's Dream*."

"See? I pay attention."

"'A Summertime Snooze.' You should be ashamed of yourself, you know that?"

"Hey, English is my second language."

"But you speak as if it were your third."

She speared a wedge of potato. "So, what do you think of the idea?"

Examining a magenta slab of roast beef, he said, "I think it's undercooked."

"Then help me out, huh?"

"Tell me why," Eddie said, fixing her with a hard look. "That's the one question no one in production ever asks, is it? Everyone is so caught up with whether a picture can get made, no one asks why they are making it or if they should."

Maria reached into her purse and took out the enemy alien registration card the Justice Department required she carry at all times. It had her photograph, signature, and index fingerprints. Her address, date of birth, and nationality. It was a miracle of efficiency, really, what scant details the government required to define a person in her totality.

"Every day since Pearl Harbor, I've gone to the studio to work on jingoist dramas about enemies in our midst," she said, studying the card. "Now and then, I wonder what it would feel like to work on a picture I wasn't ashamed of."

Eddie drained his drink. "I can't even imagine."

"The propagandist in *Devil's Bargain* at least sells his soul for a decent price. What did I get for mine? There isn't a single movie I can point to and say *I did it for this.*"

"Who do you propose to write it? Rudi Bloch?"

"You."

"Me?"

"It's your story. You tell it however you see fit. And I'll produce it."

"You'd trust me with that?"

"Eddie, you're the only person I trust with anything."

He smiled and nodded. "What will we call it?"

"What about 'The Reenactment'?" she said.

"'The Reenactment.' Maybe that's a little on the nose. How about 'The False Front'?"

"'The False Front.'" Maria nodded. "I like it."

Candlelight flickered over his face, and how unlikely, she thought, that they should have found each other. Other couples filled adjacent two-tops, older and younger, falling toward each other or drifting apart, couples who shared a look in a train compartment or a nightclub, some improbable second that in a million other universes would have never materialized, and not for the first time it occurred to Maria that the most meaningful experiences in her life were the most banal—the thrill of unexpected love, the pain of goodbye, the fear of insignificance. Working in a business dependent on cliché made her wary of its power to flatten and distort, but sitting in the restaurant's low-key lighting, Maria was content to accept that what most shaped her as a person was what made her like most people.

"Artie will never okay this," Eddie said.

"Then fuck it: I'll ask for forgiveness instead of permission."

"What, you want to shoot an entire movie on the sly?"

"Of course not," Maria said. "Just enough to convince Art that he stands to lose more money by abandoning the picture than by completing it."

PRODUCTION ON *The False Front* began when the light faded in the west. Maria supervised the skeleton crew of émigrés as they prepped the first setup: a deep-focus, low-lit shot of Eddie running into the back lot. Down the alleyway, she saw the cameraman chalking the pavement every five feet to help him pull crisp focus as Eddie ran. Maria had drawn the palette for *The False Front* directly from the blackout, using single-source lighting to capture the mood of the home front in stark chiaroscuro. The primacy of shadow aestheticized what was taken as gospel on Poverty Row sets: the less you see, the better it looks.

They weren't shooting with sound—the air traffic thrumming out of the Lockheed and Douglas aviation plants would distort it—so the assistant cameraman didn't bother snapping the chalked slate when the camera rolled.

Maria watched Eddie smash through glossy puddles as he sprinted from the Navy sailors in pursuit. He hit his marks with the fluid lope of a ballplayer tagging the bases and even at twenty-four frames per second the film felt too sluggish to capture him. In the closeups spliced in later, you'd see the entrapment the role demands, but now, on location, he was untouchable.

The next series of shots followed Eddie through the back lot. Bounding through history and geography, from Italian Piazza to Brownstone Street to Wild West Row to Jungle Forest to Tenement Alley, the legion of unseen silhouettes at his heels. Low-key lighting twisted the back lot into a labyrinth, a prison Eddie could not find his way out of. Where ambient light was unavoidable, Anna applied the shadows directly on the walls with black paint. Even Midwest Street—that idyllic serving of small-town Americana—contracted to a claustrophobia without exit. Desperate for shelter or egress, Eddie hopped white picket fences and threw open front doors. Each dead-ended into plywood walls.

The final shot of the night followed Eddie onto the set used in *Tell 'Em in Tokyo*. There, chased back into the character he tried to flee, he kept searching for an exit as the screen went black.

BY THE TIME THEY WRAPPED, it was too late to return to the Santa Monica bungalow she shared with Rudi, so Anna decided to take a shower in the main office. Because they were fundamentally meaningless status symbols, executive washroom keys were fiercely coveted. Several front office strivers had accepted them in lieu of a raise. Which was idiotic, in Anna's opinion, when everyone knew Ernst Rosner kept his under a bottle of Pepto-Bismol in his desk drawer. She showered, dried, and draped herself in a teal blue dress borrowed from the costume department. The bobby pin shortage forced her to rig her hair aloft in toothpicks. On her desk, she found the memo from Artie.

Walking back through the main office, she saw a light on in the cutting room. Vincent was already at the Moviola, working his way through newsreel footage captured from the Japanese at Midway that Rudi wanted to appropriate for a Navy training film. Over the last half year, the poor kid had documented hundreds of hours of enemy propaganda in detailed reports archived in Rudi's filing cabinet. His tolerance for cinematic monotony was genuinely impressive—he'd have made an outstanding movie critic, Anna thought. Canisters of German films rose in unsteady columns on either side of the Moviola. She'd watched them all, but none featured her son, Kurt. In memos to Mercury's military liaison, Vincent said the Propaganda Unit needed prints of Hasso Beck's recent pictures to complete *Axis Enemy: Germany*. There was one promising lead. MoMA had a print of *Victory in the East*, a 1941 Hasso Beck film, but Vincent still hadn't received it.

Perhaps the smallness of her request made him determined to fulfill it? Or perhaps the limbo he had left Concetta in, alone and without news of her son, animated his resolve to find a few frames of her child. If the world, in all its unfathomable creativity, failed to satisfy her modest plea, then it held no possibility of forgiveness for him.

"Have you heard of the Chemical Warfare Corps?" she asked.

"Nope."

She held up the memo. "Artie left this on my desk. Says to expect a visit from Colonel Macalister of the Chemical Warfare Corps on Monday."

"Regarding what?"

"It doesn't say."

Vincent shrugged. "It's probably about a training and indoctrination film."

"Probably," she said doubtfully. She tucked the memo into her purse and peeled a five-spot from her roll. "Be a good boy and buy me a Danish and two packs of Pall Malls at Vick's."

Given that her movie colony friendships were bantering alliances of temporary convenience, it still seemed strange to Anna that she had come to feel genuine maternal fondness for this lowly researcher earning $40/week. Every Sunday for months, Anna had double-parked her red Oldsmobile outside the Montclair, tapped her horn, and waited to hear the coins jingling in Vincent's pocket as he jogged out. They would then drive to the studio lot to work their way through German film reels in an increasingly frustrating, ultimately fruitless search for Kurt.

Vincent's willingness to spend his day off in the company of a chain-smoking middle-aged misanthrope and a few hundred hours of fascist propaganda suggested levels of forsakenness that even Anna found a bit depressing. The seventeen-year age difference ensured they reached platonic companionship without first weathering the turbulence of romantic possibility. He wasn't much older than Kurt. There was nothing special about him. He was no one. She could have projected the image of her son onto the face of any young man just as easily. She foisted food on him, dispensed unsolicited advice, asked when he was going to meet a nice girl and settle down, and from the way he obliged, deferred to, and encouraged her, it was clear he craved the maternal affection her doting derision implied. Almost as much as she missed Kurt, she missed the person she had been when she was a mother.

Even after they made it through the last of the German propaganda reels, Anna continued to pick Vincent up every Sunday. They'd have lunch at Musso's, catch the war news at one of the midtown newsreel theaters, play cards with a few of the other émigrés, or wander through Hollywood Memorial Park. She always dropped him back at the Montclair before curfew with leftovers wrapped in tinfoil. On those Sunday afternoons, Anna begrudgingly capitulated to California cheeriness. A bit of long-ago leached color returned to her jet-black temperament, and sometimes her mood even matched the pastels the Bullock's womenswear department had imposed on her. Rudi assumed she was having a temporary break with reality, which, in a way, was precisely what those Sunday afternoons were.

Whenever she inquired about his parents or his life in San Lorenzo, Vincent's prevarication left her with more questions. One Sunday, as they passed a poster for *Sherlock Holmes and the Voice of Terror,* in which Basil Rathbone traded his deerstalker for a fedora to ferret out a Nazi espionage ring in London, Vincent stopped and stared with a mournfulness at odds with the poster's high-spirited promises.

"What?" Anna asked.

"I was just thinking about this inspector in San Lorenzo who was always reading Sherlock Holmes stories," Vincent said.

"That seems a little pathetic, but nothing to get choked up over."

"No, of course not. It's just that he was the most corrupt policeman imaginable, but he once did something very decent for me, and I've never known why."

"What did he do?"

Vincent shook his head, made a weak joke, and said they'd better get their tickets before the picture started. Later that afternoon, she asked him why he was helping her find Kurt. They were sitting at her dining table, where she had watched with satisfaction as he devoured a dense wedge of her red velvet cake.

"Because we're friends," he told her.

"Yes, this is true." She studied him with unsparing attentiveness. "But I don't think this is why you are helping me."

"Why does it matter?"

"It matters," she said, lighting a cigarette, "because we are friends."

Vincent looked at his hands. How could he confess what he had done to Concetta to a woman whose own son had disappeared into the unknown? Anna's past reaffirmed the irredeemable in his. Perhaps the certainty that he would receive no mercy from her formed the foundation of their friendship.

"What would you do if you found yourself sitting across from the person responsible for you losing Kurt?"

"You're avoiding my question," Anna said.

"I'm answering it. What would you do?"

What would she do if she were sitting across from Hasso? She often thought back to the day he'd offered her the opportunity to become an architect if she joined the Party. Back then she could not have imagined how much she would come to regret turning the devil down.

She eyed Vincent, uncertain where the conversation was going. "I'd probably kill him," she said. "A few dozen times."

"With what?"

Anna considered the lethality of the instruments within reach: a couple spoons, a smear of buttercream frosting, a ceiling fan, two cups of ersatz coffee. She was nothing if not resourceful. "This cigarette," she said.

"What would you do with it?"

She reviewed the menu of torture she would subject her ex-husband to before settling on a classic. "To begin with, I'd put it out in his palm."

Vincent offered her his hand. Set it four inches below blazing ember. Ash flaked and fell.

Anna glanced at his open palm, then back up at him, and Vincent could see the fissures deepen in the corners of her eyes.

She looked so much older when she said, "What did you do, Vincent?"

He told her. Not the whole story, he hadn't told her his real name, hadn't even introduced himself, but she could see where it was going, and she said, "Stop telling me this," but if he stopped now he would never find his way back to where atonement begins.

Anna lowered the cigarette toward his palm. She didn't want to cause him pain, not at first, she only wanted him to stop talking, to stop telling her what she didn't want to hear, because even if he wasn't Kurt and she wasn't Concetta, she treasured the ersatz family they became on Sunday afternoons, and most of all she didn't want to hurt him, only to scare him into silence before he ruined everything, but when the hissing scent rose into the air Anna realized it was already too late.

Vincent closed his fist around the heat and squeezed until his eyes went dark.

He woke on the floor with his head in Anna's lap and his hand wrapped in a dishtowel of cubed ice. The fan unrolled cartwheeling shadows across the ceiling. He murmured words of contrition and she held his head without acknowledging what he said. Couldn't she hear him? It occurred to him as he slipped out of consciousness once more that, no, of course she couldn't. How could she? He asked for her forgiveness in Calabrian and she sang him lullabies in German.

The following Sunday he waited outside the Montclair at the usual time. Rays of summer sun filtered through smog and palm frond. His hand was bandaged in gauze and tucked into his pocket. He didn't think she would come, but at 1:00 on the nose, the red Oldsmobile coupe pulled up. She looked at him through the open passenger window.

"I quit smoking," she said. It was as near to an apology as Vincent would want.

"Probably for the best," he observed. "It's not good for my health."

Anna's white-framed sunglasses slid down her nose. "I'm bewildered," she said. "I'm utterly bewildered by my life."

"There are worse things than bewilderment," Vincent said.

"Such as?"

"Clarity, I imagine."

The first bars of a Duke Ellington tune drifted through one of the Montclair's open windows. A couple picturesque clouds floated in the crystal blue sky. The warm asphalt held the tiny imprints of children's toes. And despite her claims of quitting, Vincent could see a pack of cigarettes holstered in Anna's purse. With whom can you make your way through the wilderness, he wondered, if not another lost traveler?

"I need to pick up a print of *Sergeant York* over at the Warners lot," he said.

Anna returned her sunglasses to her eyes. "You want company?"

He did.

VINCENT PURCHASED A HALF-DOZEN PASTRIES, two packets of cigarettes, and the morning paper, and carried his haul back to the cutting room. He didn't make it past the doorway. Anna was seated behind his desk. The top drawer was open. The black photo album was splayed on her lap.

"I was searching for a pencil," she said, turning the pages. She didn't look up from the neat rows of reassembled passport photographs. "Did you take these?"

He nodded.

"Why have they been torn?"

"It's something my mother always did. Most of the emigrants who came for passport photographs couldn't read or write. She would make a second print and tear it in half. One half she kept. On the other half she would write our address. When the emigrant reached his destination, he could copy out the address on an envelope, slip his half of the photograph inside, and mail it back to San Lorenzo. When my mother pieced the two halves together, she would tell his family he had reached his destination in one piece."

When Anna reached the final page, she looked up. Her finger rested on the last entry. The only one in an album of hundreds that remained incomplete.

She took an eyebrow pencil from her purse, pressed it to the album page, and sketched in the missing half of his passport photograph above the name he had relinquished. When she finished, she passed the album back and he held in his hands the proof of his safe arrival.

"Nino Picone," she said. "It's a pleasure to finally meet you."

• • •

VEDETTE CLEMENT ARRIVED AT THE studio early that day, as she did most mornings since she began working as Miss Lagana's secretary. She greeted the night watchman, who bowed with grave European formality: "Good morning, Miss Clement."

Outside the Mill she saw a bucket of bent nails pried from old sets. The studio carpenter would straighten and reuse them because even the manufacturing of nails had been diverted for the war effort. It made you wonder, it really did. The War Production Board was so desperate for scrap that the other day it sent a man around asking for spare house keys. As if she would give a stranger a key to her front door! For all she knew, he was a burglar. It wouldn't have surprised her in the least. You can't trust anyone, can you? Why, just the other day the newscast warned mothers not to leave their children in strollers parked outside grocery stores. Apparently, hoodlums were stealing the rubber tires right off the baby carriages, if you could believe it. And Vedette could. She really could. You couldn't even buy a rubber girdle these days; now even the *new* ones were whalebone and piano wire. And they called this the twentieth century.

Her sister? Gladys? Down in Long Beach? Well, she was a manicurist, but now she worked at a converted pinball machine factory making bombs. The factory owner had recruited half the 1939 class of Mrs. Jensen's Beautician Academy. And it made sense, it really did: Who better to file and polish all those precise little pieces than a certified professional? Gladys said the crosshairs in the bombsights were threaded from black widow spider silk. Apparently, it was some kind of super thread, stronger than steel, more pliable than elastic, impervious to the temperatures of high-altitude flying. As if anyone needed another reason to fear spiders. To keep up with demand the military was paying ladies twenty cents a foot to farm black widow thread, but Vedette was gainfully employed, thank you very much. Gladys said that on the assembly line they grilled hot dogs and hamburgers on heated bombshells, and it all sounded like one big party. Too much of a party, if you believed Gladys, and you could trust her not to exaggerate this sort of thing, you really could. Apparently, there was so much whoopee-making going on in the factory bomb shelter the management had to padlock it.

Six months ago Gladys was a beautician and now she was some sort of bomb scientist. Vedette was still the secretary she'd been when the war began. Awful, wasn't it? That feeling of falling behind? Of missing your moment?

She walked through the main offices, past the projection room. She heard voices from the cutting room. She peeked in.

"Nino Picone," Anna said, looking up from a book. "It's a pleasure to finally meet you."

It looked like Anna was reading lines from a script in a black binder. Disappointing. Anna seemed too pragmatic to pin her hopes on becoming some B-movie Marlene, but Vedette was willing to concede that she may have overestimated her. Vedette had no illusions about stardom. No, the career path she wanted was the one Maria was charting for herself.

Upstairs, she passed the third-floor reception desk and stopped short at the newly installed memorial to Mercury employees in the armed services. It looked like a lobby card. The names of all those currently serving were listed at the bottom in fine print. Above that, in slightly bigger letters, came the names of the dozen employees wounded in action. Shrapnel pierced the leg of a set carpenter on Wake Island. A lab technician suffered third-degree burns when his plane went down at Midway. Then there was Don Snyder, a lecherous little publicity man who smelled of bay rum and rope cigars. He had a *reputation,* as Gladys would have put it, this being more diplomatic than saying he had a misdemeanor charge for public lewdness. A personnel department sleuth could verify his employment history by the notes of caution left on the ladies' room stalls of several studios. He'd lost both hands at Fort Hood; the Army called it a "training accident," but Vedette knew it was nothing short of divine justice.

Two names loomed over them all, boldfaced, capitalized, killed in action: HAROLD CHANDLER and GERALD FLANN.

And Vedette couldn't believe it. She really couldn't.

Harold and Gerald, thick as thieves those two. Unfailingly polite. Never passed her desk without stopping to ask how she was. Every year on her birthday, they sent a singing telegram. Once, they took her and Gladys on a double date to Ciro's and spent the night dancing. Sure, nothing really came of it, but what a lovely evening they had. Vedette didn't know why she was crying. She hardly knew them, really, a few words around the office and one night dancing. Two bit players, nobodies, really, but the way they comported themselves? The good humor? The respect and consideration they showed people even more nobody than themselves? What could you call that but grace? And their troop convoy goes down in the Pacific while all the bums in Los Angeles get to go on stealing tires from baby carriages.

She stepped back. Harold's and Gerald's names towered on the memorial, the only two legible from across the room.

Top billing at last, Gerald, Harold would say.

And Gerald, beaming, *We're leading men now, Harold.*

Among the immortals, aren't we?

We are, old boy. We are.

Turning away from the memorial, Vedette slammed her elbow into the platform displaying the model miniature of the studio lot. She cursed silently. As she inspected the model to make sure nothing had broken, she noticed the faceless figurine of the secretary sitting outside Miss Lagana's office. Very carefully, she reached into the miniature and moved the secretary behind Miss Lagana's desk. Vedette Clement had been a nobody for too long.

3

"CAN SOMEONE TELL ME WHY THE HELL I'M ANSWERING MY OWN TELEphone?"

Artie stormed out of his office. Everyone was gone. Aside from the entwined ribbons of smoke rising from a typist's ashtray, there was no sign of human habitation. Sure, ever since the war boom, the front office was going through typists the way Mildred's purse went through Life Savers, but to lose all six at once? This was something else. The Rapture. Or a fire drill.

Artie wiped his forehead with the back of his tie as he walked into the corridor. A light glinted below the door at the end. It was the ladies' room. He stood there, uncertain. This could be an emergency. People might be dying in there. He edged the bathroom door open with his toe.

The missing typists stood by the sinks in a tight circle. A séance or fertility ritual of some kind. Was this what happened in sororities? No, they were passing around pages. Whatever they were reading was engrossing enough that they didn't hear him.

Artie coughed into his fist.

One of the typists shrieked in surprise.

"Girls, it's only Mr. Feldman," Vedette said. They were spooked, Artie realized. The lot of them. Spooked. Vedette gathered the pages and sent the typists back to their desks. Unbeknownst to Artie, each had in her purse the five-spot Maria had paid for the performance.

"My apologies, Mr. Feldman," Vedette said. "We just got caught up in a story treatment that came in today."

Though loath to encourage this sort of dereliction of duty, he was curious to see what had captivated a bathroom of typists. These were his people. This was his audience.

"Let me have a look."

"AND HE FELL FOR IT?" Maria asked.

"Hook, line, and sinker," Vedette said, clinking her scotch and soda against Maria's glass. "He took Eddie's treatment out of my hands, walked directly back into his office, and shut the door."

The best way to stoke Artie's interest in *The False Front* was to make him feel he had discovered it, and only then show him the proof-of-concept chase scene she had shot two weeks earlier. Vedette's talent for militarizing gossip would serve Maria's purposes. Notoriety was the most reliable measure of excellence at Mercury, so the more Artie heard about *The False Front,* the better.

"Thank you, Vedette," Maria said. "I appreciate it."

"Your money's always good here, Miss Lagana." Vedette set down her glass. Burgundy lipstick garnished the rim. It was only half past six, but the nightclub was already filling with Air Force cadets in from Santa Ana, soldiers on leave from Camp Irwin, and sailors up from Long Beach to enjoy a late August evening in the city.

Vedette leaned forward. "Say, if Art officially bumps you to executive producer, you'll put in a good word for me, won't you?"

"For what?"

"For what. For your job."

"What, you really want to be an uncredited associate producer?"

"It sounds better than being secretary to an uncredited associate producer."

"Fair enough."

Vedette scooted her chair as uniformed airmen filed past. "I don't believe it. I really don't. Is that Betty Ludlow?"

The blonde at the bar in a victory-roll updo was indeed the paramour whom Artie had brought on the cruise to Acapulco the previous year. Though he stopped seeing her after discovering she was married, he found her husband rather memorable and ended up hiring Ralph Ludlow to play a laconic cowboy.

Shortly after Ralph became Mercury's latest handsome simpleton, the actor had quietly divorced Betty at the urging of the publicity department, which wanted to stoke fan mag speculations about the Mercury ingénues the bachelor might have eyes for.

"I thought she moved back east," Maria said.

"Maybe Mildred called in a mayday. I swear, she was more distraught than Artie when his liaisons with Betty ended. Speaking of lost souls, what happened to Anna Weber?"

"The Army recruited her. That's all I know."

Genuine ignorance relieved her of the obligation to lie. Anna left Los Angeles to join the military. She couldn't say where she had been summoned, for what purpose, when or if she would return. She slipped her resignation under Artie's door, and the next morning her desk was empty. Neither Maria nor Eddie could make sense of it. The ban on enemy aliens serving was all but insurmountable, yet the War Department saw enough military value in a miniature maker to exempt her from every hindrance and restriction. Maria was legally barred from making the seven-mile trip to visit her mother in Lincoln Heights, but Anna, whose son and ex-husband were bosom buddies with Joseph Goebbels, took a train hundreds of miles east to participate in a clandestine military program. She and Eddie sat up one night discussing this with Vincent in his room. Pinned on his walls was a selection of Robert Capa's photographs, all shot on the same model Leica Vincent had surrendered to the Enemy Aliens Property Board. It saddened Maria to think these photographs gave Vincent what Mercury's pictures gave its audience: a way to see what you cannot do and who you cannot be.

"Vedette? Is that you?" Betty Ludlow pressed through khaki uniforms to reach their table. Vedette feigned delight to see the woman who, after she transitioned from Artie's bookie to his mistress, treated Vedette as her handmaid. You had to take the long view, you really did. A stint as a Beverly Hills bankruptcy court stenographer had honed Vedette's sense of schadenfreude and dramatic irony. Here was her old tormentor, waiting for someone to buy her a drink. "It's so good to see you, Betty. It really is."

It took several rounds of drinks, and a certain amount of leading questioning, before Vedette brought out the knives.

"Are you still broken up about Ralph divorcing you?" Vedette asked hopefully. She was expecting a muted denial. She wasn't expecting Betty to laugh.

"You think *he* divorced *me*?" Betty rolled her eyes. "God no. That was my doing. Don't get me wrong, Ralph's easy enough on the eyes, but have you ever had a conversation with him? He's barbiturate incarnate. Besides, it's true what they say about a Hollywood love triangle being an actor, his wife, and himself. I wish that dimpled dullard nothing but the best. I hope he and himself are happy together."

Vedette was annoyed with Betty's cheerful disregard of her tragic circumstances. "Are you really sure you're okay?"

Betty was doing just fine. In fact, she'd already gotten remarried. Eight times. And, she was pleased to report, not a single one of those marriages had ended in divorce.

"Military wives receive a fifty-dollar monthly allotment check," she said. "Not much if you only have one husband, but if you marry often enough, and the war goes on long enough, you never have to worry about money again." She drained the dregs of her wine spritzer. "I always intended to marry rich. A few more husbands and I'll have married myself into the upper class."

Maria said, "No wonder Art was crazy for you."

Betty's shrug said *Well, he is only human.*

"So you're a bigamist?" Vedette glowered. "Isn't that illegal?"

"Only a misdemeanor in California. Besides, since time immemorial marriage has been the only means of economic advancement available to us. It's their game I'm winning." Betty exhaled a silvery beam of smoke into Vedette's eyes. "Monogamy is my sacrifice to the war effort."

"My aunts would love you," Maria said. "How do you choose who you'll marry?"

Here, Betty allowed herself a guilty little smile. "My romantic tastes run toward high-mortality occupations—airmen, cable dogs, radio carriers—with better chances of realizing the ten-grand life insurance policy the military provides the wives of enlisted men. What can I do? The heart wants what it wants."

Just then, a trio of sailors worked up the courage to approach. The first two introduced themselves as Navy seamen. Behind them stood a shy boy in a khaki cap who couldn't have been more than nineteen.

In total, Betty would marry eighteen enlisted men, drawing a nine-hundred-dollar monthly allotment and winning the top prize seven times. She might have gotten away with it if not for what occurred in a Honolulu bar in November 1944. A few troops on R&R were passing around photographs of their wives. When two exchanged photographs that were not only of the same woman, but were in fact the exact same photograph, each man concluded, not incorrectly, that the other had been screwing his wife. They mediated their dispute with the aid of a barstool, billiard cue, and several hurled coconuts, and following an investigation into the untold damage to military honor and tiki bar property, Betty was charged with fraud. When she was released in 1947, the man who had lost the fight in the Honolulu bar was waiting outside the women's prison gate. His name was Chaz Mendes. If asked, he couldn't have explained why he'd come. Only that he had already lost so much in the war; he didn't want to lose Betty too. "Can I offer you a ride?" he said. Betty looked down the empty stretch of road. There was no one else. No one at all. She said, "Yes." They moved to Modesto, where he had people, and purchased farmland. Over the decades, the walls of their ranch house filled with photographs from family vacations. Chaz Mendes died on a cool autumn morning in 2015 at the age of ninety-one, out on the porch where he liked to whittle figurines for the grandkids. Betty Mendes outlived him by six weeks. Among the unopened mail that gathered for days beneath the couple's mail slot was a check from Chaz's life insurance policy, which, unbeknownst to Betty, he'd paid into for decades. It was a sizable amount, even after it was split five ways among the sons and daughters who never knew their father was their mother's tenth husband.

"And what's your name, sailor?" Betty asked the shy boy in the khaki cap while Maria and Vedette looked on.

"Chaz Mendes."

"And what do you do, Chaz?"

"I'm in the Merchant Marines, miss."

Betty smiled because despite their JV reputation, the Merchant Marines was the most lethal of all the armed services.

"That's terribly dangerous work, isn't it?" Betty pressed her hand to her chest, and the marine brightened at the unexpected upside of his diminished life expectancy. "I'm just doing my duty, miss."

"Do you believe in love at first sight, Chaz?" Betty said as she led him toward the bar.

"I'm beginning to, miss."

"It was love at first sight," Betty would say at Chaz's funeral seventy-three years later. "Love at first sight."

4

ARTIE WAS ANNOYED MARIA HAD TAKEN IT UPON HERSELF TO PRODUCE an entire scene without his permission, to say nothing of the legal department's. Hell hath no fury like a lawyer uninformed. Nonetheless, his curiosity outweighed his vexation and he settled into his projection room armchair to watch the four-minute reel Maria had cut.

He hadn't felt comfortable in the projection room since Ned had renovated it with oak paneling, squeaky leather armchairs, and carpets thick enough to muffle an approaching assassin's footsteps. Perhaps Artie's paranoia really was getting the better of him, but his brother's recent efforts to steer production toward high-end A-pictures—the kind of million-dollar ventures that could capsize a medium-sized studio like Mercury—made him vigilant to the possibility of a putsch. He watched the reel in silence, without praise or objection, until the shot where Eddie ran into the set for *Tell 'Em in Tokyo* and the frame filled with darkness. Finally, he turned to Maria.

"I barely squeeze enough film stock from the War Production Board to justify second takes and you're wasting it on this?"

The bitterness in his voice surprised her.

"It's not enough that Ned's trying to screw me six ways to Sunday? There's already more blades in my back than in a knife block and I have to worry about you too?"

Maria said, "It's good, though, isn't it?"

"Good? *Good?*" Artie barked a laugh of disbelief. He sipped his "coffee." It was an evil cracked-wheat substitute engineered by fifth columnists to cripple civilian morale. However reluctant he was to admit it, he thought the chase scene was quite good, and that of course made it worse. "Whether it's good or bad isn't the point, the point is this isn't the Wild West: we have a legal department, we have union agreements, we have insurers, we have—"

"I already estimated the budget. Guess what the below-the-line costs would be?"

Artie couldn't help himself. "One thirty?"

"Fifty," she said. "This newsreel-style photography and low-key lighting makes everything look a couple hundred grand more expensive, doesn't it?"

"Fifty?" Artie whistled and felt the pique vent right out of him. "Are you sure?"

"Give or take a few thousand. We spend a lot of money dressing up the back lot to look like Tokyo or London or wherever. It's cheaper to let the back lot appear as itself."

Artie stroked his chin and looked down at the story treatment Eddie had written over the preceding months. "It needs a better ending," he said. "It can't end with the actor trapped on the *Tell 'Em in Tokyo* set. Too depressing. He's got to find a way out."

"I know. It needs a little work."

"Does it have to be about a Chinese actor?"

"The whole premise is an actor who's mistaken for an Axis spy."

"I suppose you're right. Until we invade Europe, the war in the Pacific is the war that matters. Okay, we'll get a Caucasian to play him."

"Sure, we could," Maria said. "But given how your brother will react, I figured you'd want to cast Eddie."

Though it appeared nowhere among the Production Code's rules and regulations, studios strove to make ethnic characters more relatable to white America by casting them with actors who supposedly brought them one degree nearer to Anglo-Saxon: Chinese actors played Japanese characters, Jewish actors played Chinese characters, Catholic actors played Jewish characters, and Protestant actors played Catholic characters. Perhaps these conventions went unwritten because even subversive producers like Artie Feldman fully accepted them. But as he paced back and forth, sinking footprints into the dense carpet, he saw the wisdom of casting Eddie as himself. Only two kinds of pictures made money: the obscenely cheap and the obscenely expensive.

That autumn Eddie Lu was set to feature in the latter, in *Guns of Midway*, an overblown A-picture Ned had been lobbying for ever since the June defeat of the Japanese at Midway Island. It was already budgeted at 1.1 million, far and away Mercury's most expensive picture to date, and if it proved a bona fide smash there was reason to think Ned's stranglehold on the board of directors would become unbreakable. Already, the board had begun treating Artie like middle management.

All of which made Artie open to a premise like *The False Front*. He liked the idea of laying bare the big-budget baloney of *Guns of Midway* by casting the villain of Ned's picture as the hero of his. He could undercut Ned's claims to realism by divulging the back lot's trade secrets, by demonstrating how cheap high-priced realism was. That alone presented opportunity for the sensationalism Artie made a career of stirring up. What's more, it might even convince the board to send Ned back to New York. If *The False Front* had a higher profit margin than *Guns of Midway*—if it even, Artie dared to hope, netted a larger gross—would the board ever trust Ned to meddle in production again? There were only two combatants on the False Front of wartime Hollywood, Artie and Ned Feldman, and as he turned to face Maria he felt the tide of battle turn in his favor.

"You're right," he said. "It has to be Eddie. Ned will lose his lunch."

5

ARTIE WAS WHITE-KNUCKLING HIS DESK PHONE WHEN LEONARD BOYD appeared at his door.

"You're fourteen. You're not wearing Coco Chanel to the goddamn Wilshire Boulevard Temple," Artie said in the death-threat whisper he usually reserved for agents. He waved Leonard Boyd in. "I don't care if the dress is French. So's a ménage à trois and I don't want you in one of those either. What's what? Good question. Ask your mother."

Artie cradled the receiver and turned to Leonard. "How did you survive your children's adolescence?"

"Habitual drunkenness," Leonard said cheerily. This was perhaps also the reason he remained one of the few Mercury board members loyal to the ancien régime of Artie Feldman; between Ned and Eastern National, who'd begun vacuuming up Mercury stock, Artie's enemies controlled over half the seats.

Leonard had recently received a commission as lieutenant commander in the Navy but thought the official uniform was a bit plain, so Artie had a costume designer fashion him a new one replete with frilly epaulettes and unearned medals.

"I visited the set of *Guns of Midway*," Leonard said, belting back the bourbon Artie offered. "Quite a production, really."

Quite. Two weeks into principal photography, Ned's prestige picture was ahead of schedule and on budget, much to Artie's consternation. It *looked* like a $1.1 million picture. Adhering to the Office of War Information's exhortation to "show democracy in action," *Guns of Midway* depicted a platoon of geographically and ethnically diverse servicemen—a Brooklyn wiseass, an emotionally repressed New Englander, a Blackfoot Indian, an Iowa hayseed, a rodeo rider everyone calls Tex, and, even though segregation ran so deep in the military that blood donations were divided by race, a Black NCO—who put aside their differences to face common danger. Eddie Lu was cast as a captured Japanese pilot who once studied chemistry in Illinois. The Office of War Information praised *Guns of Midway* for adhering to its guidelines on "Properly Directed Hatred."

"I question the wisdom of profligacy as a business strategy," Artie said, refilling Leonard's tumbler.

Leonard knocked back the bourbon. "You have to spend money to make it," he said, but if being a spendthrift was the secret to wealth creation, Leonard Boyd presumably wouldn't be a middle-aged man living on an allowance from his parents.

"That's a very . . . cerebral notion. Say, Leonard, seeing as you're a lieutenant commander in the Navy now, have you considered asking Ned to bring you on as a consultant? I think he'd really appreciate your expertise."

"But I wasn't at Midway," Leonard said.

"Sure, but didn't you sink your yacht a few years ago? That sort of firsthand experience will give *Guns of Midway* the authenticity it deserves."

"It wasn't my yacht. It was my father's," Leonard said, staring at his shoes. "And it didn't sink. I sailed it into a lighthouse."

"So you had a drink or two too many. Since when's that a crime?"

"It was fourteen felonies and eighty-two misdemeanors."

"And that only goes to show that prosecutorial overreach is one of the great injustices of our era. The important thing is bringing your . . . joie de vivre to Ned's picture."

"You really think so?" Leonard was always eager to impress

Artie. Perhaps Artie's barely disguised contempt reminded Leonard of the father he always had.

"In my heart of hearts, Leonard, I know you're the only person who can make *Guns of Midway* what it should be." Artie clapped Leonard on the back, filled his tumbler to the brim, and directed him toward Ned's office. "Your hand is on the tiller, my friend. Now sail into the light."

At the office door, Leonard turned back. "Say, Art, I'm not supposed to mention this, but there's been a lot of talk among the board about this next picture you have Eddie Lu slated for. This *False Front* number."

This was disconcerting news. He'd kept his plans limited to a close circle of allies. He intended to shoot the picture covertly, at night, exactly as Maria had the chase scene, and inform the board only once the picture was cut, scored, and ready to distribute.

"Everyone knows you and Ned have a bit of a sibling rivalry, but there's concern you're allowing it to cloud your judgment. The board is throwing around a lot of loaded terms like 'fiduciary responsibility' and 'incompetent leadership' and 'fifth columnist.'"

"Fifth columnist? They think *I'm* a fifth columnist?"

"Figuratively, and I'm sure it was said in the heat of the moment, but some board members are worried that you're trying to undermine Ned's picture with this idea."

Artie denied this with the indignation of the rightly accused.

"I'm just telling you what I'm hearing," Leonard said, placing his hand on Artie's shoulder. "Be careful, okay? You know you have my support, but I'm only one vote."

Composing himself with a deep draft from Leonard's tumbler, Artie said, "Please reassure the board their concerns are entirely misplaced. While Ned and I have had our disagreements, Mercury is my baby, and I would do nothing to imperil its financial stability nor to abuse the faith the board has in me. If *The False Front* in any way jeopardizes that, I'm happy to put it on ice."

"They'll appreciate it, Art. It'll go a long way to rebuilding trust."

"Before you go, let me ask, how did the board hear about this?"

"Why, Ned sent us the script."

"Ned did," Artie repeated, startled his brother had gotten ahold of the screenplay.

"He was very complimentary toward you in his memorandum. He said it's a bold and original B-picture premise, he's just worried it might adversely affect the investment the studio has in A-grade movies like *Guns of Midway*."

Once Leonard left, Artie punched his intercom and asked his secretary to find Maria and Eddie.

"I'm sorry," he said after breaking the news. "Really, I am. Believe me, nothing would have given me greater pleasure than sticking it to Ned, but it's out of my hands."

Maria could hear Eddie's disappointment leak out of him in a sigh. Every night, after Eddie came home from shooting *Guns of Midway,* he worked into the early hours, polishing his script. He was still stalled on the ending, unable to find a way out from the *Tell 'Em in Tokyo* set. He'd tried dozens of possible resolutions but none worked. Maria knew he would find an ending he could live with. She'd have loved to put her name on this picture, down in the lower right-hand corner: *Produced by Maria Lagana*. "There must be something we can do," she said.

"I don't think so, Maria." Artie opened his desk drawer, tapped a few antacids into his palm, swallowed without water. "It's one thing to go against the Production Code or even the US Senate. It's quite another to go against the majority opinion of your board of directors."

"We can—"

"No, Maria, we can't. We can't wage war on our enemies, our allies, and ourselves all at the same time—we're not French. We've lost *The False Front,* but we live to fight another day. Are you okay, Eddie?"

Beside her, Eddie folded his arms, sealing in his dismay. Nowhere on the Mercury lot, including the restrooms, was his sense of solitude more profound than in conversation with a producer who pretended to care if he was okay.

"The board was always going to kibosh this, wasn't it?" Eddie said. "They've staked a couple million on making me the most famous villain in the country. They were never going to let you jeopardize that."

"No," Artie conceded. "I suppose not. I'm loath to admit that we may have gotten carried away." He stared through the open door to the typing pool, where typists diligently pecked at Underwoods. "This place. The mice want to be cats and the cats want to be dogs. We got carried away is all. We forgot who we are."

"Who are we?" Maria asked.

"Bit players. Nobody at all."

On the drive home, Eddie said little. When they returned to their rooms, he flopped into the armchair and flipped through that Sunday's *Los Angeles Times*. "I was thinking I might leave California for a little while," he finally said.

Maria stood in the bathroom, in her striped nightgown, squeezing a blob of Pepsodent onto the toothbrush bristles.

"Now that *Front* is scrapped, I'm sure you can take a couple weeks off once you're finished shooting *Midway*," she said, and popped the toothbrush into her mouth. The stale residue of her two-dozen daily Luckies dissolved in the minty froth.

"I was thinking I'd leave tomorrow," Eddie said, apparently making this monumental decision between an article on meat-stretching recipes and an advertisement for grapefruit juice fortified in "Victory Vitamin C."

Several weeks later, Maria would find the Sunday edition of the *Times* behind the armchair. She would page through it without paying much attention until she saw what he must have been reading while she was brushing her teeth. The article and accompanying photographs documented the Manzanar concentration camp in the Owens Valley, where some ten thousand of Los Angeles's Japanese

Americans were interned. There were scenes of baseball played on grassless diamonds; a Boy Scout troop saluting the flag; girls in pleated skirts and bobby socks following their parents to Presbyterian services; everyone smiling, pitching in, helping out. If not for the lunar landscape, these scenes might have taken place in any small town across the country. The chipper sanitization of a concentration camp seemed to her as obscene as the most lurid anti-Japanese propaganda. One photograph depicted thousands of internees lining up to complete California absentee ballots for November's congressional election. The accompanying caption reassured concerned readers that at Manzanar only American citizens were allowed to vote.

Maria twisted the tap and tried not to think about what Eddie just said. Cool water spritzed into the porcelain basin. She washed out her mouth and dried the sink with a washcloth. Eddie was still reading the paper in his chair when she climbed into bed. Of course, he knew she couldn't come with him. It was illegal for her to travel more than five miles from her place of residence. She reached for the red-and-white cigar box on her nightstand and pulled out a letter her father had written her in 1930. There was one passage she had returned to again and again in the months since the enemy alien prohibitions were introduced:

> I still haven't grown accustomed to the sensation of being both marooned and landlocked. The San Lorenzo confino colony is without fences, barbed wire, or locks, but the borders are as clear in my mind as if the very ocean were lapping against the streets and intersections that encircle my little island. Sometimes I watch the locals cross through the unmarked threshold where the confino colony ends and think: How have they learned to walk through walls? You can't know the pleasure your descriptions of traipsing around Los Angeles have brought me. For the length of a letter, I can walk through walls too.

If these sentences carried deeper meanings now, on the thousandth read, than when she first pieced them together on the bare walls of the Italian Piazza false front, it was because now she too marked the limits of her enclosure not by barbed wire or fences but by the boulevards on which locals moved freely, without a second thought, without noticing the borders they crossed and walls they passed through. She couldn't have known what her letters meant to her father, not really, not until she finally understood how much his meant to her. With these words her father reached from the silence that swallowed him to assure her she was not alone; that everything she felt now he had once felt too; that after all these years, they had become neighbors in the same precinct of the unimaginable.

She set the letter aside and looked across the room at Eddie. "Tomorrow, huh."

Guns of Midway was halfway through its five-week shoot. If Eddie left tomorrow, he would tank the biggest production in Mercury's history, and get himself blacklisted at every studio in the city. No producer would hire him again.

"It occurred to me that I've never left Los Angeles."

"This is a hell of a time to start."

Eddie folded the newspaper, crossed the room, and sat on the edge of the bed beside her. He stroked her cheek with the flats of his fingernails. Looking up at him, she could see her face ink-blotted in his pupils. He blinked his beautiful lashes and she felt raked clean in his eyes.

"There will be other movies," she said.

"That's what I'm afraid of. The way I see it, they'll have me playing Jap villains until the end of the war, then it's back to the usual devious Chinaman shit."

"You don't know that. You were so close with *The False Front*."

"No, Maria, I wasn't."

"If you walk off, that's it. No insurer will underwrite a picture featuring you again."

"I know."

"So wait until *Guns of Midway* wraps, okay? Then do whatever you want. Don't forfeit everything you've worked for."

Eddie studied her, saddened the person who knew him best couldn't see what was so obvious to him. On the little desk across the room, surrounded by his volumes of Shakespeare, Chekhov, Ibsen, and Goethe, sat his script for *The False Front.* He'd fine-tuned every line and gesture but still hadn't come up with a satisfying ending. He couldn't get himself off the *Tell 'Em in Tokyo* set at the end of the chase scene. Every exit was blocked. Remaining in Hollywood meant remaining on that set, in that character, in one form or another, forever.

"This is how *The False Front* ends," he said. "This is how I get out."

"By walking away?"

"Exactly."

Maria tried to rein in her exasperation. She wondered if Eddie's deep-seated desire to play a tragic lead had inspired this last-stand mentality.

"*Guns of Midway* only has another two and a half weeks. It's even shooting a day ahead of schedule. Why don't you wait until then so you can leave without burning every bridge behind you?"

"Because I don't think I could live with myself if I waited that long."

Maria shook her head. "My mother warned me about idealists."

Lifting an eyebrow one impish millimeter, Eddie said, "This handsome mug of mine? You didn't stand a chance."

She settled her head into the crook of his elbow as he ran his fingers through her hair.

"Would you come with me?" he asked.

"Come where? You don't even know where you're going."

"Yeah, but would you come?"

"You know it's illegal for me to go more than five miles from here."

"I know, but would you come with me if you could?"

So this was what their future had become: a hypothetical deferred into the conditional mood. If there wasn't a war, or enemy alien restrictions, or the histories they flowed from and into, if the world was a kinder place and they were different people, then yes, she would. But in that kinder world Eddie wouldn't feel he had to leave.

They lay together while out on the window ledge finches rested their wings.

Finally, he said, "Do you have a suitcase?"

"I can't go with you."

"Not for you. For me."

It occurred to Maria that if Eddie had never left Los Angeles, there was no reason why he should have a suitcase, and of all the disparities in background and experience, this one seemed the most insurmountable.

She walked to the closet and pulled her father's brown leather suitcase from the top shelf. The leather was scratched and worn, bearing faded stickers and stamps from its long passage across an ocean, a continent, a lifetime. The brass clasps had gone green with verdigris. The musty scent of cemetery dirt no longer clung to the silk lining. For entire periods of her life, this suitcase was what she thought of when she thought of home, and now she carried it across the room and gave it to the person she loved.

6

THE FOLLOWING MORNING, EDDIE HOISTED THE SUITCASE INTO THE trunk of her Plymouth and they drove through the rush-hour streets toward Union Station. She took Sunset Boulevard east and then south, the September day pouring through the cracked window, Eddie watching her closely, trying to record this all in his memory, the breeze tugging at her curls, the pitch of her shoulders, her thumb's restless tap on the steering wheel, and the well-watered greenery washing over the windshield. Maria pulled over on a block unremarkable but for the invisible border that ran through it. The florist shop on the right marked exactly five miles from the Montclair.

Eddie stepped out, scuffing the concrete with slow footsteps. He opened the trunk and hauled out the suitcase. She walked with him as far as the florist, where, for her, the door to the world closed.

"This is as far as I can go," she said, looking down at a square of sidewalk bruised in flattened gum and soot stains. Running across it was the wall only she could see.

Eddie nodded. "Thanks for coming with me this far."

"I feel like we're getting divorced, and we were never even married."

"We were as good as."

"We were," Maria reflected. "It was a good marriage, wasn't it?"

"It was beautiful."

"I don't know how to do this. I don't know what comes next."

"I tip my hat, turn, and walk away."

They stood there, nearly touching, as the morning traffic inched past.

"Will you be okay?" he asked.

If she said no, he would stay, she was sure of it. If she said she would be lost without him, he would stay. He loved her too much to hurt her, even if it meant hurting himself instead. And she loved him too much to put him in that position. They had never cared for each other more than they did right now, as their relationship ended. As she blinked back tears and felt Eddie's arms around her one last time, it occurred to Maria the breakup was not a failure of their love but its fullest expression. It took all her strength to say, "I'll be just fine, Eddie."

Eddie's eyes were bright and wet and he flashed his matinee idol smile. "My girl," he said. Then he tipped his hat, turned, and walked away.

Watching his rangy silhouette shrink with each step, Maria recalled the distant morning in San Lorenzo, when her father accompanied her and her mother to the train station. She didn't remember what was said or not said in their final moments as a family. What she remembered was her father's footsteps falling silent beside her. He gave no warning and stopped so suddenly that she and her mother had walked another ten paces before realizing he wasn't with them. There was no razor wire demarcating the limits of his prison because its dimensions had been so firmly established, by threat and violence, inside her father's mind. She kept looking over her shoulder as her mother led her onward by the hand. Twenty miles inland, one thousand feet above sea level, her father reached the edge of the earth, and standing there, watching her journey on, his face broke into besotted disbelief, and he tipped his head back and let out a glorious whoop, as if he'd just glimpsed the impossible, as if she were not walking over cobblestone but on the water itself.

Ever since that day, her father had grown in her mind to a figure of unbridgeable distance, and yet Maria had never felt as near to him as she did while standing outside an Echo Park flower shop, on a September Tuesday in 1942, sixteen years after he watched her walk away with a suitcase he no longer needed.

7

IT WAS EDDIE'S FIRST TIME IN UNION STATION, BUT A HOMECOMING NONE-theless.

The train station had been built on the neighborhood his grandfather moved into after finishing work on the Central Pacific line. In 1933, Chinatown's opera house and temples and schools and teahouses were demolished to make way for the terminus that consolidated the multiple train lines running into Los Angeles. The neighborhood's razed bricks became Union Station's foundation stones. Beneath these gleaming floors was the house his grandfather built. The room where Eddie Lu was born.

He set down the brown leather suitcase. Stood in the bustling flow of ghosts.

Women war workers in Carmen Miranda–style turbans passed beneath the lobby's bronze chandeliers, jowly businessmen in leather club chairs unfolded broadsheets, Pullman porters ferried cabin trunks to the baggage area, and none knew what was buried beneath their feet.

Every ten minutes troop transport trains arrived with sailors and marines bound for the Pacific, eighteen years old, clean-cut, well ironed, nervy with false confidence. Scenes he'd seen a million times before, even if he was seeing them in person for the first time: the parents saying goodbye to the son, the sweetheart waving her handkerchief, the young man staring out the window long after the distances swallowed those he looked for. The teary train station farewell had become such a staple of wartime cinema that Mercury was constructing its own terminal set on the lot.

He crossed to the departures lobby. The ticket counter was a hundred feet of walnut. The ticket clerk asked his destination.

Eddie wasn't sure what to say. His destination was the means of transportation itself: "I'd like to ride east on the Central Pacific."

The clerk consulted his ledger. "There's a 10:23 to Sacramento. You can pick up the Central Pacific from there."

"Okay."

"Second class?"

"First class," Eddie said. "The whole way."

8

IN THE CUTTING ROOM, VINCENT SAT AT THE MOVIOLA AND SCROLLED through the footage from *Victory in the East,* the Hasso Beck propaganda picture MoMA had finally sent. It arrived months too late to show Anna. Nonetheless, he moved through the footage until he found Kurt. Her boy was a young man now, with neatly combed black hair and a handsome smile. Vincent stopped on a frame that interested him. It captured Kurt gazing into the camera in a moment of dawning recognition, the beat between seeing a familiar face and recalling to whom it belongs.

Rudi Bloch knocked on the door. "The War Department has finally taken Artie's advice."

"Regarding?"

"They're giving us permission to shoot a reenactment next week. We need another cameraman if you're interested in going."

"Where to?"

"Berlin," he said. "Apparently, the Chemical Warfare Corps has built one in Utah."

GERMAN VILLAGE

1

SOUTHWEST OF SALT LAKE, DUGWAY PROVING GROUND SPREADS ACROSS the high desert, horseshoed in snowcapped ridges, studded in sagebrush and saltbush, reticulated in razor wire. On the southern horizon, Anna can't tell where the bomb craters end and the canyons begin. It's the size of Rhode Island, and surely vastness has no more evocative unit of measure than an American state. On Anna's civilian map the test site is represented in the pale blankness of uncharted territory, the same leached hue of the featureless miles passing over her eyes.

The first night she wakes to rainless thunder. Red light pulses in the rattling barracks window glass. Another crack flaunts over the face of a distant escarpment. Across the gouged horizon man-made suns devour the night.

"I see you've been introduced to Dugway weather," Colonel Macalister says the next morning when Anna rubs her eyes.

"It looked like Independence Day," she says.

"We're a real patriotic bunch."

A dozen civilian engineers, architects, chemists, and set designers sit beneath a dreary storm cloud of cigarette smoke.

No one has been told anything, not even Erich Sonnenthal, the project's leader, a small dark-haired man whose inquisitive stare is magnified by steel-rimmed spectacles. Anna knows Sonnenthal by reputation. In the Great War, the ambitious German Jewish architect designed networks of trenches on the western front. Horrified by the efficiency with which his trenches transformed men into corpses, he returned from the war eager to pledge his talents to social progress. In Berlin, there was no more pressing issue than the housing shortage. Though unaffiliated with the Bauhaus, he shared its utopian creed that good design ennobles the individual and uplifts the society. If architecture is the elemental, inescapable art, the only art form that our lives unfold within, then a beautifully designed home is the vessel for human flourishing. His workers' estates were transgressively simple—clean horizontals, white walls, flat roofs, spacious interiors—privileging prefabricated materials to reduce cost and construction time as they rose across Berlin.

Sitting beside him, Anna recognizes Jürgen Behring, the foppish son of an architect who worked on Hitler's Bavarian Berghof, an unremarkable mind whose politics are purely patricidal.

The lights dim and after welcoming remarks Colonel Macalister asks if they are familiar with firestorms.

According to the slideshow, firestorms have been a feature of urban life since the Great Fire of Rome in Nero's reign. Cartoon illustrations show a thermal column drawing oxygen from the surrounding atmosphere. As the currents intensify the fire pulls in not only air but physical debris. The influx of combustible material increases heat, which in turn intensifies the wind spiraling around the updraft, eventually generating a cyclonic storm system. "A great big fucking fire tornado," as Colonel Macalister puts it, that in a few hours can consume more of a city than years of conventional ordnance. The problem is that two years of RAF bombing sorties have failed to ignite a firestorm in Berlin.

A team of Standard Oil's brightest chemists is already engineering napalm and thermite incendiaries at Dugway. However, an incendiary is not a stick of dynamite but a chemical reaction precisely calibrated to its kindling.

"If we are to burn Berlin over there, we must learn to burn it over here. And to burn it, we must build it. Which," Colonel Macalister says, "is where you folks come in."

Sonnenthal raises a hand. "I'm sorry, Colonel—you want us to build Berlin in Utah?"

"Not all of it, naturally. A representative neighborhood."

The color drains from Sonnenthal's face. "Forgive me, but I hoped, I assumed, the Army Air Force would be targeting Albert Speer's building projects."

"Satisfying though it would be, they're of limited military value. Besides, Speer mostly works in granite, which won't burn."

"What about the Berghof?" Behring adds hopefully.

"The big cheese rarely ventures there these days. Besides, he'll have dropped into its bunkers before our flyboys get within fifty miles of the Obersalzberg."

The fire-bombing campaign will target neighborhoods like Kreuzberg, Wedding, and Neukölln, communist strongholds during the Weimar years where even today you might not find a dozen Nazi Party members among its tenement blocks. Were there any justice the air raids would target Wannsee or Grunewald, but the Nazi brass live in villas too sparsely distributed to warrant area bombing runs. Densely populated urban centers where multistory tenement blocks predominate offer the highest return on investment, but even these Mietskasernen—rental barracks—prove vexingly fire-resistant. It is these tenements crowding red Berlin that the assembled émigrés are to construct in the Utah desert, no expense spared, a molecularly faithful re-creation, down to the nightstand Bibles and the carpet piles and the bassinets.

Dehousing, the colonel says, and Anna includes it among the other euphemisms—*relocation, special treatment, living space*—is never far from her mind. Dehouse Wedding and Neukölln, but Kreuzberg particularly, the most densely populated Berlin neighborhood. Does Anna mention that she grew up there? She does not. The colonel already knows this. It's why he asked her here.

"Some of you may have personal or ethical objections to this project," the colonel continues. "If so, please rest assured the US Army bears you no ill will. We'll give you a ride back to the train station this afternoon. Those of you who decide to stay will not only have the satisfaction of helping hasten the end of the war but will also have the satisfaction of working on an architectural scale that few in your profession have ever enjoyed. To say nothing of the pleasure of walking through the streets of Berlin once more."

Several architects shake their heads, offer their apologies, and shuffle out the door. Anna stands too. She understands what she relinquishes by shaking the colonel's hand and accepting his offer.

The colonel assigns them a Quonset hut so repellent to Behring's aesthetics he requests permission—not granted—to renovate it. Sonnenthal is delighted with the semi-cylinder of corrugated iron. The shape is functionalist, clean, modern. The open office space appeals to his ideals of communal living. Neither man asks Anna her thoughts. Who is she to them? A miniaturist promoted past her experience. Only when they learn she married Walter Gelb does she rise in their estimation.

"Did he get out?" Behring asks.

"Flossenbürg," she says, and in the silence they reflect on the architect perishing a slave laborer in the quarry supplying granite to Albert Speer's monstrosities.

The first order of business is stocking the Quonset hut with drafting tables, blue ground paper, T-squares, compasses, gradated scales, liner pens, and the rest of the provisions the quartermaster culls from the lists they provide.

"I ask for coffee and this toxic hickory substitute is what they send," Behring says, emptying the final crate.

"And they say they want to win this war," Sonnenthal comments, but not even a double of Café Josty's finest would improve his mood. His recovered sense of usefulness outweighs his qualms. Since emigrating he hasn't received a single commission; an architect known for Berlin-style workers' housing had limited opportunities in Manhattan, and then, following America's entry into the war, no opportunities at all. Now he works for a client with an unlimited budget and impeccable taste. His Berlin rebuilt in the Utah desert, spread over five square miles, the Berlin of his dreams, without a single swastika to sully it.

They work eighteen-hour days, fueled on hickory coffee, Benzedrine, and an endless supply of Lucky Strikes. With assistance from the Harvard Graduate School of Design, Sonnenthal conducts encyclopedic studies of the battening of Berlin's tenement blocks. The German American owner of a ceramics factory in Pittsburgh provides authentic Prussian-style roofing tiles. Behring analyzes the hardwood frames supporting the Mietskasernen's stone walls. The colonel's insistence on molecular verisimilitude is not hyperbole: the wooden frames and floorboards come from similarly designed Soviet apartment blocks dismantled and shipped out of Murmansk.

The apartment interiors fall under Anna's purview. She commissions pragmatically proletarian wardrobes from émigré costume designers at RKO. She orders cumbersome tenement furniture built by German POWs with carpentry experience. She buys out entire consignment shops in New York's Washington Heights—the "Fourth Reich"—and ships them to Dugway.

The climate is searing. Their sun-soaked complexions radiate the ochres and reds of local geology and their eyes clamp into permanent squints. Ever the clotheshorse, Behring eschews olive drab and color coordinates his ripening sunburns with mauve ascots. Anna wraps her neck in wet washcloths and walks beneath a broad-brimmed hat while distant mountains waver.

Colonel Macalister approves the blueprints for six three-story tenement blocks and the next morning buses ferrying the construction crew arrive beneath rooster tails of pale grit. Manacled men in prison pinstripes debark into the high desert heat.

To construct Deutschland in Dugway at such scale, speed, and secrecy requires replicating the labor practices Nazi architecture pioneered. Watching the stooped, sweating, chain-ganged Utah State Prison inmates conscripted to fight on behalf of freedoms denied them, Anna thinks of Walter and wonders with whom his sympathies would lie: the architects or the prisoners? Given the goal they work toward, are the architects any less guilty of murder than the prison laborers convicted of it? Are their histories any more worthy of extenuation or mercy than the misfortunes that led each prisoner to Dugway?

A dark inkling deepens to certainty. This parched patch of Utah is indeed the farthest outpost of the Third Reich, alike in the immodesty of its vision and narrowness of its humanity.

2

THOSE PRISONERS WITH EXPERIENCE IN CARPENTRY, CONSTRUCTION, roofing, and glazing receive jobs according to their specialty. Anna employs as an assistant a seventeen-year-old named Louis Harrington. Louis's father, a master woodworker whose ornately carved chessmen grace the studies and private libraries of the Boston elite, raised his son to carry on the family trade, but Louis had other notions since learning about Doris Miller, a mess attendant with no combat training who manned an antiaircraft deck gun at Pearl Harbor and became the first Black man to receive the Navy Cross. After that, Louis lost all interest in his father's chessmen.

He lied about his age and, after passing the medical examination, the recruiter shook his hand and welcomed him to the US Navy. In Norfolk he bunked with Charles Green, a reluctant draftee from Baton Rouge who considered Louis a fool for volunteering.

"You know what happened to Dorie Miller?" Charles asked. "They put him on a poster to get dummies like you to enlist, and then they sent him back to peel potatoes and fold laundry. If Dorie Miller is such a hero, then why did the Navy put him in the Steward's Branch to begin with?"

It was a reasonable question, but in their acquaintanceship Louis had learned to impute Charles's reasonableness to cynicism. How could Louis take seriously a man who claimed he would be no worse off under Japanese rule?

"Let white folks get worked over by a master race for a few centuries," Charles said. "See how they take to it."

No, Louis would not surrender to Charles's cynicism. You had to believe in a cause larger than yourself, and what cause was larger than the freedom of the world itself? What was more worthwhile than being on the front line of that fight? And so Louis was crestfallen when the inducting officer assigned him and Charles to the Steward's Branch.

"You wanted to be like Dorie Miller?" Charles said. "Now you are."

Steward's Branch training consisted of starching shirts, pressing pants, folding laundry, serving meals. Orders came to ship out to the Pacific. They took the train west, waylaid for days in nowhere rail depots while freight cars with prioritized materiel and soldiers trundled past. During a three-hour stopover in Utah, at the site of an exhausted mine so remote and desolate it served as a camp for German POWs, Charles suggested they grab breakfast.

It was a Sunday and only one restaurant was open, a roadside diner with Formica countertops and windows mottled in children's fingerprints. Red, white, and blue bunting drooped from the doorframe. Squares of butter puddled in grits and eggs opened in sizzling sheets on the smoking grill. The diner was half-filled with unobservant Christians sinking forks into soggy flapjacks. The German POW at the counter was comparing the stubby breakfast sausages to the gargantuan lengths that graced the plates of his native Mannheim when Louis and Charles walked in.

Without malice or anger—as if he was only stating the facts to two strangers who didn't know how things worked here—the grill man said he didn't serve their kind.

"You don't serve men in uniform?" Louis said, and the question, formed from genuine confusion, arose into accusation as he spoke it.

"I suppose we don't," the grill man said. "At present."

Louis looked to the German POW whose sweaty links basked in drizzled syrup—this Wehrmacht soldier who might have killed

Americans, or would have had he not been captured, who, at the very least, had pledged himself to the maniac ideology of fascism, this man, now sitting quietly, staring into a plate of sausages that didn't compare to those from Mannheim, this prisoner of war, the first enemy combatant Louis had met in the flesh, enjoyed greater rights than Louis Harrington, Steward's Branch, US Navy—and with that the whole bafflement of Louis's young life arose around him.

"You'll serve a Nazi, but you won't serve a Negro sailor?"

"You're no sailor," the grill man said, nodding to the Steward's Branch insignia. "Even on an aircraft carrier, you're a houseboy."

"Let's go," Charles urged, and Louis might have if the jocular leer in the grill man's blue eyes hadn't proved one insult too many. Louis took a stool and ordered eggs over easy, bacon, and biscuits.

The grill man reached under the cash register for his shotgun while everything on the grill burned.

The German POW stood up to leave.

"You stay right where you are," the grill man said. "It's these two gentlemen who are leaving."

"Let's go, Louis," Charles repeated.

"I'd listen to your friend." The grill man jacked a shell into the shotgun. What senseless swerve of human affairs had sent Louis skidding into a gunsight—not in the Pacific, not in Europe, not in North Africa, but in a Utah diner? The only action he would see in the entire war was over a couple eggs and biscuits? How was this permissible? Charles was pulling at Louis's elbow and Louis would have stood and followed if the waitress hadn't at that moment emerged from the washroom and, seeing her boss pointing his shotgun at two Black men—"I was sure they were robbing us," she later told the police—screamed. The grill man jerked involuntarily toward the sound, blew the German POW's head off, and the rest of Louis Harrington's life began.

• • •

IN THE DESERT HEAT GERMAN VILLAGE is a quavering city of quicksilver, unreal, hallucinatory, even as they build it.

Anna doesn't know what brought Louis to German Village. He's a reliable, confident carpenter, needs no instruction, with a father celebrated for his carved chessmen, she remembers that.

Together they construct architectural models of German Village based on Sonnenthal's and Behring's blueprints. They run chipboard through the jigsaw, and the sawdust hissing out tastes freshly chopped, exotically sylvan among the stunted sweep of desert saltbush. They roof the models in sheets of styrene shingles. They build larger, fully furnished miniatures the fire engineers use to determine the sequence of incendiaries.

"Dollhouse collectors pay decent money for this," Anna says one day, examining a three-inch bureau Louis carved. "For when you get out."

Louis doesn't tell her that he has another forty-nine years on the manslaughter sentence: no defense attorney, the judge saying his provocation caused the German POW's death, and when called to the witness stand, he said, "I just wanted breakfast," over and over again.

He's only a year younger than her son, Kurt; small for his age; submerged in coarse institutional cotton; and he looks lost when staring you in the eye. Seventeen but tried and sentenced as an adult because he lied on the recruitment paperwork to serve his country sooner.

While digging German Village's foundations, the work crew unearths frilled trilobite fossils, swirling ammonite shells, shadows of extinction stamped into rock. Louis shows Anna and she remembers Kurt collecting seashells on the Baltic shore, the five-year-old shivering with excitement as he laid his findings across the beach towel and ran his fingers over their whorled ridges. Astonished at this stone secreted by creatures that were essentially mucus, Kurt asked why mollusks wore their skeletons on their skin. "I don't know," Anna said, and instead of disappointment, Kurt laughed and exclaimed, "Then no one knows!" She hasn't thought of that afternoon in years, it could have been lost forever, and she unearths it here in a desert that was once sea.

FREIGHT TRAINS ARRIVE WITH THE tightly packed inventories of secondhand shops serving New York City's German community. Enough to rig each room in the six tenement blocks of German Village with the economic and enduring fittings typical to a Kreuzberg flat. Seeing these household furnishings stained and dented by human use unsettles Anna.

A delicately ribbed birdcage, a heavy dining table, a wall-mounted telephone.

Until this moment German Village has been a miniature, viewed from the abstracted altitude of a long-range bomber, unblemished by the animate life whose extinguishment she expedites.

A rocking horse, a rag doll, a cradle.

A pale sidewinder autographs the sand. It stares at Anna and then vanishes into the wilderness.

SCAFFOLDING CROSSHATCHES THE TENEMENT FAÇADES and through the Quonset hut window Anna watches cart-hauled bricks bow the planks spanning the braces. The speed of construction mesmerizes: forty days to build all six tenement blocks. Add another ten to paint, glaze, and furnish the apartments, and German Village will be completed in a little over seven weeks.

Tens of thousands of floorboards arrive from Soviet Russia, pried from Karelian apartment buildings constructed in the same period and of the same timber as Berlin's tenements.

"Did you want to keep this?" Louis asks.

He passes Anna a floorboard inscribed in blocky Latin letters, Germanic script, and reading the words etched into the hardwood, she quietly asks, "Where did you get this?"

"It was with all the other floorboards," Louis says.

She runs her index finger over the wood and its penmanship seems to shudder into her hand. It is addressed to *Frau Elsa Schulman, 44 Wenggasse, Rothenburg ob der Tauber, Deutschland.* She imagines a rusty nail tattooing the address into the wood grain in an ink of blood, ash, spittle, snow. Where the ink fades the score marks still make legible the signatory: *Hans Schulman, 1. Infanterie-Division.*

Behring reads the message etched into the ten inches of floorboard. He stares for two mystifying seconds before the steep understanding pitches his eyelids closed. For the first time in their acquaintanceship, he is at a loss for words.

He looks out at the strewn floorboards waiting to be hauled up the scaffolding. "The Soviets must have had German POWs pry them out," he says. "It's a letter from a labor camp."

The address is longer than the letter itself and though Louis wants to know what it says he cannot bring himself to ask. They are last words, this much is clear, the final correspondence of Hans Schulman of Rothenburg ob der Tauber, carved on a floorboard, posted into the void.

"You want to keep this?" Louis asks again.

Anna runs her finger over the floorboard once more. The coniferous chill transmitted across thousands of miles seeps into her spine and shivers out.

"I see no reason to let it go to waste," she says, ruthless with pragmatism. "Put it back with the others."

Louis does, but when the architects leave for a meeting with the chemical engineers he retrieves the floorboard, lays it across two sawhorses, and slices off the inscribed foot-long segment. He can't explain what speaks to him from this message written in a foreign language. Neither pity nor fellow feeling with its author. No, the shorn wood transfixes him with the same dread and veneration as the trilobite fossils, as if these dispatches of vanished existence reach out to him not from the past but from the barren future, as if his animate form is the improbable discovery, teeming with the mysteries of the lost age of life.

• • •

LABORERS HAUL HEAVY WOODEN FURNITURE into apartments according to the floor plans Anna provides, personalized down to the books on the shelves and the laid-out silverware.

One night she decides to sleep in one of the furnished bedrooms. Why not? They are the most comfortable accommodations in Dugway, certainly the only ones that resemble home.

She wakes to B-17s roaring overhead. Has she misremembered the test date? Or slept into it? Even the bewildered panic of German Village's sole resident is a verisimilitudinous reaction to the sound of bombers crashing through clouds.

Dark wings slice through the night, on and out of sight.

The B-17 pilots refer to every thousand feet in elevation as an angel, and as she falls back asleep, she wonders how many angels over her they fly.

The next night she wakes to rain running in cords down the newly glazed window. The first rain shower since she arrived to Dugway, first time she's seen anything but fire fall from the sky. She wrests open the sash and plunges her hands into the downpour. The water is cool and cleansing, spilling over her fingers, quenching her dry skin. It's not rain, of course, but firemen hosing down the tenement blocks to ensure authentic Berlin humidity levels in the wood-battened structures.

3

A MERCURY CAMERA CREW ARRIVES TO DOCUMENT THE FIRST INCENDIARY bombing of German Village. Given that her past rears up and reconstructs itself every day here, she isn't surprised to see Vincent among the cameramen. Or perhaps her capacity for surprise has become so arrested it takes more than Vincent Cortese to jolt her into astonishment. Nor is she surprised to see he looks well: his hair combed back into glossy quills, a spry alertness in his eyes when they meet hers.

"The only footage of the air war over Germany is shot from high-altitude bombers. You only see puffs of smoke far below, like little candles blown out," Vincent says, and without further explanation Anna understands why Mercury's Propaganda Unit is photographing tomorrow's bomb test: it wants closeups. It wants the camera to capture in the burning German Village the destructive opulence of Lana Turner's eyes. She asks how Rudi has fared in her absence.

"He's learning to cook for himself."

"How's that going?"

"He's presently recovering from salmonella poisoning."

Anna smiles for the first time in days.

They're walking through the expanse of saltbush toward German Village. The late afternoon sun leaches violet light over the western ridges. The alkali crackling beneath their boots fills the lull. It's the point in the conversation when two friends might ask about the health and welfare of each other's families, but the war contaminates the most innocuous small-talk queries.

Ahead, German Village comes into view: six tenement blocks, gabled tile-on-batten roofs, wood-framed, brick-walled. Without any suburb to mediate the transition between desert and downtown, the approach feels uncanny. The Great Salt Lake Desert rises into metropolitan blight with the abrupt geography of a back lot: Turn off Wild West Row and find yourself lost in Tenement Alley.

The incarcerated laborers trudging through German Village remind Vincent of the confinati who worked the San Lorenzo excavation site. They watch him with the same resigned loathing he once felt toward the propagandists who gathered on the bridge over the Busento. He cannot meet their eyes.

The first tenement's front door opens on raspy hinges.

"No locks," Vincent says.

"Who's going to break into a firebomb test site?"

The daily passage of two generations of Karelian workers has bowed the wooden stairs. They go to the third-floor apartment, the most comfortably appointed in German Village, where Behring is unstoppering bottles of Berliner Weisse brewed by Standard Oil chemists between batches of napalm.

"Anna, where are the glasses?" he calls out.

"The cupboard over the sink," she says, kicking the sand from her shoes.

She introduces Vincent to the two architects. Sonnenthal worries that the spirit of the evening—its verisimilitude—will be undermined by conversing in English.

"Vincent works in Hollywood," Anna says. "Of course he speaks German."

Behring returns from the kitchen. "My grandmother had glasses just like this. Herr Sonnenthal and I have been trying to find any inaccuracies in the set design."

"And?"

Sonnenthal adjusts his glasses. "Only one thing, and it's rather obvious, I'm afraid."

Anna frowns. "What?"

"The time on the wall clock is wrong."

Anna says, "It's set to Berlin time."

"Nothing is missing, then, is it?" Sonnenthal says.

No one mentions the obvious and overwhelming inaccuracy: the residents of German Village have already escaped the falling incendiaries.

Behring drizzles raspberry syrup into the sour beer. They clink cups.

"This is nearly potable," Anna tells Behring with her compliments.

As the leader of German Village, Sonnenthal feels he should make a speech but isn't sure where on the scale of wedding toast to eulogy his remarks should fall. Failing to find the right words or tone, he goes to the gramophone and slips on a record.

A few bars of piano yield to the most famous voice of the Golden Twenties.

"Lotte Lenya," Behring says. Her voice glazes a misty film on his eyes. "You know I was in the front row on the night *The Threepenny Opera* opened. Don't laugh. Brecht said that I was 'instrumental' to its success."

Vincent coughs. "*You* helped Bertolt Brecht?"

Behring doesn't miss a beat. "I helped him with the title. He wanted to call it 'The Twopenny Opera.' I said, 'Think bigger, Bert.'"

"Café culture is wherever you sit, is it?" Anna says.

Behring nods. "The Kurfürstendamm may as well be stitched to the seat of my pants."

The desert is windswept, twilit, mantled in navy. A breeze spritzes grains of sand across the window glass.

"I wonder if I will see the Ku'damm again." Sonnenthal stares into the evening.

"There is no going back," Anna says, "particularly if you go back."

"But we are architects," Sonnenthal points out. "The only reason we're getting sand in our shoes out here in God-knows-where Utah is because there's a moral imperative to defeat fascism, no matter how immoral the means. But isn't there also a moral imperative to rebuild the cities we've helped destroy, no matter how distasteful the idea seems?"

"Why must you drag your poor pummeled conscience to our drinking party?" Behring asks.

"What about you," Sonnenthal asks Vincent. "Would you return to Europe?"

Two ribbons of smoke twist from his cigarette. "I don't know," he said. "There was an actor at Mercury named Eddie Lu, and some days on the lot, he was the only native-born American I encountered. The question, for me, isn't whether to return to Europe but whether to finally leave it."

The record sputters into hissing silence. Behring returns the stylus to the outer rim of the record and Lotte Lenya's voice unspools from the flared wooden amplifying horn, once more, from the top, relieving them of the need to say anything at all.

Behring takes a paper-wrapped package from his satchel. "For you, Herr Sonnenthal. A token of gratitude for your leadership."

Now Sonnenthal really does regret not making a speech. He unwraps the package. Seeing the title, his face clouds over. He curses Behring and tosses the book on the floor.

Anna asks, "What is it?"

Sonnenthal says, "Falsehoods and fabrications."

"Oh, I don't know," Behring says, inspecting his nails. "I think the author makes some sensible points."

It is *Architecture of Folly,* a book-length survey of Sonnenthal's career by his most defamatory critic. At a generous estimate, it sold dozens of copies, but found no more dedicated reader than the architect whose work it vilified.

"Come, Herr Sonnenthal," Behring says, offering the sullen architect his hand. "Dance with me."

"You are a benighted soul," Sonnenthal says.

"So dance with me."

Improbably, Sonnenthal lets Behring pull him to his feet and Anna watches the two architects move in swaying shuffles across floorboards deconstructed by German POWs ten time zones away. She wishes she were dancing with Rudi.

4

THE ARCHITECTS AND CAMERAMEN RELOCATE TO A CONCRETE BUNKER for the incendiary test. Morning light slants golden through the slatted viewing window. Vincent opens a tripod on life preservers laid out as shock absorbers. The radio crackles with acronyms and regionalisms undecodable by Anna's book English.

"There they are." Sonnenthal draws his finger across the horizon. The stretched shadows of B-17s materialize at his fingertip. Through the propellers comes the guttural thrum of pulverized air.

Anna taps a cigarette on the pack. She strikes the match as the bomb bays open. The blockbusters tumbling from the underbellies are comically blimpish, pitching in pratfall, the metal casings as puckered and distended as inflated whoopee cushions, fundamentally ridiculous until they explode.

Foxtails of pounded clay jet from falling roofs.

The seismic force hurtles through sand, alkali, and fossil, unstitching the seams of stone it slides along. Between Anna's fingers the flame pirouettes atop its match head.

The explosion's roar chases its light. Even the unclouded endlessness of Utah sky cannot diffuse it. Anna presses her palms to her ears, but the thunder excavates hidden caverns of cranial resonance. The echo pulses against her closed lids.

The purpose of the two-ton blockbusters isn't destruction but ventilation: blowing out doors, ripping through walls, shattering windows. These tunnels and airways oxygenate the incendiaries subsequent B-17s drop on the pyre. The pilots wear insectile oxygen masks unnecessary for low-altitude bombing runs but mandated since airmen began passing out from the smell of burning flesh rising from German and Japanese cities.

At first only a few pennants of flame flap over the tenement blocks, but within minutes the inferno domes German Village in a planetarium of smoke. The afternoon sun dims to little dazzles of starlight. Incinerating wood screeches. Even a kilometer out the heat colors her skin. What surprises Anna, beyond the scale of destruction, is the vascular bloodlust it uncorks within her. More horrific than the burning city is the satisfaction it renders, the repellent and satiating specter of divine retribution. She feels no kinship with the imaginary residents whose apartments she assiduously personalized. Whose beds she made and clothes she folded. She wants them to die. It occurs to her that the project of reproducing the Nazi capital achieves its apotheosis not in the molecularly faithful German Village but in her own heart's enthralled hunger for extermination.

Vincent's camera keeps rolling. Is he thinking of the conflagration that enveloped the San Lorenzo excavation site? Anna doesn't ask.

Standing beside her, Behring and Sonnenthal press into the viewing slat, ties askew, mouths ajar, pruriently enraptured. None of them are the same people with whom she shared glasses of Berliner Weisse and stories of the city they remembered. All that is supplanted by the pheromonal intensity of communal wish fulfillment, the craving to witness the city they built burn. For an afternoon the war's vastness contracts to a few square miles of Utah desert, the miniature homeland left to them.

Sonnenthal quietly opines on the proceedings through the startled expressiveness of his eyebrows. Behring works his Wrigley's to exhaustion. In a gesture of rare tastefulness he leaves the test tube of celebratory schnapps holstered in his hip pocket. Anna offers Sonnenthal her cigarette. He accepts gratefully and passes it to Behring.

They string the silence in smoky lines, adding a teaspoon of ash to the metric tonnage while Vincent's camera rolls. Three more cigarettes and all that remains of German Village is a draftsman's sketch charcoaled on the blue-ground sky.

When the fires burn out Sonnenthal and Behring return to the barracks. Vincent leaves to consult with the other cameramen. Anna alone crosses into German Village. The melted desert sand has hardened into stained glass. Farther along comes the unmistakable, unbelievable chime of a cooking timer. The squat heft of an iron oven, galvanized against fires within and without, sits in the ruins of a tenement block. Anna hoists herself over carbonized beams that disintegrate in her grip. She folds her handkerchief into a potholder and opens the oven. Inside, a chicken sits bronzed in a pan of oil and rosemary. The scent tickles some inner gland and Anna is ravenous. She takes the sticky mass in her bare hands. The skin's caramelized crispness crackles on her incisors. Steam stirs through the toothmarks. Juice squirts down her wrists as she devours the chicken in both hands like some stupendous tropical fruit. Walking through the ruins, she tells herself that none of this is real and the chicken skeleton, loosely sewn by ligament, swings from her hand.

Mercury's Propaganda Unit ships out before she returns to her barracks. Vincent has left an envelope neatly squared on Anna's pillow. Her name, his handwriting. A letter of farewell.

She decides to shower before opening it, but after washing and drying she is too exhausted to read what he has written her. The next morning, she wakes when Sonnenthal sits at the foot of her bed.

She rubs her eyes. "What time is it?"

"Nearly eleven," Sonnenthal says. "I spoke with the colonel."

"We're being discharged?"

"No," Sonnenthal says, folding his hands in his lap. He has a niece Anna's age, a concert violinist in Vienna. "We are to rebuild German Village for the next test."

And they do.

Again and again in the coming months they rebuild Berlin for

B-17s to bomb, until even atrocity succumbs to routine. Anna falls into despair. She knows Kurt will die in the air raids, alone and without her. He is her sacrifice to the war.

For months, then one year, then two, Vincent's farewell letter remains unopened in her footlocker. Whatever he has written will cause her pain; she senses this and decides to leave his words sealed in their envelope where they cannot hurt her.

Long after Sonnenthal ceases conversing with the ghost of his niece, he continues debating the author of *Architecture of Folly*. On cool evenings, while listening to Adrian Leverkühn on the gramophone, he consults the bombing routes and damage assessments, collates broadsheet headlines, siphons the smattering of fact from fiction in Deutschlandsender dispatches. When one of his buildings is destroyed, he puts a declarative checkmark beside its entry in the monograph's index. His architecture survives, intact and complete, only in the monograph dedicated to its denigration.

Over and over and over they reconstruct German Village, until one day in 1944, a thousand B-17s flood the skies over Berlin and the fires burn for days.

Louis is among the last prison laborers to shuffle onto the idling buses and the colonel tells the architects that the mission has achieved its objective, that tonight's test will be the final one.

Anna waits for nightfall to cross through the dwindled saltbush to German Village. Where else is there for her but here? It is her Berlin, the only motherland from which she has not been exiled, the only place where she can die at home in her bed.

This is why she resisted opening Vincent's farewell letter until now: she wants someone to say goodbye to her when the time comes.

She draws the heavy curtains closed.

She settles into bed and lights the nightstand candle.

When she hears the propellers, she tears open the envelope.

It's not a letter but a photograph, no, not a photograph but a movie frame: a medium shot cropped and enlarged into a closeup. A portrait. Ten years since Hasso took him away, and look how his brown eyes peer forward, the alert curiosity, the dawning recognition the camera captures.

The antiquated dread of the camera stealing your soul. Impossible, she knows. There's no soul here, nothing but a record of light. And yet the emulsion fixes to the page an essence beyond image. Some slim spirit peers up from the print. It *sees* her. The frame records Kurt's stuttered recall, the half second between recognizing a face and remembering to whom it belongs.

Vignetting hides the surrounding scene, and even though Anna cannot selectively see, even though no darkroom trickery can obscure the horror, she is unfastened by awe to find the son she lost back in her hands.

She tries to speak. There is something she must tell Kurt before the blockbusters wrench the breath from her body.

Dark wings span the moonless sky.

The B-17s pass one angel overhead.

"It's me," she says. "It's me. I'm here."

5

THE STATE OF UTAH MAKES LOUIS HARRINGTON SERVE EACH DAY OF HIS sentence; 18,263 in a state he intended to spend four hours in. When he's released in 1992, he's sixty-seven years old with fifty dollars, a bus voucher, and a rumpled Goodwill suit. The transformed world beyond the razor wire is one he's only seen on television. At a 7-Eleven he asks for a brand of cigarettes that went out of business two decades earlier.

His parents and older sisters passed in the previous years. His record excludes him from public housing or passing a landlord's background test. He lives in a roadside motel that advertises free ice.

After Louis returned from Dugway, the warden saw the miniature furniture he decorated his cell with and offered to go into business with him. Now Louis calculates how much money the warden made selling his dollhouses over his fifty-year bid. Adjust for inflation and it rises to the low seven figures. He contacts collectors and dealers familiar with his reputation. The commissions pay well enough. Years pass blankly by. Now and then, when searching under the bed for a missing sock, he comes across the ten inches of floorboard inscribed with the German POW's last letter home. He doesn't know why he keeps it, except that for so long there was so little he called his and this alone gives it meaning. Maybe it's no more than a gesture of respect to a fellow prison laborer who carved his wishes into wood.

In 1998 Louis learns his work will be included in an exhibition at

Berlin's Bergmann Dollhouse Museum. The museum offers to cover his flights and hotel. Louis applies for a passport.

He's never been in an airplane. He presses his nose to the window as New York City falls away and the world shrinks to the scale of a monumental miniature. The sun dents the Atlantic. The ocean's crinkled gleam reminds him of his mother's reused tinfoil. In these preposterous heights, he feels boyish.

He plans to spend only two nights in Germany. He's a creature of habit, a jar of peanut butter and a loaf of white bread in his suitcase, a neighbor's promise to tape *Jeopardy!*, a photograph of his two tabbies.

The museum reception is uncomfortable. He doesn't know anyone, doesn't speak the language, certainly doesn't look like anyone there. Attempts to draw him into conversation are forced. He feels he is imposing on those who invited him. Several times he is referred to as *the American* and it's strange because he's never really thought of himself in those terms before; it's just where he lives. He endures the overfamiliarity of a PhD student explaining where his work fits into the lineage of outsider art. He tells her he'll be right back and walks out the door.

The next day he takes a train to Würzburg and connects on a local to Rothenburg ob der Tauber. Snow tinsels Bavarian conifers. Train windows pass through sunbeams like film frames through projector light. There is engine trouble and he arrives later than scheduled. The last returning train to Würzburg departs within the hour. He must be back in Berlin tomorrow morning to make his flight home.

He consults a city map laminated to the station wall and hurries toward Wenggasse, unable to help himself from pausing to admire the steep tile roofs, the rising belt tower, the crenellated town fortifications.

The woman answering the door at 44 Wenggasse is his age at least, and she studies him with the unease that attends any uninvited evening caller.

He doesn't know where to begin or how to explain himself. He should have called or written. He should have simply mailed what he's come to deliver.

"Is this yours?" he says. With that he exhausts his phrasebook German and passes her the ten inches of incised floorboard.

Frau Schulman studies what the stranger presses into her hands. Her Hans was among the hundreds of thousands of Wehrmacht soldiers who vanished on the Eastern Front. Her parents urged her to remarry, but by the time she accepted that her Hans was gone it seemed too late to begin again. The single carved sentence contains no new information, sheds no light on Hans's fate, tells her nothing she did not already know, and yet, nonetheless, he reaches across fifty-six years of silence to say *I miss you, darling. Yours, Hans.*

Watching the woman's bafflement, Louis feels self-reproach roil beneath his skin. What did he expect? Why would this piece of wood he saved from the fire a lifetime ago mean anything to anyone but him? Why, now, this late in the century, would he surrender the object that has accompanied him for his entire adulthood? Why has he come here at all?

At the same time, another thought occurs: *What if I stayed?* The PhD student told him the Bavarian towns where dollhouses originated still support a lively retail market, and its craftsmen construct dioramas for museums throughout Europe. He imagines making miniatures for minor exhibits frequented by bored schoolchildren and lost tourists. He imagines the locals would call him *the American émigré,* and it saddens him to think that only in a foreign country is he considered a full citizen of his own. *What if I stayed?* He is seventy-three years old and there is plenty of life left in his fingers.

The sky is the color of wet denim. Snow flurries twist in cones of street light. Teenagers wander past, complaining that nothing interesting ever happens in this dumb town.

If he hurries, he can still catch the train. He lifts his collar against the cold, turns his back on the woman, and wonders where he will spend the night if he misses it. He's nearly to the street when he hears her pad after him.

He turns around.

Her hands fall over his.

Her slippers are soggy in the snow.

"You dear man," she says in English. "Come in. Please come inside."

MERCURY IN RETROGRADE

1

EDDIE LU'S UNEXPECTED WALKOUT BROUGHT THE PRODUCTION OF *Guns of Midway* to a halt, a development Artie would have welcomed had the board not taken it as further proof that he was undermining Ned's production slate.

"Listen, Leonard," Artie said into the telephone. "I know I'm partly to blame for this Eddie Lu fiasco. That artistic temperament of his. But I'm taking care of it, okay? I've been in touch with Bela Lugosi's agent, and we can get him to replace Eddie for a song."

Across the line, Leonard exhaled. "It's too late."

"Too late, too schmate. It's not an ideal solution, I know, but no one doubts Bela's professionalism. We come in behind schedule and over budget, okay, not ideal, but the boys in accounting will work their voodoo on the balance sheet, and by next quarter we'll be right as rain."

"You're not hearing me, Art. It's too late. The board met last night."

"There was a board meeting? Why the hell wasn't I informed?"

Leonard's sweating was nearly audible. "I shouldn't even be talking to you."

Artie sat down. "Why wasn't I informed there was a board meeting last night?" His voice felt disembodied from his diaphragm. It was impressive that he spoke at all, given that he could barely breathe.

"Because you were the subject. Christ, I felt like the last monarchist in Versailles, walking out of the john without realizing the guillotine party had begun. No one gave me a heads-up, okay? Ned only told me to come because he needed a quorum."

"How did they vote?"

"I'm sorry, Art. I voted for you."

Artie had been staring at the telephone in his hand for ten minutes when Maria entered. "It's over," he said.

"What is?"

"I am. This is. We are."

"What the hell are you talking about?"

"Ned organized a coup. The board met last night and voted that for the health of the company my stake in Mercury should be sold to Eastern National."

"They can't do that."

"They can. They have."

"Did you hear this from anyone besides Leonard Boyd?"

Artie shook his head.

The tension released in the corners of her eyes. "Okay. Keep the cyanide capsule stowed in your false tooth for a minute more. Let's not forget this is the guy who crashed his boat into a lighthouse."

"It was his father's boat."

Maria pulled the pencil from behind her ear and performed a bit of arithmetic on the back of a call sheet. "Based on yesterday's share price, your stock is worth around two million dollars."

The number was fancifully large. Artie exhaled. His desk fan spun cool carousels in his eyes. He opened his filing drawer and pulled out the shareholders agreement. Like most legal documents he'd autographed, this one was rendered illegible via Latin. It was hard to put much faith in the vitality of a legal code written in a dead language. He read and reread the clauses and subclauses.

"It's worth three million, not two," Artie said. "If the board forces a stock sale, the price is set at fifty percent over the stock's current trading value."

"Then they can't force you to sell. They'll go broke trying," Maria said. "It wasn't a bad plan. Who would have thought that Mercury's share price would rise so high?"

That it took the worst conflict in human history to return the studio to sound financial footing bespoke the limited horizons of its business model. Artie took a hard look at his protégé. She wore a day dress patterned in high-spirited purple, her hair swept up into a pompadour, her arms folded across her chest, affection settling into her gaze. She'd been his right hand for eleven years now, the exception to the rule that he surrounded himself with yes-men and idiots. When you got down to it, outside of marrying Mildred, hiring Maria was among the best personnel decisions of his professional life.

"Thank you, Maria."

Before she could ruin his mood by saying something nice about him, he stood up, straightened his tie, and went to quell this peabrain putsch.

The Feldman brothers pitched their camps on either end of the third floor, and with limited contact beyond memoranda and intermediaries, weeks could pass without Artie venturing into his brother's zone of occupation. He crossed the lobby and entered enemy territory. He pitied the locals. Look at the painfully pleasant secretaries, the number crunchers reaping tax-deductible losses, all of them laboring under the brisk and tyrannic efficiency Ned imposed. It made you want to distribute chocolate bars and canned goods.

"Beautiful morning, isn't it, Mr. Feldman?"

A bow-tied clerk supplied this chipper optimism. Artie wondered if the bow tie was restricting his oxygen.

Ned had styled his office in the cautious inoffensiveness of a midrange hotel suite: forgettable landscapes on off-white walls, unread periodicals fanned across the coffee table, variegated carpets camouflaging stain and spill. No family photos or keepsakes; the office had feasted upon the personal life of its occupant. On the desk, Artie saw neatly stacked revenue projections and rental receipts, the prognostications of hope and human error mathematically expressed. A black top hat hung from the hat stand. A white cardboard bakery box sat on press books for next season's releases. Ned was behind the desk, the telephone receiver clutched between his shoulder and cheek.

". . . and he thinks we want *his* feedback on the adapted script?" Ned said. "No, whatever you do, don't let him into the building. Tell him I'll meet him on Soundstage 3. When he gets there, send him to the scene docks. Then to the commissary, and so on. They're not physically robust, these novelists. He won't last long in the sun."

Ned set down the receiver and rubbed his eyes. He uncapped a bottle of Pluto Water, a laxative he self-prescribed to loosen the stiffness that settled into his shoulders and lower back during long hours hunched over tiny numbers.

For a moment, Ned evoked the purest pity in Artie. Here was a man who resided in a mansion that announced with every excess and embellishment that its owner did not believe he deserved to live there. So impoverished by ambition he would banish his own brother. So knotted by insecurity he drank cathartic just to sit straight. What retribution could Artie administer that Ned had not already inflicted on himself?

Ned nodded to the chair at the foot of his desk. Artie refused it. He wanted to tower, to let his censure crash down.

Quietly sipping his Pluto Water, Ned absorbed his brother's pent-up animus, all the calumny and spittle. When the anger began to burn out, when Artie grew winded and fatigued, Ned poured a measure of the cathartic into a coffee mug and offered it. This was it. This was the end of the Brothers Feldman. The momentousness made Ned recoil, even as he rose to meet it.

"You really think the board would vote to force you to sell without knowing the price?" Ned asked. "Three million. Congratulations, Art."

"You've betrayed me." Artie's voice was raw with emotion, and in their years of combat and détente, Ned had never seen his brother so reduced by vulnerability. Stripped of his showman's pizzazz, Artie was so small he was no one at all.

That was Art's problem, Ned thought. He yielded too easily to pessimism. A newly minted multimillionaire, and rather than a mazel tov and a handshake, he reacted as if Ned had given him VD via Mildred.

"Grow the fuck up, Art. You don't betray someone by giving them three million dollars."

"Three million—and *I'm* accused of neglecting my fiduciary obligations?"

Ned would have preferred the board's counsel to carry out the sentence than perform the coup de grâce himself. "It's worth that much to me to have you gone."

Whatever resistance remained in Artie huffed out. Just like when they were children and some misdeed or misfortune veered beyond his comprehension, he looked to his brother with those big fogged-over eyes and said, "Why, Ned? *Why?*"

"You grew a beautiful thing here," Ned said gently. "And now it's outgrown you. It's time for a new generation of leadership."

"A new generation? You're going to hate to hear this, Ned, but we're twins. You're eight minutes older than me."

Ned took another sip of Pluto Water. "Metaphorically."

"You're an asshole. Metaphorically."

Ned fished a danish from the bakery box, plated it on a paper napkin, and slid it across the table. "Come on. You know what carrying on does to your blood sugar."

Artie picked up the pastry. A day-old danish was about as close as he came to a spirit animal. As dense as insulation and enameled in wincingly sweet glaze, built for endurance rather than taste, not unlike the man who consumed it.

"You're still an asshole," he maintained through a mouthful of pastry.

"C'mon. I made you filthy fucking rich. You can do whatever you want. You just can't do it here."

Artie was aware that the risk of humiliating himself rose the longer he remained in Ned's office. He wiped his mouth and stood to leave.

"You know, I used to send Ada a C-note every day," he said. "For years I did, long after I stopped hearing from her. And all that time you didn't send her a dime. Instead, you were sending your money to Senator Nye and his ilk."

"So what?"

"So if you ever feel guilty about being a piece-of-shit brother, I hope it's not over what happened today."

Artie nodded, as if coming to a sense of acceptance, or perhaps he simply recognized Marlene Dietrich's top hat on the hat stand, since he lifted it off, set it on his crown, and walked out the door with his head held high.

Even though Artie would still come into the office, and his official duties would continue until the announcement was made, for all intents and purposes this was his last day. He walked the back lot, tipping his top hat to the stagehands and workmen who greeted him, the mayor of Mercury. It was the physical space of the studio he would miss more than anything. The crowded jumble of sets, the miniaturized geographies without borders—a street of Brooklyn brownstones leading to an Italian piazza, or a Pacific island sharing the same sand as Wild West Row—and, of course, the Silesian old town, no more than a painted façade left over from the denouement of *Devil's Bargain,* when the propagandist visits his hometown following the German invasion of Poland, and, finding it empty, realizes he is in Hell. There was no reason to leave it standing, yet Artie had insisted. He stood there now, looking around the empty set. It was at the very perimeter of the back lot, directly abutting Gower Street. One step was all it took to travel from Polish Silesia to Los Angeles.

No need for visas or passports or affidavits or permits. One step. It was so far.

When he returned home, Mildred was in the living room paging through *Harper's*. She looked up, surprised to see him back so early. She asked him about his day.

"I made three million dollars this morning."

She smiled. "And I banged Clark Gable."

She fixed him a drink and left to play tennis with Edith. When she was gone, Artie dragged a chair beneath the ceiling fan. The churning blades unspooled air across the room, and he spent hours staring into the revolving whirr, wondering what he would do with the rest of his life.

2

"I APPRECIATE YOU MAKING TIME, MARIA," NED SAID WITH THE FALSE deference of the fully empowered. "As you're no doubt aware, we're in a period of transformation, and I wanted to put your mind at ease regarding your future here."

He searched her for assent or appreciation. Maria was seated across his desk. She kept her emotions stoppered behind an all-business attentiveness. Despite Ned's insistence on informality, this was a negotiation. She would give nothing away for free, least of all gratitude.

"First of all, I know how close you and my brother are, and I want to say that I share your respect for him. We may not have always seen eye to eye, but no one would deny that he is a great showman, nor would anyone deny the role you've played in the studio's recent successes. We all know who Jane Doe really is."

He let this linger a beat while he turned a few degrees in his desk chair. "Remind me, what's your weekly salary?"

"Two hundred dollars."

"Two hundred." Ned shook his head, pulled a sheet of paper from his drawer, and gave it to her. "A list of all your subordinates who make more than you."

There were two dozen male names listed, each earning between five and ninety percent more than her weekly salary. They all called her boss.

"I've always told Art that you buy the loyalty of your employees by paying them what they're worth. Nickel-and-dime them and they'll have every reason to walk away when a better opportunity comes along."

Maria's first reaction, even before anger or offense, was admiration for the deftness of Ned's emotional manipulation. He knew exactly where Maria's armor was weakest. Had she not been so experienced with boardroom battle, she would have allowed herself to feel injured by the revelation. Instead, she only felt her fondness for Artie grow numb as she scanned the salary sheet that vindicated her long-standing doubts with numerical precision.

"Loyalty isn't cheap," she agreed.

Anchoring his elbows to the blotter, his red necktie swinging between his lapels, Ned leaned forward to assess her. A sympathetic expression, even as the lively intelligence in his deep brown eyes looked for further vulnerabilities to exploit. She stared back, unblinking, annealed of every imperfection.

He uncapped his fountain pen and wrote Maria's name at the top of the salary list. Beside her name, he wrote *$400/week*. "I'm not my brother," Ned said. "I pay people what they are worth."

Maria came in expecting a raise but hadn't expected him to double her salary. If this was Ned's opening bid, she could push him to $500 a week. She sank deeper into the blank-faced impassivity that had seen her great-aunts through decades of alliances with men determined to work them over. This gesture of munificence intended to astonish her into acquiescence revealed Ned's hand. He needed her.

"That is more money," she said, noncommittally. In her experience, no negotiation tactic was more fruitful than restating the obvious.

"I'm replacing my brother with my son, Adam," Ned said. Adam, whom Artie still referred to as The Dartmouth Waterworks, would be her boss. Twenty-one years old, 4-F on account of weak lungs, no experience in the business. It explained the raise: Ned was paying her to do Adam's job for him.

She hedged her response. "I'm sure Adam will bring youthful energy to the position."

"Youthful energy, now that's exactly the way to put it. He makes up in energy what he lacks in experience. Hence, why I want us to get off on the right foot. You know the job Adam's taking over better than anyone. I'm counting on you to show him the ropes."

"If I know the job better than anyone, why wasn't I considered for it?"

"Make a girl an executive? I'd get laughed out of town."

The prospect of doing her boss's job for him wasn't new, but even with a higher salary, working for Adam after eleven years with Artie felt like a steep demotion—there was nothing she could learn from Adam.

Maria considered her words carefully. "I appreciate your faith in me."

Ned eased back in his chair. "You know, I'm genuinely worried about Art. The first rule in this business is to never make a movie with your own money, but I've heard"—he searched for the right word—"whispers that he wants to open his own independent outfit. I'm sure it's no more than hearsay, but it breaks my heart to think of him squandering his windfall. Please, allay my fears, Maria."

"I haven't asked about his retirement. It seems too painful a subject for him."

In fact, she had spoken to Artie about this at length and agreed with Ned's assessment. Artie's idea to start over at the bottom rung of Poverty Row was nuts. The up-front investment needed to bring even quickies to market could deplete Artie's bankroll. He had asked her to come with him. She had said no.

"Come on, Maria," Ned cajoled. "Let's not begin our working relationship with secrets."

"Mr. Feldman, I would hope you wouldn't ask me to begin breaking the confidences of my employer, particularly if I'm to start working for your son."

Caught off guard, Ned assured her he wouldn't dream of it. He opened a manila file folder and passed her a contract laying out the terms of her continued employment.

"This is a seven-year contract." Maria frowned as she skimmed the first page. Seven years bound to her old position. It wasn't a job offer; it was a prison sentence.

Ned studied her. The terms of the contract had the desired effect. "I have considerable faith in you."

Maria informed him that she couldn't sign without having a lawyer look it over. Ned's displeasure tautened into a mirthless smile, but he said he wouldn't dream of asking her to sign anything without consulting an attorney.

Maria had reached the doorway when he said, "One more thing. I nearly forgot."

He laid a black photo album on his desk.

"I underestimated Vedette," Ned admitted. "Your secretary is a dark horse. Apparently, she held on to this for a few months, waiting until she could use it for maximum leverage."

Maria stood very still. "What did she get?"

"A promotion," he said. "Now, would you be kind enough to return it to . . ."

Ned looked to the open page. He locked onto the face of the man everyone knew as Vincent Cortese. He tapped the name clearly printed below: *Nino Picone.* His voice was cold and triumphant.

". . . whomever it belongs to."

No threat was made. None was necessary. Amid the wartime hysteria, enemy aliens were routinely interned on unfounded accusations prosecuted with weaker evidence than this. Denied access to legal counsel, or even a summary of the charges, a detainee's hearing was designed to manufacture guilty verdicts from hearsay with the expediency of Mussolini's Special Tribunal for the Defense of the State.

Maria reached for the album. Ned raised his hand. "Once I have your signed contract."

3

VINCENT SAT AT THE MOVIOLA, MARKING FOOTAGE FROM THE GERMAN Village firebomb test, when Maria spun him around by his shoulder. There was a snarl in her voice and murder in her eyes.

"Where's your photo album?" she asked.

At first, he wondered what that had to do with anything. Of all that might have animated her ire, a collection of faded passport photographs seemed an unlikely culprit. Then he understood. He opened his desk drawer. It wasn't there.

"Ned has it," Maria said.

"I don't . . ."

"*Why* did you bring that here? To work?"

"The police searched your aunts' house," he said. "I was worried they'd come to the Montclair. I thought it was safer to keep it here."

Maria's eyes blazed with contempt. "The biggest mistake of my career was helping you. No wonder my father never made it out of San Lorenzo. With you by his side, he never had a chance."

She turned on her heels and walked out the door. It was nearly noon and she was already running late. On Mondays she had a standing lunch date with her mother at Perino's on Wilshire between Western and Wilton. It was about equidistant between their places of residence, within the last mile of permitted movement, where their radii overlapped.

Her mother had brought her great-aunts and Ciccio. They marveled at the menu with begrudging respect for Signor Perino and outright derision for customers foolish enough to pay three dollars for a plate of pasta. The place was patronized entirely by halfwits. Lala worried someone from church would see her and assume the worst.

"It's the tablecloths," Ciccio was insisting. "You lay a white tablecloth and people lose their goddamn minds . . ."

"A racket," Mimi agreed approvingly.

". . . and if you put down a couple extra forks that no one knows what the hell to do with, common sense goes right out the window."

Annunziata saw the sadness lolling in her daughter's downcast eyes. "What's eating you?"

It took Maria most of the meal to detail the choice at hand: the opportunities and hazards, the obligations and betrayals. When she finished, Mimi looked at her very seriously and said, "So you still haven't found a man willing to marry you?"

Maria stared at the ceiling in defeat. Hoping to receive the wisdom of her elders only revealed how lost she was. Over the years, she came to genuinely admire their qualities: the wily, unsentimental realpolitik with which they pursued their interests, unrestrained by morality or hypocrisy; the bone-deep and oft-vindicated faith that everyone was out to screw them over; the unflagging and unmerited confidence in their opinions. It was these qualities, passed down and tempered by California optimism, that had made Maria. They were of little use now.

"These suitors, they're Italian, no?" Pep said.

"They're not suitors," Maria said.

"But they're courting you, no?"

"In a way. I suppose."

"Which one comes from a better family?"

"They're twin brothers."

Pep made a sign of the cross. "This is how vendettas begin. Two brothers fall in love with the same fisherman's daughter and the next thing you know it's five generations of massacre."

"Neither of them are in love with me," Maria said, restraining the urge to drown her aunts in their water glasses.

"What do you expect?" Lala said. "You're not even trying. You're wearing slacks."

Chewing on a dark De Nobili cigar, scanning the room for witnesses, Ciccio mouthed, "The coast is clear."

Mimi slipped the sugar bowl into her purse.

Annunziata had been quiet this whole time. She was thinking of how far Maria had come from the world whose problems she grasped. Once when they sat on the back steps and Annunziata taught her to drink Kentucky bourbon, Maria had said she wanted to understand her mother. Ridiculous. She was proud of all she didn't understand of her daughter. Proud that Maria had gone beyond the reach of her help.

The bill arrived. Mimi, Lala, Pep, and Ciccio conveniently announced they all had to use the facilities. Annunziata took out her purse, but Maria waved her off. She peeled a couple bills and tossed them on the receipt tray.

"What about you?" Maria asked her mother. "What do you think?"

"I think I'm out of my depth, my dear."

"Come on. Didn't they used to call you Machiavelli in Mascara?"

"I've never heard that," Annunziata said, so deadpan it was clear she not only knew the moniker but had coined it herself. "I think . . . what is the term. *You are a pickle,*" she said, in English.

"I'm *in* a pickle."

The non sequitur of American idiom reaffirmed Annunziata's every doubt about the flighty character of this country. People inside pickles. What a place.

The mention of cucumbers made Annunziata think of the gardens of Lincoln Heights. The promise of cultivating your land, even these token quantities, answered the call of the generations who endured feudalism and sharecropping, subjugated to earth they did not own. And so Annunziata's advice, however irrelevant, was this: "Get something no one can steal from under your feet."

That evening, when Maria checked her mailbox at the Montclair, she found a postcard from Eddie. It was the latest of the dozen documenting his journey east. Unlike his other postcards, this one's message wouldn't make the postman blush: *Learning how to ride the ice. Love, E.*

She turned the postcard over. Illustrated ice skaters glided over a frozen expanse banked in pine trees. Below them, in a merry font: *Greetings from Lake Erie!*

4

IF MARIA FAILED TO SUMMON THE OPPROBRIUM VEDETTE DESERVED, IT was because she admired her secretary's ruthless reorientation to the studio's new power center.

"Well played," she said as she passed Vedette's desk and continued to Artie's office. It was a sad sight. The scale model of Mercury sat on his desk. Suntanned outlines of missing picture frames looked ghostly on the barren wall. The proudly displayed lobby cards and denunciatory editorials were packed away in cardboard boxes and shipping tubes. Even the lights, which usually blazed overhead, had vanished; Artie had unscrewed the bulbs from the fixtures and bundled them with the washroom hand soap, a pencil sharpener, three telephones, a few thousand paper clips. Whatever wasn't bolted to the floor, he would take. Not out of spite or parsimony, but from a desire to bring with him all he could from the studio he adored. This was the only place he'd ever felt at home. All that remained of it were a few cardboard boxes destined for the garage and a scale model gathering dust in the attic.

All he intended to leave behind were the six toupeed mannequin heads, his council of elders, his trusted confidants. The Heavyweight, The Casanova, The Optimist, The Edison, The Odysseus, The Mephistopheles. He no longer wanted their pagan luck. He seemed surprised by Maria's sudden appearance, even more so by the directness with which she said, "Make me a better offer."

"I'm sorry?"

She took the seven-year contract out of her purse and passed it to him. "If you want me to come with you, make me a better offer."

Artie flipped through the terms until he came to the salary. "I'll give you five hundred dollars a week."

"A hundred-dollar raise?"

"Six hundred dollars a week."

"Don't insult me." She took the contract, uncapped her fountain pen, and as it hovered over the signatory line, Artie's hands rose in surrender.

"What do you want? Seven hundred a week?"

"To work at a fly-by-night outfit that might fold in three days?"

"Eight hundred dollars, then. That's twice what Ned's offering. Four times what you're making now."

She uncapped the fountain pen once more.

"Okay, okay, okay. Tell me how much you want."

"There's no weekly salary that justifies the risk."

"Then what . . ." As it dawned on Artie what she wanted, he actually smiled, because you had to admire the moxie, no matter how impudent or misguided. He'd created a goddamn monster. "No way, no how."

Without looking away from him, she slowly scratched out the *M* in *Maria*.

The nib rasped on the paper.

Artie watched, agonized.

"What percentage?" he asked before she could begin the *A*.

"Fifty."

"You're a loony fucking broad, you know that? I'm putting up one hundred percent of the capital and you want a fifty percent stake?"

"Yes," she said, surprising even herself with her serene mettle. Was this what her mother felt when haggling with the neighborhood fishmonger? This zoned-out virtuosity and back-brain reflex. The countless hours of stratagem accumulating into effortless mastery. She had never felt more like her mother's daughter.

"Five percent," Artie said.

"Fifty."

"We both know that's not in the cards, Maria. Ten percent."

"Forty."

Artie laughed, shook his head, and if he wasn't getting fucked every which way, he might have appreciated how skillfully his protégée seized her moment, how closely she had paid attention. "It's like trying to negotiate with Beelzebub. Twenty."

"Thirty."

"Twenty-five. You get a twenty-five percent stake. That's more than fair. It's goddamn highway robbery is what it is."

She set down the fountain pen. "Twenty-five and the title of executive producer, both in writing."

Not wanting her to think she got the better of him, he said, "You should've held out for thirty."

"I have a condition."

"Of course you have a condition. It's called insanity."

"You said the Signal Corps is searching for competent photographers and cameramen, right? Send them Vincent Cortese."

The request was more reasonable than what Artie had already consented to. Given the close cooperation between Mercury and the military, Artie's recommendation would go a long way to relieving the War Department's concerns about enlisting enemy aliens. Mercury's previous government liaison—a man surprised to learn the Department of Labor was not a maternity ward—had been fired for gross incompetence, and now Artie dealt directly with the Army brass hats.

In Maria's limited experience, the Army was governed by a bureaucracy so vast and impenetrable, a single conscript was easily lost within it. It might put Vincent beyond exposure. Additionally, his enlistment might neuter Ned's threat. It was one thing to blackmail a civilian enemy alien in a city gripped by jingoist hysteria, quite another to cast aspersions, from the comfort of an executive suite, on a combat photographer risking life and limb. Ned was too attentive to his genteel image, she thought, to risk the satisfaction of small-minded revenge. More than that, however, it was the only request Vincent made of her during their afternoons talking about San Lorenzo: the opportunity to photograph its liberation.

"A couple months ago, you asked me not to pull any strings for him. What changed?"

Maria thought of the hours they had spent with her father's letters, how he had helped her see her father once again, and it wasn't Vincent whom she referred to when she said, "I just need to let him go."

Artie dropped an Alka-Seltzer in his glass. A hissing lather rose on the water. "I can't make any promises, but God knows those brass hat bastards owe me a few favors."

"Okay," she said. "It's a deal."

Artie reached over and plucked the fountain pen from Maria's relaxed grip. He signed the resignation letter he'd been sitting on for the last week. It was a succinct, pro forma paragraph, a courtesy the board extended him: the opportunity to resign.

In 1984, the archivist who received Ned Feldman's papers at the Margaret Herrick Library noticed two exceptions to the otherwise scrupulous alphabetization of his extensive autograph collection. The first was a signed one-dollar bill. The signature on the dollar bill was messily scrawled and the archivist would not know that it belonged to Leib Berman, the Polish night watchman who had patrolled the Mercury back lot for years. After retiring, Leib Berman opened a deli on Whittier Boulevard. Ned brought in studio searchlights for the grand opening, and arranged to have Cary Grant, Lena Horne, and Marlene Dietrich appear for the "premiere." When Leib died unmarried and childless several years later, he left $1,823—the entirety of his life savings—to his former employer. Ned donated $1,822 to the Boyle Heights library where Leib was a known delinquent borrower. The one dollar he kept had Leib's signature on it, a souvenir of the first customer on the opening night of his deli. It had been Ned's dollar bill to begin with.

Unable to decipher Leib's rickety signature, the archivist filed it under *M* for *miscellaneous*. She had no difficulty making out the second exception. It was Art Feldman's resignation letter. She should have filed the letter under *F* for *Feldman* but was bemused that of all the luminaries and notables whose autographs Ned collected, he broke with alphabetical order to keep his brother's first.

The ink was still wet on the resignation letter when Maria peered into the miniature of Mercury. She could see herself in this very office, the faceless, featureless figurine peering out the window. She carefully pried the figurine off its mounting, pulled it through the little window, and slipped it into her purse. It was all she would take with her from Mercury Pictures International.

Artie slapped his forehead. "I nearly forgot our final bit of business."

In his last act as the head of production, Art Feldman discharged Maria Lagana.

"You're fired," he said, and offered her his hand. "Welcome aboard."

SAN LORENZO

1

THE FIRST AMERICAN TO PARACHUTE INTO SAN LORENZO WAS A COW. Strapped into a canvas harness, its legs paddling placidly, the cow surveyed the land with an equanimity induced by five syrettes of morphine. From its omniscient altitude, it would have seen the sunbaked slopes of La Sila, the valleys of rippling wheat, the coastal crags patrolled by peregrines, the Aeolian Islands skirted in mist and garnished in green. It would have seen white phosphorus pluming from Aspromonte ridges, feral dogs lapping human fat rendered from torched Panzers, British infantrymen playing William Tell with marble church saints, and a Signal Corps corporal standing on a dusty road, snapping its picture. The quartermaster's excessively creative effort to furnish the front line with fresh chow was short-lived, but for a few hours in September 1943, cattle parachuted into Southern Italy.

A moment after Vincent released the shutter, the wind caught the parachute and dragged the cow from the viewfinder. He'd photographed surgeons operating on baccarat tables in Casablanca, passengers riding the roofs of plodding Algerian trains, Wehrmacht soldiers crossing the front line to watch Marlene Dietrich's USO show in Sicily, and now, a cow domed in rippling silk high in the Calabrian sky. Of the improbable places the war had taken him, this seemed least believable of all: he was nearly home.

It struck him as strange that his journey to San Lorenzo should have begun while awaiting another man's judgment. Only two weeks earlier he had been sitting beside Myles Sullivan, his superior in rank only, in a Palermo palazzo requisitioned by the Seventh Army.

"So I have a passion for Baroque art," Myles had said in his defense. "Since when is that a crime?"

"You stole a Caravaggio."

"I wish." Myles eased another inch into his slouch. "It was only a reproduction."

Myles was a pool shark, card cheat, and New Jersey native. Desperate for competent cameramen, the Signal Corps decided to view his misdemeanor charge for distributing photographs of "a prurient nature" as professional experience. After Myles's previous corporal gave himself a million-dollar wound—point blank, pinky toe—Vincent had taken his place in the 163rd Signal Photographic Company. For nine months, Vincent and Myles had lived off the land, delivering film to company HQ through carrier pigeons and couriers, a couple hobos hitching their way through Hell. Vincent had become an itinerant photographer once again. As front-line photographers, Vincent and Myles were regularly the first American soldiers to enter liberated territory. Thus, they had their pick of the plunder. At least Myles did. Vincent had no interest in his campaign of cultural ransacking. A postal clerk whom Myles cut in for a percentage of the proceeds shipped his "souvenirs" to a Manhattan art dealer with a laissez-faire attitude toward provenance. Only a matter of time before Myles was court-martialed. According to a radio operator who owed Myles fifty bucks, two MPs had come around asking after the two-man photographic team the previous afternoon.

That was, Vincent assumed, why they had been abruptly summoned to the major's office that morning.

"Look at this place." Myles contemplated the mosaics vaulting over the palazzo ceiling. "Seventh Army command steals an entire *palace* and they want to court-martial me for helping myself to a few square feet of moldy canvas."

"My heart breaks for you," Vincent said, offering Myles a cigarette.

Myles helped himself to the entire pack. In the corner, soldiers battled gladiatorial scorpions in a private's upturned helmet. Vincent caught the scent of chickpea fritters, lamb spleen, and roasted pumpkin seeds drifting from the street below. Arab cognates, Spanish loanwords, the three-millennia history of invasion lived in the etymology of market banter. On that palimpsest the newest language of occupation scratched out its additions: *hubba hubba, this way, pay first.*

Myles was still staring up at the mosaics. "You think a fella could jimmy these things out with a flathead?"

Vincent laughed. As with Antarctic exploration and third marriages, there was something inspiring about the indomitability of human folly that governed Myles Sullivan. "You're an asshole, you know that, Myles?"

"I'm still your superior officer, Corporal."

"An asshole, *sir.*"

The heavy wooden door swung open.

A bespectacled adjutant with soft, clean hands peered into the antechamber. "The major will see you now."

A CRYSTAL CHANDELIER DRIPPED LIGHT, knights rode bug-eyed stallions across wall tapestries, and cherubs congregated in the ceiling's frescoed corners. The major glowered from a lordly desk. His skull was spherical and hairless, as if molded by battle helmet, and he possessed a nearly athletic faculty for frowning. To Vincent's mild disappointment, there were no MPs waiting to take Myles into custody. Instead, the major had summoned them to his office to discuss his latest communiqué from the War Department.

"For five weeks, we've had cameramen scattered across this godforsaken island." The major searched for a receptacle to deposit his spent chaw and settled for a flower vase. "Washington wants to know why our efforts haven't produced enough usable combat footage to fill a two-reeler."

It was less a question than the contradiction defining Vincent's military service: he was a combat photographer in a war where combat was unphotographable.

He explained that the most dramatic incursions occurred at night when conditions made photography impossible. During the day, the field of battle consisted of barren expanses between camouflaged and concealed positions. Their chrome-clad cameras were irresistible targets for German snipers, hence rank-and-file grunts gave them wide berth. Furthermore, even if by some stroke of military blunder and fortuitous timing they found themselves within a picture-perfect battle, the spring-driven Eyemo camera had to be rewound every thirty seconds and reloaded every minute, making it all but impossible to film more than fleeting moments unmoored from continuity. Ninety percent of the shots the moviegoing public associated with war drama realism were physically impossible outside a soundstage. The other ten percent were only possible by sacrificing the cameraman.

"And yet the Brits figured out how to do it in *Desert Victory*," the major said.

"With respect, sir," Vincent said, "*Desert Victory* is no more a documentary than *Casablanca*."

"How do you know?"

Vincent didn't know how to answer without risking impertinence. "I saw it, sir."

Desert Victory, the British propaganda documentary chronicling

Montgomery's triumph over Rommel in North Africa, had received universal acclaim when it reached American theaters three months before the invasion of Sicily. But the cinematic grammar that made it watchable revealed its inauthenticity. The filmmakers had supplemented combat footage with staged reenactments, which provided the patina of realism to the back-lot battle moviegoers expected.

"You saw it. The entire country saw it. That's the whole goddamn problem." The major plopped a fresh wad of tobacco into his mouth. "That picture's done more harm to home-front morale than Leni Riefenstahl's entire oeuvre. It makes us look like the *junior* partner in the US-UK alliance."

A jeep drove past wearing an SS captain's peaked cap as a hood ornament.

"President Roosevelt is concerned the public won't fully mobilize to support a war it can neither witness nor imagine. He wants pictures that bring the front line to the home front, that depict authentic battle *as it happens*."

Vincent said, "You can only film battle as it happen*ed,* sir."

The major's window overlooked a courtyard pool stocked in exotic fish. Shoeless GIs hoisted rods fashioned from radio antennae and surgical thread. The most marvelous creatures shimmered and died on their lines.

"Washington has ordered us to scale down the Italian campaign to a digestible narrative small-town America can rally behind. Something that will play in Peoria: evil German occupiers, heroic American liberators, grateful Italian villagers, and no goddamn Brits."

The capitulating Italian Army so swamped Allied POW–processing capacity that its soldiers had to reserve their surrender days in advance, and now Italy was no longer viewed an enemy but a country under enemy occupation. It bothered Vincent that the cinematic expression of these shifting geopolitical alliances was no more impervious to the flattening of genre convention than the average John Wayne Western.

The major steepled his fingers and turned to Vincent. "It occurred to me that Corporal Cortese's familiarity with studio warfare might prove advantageous. I'd like you two to photograph an incursion into Castellalto, a village in northeast Sicily."

Myles asked when the incursion would begin.

"It's already over."

Though fluent in the bureaucratic idiom of plausible deniability, Vincent still asked, "Are our orders to stage a reenactment, sir?"

For the first time that morning the major smiled. "Who said anything about reenactments? We have a policy against reenactments. I'm simply asking you to film the liberation as it happened."

Within his first few weeks photographing in Tunisia, Vincent understood that Robert Capa's *The Falling Soldier* was staged. Had to be. The idea that Capa had his Leica focused, on the right f-stop, pointed in the correct direction, in the heat of battle, just in time to capture a bullet passing through the Republican guerrilla was vanishingly improbable. And even if it was staged, it remained the most powerful indictment of political violence Vincent had ever seen, the very image that years earlier had put into the head of a Rome law student the idea of traveling to Barcelona to photograph the Spanish Civil War with the camera his closest friend had given him. Which was why he had few qualms about traveling to eastern Sicily to begin shooting a battle that had already ended.

CASTELLALTO WAS TUCKED IN A valley pitted with sulfur mines and smattered with plots of arable land no larger than living room rugs. By the time Vincent and Myles arrived, the Germans had long since retreated. The remaining locals scrambled over hillocks of fallen stone and pawed up rockslides. Walking down those bombed-out streets was a kind of horizontal mountaineering.

"We should have held out for the Liberation of Capri," Myles said.

The captain who made his three platoons available for the reenactment had meticulously chronicled the battle to ensure against the scapegoating and credit theft of his superiors. With the aid of his notes, and interviews with a dozen infantrymen, Vincent and Myles worked up an outline over the next several days. They strove for verisimilitude, but that standard soon proved its own guarantor of inaccuracy. Was fidelity to unreliable memories and contradictory accounts any less flawed than outright fabrication?

The solution was the camera itself. Long hours poring over real and staged combat footage as Mercury's Propaganda Unit researcher had taught Vincent that no matter how meticulously reenacted, verisimilitude was not a matter of *what* but *how* a photographer shot. It was the unsteady presence of the photographer's mortality—the camera jerking under incoming ordnance, veering toward the explosion but only capturing its aftermath—that created a sense of authenticity. It was a realism perfected by error. The constant reminder that you were watching a faulty record made it viscerally trustworthy. And this, of course, was manipulable.

Vincent shot *The Liberation of Castellalto* in a palette of lurches, jolts, and swerves that trailed rather than anticipated dramatic action. All of northeastern Sicily was his soundstage. Cecil B. DeMille had never worked on such an epic scale. But even with the manpower and materiel of the US Army at his disposal, he couldn't credibly re-create the most cinematic moments of combat without risking civilian casualties and left them suggested rather than shown. What had been true on Mercury's back lot was true on Sicily's battlefield: the less you saw, the better it looked.

Over the ten-day shoot, Vincent pushed this cinematography of turbulence and omission to its graphic limits. A staged firefight provided *The Liberation of Castellalto*'s most harrowing moments. To conserve bullets, the captain supplied his soldiers with blanks, and they shot into the village, unable to bring down whatever phantoms still lingered for them there. At the end of the scene, Vincent let his camera drop: the sun swung through the viewfinder, the sky somersaulted, the ground tumbled upward. A self-portrait of sorts, *The Falling Photographer*. The camera continued filming on its side, the world capsized in its lens. A pair of general-issue boots stepped into the frame, some Samaritan trying to help the cameraman up, perhaps. You could see no higher than the ankle. Home-front moviegoers would fill those boots with whomever they most feared losing. A sound man would loop in a single gunshot and let the image carry the audience into silence: the boots suddenly tipped over, lay inert, and the motion picture became as still as a portrait photograph.

In the emotional denouement of *The Liberation of Castellalto*, four GIs carried a woman's body from a church destroyed in an Army air raid. ("We'll say the Germans bombed it as they retreated," Myles suggested. "More believable.") The woman was played by an actress cast from the part-time prostitutes on Via Fratelli Bandiera at twice her hourly rate.

GIs lifted her on a wooden door, pallbearers in muddy battle fatigues. The camera captured a child sledding down an avalanche of pulverized plaster, a wrought-iron railing wrapped around a pillar, the bleak refashioning of the recognizable.

To Vincent's surprise, rubberneckers soon glommed on to the advancing cortege. Ones and twos, then dozens. They clutched medallions and amulets, rosaries and candles, and armed with these accoutrements of mourning, they harnessed wails of private grief to the public procession.

At the head of the line, a mustachioed man leaned toward the actress. "She's still breathing," he said. There was no eureka in his words, no surprise that a dead woman would still possess the power of respiration, not from the mustachioed man, who knew full well he would be dead for the rest of his life.

"She's still breathing," the mustachioed man said again. Myles moved to pull the man away, lest he disturb the impromptu procession, but Vincent stopped him. The reenactment had ended. This was something else.

"She's alive," the mustachioed man said, shaking with fury and despair for this place where the living were dead and the dead would not die. His words radiated through the assemblage, a fervor multiplying with each reiteration, and not only alive, but sitting up now, without injury or breakage, a flawlessness reified in flesh and heartbeat.

She was the most natural performer Vincent had ever seen. Intuiting that the audience had shifted from the camera to the crowd, understanding the power she wielded over them, she rose to her feet, magisterial, numinous, towering into the enlarged dimensions of the role. An affirmation of unfathomable mystery moved through the ragtag procession, rising from the artillery-gouged streets to the vivid blue oblivion above. She stepped into the throng. Reentered the land of the living to bless her mourners.

Even as they asked for her benediction, the practical concerns were never far from mind: the need of food, shelter, medicine. The privations no saint's blessing would relieve. But the relics of a saint, a toe or an ear—even a fingernail or an eyelid, whatever you could peel off—would fetch enough on the black market to feed a family for weeks. What good is an angel you can't eat? A human body selling herself for a few lire an hour earlier was now worth thousands. It was the only miracle that mattered to the mourners gathered in Castellalto on that bright September day.

The rings of the audience cinched around the actress. The hands that had reached for her in supplication would devour her. She told them to stand back, but what authority does a saint have here in Hell?

On the cusp of this public dismemberment, the captain ordered his men to fire on the crowd. The rifle reports batted between valley slopes. The bitter tang of cordite sprouted into the air. In the echoing stillness Vincent listened for cries of pain but heard only the lunatic laughter of the living as they searched themselves for the shafts the bullets should have sunk. Even the mustachioed man standing six inches from a rifle muzzle had dodged its discharge. Before the crowd realized the soldiers were armed with blanks, the captain escorted the actress away.

The spectators were still staring at their fingers, wondering what each was worth now that they were saints too, when a jeep pulled up. Two MPs climbed out, scanned the scene, and strode toward the cameramen.

Myles sighed. "Well, my friend, it looks like this is the end of the line for me."

Vincent offered Myles his hand. "Good luck."

"You'll put in a good word for me at the court-martial, won't you?"

"You really want me testifying to your character under oath?" Vincent asked and passed Myles the rest of his cigarettes.

"If you put it that way, I suppose not."

They turned to the approaching MPs. The taller of the two, a blond-haired lieutenant, asked which one of the cameramen was Vincent Cortese.

Myles laughed, as incredulous as any in the crowd who had dodged a bullet, astounded that he too was spared on that bright Sicilian afternoon. "You're here for *him*?"

2

THE CEILING GLIDES OVER ROCCO FERRANDO'S GLAZED EYES. HE IS IN Bellino's arms, carried like a child. Has he lost that much weight? Each of Bellino's footsteps ricochets pain through Ferrando's body, which is no longer a body so much as the ruins where his spirit waits out the storm.

"Where am I?" he asks.

"You're with us now," a woman's voice says.

Velvet curtains, trimmed in silk valances and frilly tiebacks, keep the room steeped in perpetual midnight. The scent of agave rises from freshly laundered linens. Elisabetta's closed house.

"You brought me to a brothel to die?" Ferrando would laugh if he could breathe.

"Business isn't so good these days, what with most of the johns conscripted for the war," Bellino says. "A couple of Elisabetta's girls agreed to double up until, well, uh—"

"For as long as you need," Elisabetta chimes in.

The mattress cups his wasted, cadaverous body so softly, so gently, and despite the pain crowding out articulate thought, he emits a bleat of pleasure. Why hadn't he come to Elisabetta's closed house before? Just to sleep?

Bellino pulls a stool beside the bed. "How do you feel?"

"It hurts," Ferrando admits.

Bellino stares dolefully at his former boss, and that's when Ferrando knows that he will never leave this bed. The thought doesn't trouble him. On a mattress this soft a paper pusher who has spent months sleeping on a jail cell bunk might finally get a good night's rest.

"I know it hurts, pal," Bellino finally says. "I know it does."

"Michele had the right idea. Just jump. Just be done with it."

"Who's Michele?" Elisabetta says from somewhere impossibly distant. A cool washcloth drapes over his forehead.

"No idea," Bellino says. "He talks to himself sometimes. He's not all there."

Ferrando would second that opinion if there was enough of him here to reply.

Bellino unstoppers an amber bottle. Thirty drops of laudanum plink into a small glass of wine. He brings the glass to Ferrando's lips. "C'mon, pal. This will help."

Ferrando takes a sip, his lids scrape down his eyes, the laudanum swallows him whole.

HE CAN NEITHER SLEEP NOR wake, and trapped in this twenty-four-hour twilight, there's little discernible difference between states of consciousness, just a cusp he drifts along.

"How you feeling?" Bellino asks.

His capacity to feel pain has surpassed his capacity to describe it. His sweltering brain swells against his skull; a fat man tightrope walks on his spinal cord; so little breath reaches his lungs. "More laudanum," he says.

"Hey, look. I was cleaning out my—your—office and found this." Bellino shows Ferrando a collection of Sherlock Holmes stories. "I thought I'd take the day off and read to you."

"Isn't this your first day as inspector?"

"Let the brigands have a head start. Only fair to give them a sporting chance," says the newly promoted Inspector Bellino. With that kind of initiative, Bellino will more than live up to the standard set by his predecessor.

"Your eyes," Ferrando manages.

"My eyes?"

Straining to form a smile is the most vigorous exercise Ferrando has had in days. "You'll ruin your eyes with all those little words."

"For you, I'll risk it."

All day, Bellino reads him Sherlock Holmes stories. Ferrando tries to pay attention, but he can only concentrate on the dissipating efficacy of dissolved morphine, the slow, splintering pain breaching the narcotic numbness.

At some point, he says, "I'd like to speak with Signora Concetta Cortese."

"I don't think that's such a good idea, Rocco."

"Please."

"YOU WANT A GRAPE?" SIGNORA Concetta asks.

A grape? He realizes he's staring at the green grapes Bellino left him. All morning he has watched the sunlight swell within the golden skins. The soggy brown ring where the grape meets the stem's damp tuft changes colors as the sun approaches the windowpane. The flesh ripens to a vernal luminescence filigreed with fibers of even lighter green. Whether being moved to tears by a bowl of grapes means he has too much or too little opiate in his system is unclear.

"Thank you, but no. They're too difficult to chew," he says. "Why have you come?"

"You invited me."

Yes, of course he did. The laudanum blunting his pain also dulls his mind. Diminished to an accumulation of leaky secretions and inchoate groans, he fears his mind is too hobbled by pain and clouded by painkillers to speak sensibly.

"Yes, I did," he manages. "I wanted to tell you about your son."

Concetta is motionless but for the hungering look that leaps out of her eyes. On the day she and Vincenzo were due to sail to New York, she finally, reluctantly reported her son missing, even though she knew her son was a good boy, no matter the trouble he got himself into, and would never leave her unless he was never coming back. Inspector Ferrando wrote it all in his notebook, promised to investigate it and get back to her, and she never heard from him until now.

Ferrando tries to tell her about everything that happened over those twenty-four hours in 1938: the German murderer, the body he and Bellino buried beneath two meters of unconsecrated riverbank, Nino rowing beneath the bridge abutments, the evidence of a forged passport later found in the darkroom of Picone Photography.

"Your son didn't have any papers on him," he explains. "We didn't know who he was."

"He always kept his papers on him. I don't understand," Concetta said, but by then she understood well enough: a German stole her son's life and Nino stole her son's name.

Ferrando doesn't know if his words come out in the right order. Within a few minutes, he's so depleted he can't fit more than two into a sentence, but two are enough for the last thing he must tell her: "I'm sorry."

Concetta's revulsion is tempered with pity for the states of suffering to which life will reduce even one's enemies. She pushes one of the grapes between her lips. Ferrando can hear it pop and squirt between her molars. She spits the pulp into her palm, gently tips his head forward, and he receives the mash of grape flesh and spittle. The sliding wetness sparkles on his tongue: the bright juice, the fibrous tartness of the seed, a fragrant spice smuggled from Concetta's last meal into Ferrando's mouth via the grape she chewed for him. He doesn't dare swallow. He will never taste anything this sweet again. He moves the pulp from one side of his mouth to the other. He would like to thank her for her kindness, but by the time the last of the grape slurry travels down his throat, she has gone.

• • •

THE VOICES FILTER THROUGH DENSE FOG.

"Madonna, it's an oven in here," Bellino says.

"This heat spell has to break one of these days," Elisabetta says.

"Look at him. He's sweated through the sheets."

Silence. Then, "I'm sorry, darling. There's nothing more we can do."

"We just need to cool him down and he'll pep up."

"It's too late for that."

"But I brought a desk fan from the station. You hear that, boss? I have your desk fan."

"He can't hear you."

"We just need to cool him down a bit."

For Rocco Ferrando, the cold is already here. It seeps from his failing organs and into his feverish brain. In the summer heat, winter enters his bones. What lies ahead isn't darkness but a white void. There's just enough of him left to feel the fan's oscillating current slide over him, churning the whiteness ahead into a spinning August snowstorm. The cold is everywhere now. Within the freezing whiteness he sees Michele with sugar clumped on his lashes. Michele's eyes are the translucent green of grape flesh, the last color in the whiteout. Rocco steps into the blizzard.

3

THE IMPORTANT THING, VINCENT REMINDED HIMSELF, WAS THAT HE wasn't under arrest. Not yet, at any rate. The military police escorting him to San Lorenzo simply needed to clear up the allegation referred by the FBI's Los Angeles office. Usually the MPs wouldn't have bothered, but the man who lodged the allegation—one Mr. Ned Feldman—donated to the campaigns of several prominent senators and couldn't be brushed aside. A routine matter, the MPs assured Vincent. Merely verifying his identity to satisfy the higher-ups.

"C'mon, Corporal Picasso," the blond-haired lieutenant called. "We need a local guide."

An hour earlier, as he photographed the parachuting cow, Vincent had told the lieutenant that Picasso was neither a photographer nor Italian, but nothing anchored an officer to his errors like a subordinate's correction.

Vincent walked over. The lieutenant's soft-spoken sergeant had spread a map on the jeep hood. Ahead the road jagged into dirt paths flanked with embankments of blighted tussock grass and thistle. Scraggly copses of olive and manna ash huddled amid the boulder-strewn expanse. The late summer heat desiccated the earth to a fine powder that invaded each inhalation.

The blond-haired lieutenant said, "Which way do you suggest?"

Intelligence had no reports of mined roads along the coastal mountains but serving in the 163rd required taking on faith that information supplied by liars and compiled by idiots would keep your chestnuts from the fire. Earlier that day they passed a crate of pressure-fuse Teller mines abandoned on the side of the road by the sapper charged with planting them. Whether this dereliction of duty was exception or rule on the roads of southern Calabria was a question of immediate concern.

Vincent studied the map, a surveyor's chart not unlike the one Giuseppe had used to plan their flight. He could lead the MPs deeper into the interior and disappear into the mountains. Why not? What mercy could he expect in San Lorenzo?

"Well?" the soft-spoken sergeant asked.

Vincent crossed the clearing to the eastern dogleg and knelt. Hoofprints scalloped the dried dirt. In the North African campaign, he learned herd animals were nature's mine detectors. The afternoon heat collared him in perspiration and a soul-sapping resignation slackened his spirit. *We keep pursuing our lies,* he thought, *even after they begin pursuing us.* He was Vincent Cortese, come what may.

He stood and brushed the dust from his knees. "Let's follow the sheep."

The blond-haired lieutenant smiled at his sergeant. "And they think he's not a real GI."

They returned to the jeep and drove on. It wasn't clear when or if they crossed into Axis-controlled territory. The war mobilized national borders. You needn't move to emigrate. Hoofprints tunneled beneath arched cypress boughs. The sheep would lie down in one country and rise in another, where the wolves have new names.

VINCENT'S STOMACH CANNONBALLED INTO HIS pelvis as the MP jeep thunked over the crest. They were nearly there now. As they descended the ridge, he could see San Lorenzo in the distance, widening over the windshield in smears of navy river, black smoke, gray stone. In the passenger seat, the blond-haired lieutenant was humming a Benny Goodman tune, but Vincent could not hear him. He could hear nothing but the air whooshing into his ears and his growing voice of doubt. The jeep tires pulverized sprigs of sage spearing through the gravel. Ahead, missing buildings left gaps in San Lorenzo's familiar, clay-tiled horizon. The road between here and there was layered with Allied leaflets promising that *Germany will fight to the last Italian.* They drove on, through barriers thrown open in hasty retreat, over bomb craters spanned in I-beams. Every passing meter added accelerant to the panic blazing in Vincent's chest. They crossed the invisible line marking the border of the confino colony.

It was only five years since he'd left, but Vincent felt more estranged from San Lorenzo now than while reconstructing it in daydream and nightmare nine time zones away. The broken abutments and piers of the Ponte Zupi still jutted through the water. German sappers had dynamited its arches as the Wehrmacht armored division pulled back. The bridge where Giuseppe had leapt, and Himmler had stood, had fallen into the Busento. Whatever treasure remained in the riverbed was now entombed beneath a hundred thousand pounds of stone. They drove on.

The sergeant eased the jeep into the Piazza Vittorio Veneto, where Army bootleggers had refashioned a Sherman fuel tank into an immense distillery. Canned peaches, fresh oranges, and kerosene fermented for all of thirty minutes before being christened with colorful monikers—Finito Benito, Prego Dago—and ladled into artillery casings doubling for shot glasses.

The blond-haired lieutenant stopped humming Benny Goodman long enough to wave over a tout and order a round of whiskey sours—rubbing alcohol and powdered lemonade, as it turned out.

A festive bedlam spilled across the piazza. From the backseat of the jeep, Vincent scanned the crowd through his viewfinder, searching for a familiar face, for anyone he recognized, but San Lorenzo had been repopulated by madmen and animals. Vendors hawked watermelon, soppressata, and dresses sewn from parachute silk to the Allied soldiers. Monks raided abbey catacombs and sold the relics of saints on a sliding scale of patronage and power. That many of these relics seemed to have regenerated their own flesh—one with a tattoo of Betty Grable—was, the monks assured, proof of their miraculous powers. An argument erupted when a Canadian amputee found his arm for sale as a relic of Saint Calogerus the Anchorite.

Vincent felt as if he were photographing a demented Bruegelian apocalypse where every figure, no matter how minor, was burdened with amusingly particular torments. Women hung curtains in a razed church to ensure a modicum of dignity while taking customers in the alcoves. Infantrymen persuaded destitute vendors that Monopoly money was the official occupational currency. Snipers staged a safari with a looted taxidermy collection, shooting stuffed lemurs and ocelots from the shoulders of street urchins paid in chocolate bars. Brigands executed local fascist officials in the podestà's office while old men wearing trousers patched in bright scraps of old tapestries sang love songs.

There was nothing in the ghastly tableaux Vincent hadn't already photographed, in one permutation or another, in Palermo or Tunis, Algiers or Castellalto. Why would it be different here? Stretcher-bearers carried a soldier waffled in Panzer treads to a field hospital designated with a red cross drawn in iodine on a pillowcase. Next to the field hospital, a monk slipped into a tent labeled *SPARE PARTS*. The relentless diversity of affliction pouring through the camera lens benumbed the senses, deadened the heart, and while the two MPs who devoured round steak parachuted into San Lorenzo via the ass of a terrified cow, Vincent walked home.

Afternoon shadows stretched across the cramped alleyways. Paving stones passed quietly under his boots. At every turn, he considered turning back. What did he hope to find in the home he once shared with Giuseppe Lagana? Each year of silence reaffirmed what he knew the moment Giuseppe pushed the rowboat into the Busento. There was nothing and no one waiting for him here.

The portrait studio's sign had been torn down and chopped for firewood, but at the sight of its whitewashed façade, Vincent's mind went motionless. He pushed open the front door. He crossed the threshold where one afternoon a lifetime ago his mother had made the most respected defense attorney in Rome strip to his underpants. Inside, the scurrying pawprints of small rodents indented the floor dust. The calendar on the wall still read *March 1938.* Enterprising neighbors had seen to it that nothing went to waste—the furniture, the darkroom equipment, anything that could be moved had been pried out, hauled off, repurposed, or sold.

He rummaged through the debris until he found an intact picture frame. He took a photograph from his billfold, slipped it into the frame, and hung the frame on the wall. He stepped back and studied the passport photograph he'd taken of the girl in this very room nearly two decades earlier, when she had come to say goodbye to her father before journeying to Los Angeles. Should Giuseppe ever find his way back, he would be welcomed home by the daughter whom he'd tried so hard to reach.

THE TWO MPS HAD JUST finished eating when Vincent returned to the piazza. They drove to the parish archive, and with the help of an Army interpreter, the blond-haired lieutenant found Vincenzo Cortese's baptismal record. It went some way to discrediting the allegation the Los Angeles office of the FBI had passed on.

"And you've never heard of a fellow named Antonio 'Nino' Picone?" the lieutenant asked Vincent.

"No."

The lieutenant was inclined to believe him. In the lieutenant's experience, the FBI found no rumor too baseless to resist forwarding to the Military Police Corps. And from there the investigatory apparatus ran its rickety course. Traipsing across the field of battle to disprove hearsay. Risking life and limb to investigate a denunciation that was likely little more than the score-settling of some vindictive piece of work in Los Angeles.

The sergeant popped his head into the office the lieutenant was using. "I found something, sir."

At the local police station, the sergeant had found a report written by an Inspector Rocco Ferrando in March 1938: *One shot fired. Picone hit. Presumed drowned. Manhunt called off.* "Unbelievable," the lieutenant said, fed up with superiors who were forever ordering him to pursue unfounded allegations to their inevitable discrediting. "It's not that hard to find actual goddamn fascists around here, and we're chasing hither and yon for an antifascist killed five years ago."

It might have ended there, but the soft-spoken sergeant, a tax accountant in civilian life, was a stickler for double-checking his arithmetic. "We can clear this up easily enough, Lieutenant," the sergeant said. "The mother, Mrs. Concetta Cortese, lives down the river, right? Let's all pay her a visit."

4

CONCETTA WOKE WITH AN ACHE IN HER LOWER BACK, A RASP IN HER knees, the old complaints. She made her bed, smoothed the lingering wrinkles from the sheet, and tucked the corners beneath the mattress. Life offered few pleasures as affordable as a well-made bed. Her basket still hung on the rafter overhead. She pushed it once and watched it sway while the river breeze whistled through the cracked stone wall. Outside, the ground churned with the thousands of leaflets Allied aircraft had dropped on San Lorenzo. Concetta took her broom to the churchyard to sweep them from her children's graves.

She started with Andrea's. First born and forever her youngest. Two days after entering the world he turned around and departed before Father Mancuso had even baptized him. But the priest had fathered innumerable illegitimate children, understood a parent's grief, and allowed Concetta to bury Andrea on consecrated ground so the newborn wouldn't be forgotten in the great hullabaloo at the end of time.

An easy grave to sweep. So small it took no more than one swipe of the broom.

Next came Mario and Giulia, eighteen months and three years. How her husband, that magnificent liar, had doted on Giulia, balancing her on his feet while he goose-stepped about the room, laying prayer cards on her chest when she fell ill, holding her hands until the last of her heat seeped into him. The typhoid had taken him too.

I feel better: the magnificent liar's last words. Back then the local doctor was a charlatan wanted for murder in Bari, and the only trusted medical authority was the village witch who treated typhoid with an elixir brewed from the ashes of lemon peels and six strands of a virgin's hair. No one expected miracles. Everyone knew she specialized in curses.

A cyclist pedaled past the churchyard. The rear bicycle tire was a garden hose packed with sawdust.

The leaflets gathered weight under Concetta's broom. Come winter she would burn them in the stove to keep away the cold for a moment more.

Giovanna was twelve years old: malaria. Salvatore was twenty-three when the taxman knifed him in a dispute. Concetta wore the same black veil and dress as her mother and grandmother, lived in the same style house, farmed the same clay- and rock- and bone-strewn plots for the same rapacious latifondisti, and no matter the centuries that had passed since Christ's birth, it remained the Dark Ages here, and yet one day last winter she had stumbled into a grove of towering citrus trees and spent the afternoon eating oranges until she was so full she had to lie on the ground, and enveloped in the invigorating fragrance of peeled rinds, she couldn't imagine anywhere on earth was more hospitable to human life.

Father Mancuso saw her sweeping the leaflets and walked over. He'd spent the morning reburying bodies disinterred by artillery fire at the western end of the churchyard. Over the years, the priest had lost three children and eight grandchildren. The surviving ones went to school in Reggio. No one thought any less of the priest for disgracing his vows. Father Mancuso had attended seminary in Catania. The bishop there thought he was too weak-hearted and recommended him posted to San Lorenzo where the souls were well past saving. "He can do no harm there," the bishop in Catania had written before enjoying a five-course lunch.

Father Mancuso knelt at Concetta's graves and prayed. Several times he forgot the Latin and ad-libbed. It was all the same to her.

Once she imagined buying a parcel of land to till. Nothing valuable, nothing large. Just a little piece of earth to make her own. But what little money she saved had gone to buy her children's cemetery plots. The only land in this world that was hers was right here: five swept rectangles blessed by a drunken priest in misconjugated Latin.

Vincenzo was born her youngest and died her oldest. Three years ago, on his deathbed, Rocco Ferrando had told her what happened to her son. Told her even where in the Busento he had interred him. For weeks she'd gone to the riverside with a shovel, knee-deep in muck, never discovering the body, still waiting for her son's ghost to come home to her.

5

IF THE PEASANTS REMEMBERED ANYTHING OF THE PRISONER THE TWO Americans led down the lane, they would remember his sturdy leather boots. A person could go far in a pair of fine boots like that. None recognized him as the sweet-tempered young fellow who once made his way down this lane every week to read aloud and transcribe Concetta's letters to her son. The prisoner had the look of a man on his way to the gallows, and a few of the peasants watched him enviously, wondering who would get his boots when he died.

One of the dogs lazing beside the dirt road caught a familiar scent as the prisoner passed, but it was only a whiff, and it was too hot to get excited. A peasant woman on her way to the fields recognized the prisoner as the young man who drowned in the Busento, but there was nothing notable about that. Since time immemorial the dead had roamed San Lorenzo as senselessly as the living.

The peasant woman set a jar of water on her daughter's head and they began their four-mile trudge to a latifondista's field. The girl was nine years old, the fruit of an evening beneath the traveling circus bleachers with a left-handed militiaman. When the peasant woman was three months with child, she tried to instigate a liaison with Father Mancuso, knowing the opportunities her child would receive as a priest's bastard, but the priest did not fall for her southern wiles. The girl walked down the lane with four liters of water balanced on her head. Without spilling one drop, she turned to watch the Americans lead the prisoner to Signora Concetta Cortese's house.

The blond-haired lieutenant knocked on the door left open to air out the infernal summer heat. Concetta rose. She frowned at the Americans. She couldn't place the prisoner staring at his feet.

"Excuse me, signora," the soft-spoken sergeant said in phrasebook Italian. "Is this your son?"

Concetta stepped over the threshold. When the prisoner met her gaze, the breath left her body. The young man who lied to her, betrayed her, stole her son's death from her. Who stole his very name. Whom she once loved and now loathed. His eyes were red-rimmed, repentant, deserving of her retribution. Never has she had more power over another human soul.

Thinking he must have mispronounced the words, the sergeant consulted his pocket phrasebook and repeated the question. "Is this your son, signora?"

One word is all it takes. She can damn him with a single spoken syllable.

The lieutenant took the phrasebook from his colleague and repeated the question.

The girl with four liters of water on her head was still watching from the lane. Her name was Teresa, and even though she couldn't hear what the MPs were asking, she would recall this moment seventy-four years later while watching her great-granddaughter jump into a park fountain on a sweltering summer day in Melbourne. There was no reason why the memory would return to her then, so long after its participants and witnesses had passed, it was just one of those things, and she would suppose that no matter how far into the world she had gone, she was always going back. The five sinks and two baths in her Melbourne house provided all the water she would ever need. Into her nineties Teresa would fill her water glass to the very brim and bring it to her lips without spilling a drop. After that moment in the park, she wouldn't think of Concetta again. When her great-granddaughter called for her, Teresa sat up from her reverie and that distant day would vanish forever.

Concetta steps outside. Her ruthless grief, her vindicated cynicism, every wasted prayer for leniency, all of it focuses on the penitent before her, and standing amid the despoilment and blight of this heavily haunted country, she wonders if her ghosts are the very mirages chased by this traveler, this revenant journeying from distant lands to find her.

The word she searches for comes. Its immensity spreads within her. She cannot imagine bestowing the mercy God has time and again denied her. What then remains but surrendering to the unimaginable?

The sight of the little woman in a black mourning dress embracing the Signal Corps photographer is enough to satisfy the lingering doubts of the sergeant, who looks away, a bit bashful at intruding on this moment of homecoming. Glancing toward the lane, he marvels at the little girl balancing a water jug on her head. The girl steps lightly through the thorn grass sprouting in sparse patches and follows her mother down the lane. Long after the girl lost sight of the house, she would still hear its resident crying, "Yes," but she could never decide if this was a cry of loss or triumph.

It would depend, she supposed, on what had been asked of Concetta Cortese.

EPILOGUE: 1946

"WHAT YOU HAVE TO REMEMBER IS THAT MY BROTHER, GOD REST HIS soul, was never a showman," Artie told the reporter on the telephone. "He never knew what the public wanted, nor how to give it to them. How could he have known what people like, given that he was so unlikable himself? You can quote me on that."

The reporter asked why Artie was referring to his brother in the past tense.

"Because he's been dead to me for years." Artie saw Maria standing in his doorway. He cupped his hand over the receiver. "The *Daily Variety* is doing Ned's obituary. Anything you want to add?"

The rumor of Ned's ouster from Mercury the previous week had been received in the executive offices of Jupiter Pictures with a sense of divine justice, but nothing in Hollywood was real until the trades reported it.

"I trust you to make my feelings known," Maria said.

"You sure? There's no better time to kick a man than when he's down."

"Tell them Ned's got no class," Maria said, and turned back to her office.

Artie gave her a thumbs-up and shouldered the receiver. "You know what Mercury's board gave Ned to walk, don't you?" Artie asked the reporter. "A goose egg. You know what they paid me? Three million. That's right. Three with six zeros. Be sure to put that in your piece."

Jupiter Pictures' executive offices occupied the second and third floors of a Highland Avenue building that had previously housed several dental practices and a podiatry office. Supposedly it was a temporary base camp until they could afford grander accommodations, but three years after moving in, it still suited their needs. The institutional cabinets and built-in countertop cast a clinical atmosphere over Maria's office, but it had two windows and a private bathroom that in the strictest, technical sense had become her executive washroom.

Maria flipped on the radio. It was nearly noon and KECA would be rerunning last night's *The World's a Stage.* The drama, recorded in ABC's New York offices, featured a repertoire of classic plays—Shakespeare, Ibsen, Chekhov—adapted for one-hour radio broadcast. Among the standing five-person cast was a voice actor billed as Eddie Lewis, who took the leading role every few weeks.

When Artie walked in, Maria dialed down the radio volume. He looked out the window. It was a beautiful morning. A flotilla of cumuli sailed on blue skies. On the street below, a pool shark sporting the sort of sparse mustache that comes with a snake tattoo was sharing a smoke with a couple soda jerks. And a pigeon was taking a crap on Maria's brand-new convertible. Someone really should tell her to put the top up, Artie thought.

"The great Ned Feldman is out on his ass," he said, shaking his head. The showboating pizzazz had drained out of him, and he seemed puzzled and saddened by the turn of events. "Who would have thought? All Ned's conniving and all he did was force me to sell when Mercury's stock was at its peak. You'll never guess the cause of termination. Nepotism."

"For hiring his son?"

"No, for cashing me out with such a big payout."

Maria laughed. "Jesus. What a world."

"I know. I can't wrap my head around it."

"There's no better luck than getting screwed over at the right time."

"That, Miss Lagana, is a fact."

Since 1942, Ned had courted considerable debt to capitalize Mercury's expansion into theatrical exhibition and bankroll its A-class talent. For a time, Ned's gamble looked like it was paying off. *Guns of Midway*, entirely reshot following Eddie's departure, was nominated for five Academy Awards. But with each new series of investment, Ned diluted his ownership stake until not even the erstwhile allegiance of Leonard Boyd—presently the commanding officer of the aircraft carrier USS *Monroe*—could have restored his control over the board. When Vedette Clement was named executive producer of Mercury Pictures International, she sent Maria a note thanking her for all she had taught her.

"You should get in touch with your brother."

"Sure. I'll send him the classifieds."

Despite the champagne-popping merriment with which Artie greeted the news of Ned's dismissal, the toll losing his brother had taken was evident in his downcast eyes. Ned was his only surviving sibling. Last year, Artie learned that Ada died long before he had finally stopped writing her. The hundred-dollar bills he'd sent had continued to pile up beneath Ada's mail slot for months after her death, but Artie never regretted the thousands of dollars he'd posted into the void. Decades later, long after Artie was laid to rest in Hillside Memorial Park, his son, Billy, received a letter from Tel Aviv. The letter was from an Israeli woman who'd grown up in Silesia near Billy's aunt Ada. During the German occupation, the woman had broken into Ada's home to search for food and instead found the small mountain of envelopes filled with C-notes, more than enough to purchase false papers for her family. Billy's relationship with his father had only deteriorated from the days when he used Artie's laundry hamper as a latrine. His father was distant, self-centered, and domineering, and it had been a long time since he'd stopped looking for a reason to love the man. But when he finished reading the letter for the third time, Billy left for the video store to see if he could find any of his father's old movies.

"You should buy your brother a drink," Maria told Artie. "I'm sure he could use one."

Artie shook his head. "There's too much history there."

"This is California, Art. History begins tomorrow."

Grunting noncommittally, he reached for the magazine on Maria's desk. "You see this bullshit?" he asked. "*The Hollywood Reporter* is publishing a blacklist of communist sympathizers. These poor bastards are losing their jobs for being 'prematurely anti-fascist.' At this rate they'll start denouncing veterans for fighting on the same side of the war as the Soviets. Look at this, they're even going after Rudi Bloch."

"We should hire him. I'll bet we can get him for a song."

"And have the likes of *The Hollywood Reporter* dumping on us all the livelong day?"

"Who says they have to know?" Maria asked. "We can credit Rudi under a pseudonym."

"John Doe, for example?" Artie said archly.

Maria smiled. "I was thinking he could choose his own front name."

Her secretary knocked on the door. "There's a Mr. Cortese here to see you."

It had been two months since Vincent returned from Tokyo and he was still acclimating to civilian life. Four years of C-rations and mess fare had made him nostalgic for those innocent days when he knew of no culinary abomination more offensive than tuna salad. Following the invasion of Italy, he had accompanied the Seventh Army into France, over the Ardennes, across the Rhine, into Germany. He remained with the Signal Corps for eight months after V-J Day, documenting the reconstruction of German and Japanese cities. Following his honorable discharge, he placed one hand on a Protestant Bible in the General Headquarters of the occupational authority in Tokyo. In his first act as a citizen, he asked how he could go about securing a visa for his mother.

That morning, he wrote a letter to Concetta telling her that with an interest-free mortgage courtesy of the GI Bill, he purchased a Lincoln Heights bungalow with a great big orange tree in the backyard. He put the deed in Concetta's name. A little piece of land to call her own, if she wanted it. He told her about the gardens of Lincoln Heights, with mulch and fertilizer and hose water so abundant she could grow anything. He would care for her. He would spend the rest of his life repaying what he owed. He signed the letter *Nino Picone,* the first time he'd used that name in years. Now, several hours after he sealed the letter in its envelope, he could still feel the signature of that stranger's name vibrating in his hand. The letter was in his pocket. He hadn't mailed it yet. He knew he never would. He was too afraid of learning how little the promises of Nino Picone meant to Concetta.

Artie stood and shook Vincent's hand. "Maria told me you'd been discharged. How the hell are you?"

"I'm all right, Mr. Feldman." Vincent tried to dislodge his hand from Artie's enthusiastic grip. He scanned the room. "Is this a dentist's office?"

"Dr. Henderson was a bit of a . . . what's the word I'm looking for?" Artie turned to Maria.

"Convicted felon."

"Yes, I suppose he was, wasn't he? Maria read about the trial in the papers and I immediately called the landlord. It's amazing, really, the agreeable leasing terms you can get on a crime scene. What are you doing these days?"

"Next week I'm starting a job as a photographer for *L'Italo Americano.*" He looked at Maria. "In fact, that's why I'm here."

"Then I'll leave you to it," Artie said, and went to his office to call Rudi Bloch's agent.

Maria opened her desk drawer and pulled out a paper bag. She handed it to him. Inside sat the Leica that Vincenzo had given him, the camera that had accompanied him for thousands of miles until he surrendered it at the Enemy Aliens Property Board in December 1941. He'd loved this camera. He'd seen so many faces through its lens.

"Can I buy you a sandwich?" he asked.

"Afraid not." Maria grabbed her purse. "I've got lunch with my family."

For years Maria and her mother would keep their standing weekly lunch at Perino's, often with the company of Mimi, Lala, and Pep. Sadly, Ciccio was no longer among them. His long love affair with Mimi began when he assured her that the Lincoln Heights Funerary Society was the only lottery she was guaranteed to win, and death was always there, a constant chaperone trailing them from church to cemetery to bed to breakfast. No love triangle is equilateral, and Death loomed at the apex of theirs. On a cool autumn evening, while double-parked outside St. Peter's, Ciccio treated Mimi to a bit of barstool philosophizing: "If you're tall, everyone and their brother assumes you're good at basketball, right? So why's it that if you got big feet, no one assumes you're good at soccer?" With these last words, his smile slackened, his shoulders drooped, and he slumped against the steering wheel. Life left his body like a hand leaving a glove. All around, autumn leaves rustled. Just like that, Death and Ciccio eloped, and Mimi was left with the losing ticket.

Ciccio's funeral was the most lavish in the history of the Lincoln Heights Funerary Society. He was laid to rest in the suit he'd been married in. Once again, Mimi waited for God to take her, but Ciccio was only the first of six funeral directors she would outlive.

In the last years of the war, Maria's mother had gone into business for herself by exploiting inefficiencies within the rationing system. Ration stamps had become a second, concurrent monetary system to the dollar. Some, such as gasoline coupons, were prorated based on an individual's value to the war effort, but most were democratically distributed regardless of need or inclination. Recognizing the unrealized value of a liquor stamp in the wallet of a teetotaler, or a coffee stamp in a tea drinker's purse, Annunziata ran a black-market clearinghouse for unused stamps. It did surprisingly brisk business, and by 1946, she had stashed away nearly twelve thousand dollars.

The following year, Maria returned to Italy with her mother to search for news of her father. When they had visited San Lorenzo twenty-one years earlier, Annunziata had taken Maria by the hand and led her into the confino colony. Now Maria was nearly the age Annunziata had been back then, and she had to help her mother up the steep stone streets. At the San Lorenzo police station, they spoke with Inspector Bellino, a well-dressed official who sneezed his way through three handkerchiefs during their brief visit. "I'm sorry, signora," Bellino said. "The podestà's records were destroyed in the war. We don't know what happened to Signor Lagana." As Maria and her mother left Inspector Bellino's office, a cat sauntered in.

Nothing in Picone Photography offered any indication of what had befallen Giuseppe. Aside from the picture of Maria on the wall and the cardboard box beneath the bed, there was nothing to suggest he had ever lived here. When Maria lifted the lid off the cardboard box and saw hundreds of international mail envelopes ordered in neat rows, she felt raised out of her dread and shame and remorse into a state of unforeseen elation. It had been nine years since she last received a letter from him, and for the briefest moment, she imagined these were all the letters her father hadn't sent, that each contained news she'd never heard and greetings she'd never received. That within them she would find the answers to her every question. But no, of course not: Inside those hundreds of envelopes were the letters she had written him from Los Angeles. Her father had saved them all. This was what he left behind. All that remained of him was her.

For several days, Maria and Annunziata wandered through the ruins of San Lorenzo, but anyone who might have known Giuseppe was gone. On their last evening, after Maria fell asleep, Annunziata walked to the Busento excavation site. The river had long ago flooded the tunnels, and if not for the ramshackle shed where diggers once checked out shovels and pickaxes, she wouldn't have found the site at all. She plodded to the river's edge. Her high heels punctured the silted bank. She watched her reflection waver on the moonlit water. Who lay in that underworld below her rippling eyes? What were their names? She tried to imagine the numberless souls who diverted the river, who dug Alaric's tomb, who laid his plunder in the riverbed, who were slaughtered and buried in the tomb they built, and if history remembered them at all, it remembered only how they died. What justice exists in a world where villains enjoy the afterlives their victims are denied? There is no justice, not for bit players, not in this or any other world. Fifteen centuries after his death, every citizen of San Lorenzo knew Alaric's name, yet none could recall the name of the defense lawyer with a love of Tuscan cigars who had been alive here just a few years earlier.

Annunziata stepped out of her shoes and sloughed off her stockings. Her toes touched the lapping river edge. Over the years she often imagined Giuseppe's nocturnal swims in the Busento, diving for gold coins no one else knew were there. Where in San Lorenzo would she find the memory of him if not here, where he felt most free? Wearing only her slip and her wedding band, she stepped in. Her footprints sank into soft sand. She was fifty-six years old and hadn't entered a body of water larger than a bathtub since the morning of the earthquake in 1908 when the ocean roared up from the shuddering seafloor. Would she still know how to swim? Somewhere a young Romeo sang love serenades beneath a darkened window. Moonbeams wobbled on the current. The taste of woodsmoke twisted through the air. She had been lost for so long. She closed her eyes, leaned back, and as she spread her arms, her weight bobbed on the rippling river. Her hair fanned out. The water puckered and creased in little wavelets on her skin. She opened her eyes. Directly overhead, stars burned in the depths of the universe. After twenty years in Los Angeles, she'd forgotten the dark sky held so much light. The current cradled her, and afloat in these purifying waters, she could feel her mind gradually quiet until there was nothing inside her but absolute silence, and in that absolute silence there was peace.

The next morning, they took the train back to Rome. The same landscapes they had traversed two decades earlier once again passed over their eyes. They buried the cardboard box filled with Maria's letters in the Verano cemetery plot Annunziata had purchased for herself long ago. Standing at the grave on that warm autumn morning, Maria and Annunziata told Giuseppe all the things they'd wanted to tell him over the years. They talked with him well into the afternoon, long after they finished saying what needed to be said. Twenty-one years since they last saw him, and they still couldn't say goodbye. Even though he would have disapproved of the pageantry, Maria and Annunziata erected an extravagant marble cenotaph with his name carved in foot-tall letters. They would never again have any trouble finding Giuseppe Lagana.

"ALL RIGHT," MARIA TOLD VINCENT. "Andiamo."

He followed Maria outside to the blue skies and the humming neon signage and the stifled horsepower of convertibles idling in midday traffic. Bela Lugosi, Clark Gable, and Judy Garland crossed the street in animated conversation. "Oh, come on, Bruce," Judy Garland was saying. "No one in their right mind would pay five dollars for Bela Lugosi's photograph."

Vincent turned to Maria, bemused.

"Don't get too excited. They're only lookalikes."

He'd forgotten about the impersonators who came out to pose for photographs with sightseers in Bermuda shorts and practical shoes.

"I'm parked off Sunset," Maria said. "Where are you going?"

The afternoon was his, the city wide open, without zones of exclusion or the invisible borders beyond which an enemy alien could not travel. There were so many places he still wanted to see. He'd never been to Palm Springs or Santa Barbara. He'd still never stepped foot in the Pacific Ocean. He could drive to Santa Monica and afterward stop by Woodlawn Cemetery, where the small headstone bearing the name of a German miniaturist gave no indication of the scope of her work. For the first time in years, he could go anywhere.

"I think I'll go see the impersonators."

At the intersection of Hollywood and Highland no one went by their real name. There were the marquee stars and matinee idols, the tubby comedians in tight suits, the actresses in bumper bangs and evening gowns, the jubilantly costumed, haphazardly sober, and unrecognizably transformed. The starlets made famous via fatal mishandling of pills and liquor. The aspirants turned celebrity through the grisly details of their downfall. The tragic immortals: Jean Harlow, Peg Entwistle, Carole Lombard, Rudolph Valentino. All the beautiful ghosts are out. They line the street. They welcome you home.

And Nino decides to leave Vincent Cortese in their radiant company.

A tourist snapping photographs notices the Italian fellow among the impersonators. All the others she recognizes; him she can't place. She peers into her viewfinder and realizes he's not an impersonator. He's no one at all. Just a man dropping a letter into a mailbox as he walks out of the frame.

Acknowledgments

Paris is over a hundred miles from the nearest coastline, but this fact—supported by the various maps his assistant showed him—wasn't enough to persuade Irving Thalberg, MGM's head of production, to cut a romantic Parisian seascape scene from a script. He defended the decision by saying, "We can't cater to a handful of people who know Paris."

I'm grateful to the following sources, which served as atlases to the worlds within this novel. From them I drew anecdotes, details, and textures, and, above all, a great deal of joy. Any remaining Parisian seascapes are mine alone.

The Thalberg story comes from Otto Friedrich's endlessly entertaining and insightful *City of Nets: A Portrait of Hollywood in the 1940's,* which chronicles European émigrés in the wartime movie business. At Mercury's exiles' table, Anna Weber suggests that an anthropologist would do well to study the rituals and taboos of the Hollywood commissary; in the late 1940s Hortense Powdermaker did just that in *Hollywood, the Dream Factory: An Anthropologist Looks at the Movie-Makers*. Earlier in the decade, Leo C. Rosten brought a team of social scientists to study the picture business, resulting in his superb *Hollywood: The Movie Colony, the Movie Makers*. The battles Jack and Harry Warner waged against the Production Code, the US Senate, and finally each other provided models for Artie and Ned Feldman, and I'm particularly indebted to *An Empire of Their Own: How the Jews*

Invented Hollywood, Neal Gabler's magisterial portrait of Hollywood's founding fathers, as well as *Celluloid Soldiers: Warner Bros.'s Campaign Against Nazism* by Michael E. Birdwell, *Hollywood Hates Hitler!: Jew-Baiting, Anti-Nazism, and the Senate Investigation into Warmongering in Motion Pictures* by Chris Yogerst, and *Warner Bros.: Hollywood's Ultimate Backlot* by Steven Bingen. Additionally, I'm grateful to *Crab Monsters, Teenage Cavemen, and Candy Stripe Nurses: Roger Corman: King of the B Movie* by Chris Nashawaty, *Poverty Row Horrors!: Monogram, PRC and Republic Horror Films of the Forties* by Tom Weaver, *The Immortal Count: The Life and Films of Bela Lugosi* by Arthur Lennig, and *Blackout: World War II and the Origins of Film Noir* by Sheri Chinen Biesen.

Anna May Wong and Philip Ahn were among the most charismatic classical-age actors, even if they rarely received parts worthy of their talents. *Anna May Wong: From Laundryman's Daughter to Hollywood Legend* by Graham Russell Gao Hodges and *Hollywood Asian: Philip Ahn and the Politics of Cross-Ethnic Performance* by Hye Seung Chung offer incisive portraits of their complicated lives and careers. If Eddie Lu's story interested you, I'd encourage you to check out *The Fortunes* by Peter Ho Davies, *Delayed Rays of a Star* by Amanda Lee Koe, and *Interior Chinatown* by Charles Yu.

The political, cultural, and economic contradictions the film industry navigated in the years leading up to and through World War II are brilliantly laid out in three works by Thomas Doherty that I regularly drew from: *Hollywood and Hitler, 1933–1939; Projections of War: Hollywood, American Culture, and World War II;* and *Hollywood Censor: Joseph I. Breen and the Production Code Administration.* Additionally, *Hollywood Goes to War: How Politics, Profits and Propaganda Shaped World War II Movies* by Clayton R. Koppes and Gregory D. Black, *Boom and Bust: American Cinema in the 1940s* by Thomas Schatz, *The World War II Combat Film: Anatomy of a Genre* by Jeanine Basinger, and *We'll Always Have the Movies: American Cinema During World War II* by Robert L. McLaughlin and Sally E. Parry provided insightful analysis into how the war shaped the movies of its era and how, in turn, those movies shaped the public. I'm grateful to Mark Harris's *Five Came Back: A*

Story of Hollywood and the Second World War, particularly its chapters on Frank Capra and John Huston. In his *Why We Fight* documentary series, Capra waged an ideological war against fascism by appropriating and contextualizing its own propaganda, which Joseph McBride describes at length in *Frank Capra: The Catastrophe of Success.*

Like Maria Lagana, Frank Capra immigrated from Italy to Los Angeles as a child. The Italian American Museum of Los Angeles has documented the history of the city's Italian community in rigorous detail. In its collection, you will find the June 16, 1917, issue of *L'Italo Americano,* the only pre-war issue that survives after the publisher, fearing internment, destroyed his archive. The paper survived and still publishes twice a month (italoamericano.org). The history of California's Italian enemy aliens receives overdue attention in *Searching for Subversives: The Story of Italian Internment in Wartime America* by Mary Elizabeth Basile Chopas, *UnCivil Liberties: Italian Americans Under Siege During World War II* by Stephen Fox, and *Una Storia Segreta: The Secret History of Italian American Evacuation and Internment During World War II* edited by Lawrence DiStasi.

In portraying midcentury Los Angeles, I relied on *Southern California: An Island on the Land* by Carey McWilliams, *Material Dreams: Southern California Through the 1920s* and *Embattled Dreams: California in War and Peace, 1940–1950* by Kevin Starr, and *American Chinatown: A People's History in Five Neighborhoods* by Bonnie Tsui. I'm particularly indebted to *Los Angeles in the 1930s: The WPA Guide to the City of Angels* by the Federal Writers Project and *The Darkest Year: The American Homefront, 1941–1942* by William K. Klingaman. The means by which Betty Ludlow's many marriages come to light is taken directly from the case of a notorious "Allotment Annie" described in *Don't You Know There's a War On?: The American Home Front 1941–1945* by Richard Lingeman.

Christ Stopped at Eboli: The Story of a Year, Carlo Levi's classic memoir of political internment under Mussolini, was always at hand while I worked on the San Lorenzo chapters, as was *A Bold and Dangerous Family: The Remarkable Story of an Italian Mother, Her Sons, and*

Their Fight Against Fascism by Caroline Moorehead, *Ordinary Violence in Mussolini's Italy* by Michael R. Ebner, *The Stone Boudoir: Travels Through the Hidden Villages of Sicily* by Theresa Maggio, *Women of the Shadows: Wives and Mothers of Southern Italy* by Ann Cornelisen, *My Two Italies* by Joseph Luzzi, and *Unto the Sons* by Gay Talese. San Lorenzo is very loosely based on Cosenza, Calabria, which Himmler visited in 1937. Alaric's tomb in the Busento River has never been discovered, but Daniel Costa offers a history of failed searches (including Himmler's) in *The Lost Gold of Rome: The Hunt for Alaric's Treasure*. Nino's torn photographs originate in a practice common among Portuguese migrants during the Salazar regime, which I first learned about from Hugo Gonçalves. While describing the Italian Campaign, I drew heavily from *The Day of Battle: The War in Sicily and Italy, 1943–1944* by Rick Atkinson, *Slightly Out of Focus* by Robert Capa, and *The Skin* by Curzio Malaparte. In *Armed with Cameras: The American Military Photographers of World War II*, Peter Maslowski documents how John Huston relied on reenactments for his combat "documentary" *San Pietro*, which is hardly less powerful for being largely staged. *New Yorker* writer Lillian Ross was given unprecedented access to the production of John Huston's postwar adaptation of *The Red Badge of Courage* in her classic work *Picture;* Harold and Gerald were inspired by her account of an extra who "fought in every war there was in history since the Philistines."

In describing interwar Berlin, I drew details from *Before the Deluge: A Portrait of Berlin in the 1920s* by Otto Friedrich. *Weimar on the Pacific: German Exile Culture in Los Angeles and the Crisis of Modernism* by Ehrhard Bahr, *Hitler's Exiles: Personal Stories of the Flight from Nazi Germany to America* edited by Mark M. Anderson, *The Sun and Her Stars: Salka Viertel and Hitler's Exiles in the Golden Age of Hollywood* by Donna Rifkind, *The Kindness of Strangers* by Salka Viertel, *On Sunset Boulevard: The Life and Times of Billy Wilder* by Ed Sikov, and *Weimar in Exile: The Antifascist Emigration in Europe and America* by Jean-Michel Palmier were all sources I regularly consulted when depicting the émigré community in Los Angeles. I'm particularly grateful to *Exiled in Paradise: German Refugee Artists and Intellectuals in America from the 1930s to the Present* by Anthony Heilbut, which is as erudite as it is morally forceful. "Berlin's Skeleton in Utah's Closet" in Mike Davis's *Dead Cities: And Other Tales* was indispensable while writing the German Village chapter. Anna Weber's backstory is partly modeled on émigré filmmaker Douglas Sirk; Sirk's first wife joined the Nazi Party and kept their son in Berlin, where he was a well-known child actor before being drafted into the Wehrmacht and dying on the Eastern Front.

In addition to nonfiction sources, I'm indebted to the following works of fiction for their influence, inspiration, and companionship: *Doctor Faustus* by Thomas Mann, *Mephisto* by Klaus Mann, *Transit* by Anna Seghers, *The Day of the Locust* by Nathanael West, *Ragtime* by E. L. Doctorow, *The Amazing Adventures of Kavalier and Clay* by Michael Chabon, *Manhattan Beach* by Jennifer Egan, *Beautiful Ruins* by Jess Walter, *A Fine Balance* by Rohinton Mistry, *All Our Yesterdays* by Natalia Ginzburg, *Underworld* by Don DeLillo, *The Plot Against America* by Philip Roth, *The Count of Monte Cristo* by Alexandre Dumas, the detective novels of Andrea Camilleri and Philip Kerr, and the movies *His Girl Friday* (1940), *To Be or Not to Be* (1942), and *Sunset Boulevard* (1950).

Thank you to the Guggenheim Foundation, the American Academy in Berlin, the National Endowment for the Arts, the Simpson Literary Project, and the Jeannette Haien Ballard Trust for supporting this project. This book has had three editors: Lindsay Sagnette welcomed it to Hogarth, Alexis Washam saw it through the middle stretch, and David Ebershoff brought it over the finish line; I'm enormously grateful to each. Additionally, a big thank-you to Andy Ward, Avideh Bashirrad, Rachel Rokicki, Julie Cepler, Ruth Liebmann, Michael Hoak, Darryl Oliver, Paolo Pepe, Anna Kochman, Mark Birkey, and Evan Gaffne at Hogarth and Random House. Janet Silver, my agent, has been a cherished consigliere and friend for over ten years now. Thank you to Celeste Ng, Ching-chun Shih, and Bob Bookman for their invaluable early reads. Linh Tran at A'cuppa Tea in Berkeley provided not only a place to write but much needed encouragement.

My father and his sisters descend in part from Calabrian and Sicilian emigrants, and the most rewarding aspect of researching this book was the opportunity to hear the stories and see the photographs they inherited. My great-aunts Mimi, Lala, and Pep were far too individualistic to saddle with pseudonyms; the characters bearing their names share few of their personal details, but a lot of their personality. Pep died in 2003 at the age of ninety-seven; Lala died in 2010 at the age of ninety-five; Mimi died in 2015 at the age of ninety-eight; but in another world, one where Paris is on the ocean, they are driving Maria bonkers right now. Should you find yourself in San Francisco, you can visit the real Trattoria Contadina, owned and operated by my cousin Gina Correnti and her husband, Kevin; their "Carlesimo" is an even better version of the Mimissima described on page 40.

To end at the beginning: on a drizzly day in 2014 when I met a brilliant art historian from Long Beach who specializes in—what else?—photography. Two stories began that day, one on the page and one off, and both are love stories because of you, Kap.

ABOUT THE AUTHOR

ANTHONY MARRA is the *New York Times* bestselling author of *The Tsar of Love and Techno* and *A Constellation of Vital Phenomena,* winner of the National Book Critics Circle's John Leonard Prize and the Anisfield-Wolf Book Award, and longlisted for the National Book Award. He lives in Connecticut.

ABOUT THE TYPE

This book was set in Baskerville, a typeface designed by John Baskerville (1706–75), an amateur printer and typefounder, and cut for him by John Handy in 1750. The type became popular again when the Lanston Monotype Corporation of London revived the classic roman face in 1923. The Mergenthaler Linotype Company in England and the United States cut a version of Baskerville in 1931, making it one of the most widely used typefaces today.